The Rogues of Regent Street

In her acclaimed novel The Dangerous Gentleman, *Julia London introduced the infamous Rogues of Regent Street, three aristocratic rakes whose escapades are the talk of the* ton. *The dashing Julian Dane, Earl of Kettering, has cut a swath through London's finest ballrooms, boudoirs, and dueling grounds. This is his story. . . .*

THE RUTHLESS CHARMER

No woman could resist Julian Dane—except Lady Claudia Whitney. Julian had known her since childhood: the only beauty ever to refuse the dark Adonis whose rakish exploits were legend—but whose kind heart was a closed book. Now the headstrong lass had grown into a beautiful woman and Julian was determined to have her. But the sparks that fly between them ignite a moment of reckless abandon that threatens scandal and assures Claudia's certain ruin. The only solution is marriage. Julian vows to teach her everything he knows of passion. But Claudia, in her innocent ardor, promises to challenge him to the most dangerous emotion of all: wild, all-consuming love.

THE ROGUES OF REGENT STREET

The Ruthless Charmer

Julia London

A DELL BOOK

Published by
Dell Publishing
a division of
Random House, Inc.
1540 Broadway
New York, New York 10036

Copyright © 2000 by Dinah Dinwiddie.
Cover art by John Ennis.
Hand lettering by David Gatti.

Dell® is a registered trademark of Random House, Inc., and the colophon is a trademark of Random House, Inc.

ISBN: 0-440-23562-6

Printed in the United States of America

Published simultaneously in Canada

October 2000

10 9 8 7 6 5 4 3 2 1

OPM

For Matt.
And Jimmy and Duane and Raymond and David . . .
For all of them who helped to shape my life yet didn't live
long enough to shape their own.

*Of all the pains, the greatest pain
is to love, and love in vain.*

"THE HAPPIEST MORTALS ONCE WERE WEE"
GEORGE GRANVILLE, BARON LANSDOWNE

The Ruthless Charmer

Prologue

"Know ye in this death the light of our Lord,
the quality of love, and the quality of life,
And know ye the quality of mercy, Amen . . ."

THE VICAR'S WORDS scarcely penetrated his consciousness. Standing over Phillip Rothembow's open grave, Julian Dane felt as if he were trapped in some sort of macabre dream, for what had happened on that yellow field was simply inconceivable. One shot fired—Adrian deloping, bowing to Phillip's inebriation and the absurdity of the duel. It should have ended at that moment, but Phillip had actually *fired* on Adrian—had tried to kill him—and Julian had been stunned almost beyond comprehension.

Phillip's shot was absurdly wide; he could barely hold the gun straight. Yet in the blurred moment that followed, he seemed to regain his balance, twisting around and lunging for Fitzhugh's double-barreled German pistol, which protruded from that fool's coat. Phillip had looked wild, almost maniacal as he turned on Adrian then, and Julian had tried to stop him, but his legs and arms had felt as if there were weights tied to them, and everything happened so *quickly*.

In what seemed like the blink of an eye, Lord Phillip Rothembow was dead. Shot through the heart by his very own cousin, Adrian Spence, the Earl of Albright, who had fired in self-defense.

Julian remembered seeing his shock and disbelief mirrored on Lord Arthur Christian's face. He remembered falling onto Phillip's body, pressing his ear against the blood-soaked waistcoat, and hearing the words from his own mouth, *"He is dead."*

That was the moment the dream had taken hold of him, deepening every hour since, holding him down and refusing to let him wake fully. But even the dream could not spare him from the ugly realization that Phillip had actually *meant* for Adrian to kill him, that he had sought to end his own life after months of drowning in debt and drink and Madam Farantino's women. Months Julian had spent with him, duly concerned about his excesses . . . but never in his wildest imaginings did he suspect Phillip so desperately wanted to end his life.

How could he have possibly imagined it? Phillip, Lord Rothembow, was one of the bloody Rogues of Regent Street! An idol of every man of the Quality, just like Julian Dane and Adrian Spence and Arthur Christian. They were the *Rogues* for God's sake, living by their own code, risking their wealth to make more wealth, never fearing the law or society. They were men who purportedly broke young hearts among the clientele of the upscale Regent Street shops by day, extracted intended dowries from their papas in the Regent Street gentlemen's clubs at night, and saved the best of themselves for the notorious Regent Street boudoirs. They had pushed every limit, but this time Phillip had pushed too far, falling like an angel at their feet.

And Julian had tasted his own mortality.

He understood that he was, in part, responsible for this tragedy. He stared blankly at the pine box in the gaping hole before him, wondering if this dream would find its end. What had the vicar said? *Know ye in this death the light of our Lord and the quality of love . . .*

The notion was so absurd that he almost laughed out loud. He knew what it was to love a father so much that he would swear to almost anything as the throes of death descended. He knew what it was to love a sister like his own child and have his heart wrenched clean from his body as she lay dying in his arms. And God help him, he knew what it was to love a man like a brother and watch helplessly as he spiraled down into the clutches of madness and suicide.

He knew the quality of love, all right, and it was of little comfort.

Julian tore his gaze from the grave and looked at Arthur standing rigidly as the gravediggers pushed earth into the hole. Arthur, the peacemaker, the one with the admirable ability to fall into pace with any of them. Arthur, who had broken down last night as they drowned their sorrows in a bottle of brandy, confessing he'd noticed the downward slide, but did not understand the depth of Phillip's trouble until it was too late.

Neither had Adrian.

Julian shifted his gaze to their unofficial leader, Adrian Spence, who wore the horror and disbelief of what had happened etched deeply in lines around his eyes. Adrian hadn't seen Phillip's slide, he had said, because he had been blind to all but his, his ongoing war with his father.

And while his friends had grieved, he, Julian Dane, the Earl of Kettering, had sat there ruminating, thoroughly numbed by guilt and despair.

A fine rain was falling now, but Julian's gaze remained transfixed on the mound of dirt that was quickly turning to mud. It was hard to believe that the man who had been his constant companion since the four of them had met at Eton so many years ago was lying in that grave. *God!* It was so bloody difficult to understand how this could have happened. How could he have *allowed* it to happen? Had he been too mindful of Phillip's pride? Too sure of his strength? Had he not been forceful enough with Phillip, not made his concerns clear?

Had he perhaps been too infatuated with Claudia?

It hardly mattered. It remained that he hadn't done enough to stop Phillip's decline, and death was his reward. The misfortune being, of course, that it was not his own.

One

Aha! HE WAS being smothered by a pair of breasts.

That at least explained the strong scent of a woman. Julian shifted between the two luscious mounds and gasped for air as a most delectable female creature murmured unintelligible phrases in his ear. Unfortunately, even the touch of the little French goddess couldn't raise him higher than half-mast. A *crane* couldn't raise him higher than half-mast—damned appendage was nothing but trouble of late.

Julian sighed, realized he was still holding a bottle of whiskey, and managed to take a good swig of it before burying his face between her breasts again. A bead of perspiration trickled down his temple and he couldn't help smiling; perhaps he just wasn't trying hard enough. As if on cue, sweet Lisette sighed longingly, inflaming all of his masculine senses—except *that* one, curse it to hell—and Julian attempted to position himself for another go at it. His fingertips brushed a taut nipple; his palm cupped the firm swell of her breast—

The cold hands on his shoulders startled him so badly he couldn't even cry out. Suddenly, he felt himself being lifted and heard Lisette's muffled shriek as the bottle of whiskey flew out of his hand and scudded across the bed.

He caught just a glimpse of the elaborate frieze moldings on the ceiling before he hit the hard wood floor with a resounding *thud*.

Now that hurt. Wincing painfully, Julian glanced up at his assailant. "What in blazes did you do that for?" The response was the toss of his shirt onto his head. He yanked it from his face and glared up at the infidel towering high above him—Louis Renault, otherwise known in this godforsaken country as Monsieur le Comte de Claire. A scoundrel if Julian had ever known one, an insufferable Frog with all the manners of a toad, and most unfortunately, the husband of his sister Eugenie.

Unsteadily, Julian gained his feet.

With disapproval seeping through every pore, Louis let his gaze sweep over Julian as he folded his arms across his chest. "Did you come to Paris to make trouble for me? Is that how you repay my kindness to your sister?" he demanded in that smooth, silky way he had of speaking English, and stooped to pick up Julian's trousers. "Come. Your frolic is *fini*. You must go from here."

Go? Julian glanced at Lisette, who smiled seductively and twisted a blonde lock around one finger. From *here*? His focus slipped to the rumpled bedding—*ho there! Where was his whiskey?*

"Kettering, listen to me!" With supreme effort, Julian forced himself to look at the Frog—no small feat given that there appeared to be at least two of him. "You are in danger. . . . Do you understand?"

He understood all right. "Ridiculous," he mumbled, and waved dramatically at the little French goddess. "What danger is Lisette?"

With a snort, Louis tossed his trousers to him, which Julian caught clumsily against his chest. "If you do not leave Paris at once, Monsieur LeBeau will see you shot. Or worse. Dress, will you?"

Dress. One glance down his naked body and Julian silently agreed that he ought to at least cover up the offending parts. All right, he'd dress, but he wasn't going anywhere with Louis. He was going to crawl right back into that bed and pick up where he had left off. Needing both hands to attempt the trousers, he dropped his shirt and lifted one leg. He missed.

This would, apparently, require some keen navigational skills.

"*Mon Dieu!* I'll be forced to carry you from here!" Louis exclaimed, and grabbing Julian's arm—rather *tightly*—steadied him so that he could get his trousers on. "I distinctly warned you of the trouble you were causing, didn't I? LeBeau is a hateful man. I told you this, more than once I told you this, but would you listen? No! I ask you now—Madame LeBeau, is she so appealing for all the trouble you've caused?"

Julian paused with one leg in and one leg out of his trousers to ponder that. He could vaguely recall seeing Gisele LeBeau. Had she actually kissed him again? Probably. The woman could fill an ocean with her gall.

"What, so you think he would ignore this?" Louis heatedly continued. "Some of the most important names in Paris attend the balls on the Boulevard St Michel. How could you humiliate him so? Dallying with his very own wife!"

Actually, Gisele had cornered him when he wasn't looking, not the other way around. And what was he to do? When a comely woman pressed her breasts against him, he was only human. "Ha!" Julian interjected, thrusting the second leg into his trousers with such force that he swerved right into Louis's chest. "LeBeau is a . . ." —he had to think about this—"a shrimp. With ears," he added firmly, and clumsily attempted the buttons.

A hard jerk of his arm, and Louis was suddenly standing so close that Julian had trouble focusing on his flaring nostrils. "You would do well to heed my advice, *mon ami*. In France, a discreet affair is something a man expects and may tolerate, but to publicly *coqueter* with his wife in the most crowded ballroom in all of Paris is another thing entirely. These things turn deadly when a man's honor has been compromised! Trust me, LeBeau will see you dead if you remain here!"

The image that conjured up suddenly made Julian laugh. For some unknown reason, so did Lisette.

A rapid-fire, heated string of French fairly burst from Louis's lips. Although Julian thought he spoke French fairly well, when Louis was in a mood, he spoke that fast, never-let-an-Englishman-understand-you French. Hell, even Lisette seemed to be having trouble keeping up with him. With an impatient flick of his wrist, Julian said, "You fret like an old woman, Renault. Off with you now."

What was amazing, Julian would later recall, was that he never saw Louis move. He never even felt the impact of Louis's fist against his jaw. He just had the strange sensation of flying before everything went black.

Barefoot, Claudia was walking toward him across the wide green lawn at Château la Claire, her skirts free of stiff petticoats and dragging the grass behind her. Her hair was loose and flowing, skimming over creamy white shoulders and down her back. His longing for her was so great that it threatened to choke him—and in fact, he could scarcely breathe. . . .

Because there was a blasted *noose* tied tightly about his neck, and obviously, he had been strangling for sometime. As Julian roused himself from the deepest remnants of sleep before he choked to death, he slowly comprehended that not only was his head pounding and threatening to split wide open, but everything was *moving*—up and down, up and down. Or maybe sideways. He couldn't be entirely certain.

Miraculously, he managed to force an eye open and struggled to push himself to a sitting position, propping himself against . . . God, who knew? *Everything* hurt. A vague memory of Lisette and Louis came to him, but the only explanation his aching brain could conceive was that he had been beaten within an inch of his life—pummeled and kicked and stomped.

Expecting to find nothing but pulp, he very gingerly probed his nose, his face, and even his eyes. Oddly enough, nothing seemed too terribly damaged. But he *was* suffocating, and therefore, the first order of business was to get the bloody noose from his neck. The thing was pulled so tightly it was a wonder he was able to breathe at all.

He felt for the rope, feeling everything from his ears to his shoulders, but there was no noose. Nothing at all unusual, just a collar and a neckcloth—which had been knotted very tightly. Good God, he was choking to death on his neckcloth! Not only that, he noticed as he clawed at the offending piece of linen, his waistcoat was fitted strangely, too—all hiked up in the wrong places and buttoned in a very odd way.

Able to breathe again, Julian squinted, peering into the dark around him until he recognized the interior of a coach. He suddenly jerked his gaze to a window, wincing painfully. It was pitch black outside, no lights from gas lamps or drawing room windows. *Damn!* The coach was hurtling through the night, well gone from Paris, no doubt en route to Château la Claire, where *she* would be, waiting to torment him. . . .

An abrupt and loud snore caught Julian's attention; he slowly turned his head, peering bleary-eyed through the dark at a sleeping figure across from him. *Louis,* Ah, but he would kill the scoundrel this time! Clutching the squabs on either side of his legs, Julian lifted a booted foot and thrust it at the sleeping traitor, making contact with a soft part of his body. Louis shot up with a start, sputtering his surprise. *"Qu'est-ce qui s'est passé?"*

"I'll tell you what has happened, you degenerate Frog. You have abducted me!" Julian croaked.

A moment of silence passed. *"Oui.* So I have," Louis replied wearily and fumbled in the dark, blinding Julian with the sudden flare of a tinderbox he used to light the crystal kerosene lamps, illuminating the plush interior of the expensive travelling chaise.

"You might have *asked* me to take my leave of Paris, you know," Julian exclaimed irritably, blinking at the stark light. "There was no reason to resort to abduction. Don't you people have laws about this sort of thing?"

"There was every reason," Louis amicably disagreed. "One day you will thank me, for I do you an enormous favor. Monsieur LeBeau is quite determined to kill you—not that I have any particular objection to it, but I believe Genie would be quite displeased."

"LeBeau!" Julian snorted. It was hardly his fault that LeBeau's comely wife could not abide the tiny peacock she had married. Or that the imbecile couldn't play cards to save his fool life. Or that he took offense to being called a Little Bit.

"*Oui,* LeBeau. A leader in the Republic, a strong critic of the monarchy, and a sworn enemy of mine! He's quite ruthless, Kettering. I shouldn't be surprised if he is pursuing you even now."

Part of Julian hoped that was so—he would very much like to take his irritation out on the peacock. But he surmised Louis didn't particularly want to hear that, and closed his eyes, carefully resting his throbbing head against the velvet squabs.

"It is time, I think, for you to return home," Louis announced impassively.

Julian forced one eye open. His brother-in-law was casually studying a cuticle, his legs comfortably crossed—all in all, looking rather inflexible on that point. "In the seventeen years I have known you, I've never seen you quite so . . . aimless. Rudderless, so to speak. Without purpose. A ship without a—"

"All right, all right!" Julian growled, and refrained from pointing out that in the seventeen years he had known Louis, he had never known him to be as *motherly* as he had been this last fortnight.

"I suppose you are suffering a bit from ennui, and who can blame you?" Louis blithely continued.

Julian blinked. "Pardon?"

"You raised your sisters from the time you were sixteen and now they are all grown and gone. Your estate and affairs seem to manage themselves, and Lord knows the Rogues are not the same force they once were. It seems your only worthwhile activity is the occasional lecture at university, but that is hardly enough to fill one's days, *n'est-ce pas?*"

With an impatient grunt, Julian waved a hand dismissively. Louis was bloody well right that he was bored, but he had no hope the Frog could fathom just how bored. Because this wasn't merely boredom, *this* was everything and nothing, a struggle to survive in his own skin, an increasingly uncomfortable feeling as if he was forever trapped in an ill-fitted suit of clothes. Unfortunately, nothing could make the feeling go away. Not drink—although the Lord knew he had tried hard enough to drown the feeling—not travel, not study, not gaming or whoring. *Nothing.*

Louis's eyes narrowed, and he muttered under his breath. Julian closed his eyes, hardly in a mood to try to explain that the insufferable itch had started the day his sister Valerie had slipped the bonds of earth and had mushroomed into an internal rash the morning he laid his head to Phillip's bloodied chest. Or that the rash had turned into a cancer that had begun to ravage him in the months afterward, because even though he had offered to help Phillip and was rebuffed several times, Julian knew the truth. He hadn't really done enough to save Phillip, and he rather doubted Louis would want to hear his darkest suspicion—that in actuality, he hadn't tried so very hard at all because he knew if Phillip was in some gaming hell or on top of some whore, he was not with Claudia.

"Very well then," Louis huffed. "If the Divine Dane is offended with the notion that perhaps he is human after all, I cannot help him."

Ha! If only he were human! Julian slumped down against the squabs and slung an arm over his eyes, ignoring Louis's loud sigh of frustration.

"*Ach!* You care so little for what *I* think? What of Genie? She frets terribly. At least think of your sisters!"

Oh, now that was almost laughable. From the

moment his father, in the throes of death, had begged him to keep his sisters safe and well, he had thought of little else. "I think of them, Louis. Every day," he muttered.

"I apologize—naturally, you are right, Kettering. You have always indulged them shamelessly—"

"Please. I've done no such thing."

"You have always given them whatever they want. If they wanted new gowns and slippers, you supplied them. If they preferred sweets to break their fast, you merely smiled. If they complained there were not enough ribbons to go around, you commissioned a seamstress that very day!"

Julian shifted his arm slightly to peer at Louis from beneath it. "All right, so I might have pampered them a bit—"

"*Pampered* them?" Louis rolled his eyes. "They were incorrigible—"

"They were hardly incorrigible—"

"And the screams! I shall never forget the screams. The trunk from London—*mon Dieu,* my head ached for days!"

An inadvertent chuckle escaped Julian. He remembered, all right. The modiste he had paid so handsomely to have his sisters properly outfitted in the finest fabrics had done splendid work. Each time a dress was pulled from the trunk, the girls screamed their approval. "I am thankful that you recovered sufficiently from your horror to beg me for Eugenie's hand."

"On both knees," Louis reminded him, trying gamely to keep the grin from his face. "You forced me to crawl. Rather proud of yourself then, hmmm? Strutting around my wedding breakfast like a gamecock—as if *you* had given life to those four girls!"

He had not given Valerie life. He had taken it. A weight suddenly settled on Julian's chest, and with a shrug, he closed his eyes again. "I did what I could for them."

"*Oui,* this too is obvious. It was a brilliant match you made for Ann—Viscount Boxworth rather adores her.

And Sophie has benefited greatly from the finishing school in Geneva. But they are grown now, and your restlessness surely comes from trying to fill the space they once occupied."

"That's absurd," Julian snapped. "Now that they are grown, I have the luxury of time to engage in my own interests. I lecture at Cambridge and Oxford—"

"I beg your pardon, you may be quite renowned for your expertise in medieval languages, but an occasional lecture about old documents is hardly enough to fill the days of a grown man."

Julian did not like the direction this conversation was taking, not one bit. Suddenly he sat upright, propping his forearms on his knees and swallowing past the nausea his sudden movement caused. "Good *God* this conveyance is uncomfortable!" he complained. "I should think you could afford better, Renault."

"I warn you, *mon ami,* that a restlessness such as yours can get a man killed in France."

"How long to Château la Claire?" Julian interrupted, lifting his head to glare at his brother-in-law.

Louis brushed a wrinkle from his trouser leg. "Our destination is not Château la Claire. We are to Dieppe."

"Dieppe?" He was liking this less and less. "As I don't suppose you intend to take the healing seawaters there, might I conclude we are going on from there?"

"Not we. You. To England."

"You are throwing me out of France." It was not a question; it was a statement of fact.

"I am," Louis shamelessly admitted. "Fortunately, Christian runs a rather accommodating enterprise. When I spoke with his man last week, he assured me there would be room for you on the daily packet boat."

With a snort of indignation, Julian folded his arms across his chest. "And if I refuse?"

Louis shrugged indifferently. "His man also promised to return your gun and purse the moment you set foot on English soil."

Instantly, Julian clutched his side, his frown deepening when he discovered his pistol and purse were missing.

"These things you will not need on the boat."

The pulse at Julian's temple was throbbing painfully now. "On my honor, if it weren't for this spectacular pain in my head, I would gladly beat my purse out of you."

"Ah, but you are hardly in any condition to do so, and I am compelled to force you from France before your sister finds that fool head of yours piked on the gate at la Claire. Do not doubt that LeBeau will make good on his threats, Kettering. He is a vicious little man who will not tolerate the humiliation you've caused him. You are going to England."

Julian's response to that declaration was a cold glare.

"Tonight you escape with your life," Louis warned him. "Take my advice and mend your ways before someone actually succeeds in killing you."

A rumble of bitter laughter lodged in Julian's throat. "Perhaps my ways are best mended if someone *does* manage to kill me, have you considered that?"

Louis responded by pressing his lips firmly together and frowning at his lap. Julian slid down onto the bench. "Wake me when we arrive, will you?" he muttered.

Louis woke him, all right, just in time to push him out of the coach and toss a small bag after him. Standing on the main thoroughfare in Dieppe, Julian stared daggers at the Frenchman as he explained that the *Maiden's Heart* would sail at midnight, and that the captain would return his pistol and his purse when they docked at Newhaven. And just before he pulled the coach door closed, Louis tossed a coin that Julian caught in mid-air. He glanced at his palm—one gold franc—and sliced a murderous gaze across Louis.

"Eat something, won't you? You look as if you could use it. May I recommend the *Hôtel la Diligence*? Seems rather the perfect place for a Rogue."

Lifting two fingers to his temple, Julian bowed.

"You've been a most gracious host, Monsieur Renault. I look forward to treating you in kind," he mocked.

Louis laughed. "I don't doubt it for a moment. Until then, *au revoir!*" Grinning, he signaled the driver and pulled the coach door shut, leaving Julian standing with a satchel at his feet, a waistcoat buttoned unevenly, and a heavy shadow of a beard chafing his face.

"Bloody Frog," Julian muttered irritably as the coach disappeared around a corner. He adjusted his clothing as best he could, quickly tying the neckcloth into something barely resembling a knot, slapping the dust from his trouser legs, and thrusting both hands through his hair in an attempt to comb it. He rather imagined he looked like hell, but he hardly cared. There was nothing to be done for it, so picking up the satchel, he dragged himself to the *Hôtel la Diligence.*

Two

SLOGGING ALONG a rutted French road in a carriage that had seen better days, Claudia Whitney frowned at the man sitting beside her. "I tried to warn you, Herbert, you know I did. I told you I was hardly in need of a driver, and I distinctly recall saying *non* when you started running after me."

Herbert peered so intently at her she could almost see the rusty wheels turning in his feeble brain. *"Qu'est-ce que ça veut dire?"*

"Oh *Lord*," Claudia moaned, and impatiently snapped the reins against the back of the hapless mare, urging her to please go faster than a stroll. This drive was quickly approaching the longest of her life. Unfortunately, she knew very little French—all right, she had never been particularly studious, but she would pay a grand sum to know it now. When she had accidentally run over the footman's foot and therefore had been forced to bring him along—she could hardly leave him hobbled in the road like that—he had been polite enough to pretend he knew some English. So she had talked for the sake of it, filling the space and time, until the last fifteen miles or so when Herbert had begun his wild gesticulating to the ankle and the horse and the reins all over again.

She stole a glance at his swollen ankle. Blasted footman shouldn't have tried to stop the mare anyway! "If I wasn't exactly clear when I said I did not want a driver and to please not follow me, I was most decidedly clear when I asked you to *move*," she reminded him. "Honestly, what sort of man stands in the middle of the road when a carriage is bearing down on him?"

"Madame, parlez un peu plus lentement, s'il vous plaît!"

"Don't blame me for your predicament, sir!" she said sharply. "Oh, look! There is Dieppe just ahead! You see? We'll get that foot looked after in a trice now." She smiled brightly at him.

With a shake of his head, Herbert tossed his hands in the air and looked off into the distance. *"Je ne comprends rien,"* he muttered.

In spite of the fact that they could actually *see* Dieppe, Claudia had no hope they would ever reach it. Not at this rate, anyway. One would think a man of Renault's considerable fortune would have more than an old nag in his stables, and she spent the remaining half-hour silently cursing him.

When they coasted onto the main thoroughfare in Dieppe, Claudia reined the mare to a stop and helped herself down from the carriage—over the loud French protests of Herbert—and stood, hands on hips, surveying him, his ankle, and the drop to the ground. "Rather a long way down, sir," she informed him. "I think you'll have to put your hands on my shoulder, whilst I put my hands on your waist," she said, reaching for him. "And then, we might—"

Herbert shrieked when she touched his waist, then followed it up by bellowing in French like a madman. With a quick, mortified look around, Claudia opened her mouth to tell him to stop it at once, but two rather large men actually paused and exchanged words with Herbert. The footman gestured wildly, pointing frequently to his ankle and making all sorts of expressions of agony. A heat began to creep up Claudia's neck; she glared at the ridiculous footman.

"*Pardon, madame,*" one of the men said, motioning her away. When Claudia did not move, he gave her a gentle bump and moved to help Herbert down. Swinging his arm under Herbert's shoulders, he bowed to Claudia and gestured toward the *Hôtel la Diligence* as his companion fetched her bags.

"Oh!" Claudia exclaimed, realizing they meant to help them inside. "*Merci beaucoup!*" she chirped, and marched forward, leaving the hobbling Herbert to the two Frenchmen.

Nursing his second ale instead of the fourth of five he would have liked—no thanks to Louis—Julian turned apathetically toward the sound of a commotion. Two men pushed through the small door of the inn assisting a hobbled footman between them. Julian instantly recognized the livery of Château la Claire and fumbled in his coat for his spectacles. As he donned them, he slowly came up from his slouch, his eyes narrowing on the woman who followed behind. He abruptly lurched backward, snatching the eyeglasses from the bridge of his nose.

Bloody hell, was this some sort of nightmare, some horrid dream from which he would never awake? He jerked forward again just to be sure he wasn't seeing things, but oh no, he wasn't imagining it. *That* was the wench, all right—the impossible, willful, extraordinarily difficult Lady Claudia Whitney! Was he being punished? Did God find his sins so great that He should put her in his path to torment him for eternity? Or was this God's idea of a jest?

He watched as the innkeeper hurried forward to greet her. Absently smoothing a strand of the impossibly thick auburn hair gathered at her nape, she smiled and motioned toward the footman. The innkeeper spoke; she shrugged faintly and gestured again toward the footman. The footman frantically waved both hands at the innkeeper, his cries of "*non, non!*" audible even to Julian.

Claudia fell gracefully in a cloud of dark green silk

onto the chair across from the nervous footman and leaned across the table, looking earnestly at him. After a moment of animated conversation between the footman and the innkeeper, the innkeeper hurried away. She smiled fully at the footman then, and Julian felt the force of it from clear across the room. *She had smiled at Phillip like that once, across the table at a Christian family fete.*

He shook his head, jerking at his collar as it had gotten incredibly warm all of a sudden, and decided that he was hardly in a mood to suffer the Demon's Spawn just now, particularly after she had made it quite clear at Château la Claire that she despised him. Well good *God*, when he had come to France to surprise his sister Eugenie with an impromptu visit, he had no idea *she* would be at Château la Claire. With the exception of an occasional glimpse of her from across a crowded ballroom, he had not seen her since Phillip's death almost eighteen months ago. He would never have even ventured across the Channel if he thought it *remotely* possible she would be here!

And just how in the hell was it that she could look even more luminous now than she had a fortnight ago when he had encountered her so unexpectedly?

Sighing heavily, Julian pinched the bridge of his nose. It wasn't possible for her to look any more beautiful than she had that day when she had appeared as if walking out of his dreams, gliding barefoot across that wide green lawn with his two nieces, who were dressed in little medieval costumes. The whole scene had been so surprising that it had literally taken his breath away. His heart had begun to pound like a drum, his palms had gone all sweaty, and he had stood there like a dolt, completely mesmerized as she came to the fountain terrace where he was standing.

He had smiled at her—at least he thought he had. Her blue-gray eyes had warily assessed him, a probing gaze that unexpectedly unnerved him, and he had quickly leaned down to hide his discomfort behind a kiss for little

Jeannine. "You look like a princess, my love," he had remarked.

"I'm a knight."

"Me, too," chirped Dierdre, lifting a child's wooden sword for his inspection.

"Ah, I see," Julian drawled, and flicked his gaze to Claudia. "And you are . . . ?"

The girls giggled; the briefest hint of a smile graced Claudia's lips. "Merlin, of course. This is Sir Lancelot," she said, motioning to Jeannine, "and Sir Gawain."

Dierdre suddenly smacked his shin with her sword; the two girls looked at him, their faces turned up like daisies as they waited for his reaction. Julian grimaced. "Slaying dragons, I take it."

Claudia smiled then, and Julian felt his fool heart plunge to his toes. "You might say that," she said, laughing when Dierdre whacked him again. Only harder.

"Darling, I am not a dragon," he kindly informed his niece, restraining the urge to snatch the wooden sword from her chubby little hand and break it over his knee.

"In France you are," Claudia blithely informed him, and Jeannine walloped him with her sword, mimicking her sister. Julian hastily stepped out of their reach as Claudia asked, "What brings you to Château la Claire?"

God, if only he knew. "You might say the wind blew me here," he said with a shrug, and suddenly found himself captivated by the shades of dark gold mixed with the earth brown of her hair.

"It must have been a gale," Claudia remarked. Her lips moved erotically over those words, and the desire to touch those lips with his own was almost overwhelming . . . until Dierdre poked him in the gut with the tip of her sword. "Are you passing through, then?"

Wincing, Julian lied, "For a time." In truth, he hadn't the slightest notion of what he was doing in France, or for how long, or what came next. The only thing he knew for certain was that the London Season had ended, and with it, the distraction of the festivities surrounding Parliament.

She had cocked her head thoughtfully to one side, and aware that he was gazing at her too intently, Julian smiled down at his nieces, grabbing Jeannine's sword before she slammed the tip into the toe of his boot. "Shall I show the knights a bit of swordplay?"

That pleased Sirs Lancelot and Gawain enormously, but much to Julian's chagrin, Claudia was quick to relinquish her claim on the little knights. She stepped back, bid the girls mind they not hurt their uncle too terribly much, and with one last flick of her blue-gray eyes across him, had abruptly turned toward the château. Julian had watched her walk away, a thousand questions on the tip of his tongue and a longing unfurling through his body until his nieces had demanded his attention.

Now, in Dieppe, Claudia chatted with the footman over two tankards of ale as if they were old friends. Fine. She chatted with a footman, but she had barely spoken to *him* at all those few days at Château la Claire.

Not that he wasn't glad for it. He had felt like a clumsy oaf around her, his tongue like leather, unable to speak French *or* English. He, Julian Dane, a man who had seduced and bedded more women than he could count reduced to a blathering idiot in her presence.

And exactly when had *that* malady stricken him?

He hadn't always felt such yearning for Claudia Whitney. Years ago he had thought her an amusing child, then an annoying miss, and then a shy young lady. She had practically grown up with his sisters. The only child of the powerful Earl of Redbourne—her mother having died in childbirth—Claudia met Eugenie and Valerie at an exclusive school for girls shortly after Julian's father had died, and the three became fast friends. When Julian decided the girls' education would be better delivered—and received—under his supervision and with a host of tutors at Kettering Hall, Eugenie and Valerie had pined for their friend until Julian wrote Lord Redbourne to request Lady Claudia visit the country for a month or so. Thus began what was to become an annual summer

event for the Dane sisters and Lady Claudia until they
were grown.

He certainly hadn't longed for her then, he thought,
noticing a man at a nearby table looking at her like a dog
salivating over a piece of meat. He could hardly blame
the poor chap—Claudia had a way of capturing a man's
attention. She was strikingly beautiful—a little taller
than average, slender, and terribly curvaceous. She followed her own rules and set her own standards. If
Claudia Whitney determined the grass would be blue,
half the bloody *ton* would follow suit. She refused to bow
to the latest fashions, yet she possessed more grace than
the most fashionable. Somewhere along the way, when he
wasn't looking, the little demon had blossomed into a
beautiful and poised woman.

In the last few years, Lord Redbourne, as a member of
the Privy Council, had King William's ear on most matters. His home on Berkeley Street was one of the most
popular London residences on which to call, and that was
due, in large part, to Claudia. It was said that an invitation to one of her supper parties was as coveted as an
invitation to Carlton House. She was witty and clever
and not afraid to enjoy life. Yet for all her bravado, she
had a soft heart and eagerly used her position to gather
donations for various worthy causes. It was that which
Julian admired most about her—not that he didn't
appreciate her beauty enormously—but he admired her
even more for being her own woman, and an alluring one
at that.

It was funny, he mused, that he had never really
noticed her until two or three years ago. But one evening
at some ball or another, he had seen her as if for the first
time. He could recall it vividly—she was dressed in a
gown of gray velvet, decorated with tiny little sequins
that reflected the light around her. Her hair was artfully
done in a simple twist and fastened with jewel-tipped
pins that rivaled the sparkle in her dress. When she had
entered the ballroom on her father's arm, it had seemed
as if the world had stopped to catch its breath. She had

been a brilliant, ravishing young woman with clear blue-gray eyes that could pierce a man's very soul and a voluptuous shape that begged for his arms.

In the space of that single evening, Julian's esteem for Claudia the Woman had rooted in his heart and sprouted like a weed.

Unfortunately, so had Phillip's.

The strange sense of discomfort came over him again, the odd feeling that he was packed into his skin too tightly, and he wondered for the thousandth time what might have happened had he noticed her first. But Phillip had beaten him to it, and the unwritten code of honor the Rogues had forged through twenty years of friendship had demanded he deny his growing attraction to Claudia.

Heaven help him, he had tried desperately to deny it—had pushed it down, tried drowning it with whiskey and an endless round of parties—but none of it had worked, and he despised himself for his inability to stay completely away from her. Even after Phillip was dead, he felt guilty for even *thinking* of her.

Julian suddenly drained the last of his tankard. Guilt had eaten at him these long months, and when he had seen Claudia at Eugenie's, the discomfort had seized him with a vengeance. Unfortunately, it had only gotten worse in the course of the next few days at Château la Claire when he realized that Claudia was completely indifferent to him. Good Lord, she seemed to prefer the company of *sheep* to him, taking long walks where no one could find her, eating her meals in the solitude of her rooms. After enduring several days of her aloofness, he had eagerly accepted an invitation to accompany Louis to Paris where he had enthusiastically numbed himself until that Frog had intervened.

Thinking of which, he could certainly use a whiskey now, and tugged again at his insufferable collar.

He was sick to death of denying his longing for her. Phillip had been dead for more than a year. Whatever he thought he might have done differently, however he may have contributed to his friend's tragic death, the fact remained that Phillip was gone and there was no earthly reason why he should deny what was in his heart any longer. If Claudia could befriend a lowly footman, he thought irritably as she lifted her tankard to her lips, then she could very well treat him as if he were someone other than a malevolent stranger. Frankly, he could not remember a time when a woman had ever treated him with such disdain. Ridiculous little chit—who did she think she was?

Julian looked away, searching for the innkeeper. Catching that man's attention, he signaled for another tankard, then glanced toward Claudia's table again, and started badly. She was looking straight at him; her clear blue-gray eyes boring a hole clean through him.

Unbelievable!

How was it possible that of all the days, the hours, the *moments* in villages and countries around the world, *he* should appear *here,* in a small inn in an even smaller French village? He was supposed to be in Paris! her mind screamed, and after all the trouble she had gone to just to make *doubly* sure she would not see him, here he was!

Maybe her mind was playing a trick on her. Maybe that handsome gentleman was actually unknown to her—after all, it was growing rather dark, and he was sitting in the shadows. She pivoted in her seat. "Herbert," she said to the footman, indicating the man in question, *"Qui est-ce?"*

Herbert squinted at the gentleman; a smile spread across his face. "Monsieur le Comte de Kettering, madame."

Oh, *honestly!* Claudia turned toward the wastrel again and he smoothly acknowledged her with a nod. All right, all right, how long until the packet boat sailed? Three hours? Maybe four? She was *not* going to invite him to her table. She would preempt him, have Herbert send the innkeeper to tell him he was not welcome!

"Herbert," she began, then paused, pressing her palm

to her forehead as she racked her brain for an appropriate French phrase. As none was forthcoming, she slid her gaze to the rogue again as the innkeeper placed another tankard in front of him. One corner of his mouth lifted in a lazy smile; he lifted his tankard in silent salute.

Lord *God,* the man was impossibly handsome, she thought as he came indolently to his feet. An Adonis, really. He was tall, two or three inches over six feet. His wavy black hair was far too long, nearly to his shoulders but terribly appealing—particularly as unkempt as it was, with one thick lock draping his forehead. His coal black eyes reminded her of a raven, keen and glittering as if they focused on his prey. His nose was perfectly straight and patrician, his face sculpted into high cheekbones and a square jaw that was covered with the shadow of a beard. He possessed a pair of broad shoulders, but even more startling, she thought wildly as he started toward her, was that his legs looked to be all muscle in the form-fitting trousers he was wearing, impossibly long—and the unmistakable protrusion between them . . . oh, *Lord. . . .* Suddenly frantic, Claudia turned to Herbert and whispered loudly, "Herbert! Ah . . . *aidez-moi, s'il vous plaît!*"

Her clumsy request for help startled Herbert *"Pardon?"*

She could hear each *clop clop clop* of his boots on the oak planks as he neared them. "Don't let him sit here!" she whispered madly.

A light dawned on Herbert's face. "Ah!" he exclaimed, and nodding eagerly, straightened in his chair as Kettering came to a halt next to their table. Herbert fairly exploded into French, gesturing wildly at Claudia, then his foot. Kettering folded his arms across his chest and shifted his weight to one hip as he listened patiently to the footman, nodding occasionally. His casual stance belied his appearance; his neckcloth was stained, his coat rumpled, and the heavy stubble of his beard suggested that he hadn't shaved in more than a day. Actually, he looked as if he had been involved in some altercation. As Claudia was pondering that, his gaze slid to her and one brow arched quizzically. From the sound of it, Herbert was now explaining the unfortunate accident—mimicking *his* version of events, naturally—and then he made the unmistakable gesture for Kettering to sit.

"No!" she cried, and grabbed the back of the empty chair as she jerked her gaze to the blackguard. His black eyes were gleaming with delight. *"Merci bien, monsieur, je vous suis très reconnaissant,"* he said to the footman, and then to her, "You don't understand a word, do you?"

Her shoulders sagged. "Not many," she confessed irritably.

He laughed then, crinkling the corners of his eyes and revealing straight, white teeth. "I always suspected you were lax in your studies," he remarked as he pulled the chair away from her and sat. Before she could respond that she was *not* lax in her studies, but preferred to study something more exciting than dead languages and needlework, he had turned to Herbert and spoke what sounded like flawless French.

The poor footman, having spent the better part of the afternoon unable to communicate, responded excitedly, gesticulating toward the table and the ale and at her—undoubtedly revealing everything about her flight from la Claire. Judging by the way Kettering cast looks of amusement at her, Herbert was embellishing the whole, rather innocent story. After all, she had left Eugenie a perfectly suitable letter explaining her need to return to England, etc., etc., etc. What harm was there? Eugenie might have been gone for *weeks* visiting Louis's ailing aunt! Oh, but she had to leave—she had to be gone from Château la Claire before *he* returned. Before his presence dredged up all the regret and sorrow she'd felt over Phillip's death. She had explained all that to the ridiculous footman.

Herbert abruptly collapsed against the back of his chair, exhausted. He had, apparently, finished his explanation of what they were doing in Dieppe and why his foot was wounded.

Kettering shot her a sidelong glance. "Are you in the

habit of running over all footmen, or do you reserve that for the French ones alone?" he asked casually.

Claudia frowned at Herbert. "Well, I certainly didn't *ask* him to drive me, and I hardly meant to run over his foot, but . . ." *Wait. What was she doing? She did not owe this rogue any explanation!* He was looking quite amused, and she was suddenly reminded of the many times she and Eugenie and Valerie had been called to his study to account for some misdeed. *Would you care to try and explain your behavior? Or shall we move directly to your punishment?*

She looked him square in the eye. "How is it that you are now in Dieppe? Did the tide wash you up?"

He laughed roundly at that, and though she was loath to acknowledge it, the rich sound of his laughter actually made her skin tingle. "Something like that," he said, grinning.

"Well. It was awfully kind of you to stop by and inquire after us, but I—"

The brow arched again. "Actually, I thought to join you."

Oh, *fine!* Claudia frowned. "I don't mean to be discourteous, my lord, but I prefer not to have company presently."

He ignored her and glanced curiously at her tankard. "Ale, Claudia? Rather pedestrian for you, isn't it?"

"I adore ale!"

"Really? I wouldn't have guessed."

"Yes, indeed. I drink buckets of it every day." *Oh good Lord, what a ridiculous thing to have said!*

Smiling, Kettering said something to the footman. Whatever it was, the two of them shared a belly laugh over it. "Might I inquire what you find so terribly amusing, sir?" she asked, glowering at him.

He surprised her by suddenly leaning forward. "Why do you address me so formally, Claudia? You have called me by my Christian name since you were a girl, when you most certainly *should* have addressed me formally." His gaze dropped to her lips. "Don't you suppose we are acquainted well enough to dispense with the formalities?"

No! Well . . . *maybe.* Honestly, she hardly knew him well enough anymore to know what to call him. He wasn't the same man she had known in her childhood, something she realized the day he had called on her to explain in that condescending way of his that she wasn't good enough for Lord Rothembow and should therefore set her sights on other men. This from the man who led Phillip to his demise with the constant gambling and drinking and Lord knew what else. Granted, sitting beside her now he looked the very same as the Julian Dane she had known all those years ago. The same Julian Dane who *still* made her insides turn to jelly. But he couldn't possibly be the same man, because *that* Julian Dane had disappeared when Valerie died, only to be replaced by this imposter. This incredibly handsome, exceedingly *virile* imposter.

Kettering chuckled softly to himself when she did not respond and turned his attention to Herbert, posing a question that Claudia did not quite catch. Herbert responded with much enthusiasm, and after several moments of unintelligible chatter between the two of them—really, she would be quite able to understand if everyone just slowed down a bit—Kettering signaled for the innkeeper. Smiling in that particularly charming way of his, he explained something to the innkeeper that included a gesture toward Herbert and a coin fished from his pocket.

"Certainement, monsieur," the innkeeper replied with an enthusiastic nod, and taking the coin, pivoted sharply on his heel. *"François! Où est François!"* he bellowed, and hurried away, disappearing through a door as Herbert braced his hands against the table and pushed himself to his feet.

Alarmed, Claudia looked frantically from Kettering to Herbert and back again. "Wh–what are you doing, Herbert? Where are you going? You can't walk!"

Herbert grinned and bowed. *"Bon voyage, madame."*

"Not to worry," Kettering cheerfully offered. "Herbert tells me you are returning to England tonight. As luck would have it, you and I are crossing on the same packet. I naturally offered my escort so that he might get an early start for la Claire. He is most appreciative, I assure you—particularly since he had not intended to come so far today."

She ignored that barb because her mind was trying to absorb the idea that the scoundrel was returning to England . . . *tonight!* On the same boat as she? How much worse could this be? She felt a bit of panic and opened her mouth to protest, but Kettering quickly interjected, "I am quite certain you will agree that Herbert has a long journey ahead of him. We wouldn't want to see him start in the middle of the night unnecessarily, would we?"

A young man suddenly appeared, and with one look at Herbert, the two men burst into simultaneous chatter. As Herbert put his arm around the man's shoulder, talking excitedly and gesturing to everyone around him, Kettering turned to Claudia. "Say *au revoir* to Herbert."

"*Au revoir, madame!*" Herbert sang out, and gestured for the other man to proceed. The two Frenchmen began to work their way across the common room, each talking rapidly over the other.

"But—"

"It seems François is a friend of Herbert's cousin," Kettering explained.

"But he can't drive the carriage!" she blustered as Herbert disappeared through the door.

"Ah, but he can. As he apparently tried to tell you all the way to Dieppe, the carriage has a hand brake, and he is quite confident that he can use it, seeing as how it was his foot you mangled, not his hand."

That gave her a moment's pause—come to think of it, Herbert *had* gestured to the brake quite a lot.

Kettering grinned. "Seems you had yourself a rather exciting escape."

Blast it all, how on earth had she ended up alone with

him? "It was not an escape," she insisted, noticing how his eyes danced with amusement. A nightmare—this was a bloody nightmare, she thought madly, because there was no one in Europe who could confound her like the Earl of Kettering!

She frowned; he casually sipped his ale.

As a girl she had worshipped him, had prayed nightly for an older brother just like him—strong and handsome and eager to shower her with gifts and attention, just as he did Eugenie and Valerie and Ann and Sophie. As an adolescent, she had felt the pangs of a deep infatuation turn to horrifying mortification when she impetuously kissed him on the terrace one night. She hadn't really meant to do it, but he had been teaching them how to waltz, and she had been so moved by the magic of it that she had felt compelled to kiss him, bouncing up on her toes and bussing him on the lips. He had all but banished her from Kettering Hall then, but it hadn't stopped her desire. As she grew older, she hung on every rumor and story surrounding the Rogues of Regent Street. Of all of them, the Earl of Kettering was the one with the reputation of being the suave lady-killer, and Lord, what she would have given to be slain by him!

But he never showed her any interest. Worse, he crushed her hopes when she was seventeen. At a ball given in honor of Eugenie's wedding, Julian had smiled at her, told her she looked beautiful, then stood up with her for the first waltz. With effortless grace, he twirled her about the dance floor, all the while smiling down at her and arresting her heart with those black eyes. He spoke of how she had grown, how lovely she appeared in her gown, how very well she danced. If he hadn't been holding her so close, she would have swooned right onto the ballroom floor. And when it ended, he lifted her hand to his lips and kissed her gloved knuckles. "Will you save me another dance?" he had asked. Too dazzled to speak, she had nodded dumbly, then waited all night for him to approach her again.

He never did.

He never so much as glanced in her direction again. And when Claudia saw him slip out a side door into the gardens with Miss Roberta Dalhart on his arm, she had been crushed.

That's right, he had crushed her foolish heart, and she wasn't about to idle away the hours with him. Claudia suddenly came to her feet. "*Au revoir,* Lord Kettering, I believe I shall wait alone," she said coolly, and started to turn.

He caught her wrist in something of a vise-like grip. "Claudia. Sit," he said low. "I may not be the perfect companion, but I'd wager I'm quite a bit more desirable than some drunken Frenchman you cannot understand."

The *arrogance!* She had labeled him a Rake with a capital R seven years ago and could hardly abide the thought of being in the same room with such a terribly arrogant *Rogue,* especially one so full of esteem for himself.

She sat.

It seemed to her that his fingers lingered on her wrist a moment longer. But then he abruptly let go and smiled. "My, my," he said as he settled back to observe her. "The last time I was successful at making you heed my word, you were twelve years old —and it was a rather shallow victory at that."

"What are you talking about?" she asked warily.

"My horse."

The heat immediately crept into her cheeks. "Oh honestly. My father allowed me to ride any mount I preferred. I naturally assumed you would, too," she said with a dismissive flick of her wrist.

"Your father allowed you on the back of stallions accustomed to the weight and crop of a man?" he asked incredulously.

Claudia shrugged slightly and looked at her tankard. *Not precisely.*

"And though I would like to think you never attempted to ride Apollyon again because of my sound advice, I rather think it was the tumble onto your bum that did the trick."

She couldn't keep the thin smile from her lips. "You may be correct, sir," she conceded. "But as I recall, your so-called advice was just as painful."

Kettering laughed. "You were quite an extraordinary lass, Claudia."

Please. She had been a plain little girl with knobby knees and a mouth that was too big for her face.

"And you are an extraordinary woman," he added.

That caused her to choke on her ale. He might as well have called her a traitor, a whore—it was just as shocking. Conscious that he was watching her, she lifted the tankard and took a long, generous swig of the bitter stuff as her mind reeled. He had never thought her extraordinary when she was a child, and he certainly had not thought her extraordinary during her coming-out Season. Even after Valerie's death, on those rare occasions she would encounter him at some ball or rout, he acted as if he hardly knew her. Ah, but all that had changed when Phillip began to court her, hadn't it?

"On my word, some things never change."

Claudia jerked her head up—Kettering was looking at the tear in the sleeve of her gown, an unfortunate mishap when she had tried to force the carriage backward and off Herbert's foot. He leaned forward and probed the tear with his fingers, singeing the bare skin beneath it. "I rather imagine it had something to do with Herbert's accident," he surmised, and lifted his glittering gaze to hers. "Care to tell me why you were running away from Château la Claire?"

Or shall we move directly to your punishment?

Claudia moved her arm away from his touch. "You know, you have a very peculiar way of appearing when I least expect you."

"I was just thinking the same of you. You didn't leave without bidding Eugenie a farewell—the two of you haven't fought again, have you?"

She rolled her eyes at that ridiculous conclusion.

"Although it is hardly any of your concern, ̶ inform you that we do not *fight*—Eugenie and I ̶ longer girls."

"That," he drawled, "is quite evident, madam. If you don't want to tell me, I shall have it from Eugenie, you know, so you may as well 'fess up."

Squirming uncomfortably, Claudia glanced over her shoulder in search of the innkeeper.

"Very well, then, I shall have to conclude it was me," he said cheerfully.

Oh, it was him, all right, everything about him. It was the way he looked, the polished way he spoke, the deadly charming way in which he smiled. It was that his name had been linked with every beauty among the *ton,* married or not—but never hers. And it was the way he had denigrated her when he told her she wasn't good enough for Phillip, then had turned around and led Phillip to his demise. It was all of that and a sense of urgency to flee before she was forced to confront those demons again, relive Phillip's death again, and the events leading up to it. She really did not want to despise Julian.

But she did.

"I confess I am rather keen to know why you would so desperately want to avoid me that you would run a man down. It rather injures my feelings."

As if anything could injure his black heart. "I did not run a man down. I didn't actually *see* him until it was too late. Really, I am not obliged to answer."

A chuckle rumbled through his chest. "But you will," he said in that terribly silky way of his.

Claudia made a frantic motion for the innkeeper then, and when he acknowledged her, she turned to face her new escort. His black eyes locked with hers; a smile lazily lifted one corner of his mouth, and her insides somersaulted in response. That was *exactly* the problem—her insides *always* somersaulted when he smiled. But that didn't change who he was, and he couldn't sit with her, even if they were the last two people on the face of the earth. He was a selfish, arrogant, irresponsible rogue, and though Adrian Spence may have pulled the trigger, Phillip wouldn't have been standing on that field at all had it not been for Julian Dane.

But God in heaven, why did he have to *smile* like that?

"Oh, *please!*" she muttered hopelessly.

With a slight frown of worry, Julian leaned forward. "What is it, Claudia?" he asked, managing to sound genuinely concerned.

"Might we at least have a bottle of wine if we are to wait?" she asked, and immediately closed her eyes, mortified that those words had come out of her mouth.

Three

CLAUDIA COULD HAVE a whole bloody barrel of wine if she wanted it, as far as Julian was concerned—anything to keep her exactly where she was. The innkeeper beamed with pleasure when Julian asked for his finest bottle of wine and quickly suggested a platter of cheese and bread to accompany it. Julian nodded absently to that as his attention was sharply focused on the woman beside him. As her gaze darted to other patrons around the room, she drummed long, tapered fingers on the scarred table, then fingered the gold cross around her neck—

Phillip again. The obscure, demented feeling that he is watching.

Was she thinking of Phillip, too? Remembering what might have been? It had been only eighteen months—perhaps she still mourned him.

Bloody marvelous. It had been and was Julian's grave misfortune to want her, more than he had a right to. More than common sense could justify, even now. Yet he desired her, completely and miserably, and although he *knew* she would never be his when Phillip lived, he could not bear to see her make the dreadful, irrevocable mistake of shackling herself to Phillip. For all of Claudia's sophistication, she was an innocent. She had no way of knowing that if she agreed to Phillip's suit she would be marrying a drunkard facing staggering debt and certain ruin.

So Julian had felt compelled to go to Claudia and

explain that Phillip was not the sort of man for her. He had done it for her sake . . . he was *certain* he had done it for her sake. Claudia, however, had not exactly thanked him for his advice. Actually, she had come dangerously close to hitting him, and Julian was not anxious to resurrect that memory.

He waited until the wine had been brought, and as he filled her goblet, he remarked, "I had occasion to visit the Jardin du Luxembourg while I was in Paris and happened upon one of the finest displays of roses I have ever seen."

Immediately, Claudia shot him a look of suspicion. "Roses?"

"It brought to mind a garden that once boasted England's finest roses. Not as brilliant, perhaps, but nonetheless quite pleasing to the eye and rather well thought upon by residents of that particular parish." He smiled and handed her the goblet of wine.

Her eyes narrowed. "And?"

Very deliberately, Julian poured wine for himself. "And, I was reminded of its unfortunate demise." He lifted his glass and touched the rim of hers with it. "All for the sake of an imaginary castle. You were incorrigible, Claudia."

The memory danced across her eyes. "I beg your pardon, you are mistaken," she said politely. "It was not for the sake of an imaginary castle, but the castle's imaginary bailey, where the imaginary knights housed their steeds. And by the bye, I was *not* incorrigible, I was creative. You, on the other hand, were quite rigid."

"Rigid? Me?" He chuckled, lifted the goblet, and sipped. "Do not confuse discipline with austerity. I assure you, instilling a little discipline into five young girls was not an easy task. I am quite certain you recall the rainbow incident? No doubt you thought me rigid, but I should have taken a switch to all five backsides for running off like that, and at the very least to *yours*."

Claudia almost sputtered her wine. "You think *I* was responsible? I'll have you know that it was all Genie's idea to find the end of the rainbow. I merely claimed it was my doing to protect her from your wrath, as I was often forced to do."

Now that made him laugh. "You would have me believe that? Should I take it then that *Eugenie* chopped down the rosebushes? Or frightened poor Sophie nearly to death?"

"It was hardly my fault that you coddled Sophie so shamelessly," she said, trying to hide an impudent smile behind her goblet.

"I hardly coddled her. But when an eight-year-old girl climbs into one's bed, and clings to one's nightshirt with the grip of ten men because she is frightened out of her wits, one is inclined to allow her to stay."

Claudia actually laughed at him. "All right, I shall concede that point," she said cheerfully. "But I was only twelve! And it really wasn't such a terribly scary story!"

But it wasn't a very scary story! For a brief moment, Julian was transported back in time to where the twelve-year-old Claudia stood before him in his study, her little hands fisted at her sides, her chin raised defiantly, Eugenie and Valerie cowering behind her. *But didn't you think the child would be frightened when Eugenie pretended to be a ghost?* Claudia's pert little nose had wrinkled at that and she had stolen a glance at her partner in crime. *I didn't think she was very scary a'tall. I thought she should have made some noises.*

"It was frightening enough for an eight-year-old. Sophie slept in my bed for three nights before I finally convinced her it was Eugenie underneath that linen."

With a sheepish smile, Claudia dropped her gaze; thick, chocolate lashes dusted her cheeks. "I suppose we might have been a bit careless," she admitted, "but that doesn't mean you weren't terribly rigid."

"What, rigid again?"

"I rather imagine old Tinley had to screw your boots on every morning."

Julian smiled broadly. "Is that so? Then what have you to say about the ponies?"

"Oh! That was hardly my fault!" Claudia insisted with an indignant gasp. "What of Genie? Why is it that you don't recall *her* wretched behavior?"

"My dear Eugenie was a veritable saint. And I suppose the disaster with the rabbits was hardly your doing, either?"

She threw up her hand, palm outward. "On my honor, *that* was most assuredly Genie."

Julian laughed for the first time in weeks, a laugh that started somewhere deep in his belly and twirled about his heart before escaping him. "You were a willful child, and it is a wonder to me that Redbourne didn't lock you up in some convent."

Her smile brightened considerably. *Lord, but her eyes were arresting.* Julian lowered his goblet and looked about the room as he gathered his composure. "What brings you to France?" he asked. "I had heard you were nettling poor Lord Dillbey to draft a parliamentary bill that would allow labor organizations for women and children."

Color crept into Claudia's fair cheeks and she sobered somewhat. "Is that such a horrible thing? Men have them. There is talk in France of allowing them for women."

"And exactly how would you know that? As you can scarcely speak French, I rather doubt you can read it."

That earned him a saucy grin. "Why, Lord Kettering! There are other ways of communicating—one does not necessarily *have* to speak French."

Oh, yes, he could only imagine that was true. "I suppose your considerable charms were enough to convince Dillbey?"

With a rather unladylike snort, Claudia shook her head. "The *king* could not convince Dillbey! That man is *impossible!* Rather pleased with himself, if you ask me, and fancies the rest of us should be just as pleased. . . ."

Lord Dillbey was, apparently, often on Claudia's mind, as she spent the better part of the next quarter of an hour detailing his many idiosyncrasies, not the least of which was his apparent disregard for womankind in general. That was not entirely true—Dillbey was a regular customer at Madame Farantino's, a rather expensive and clandestine gentlemen's club—but he *was* rather odious. Although not as odious as Claudia found him, and Julian was terribly amused by her description of his long, thin neck and peculiar walk as resembling an ostrich all dressed up for Christmas.

The more she talked of Dillbey and her causes, the more she seemed to relax. He would have thought it impossible, but Julian grew increasingly enchanted. The aloofness he had suffered from her at Château la Claire seemed to dissipate altogether, and it was easy to see why Claudia was so popular among the *ton*'s eligible bachelors. She had a dozen ways of smiling that made a man feel as if he was on top of the world. When her eyes glittered with amusement, that same man could not help but wonder how they might glitter in the tumult of love-making.

God Almighty, was there *nothing* he could do to steel his heart against this impertinent, charming, stubborn, and beautiful woman?

Phillip never had her.

He was ashamed to think it, but the knowledge kept creeping into his thoughts, unwanted, unfounded. Yet Julian was glad for it. *He* wanted the privilege of holding her, of making passionate love to her. He wanted her all to himself, and at this moment, he didn't give a damn what that said about his character or his actions almost two years ago. He wanted her so badly, *had* wanted her for so long now, that sometimes he actually felt paralyzed with a longing he could hardly contain. That didn't stop him from feeling like a traitor to Phillip, even now, but he couldn't make himself care any longer.

He just wanted her.

Claudia was in deep trouble. Oh, yes, *very* deep. Ocean deep.

She swirled the contents of her goblet with one hand

and watched his fingers caress the lines on the palm of her other as he pretended to read it, the skill dubiously gained during a particularly memorable trip to Madrid some years ago.

She had tried to remain aloof from the arrogant rake, but he had to go and be insufferably clever and charming and witty, and good *God* was he handsome! Ah, but she knew what he was about. At five and twenty, she was well acquainted with the signs of subtle seduction—reading her palm, indeed! It galled her to think that she might still succumb to such adolescent games!

"Ah. See this line? It means you will love well and be well loved in return," he said, and lifted his raven eyes to hers.

"Rather, you *wish* that's what it meant."

"You've no idea how much," he easily agreed, and dropped his gaze to her palm again as he languidly traced the line with the tips of his fingers, his touch feather light. Her skin tingled deliciously, and she recalled. Beatrice Heather-Pratt, the wife of the invidious Viscount Dillbey, whispering to her, *"No man can pleasure a woman like Kettering—dear me, what that man can do with his hands!"* This, she had said breathlessly to Claudia as she tried to adjust her coif, having just come from the closed morning room at a Harrison Green party. She and Beatrice had been standing along one wall, both of them surreptitiously watching Kettering saunter across the crowded room like a bantam cock upon his exit from the very same morning room.

"And this line means you will live a long life, apparently with many grandchildren to comfort you in your old age."

Her skin was on fire.

"What nonsense, your palmistry!" she scoffed, and withdrew her hand.

"Perhaps, but I think there is something to be said for it. After all, one's skin reveals many things about one's character."

Her scalp prickled; she took a gulp of wine. "By one's *skin?*" she asked, feeling a little light-headed.

"Yes, indeed." He leaned forward, only inches from her face, and peered closely. "For example, the fine lines around a woman's eyes," he murmured, lifting his hand to brush her temple, "tell a man that she likes to laugh, that she is happy." Heat shot down Claudia's neck and into her chest as he traced a line around the corner of her eye. "And the fine lines around her mouth," he continued, his gaze and his finger dropping to her lips, "tell a man when she is not happy." He touched the corner of her mouth so lightly that Claudia's pulse was suddenly racing. Impossibly, he leaned closer. He meant to kiss her. Her mind screamed to pull back, but Claudia froze, unable to stop him, *wanting* him to touch her with his lips—

"Pardon, monsieur."

Claudia started, her cheeks flaming, but Julian calmly leaned back and removed his hand from her cheek, his gaze still riveted on her lips. *"Oui?"*

The innkeeper reported something in rapid-fire French.

"Merci," Julian said, his gaze still locked on her. "It would seem the *Maiden's Heart* is ready for boarding."

"Oh! That's very good news," she blustered clumsily, and looked down as she tried to fit her hand into a glove that Julian had somehow coaxed off her. The innkeeper said something more, and by the time Claudia had managed to stuff her hand into the tight kid leather glove, Julian had come to his feet, was shoving a hand through the thick tousle of his hair as the innkeeper walked away. He regarded her rather sheepishly. "We've a bit of a problem, I'm afraid."

She didn't like the sound of that.

"It would seem we owe the man a little more than a franc. Claims we drank from his finest stock," he said, and motioned lamely toward the empty bottle.

Judging by the trouble she was having getting to her feet, Claudia thought that she in *particular* had drunk

from his finest stock. Grasping the table for support, she
hauled herself up, smiled broadly at Julian, and could
have sworn she heard something very much like a groan.
"Claudia . . . it's rather a long story, but the short of it is,
I'm afraid you find me without my purse."

She blinked.

He frowned. "I have no money."

That sobered her. A thousand things tumbled through
her mind, not the least of which was the distasteful notion
that he had insisted on keeping her company because he
had no money. And exactly how was it that one of the
richest men in England could find himself in such a
predicament? She did not want to know. "I see," she said,
and snatched up her reticule.

"No, you really don't."

She raked a look across him, and with surprising dex-
terity given her state, managed to pull open the little bag
and produce several coins that she tossed onto the table.

"That is very kind of you," he muttered.

"Think nothing of it," she responded tightly. The man
was a *rake,* had always been and undoubtedly would
remain so for the rest of his bloody life! She should have
known his interest was insincere, his attentions self-
serving!

She stooped to fetch her portmanteau, but Julian was
there before her, and easily hoisted it onto his shoulder.
"Please allow me," he said, balancing himself with his
small satchel in his other hand.

Oh, but she already had. She had allowed him to
make a fool of her. *Again.* Claudia started walking—
weaving, really—out the door, her heart thumping angrily in her chest, and marched indignantly down the
pedestrian walkway toward the pier.

"Claudia, I'm as anxious to get to England as you,
believe me, but I can't fly," he said somewhere behind her.

She realized she was practically sprinting and
stopped, folded her arms across her chest, and glared out
across the Avant-port. Julian paused to catch his breath,

adjusting the heavy bag on his shoulder. "It's not what you think," he said, reading her mind.

Bloody hell if it wasn't.

"The Captain has my purse—*and* my pistol—it's Renault's way of aggravating me. When we reach Newhaven, I'll repay your generosity, every last franc of it."

"You must think my manners quite appalling if you think I would begrudge a fellow traveler some wine," she said in her best aristocratic voice. "There is the *Maiden's Heart*," she quickly interjected before he could speak further, and marched onward, not caring if he kept up or not.

Fortunately, the captain was the same one who had brought her to France, and was quick to show her to his best cabin—a small, airless pocket, really. Lying on the hammock that served as a bed, Claudia battled herself, trying not to think about The Rake. That man was one of the original Rogues of Regent Street, a libertine with a nasty reputation for breaking hearts, a ruthless charmer. Her biggest mistake was sharing a bottle of wine with him in the first place.

That was true in more ways than one, she realized as soon as the ship began to move. She'd never been terribly good at sea, particularly in the fast little clippers, and with a good amount of wine in her, she was feeling ill before the ship had hardly put to sea. She tried to brave it as best she could, but an hour into the voyage, she was in desperate need of air.

She hurried up onto the deck, smiled thinly at two sailors who were coiling a rope as thick as a man's arm, and frantically sought a place where she might be alone. On the lee side of the ship, she found a spot that seemed about as private as one could hope, and leaned over the railing, taking deep gulps of the salt air. That helped to steady her roiling stomach, and after a few moments, she was feeling much improved, her head clearer. She glanced up; the night sky formed a brilliant canopy above her. The full moon illuminated their course and stars glittered like diamonds suspended from the heavens. It was a vast, natural wonder that she never tired of, and for a few moments, she forgot everything else.

"Few things are as breathtakingly beautiful as a starlit night on the Channel."

Slowly, she lowered her head and turned toward the sound of his voice. He was standing several feet away with one foot propped on a barrel, his arm resting on his knee, and a cheroot dangling carelessly from his hand. He had loosened his collar and untied the neckcloth; in the moonlight, the tails of it fairly glowed down the front of his chest. He dragged on the cheroot; its tip flared red hot against the backdrop of the night before he flicked the remainder over the railing. "I know of only one other sight with the power to seize my heart so."

A good Scotch whiskey and a demimondaine at Madame Farantino's, she would wager.

Julian dropped his foot from the barrel and, shoving his hands in his pockets, strolled toward her. "There is another beauty that takes my breath away time and again."

Perhaps it was the starry night or the lingering warmth of the wine—Claudia didn't know exactly—but she couldn't seem to stop herself.

She laughed—a rather loud belly laugh.

One of his thick brows floated upward, but he kept on, closing the distance between them. Her heart did a strange little flutter, an internal warning of danger. It was the wine. It was the wine making her heart beat so.

She laughed again.

"And now," he said softly, ignoring her snicker, "I see that beauty in the moonlight." He lifted his hand to touch her neck; Claudia flinched as if he'd scorched her. A smug smile curved his lips, and he leaned into her so that she could feel his breath on her neck. "I see that beauty in the moonlight, and I am compelled by an unearthly desire to hold it in my arms," he murmured.

And the sudden desire to be held in his arms stunned her—Claudia promptly took one very large step backward. "My, my," she said behind a nervous little laugh, "I thought I had drunk most of the wine, but apparently, my lord, you indulged in a goblet or two. You must think me terribly naïve."

"Naïve? No. Innocent, yes."

"Not so innocent that I don't know what you are doing."

He grinned. "I wear my admiration openly." And his gaze casually swept the length of her as if to prove it. "You are as stunning in moonbeams as you are by morning's light, Claudia."

With a shout of laughter, Claudia wildly shook her head. "Please God, would you stop? I'm quite fearful you will cause me to snap a rib or some such injury."

"I can't stop."

Curse her knees, but they were starting to shake, giving credence to the ridiculous theory circulating around London salons that his smile could actually melt a woman. "Look here, I know what men are about, and I am *not* a wanton, Julian."

"Ah, so you *do* remember my name," he said as he took another step toward her. And another. There was suddenly nothing but a sliver of moonlight between them. "So tell me, fair Claudia, what are men about?"

She knew *exactly* what they were about, but she was having trouble speaking up at the moment because his dark eyes were piercing hers, boring down into her, past the façade of propriety and well into the very core of the heat that was suddenly creeping into her neck and face. "P-pleasure," she stammered.

"Hmm," he mused, and one hand appeared from behind his back to clasp her elbow. "Not a bad pursuit all in all. Perhaps," he said thoughtfully as the other hand snaked very casually around her waist, "you are a bit jealous of men and all that pleasure?"

She would have protested, but she was caught off guard by the grain of truth in his statement, and besides, his head descended so quickly that she was being swept away on a tide of pleasure before she even knew what had happened. The soft pressure of his lips on hers threw her completely off balance and turned everything upside down; she lost all sense of reason when his tongue touched the seam of her lips, at once shaping and devouring them. The faint taste of tobacco mingled with the masculine smell of him, and the tingling sensation in her lips was suddenly spreading like wild fire through her entire body.

His hands came up and cupped her face; through no accord of her own, Claudia opened her mouth beneath his, and he thrust his tongue deep inside, swirling over her teeth, the soft skin inside her cheeks, around her tongue. She stumbled backward—he caught her with an arm tight around her back and crushed her to him.

Never in her wildest dreams did she think a kiss could be so shamelessly erotic! Her body squirmed for more, all of a sudden pushing against him, her hands around his neck, her tongue darting around his. It felt as if she had drifted into a strange fog and she was suddenly pushed up against the railing, his thigh wedged deep between hers while his tongue thrust into her mouth in an ancient rhythm she instinctively understood and responded to in kind. His hand fell to her leg and he grasped a handful of her skirts, inching the brocade up. A primordial warning sounded in Claudia's fogged mind and she tried to push his hand away.

Julian responded by hoisting her up until she was sitting on the railing, her legs on either side of him, one of his sinewy arms anchoring her firmly to him. With his free hand, he gathered her skirts until his hand found her leg beneath.

If it weren't for his iron grip around her, Claudia would have tumbled right into the sea and drowned in a state of happy delirium. The gentle caress on the inside of her knee—the forbidden touch of a man—sent a current of desire through her that culminated in a raw, moist heat between her legs. Her heart thrashed madly about in her chest and, scarcely able to breathe, she gasped against his mouth. Julian dragged his lips from hers and buried his face in the crook of her neck. "Let me show you pleasure, Claudia," he murmured. "Let me show you pleasure you've never dreamed of."

The passion in his voice made her shudder. But though her body ached for more—*begged* for more—her conscience squeaked a faint protest. This was Julian Dane, a man who had once crushed her tender heart and then killed her intended, no matter how much she didn't want to think of that now. Julian was right—she might be innocent, but she wasn't naïve.

His skill at seduction far surpassed that of any man she had ever known and it frightened her to know how quickly and easily she had surrendered to it. But he was still a rogue polished in the art of seducing women, and the sensual words whispered in her ear were firm evidence of it.

"Let me down," she muttered.

A moment's hesitation and he lifted her from the railing, held her against him while her body slid through his arms till she stood. He didn't let her go immediately, but kissed her forehead and the place on her cheek rubbed raw from the bristle of his beard. "Where is your cabin?"

Claudia shoved against his chest, clearly startling him. "I won't be one of your conquests. I will not be swayed by your charms! Save your kisses for someone who wants them, Julian." And with that, she stepped free of him and walked away, silently castigating herself for being so weak and almost yielding to his charms. What a *fool* she could be! There was not a more celebrated rogue in all of England! What, would she fall into a man's arms just because he spoke prettily to her? Certainly not, and least of all *his* arms!

She despised him!

She *did*, didn't she?

Four

Mₐʀsʜᴀʟʟ Wʜɪᴛɴᴇʏ, ᴛʜᴇ Earl of Redbourne, had just returned from St. James Palace and was holding his own court in the south drawing room of his rather impressive town house on Berkeley Street. The men of the King's Privy Council gathered here every afternoon at precisely six o'clock, and Randall, the earl's butler, served brandies all around.

That's where Claudia found her father upon arrival from Newhaven, where the *Maiden's Heart* had weighed anchor that morning in a steady downpour. Claudia's father and his guests came to their feet the moment they saw her. "I wasn't expecting you today, moppet," he said as she ignored his outstretched hand and embraced him. "I understood you would remain at Madame Renault's another fortnight."

"Renault's aunt is failing, and I felt rather in the way," she said, and pressed her cheek to her father's shoulder.

"Ah, pity, that. You shall tell me all about your little adventure into France over supper." He stepped back, out of her embrace, and smiled. "You know my guests?"

She dipped a polite curtsy. "Good afternoon, Your Grace," she said to the Duke of Dartmoor.

"Lady Claudia," he mumbled with a quick bob of his head.

"My Lord Hatcliffe, how good to see that your ankle is much improved."

The smaller of the two men, Lord Hatcliffe smiled sheepishly and wiggled his ankle. "Much improved indeed, my lady. Nasty twist of the thing."

"My dear, you will want to rest now," her father interjected, and grasping her elbow, steered her toward the door and rapped softly. It was immediately swung open by a footman who stood ready to attend. "Rest now, and I shall see you at supper," he said, and releasing her elbow, turned back into the room. "Randall?" As the door swung shut, Claudia saw him motion his guests to be seated as he resumed his seat, extending his hand so that Randall could fill it with his snifter.

Dismissed. It was the same scene that had been played out hundreds of times in this house and one that never failed to embarrass her. She was to retire to her rooms, fret over hats and gowns and teas while they, the men, talked about the king and the affairs of the monarchy, and reforms and—

"Madam? Shall I ring for your maid?"

She realized she was still standing in the corridor, staring at the closed oak door. Claudia glanced at the footman from the corner of her eye. "Thank you, Richard, that won't be necessary." Pivoting on her heel, she marched smartly down the corridor.

Even the footmen were trained to think her helpless and fragile, she thought irritably as she bounced up the wide, curving staircase to the floors above. Fragile and empty-headed and useful for only one thing in particular. Ah, but it was the way of the man's world—a little fact of life she had never realized until Phillip was gone.

She supposed that at the very least, she could thank the Rake for waking her up to the inequities between men and women.

That, and the passion between them.

Claudia paused at the door of her suite and laid her forehead against the cool oak as she recalled that wondrous, searing kiss. She hadn't been able to stop thinking about it for even a moment all day, and every time she closed her eyes, she saw his tousled hair, the glitter in his black eyes, the dark stubble on his chin. Worse, she felt him—oh God, she *felt* him—his hands on her skin, his tongue in her mouth, his breath in her ear. . . .

She abruptly straightened and frowned at the door. She had never felt such gut-wrenching yearning for Phillip. *Phillip!* Lord above, she was making herself insane! Shoving the heavy door open, she stepped across the threshold and headed straight for her bedchamber, not bothering to ring for her maid. She peeled off her pelisse, untied the sash at her waist, and unbuttoned the front of her travelling gown as she went, then collapsed, facedown, on her bed.

There he was again. That devilish smile haunted her mind's eye. Why did he have to charm her so? Why must he be such a rotten rogue? Seeing him again in France had dredged up old feelings for him that she had thought long dead. If he hadn't kissed her like that, she was quite certain she could have buried them again. She *had* to bury them, because, unfortunately, the passage of time has not really changed her opinion: Julian Dane had led Phillip on that fatal course with no regard for anyone but himself, and least of all, her. But then, he had made it quite clear that she was not worthy of Phillip's affections . . . just as he had once made it abundantly clear she was not worthy of his.

All right. In truth—not that she would ever admit it—no one was more surprised than she when she caught Phillip's eye at the Sutherland ball. It had astounded her that Lord Rothembow, one of the Rogues of Regent Street, the elite of the *ton*'s most eligible bachelors, would be interested in her. As charming as he reputedly was reckless, he was a figure bigger than life to her, terribly handsome with his blond curls and laughing blue eyes. She had thoroughly enjoyed his attentions, but who wouldn't? In the beginning, Phillip made her feel as if she meant something to him, as if she were important. He escorted her to a number of events, gave her trinkets as a token of his admiration, and seemed truly genuine in his affection.

Naturally, it hadn't been very long before her friends were whispering that Phillip would offer for her. Even Phillip hinted at it once—nothing very direct, really, but just a casual remark of their future together. God knew she was certainly open to the possibility. Rather hoped for it, actually. But then, in the last few weeks of his life, Phillip grew distant—even belligerent—and that could only be blamed on the Almighty Lord Kettering. She remained quite convinced that Phillip *never* would have fallen so far had it not been for him. Even that horrible, wretched night Phillip had called unexpectedly, well into his cups—even *then* he had been out with Julian.

That night was her worst memory. Phillip was obviously quite inebriated, although he was usually a master at masking it. But she hadn't really known just *how* inebriated until she did not receive him as ardently as he thought she should. Angered, he had lunged at her, trapping her against the door in an attempt to force her affection.

A shiver ran down Claudia's spine as she recalled how he had shoved his hand into her bodice, cruelly squeezing her breast while his other hand groped for the most private part of her. Fear had quickly turned to terror when she could not stop him, could not stop him from taking her like *that*, in her father's house, like a whore.

By some miracle, she had managed to wrench her arm free and slap him, hard, with every ounce of strength she possessed. Stunned by the blow, Phillip had staggered backward as he lifted a hand to his face. And then he had laughed. Had laughed at her in that same indolent way Julian had laughed when she insisted Phillip cared deeply for her.

She never saw Phillip again. He was dead a scant two weeks later, having followed Julian Dane and the others to some remote hunting lodge for a weekend of debauchery.

Adrian Spence pulled the trigger, but Julian Dane put him in the line of fire.

And she could not, *would* not, forgive it, no matter how hotly he made her blood run.

But really, with the extraordinary exception of last night, he had never shown her the slightest bit of attention in all the years she had known him. If anything, he had run with horror in the other direction. She couldn't help but recall the summer of her twelfth year and the night she had done the unthinkable by kissing him full on the lips. She scarcely had a moment to wonder at her own madness before he jerked her away from him so hard that her arms felt as if they had been yanked from their sockets. "If you ever do something so foolish again, I will send you home at once with a letter explaining to your father exactly *why* you are being sent home from Kettering Hall!" he snapped in a terrifying voice.

Her stomach had twisted with the horror of her mistake, and she had whirled away from him, fleeing the terrace with tears of shame blinding her.

Thirteen years later and it was *still* a painful memory.

Claudia restlessly pushed herself off the bed and crossed to the window.

Even though she continued on at Kettering Hall each summer, she saw him less frequently after that—rarely, if at all, by the time she was grown. But oh, how she had relished the many rumors that circulated about the Rogues of Regent Street! Julian was considered the most handsome scoundrel among them, the one who could turn a woman to butter with just a smile, which he apparently did with alarming frequency—if one listened to gossip, one would think he changed his attentions as often as he changed his shirt. Of course, now that she was older and more experienced in the ways of the world, Claudia understood men like Julian ultimately loved themselves above all else.

Devil take him.

Oh, all *right*. She *had* seen a different Julian when Valerie died. The Julian who stood vigil at Valerie's coffin in the black-draped drawing room as friends and family came to pay their last respects. He would not eat or drink for two days. When Louis Renault tried to coax him to come away, if only to rest, he had lashed out in grief, assailing those around him, begging them to leave him be.

When the Redbourne coach pulled away from Kettering Hall two days later with her in it, Claudia had seen him in the chapel graveyard, down on his knees next to a fresh earthen mound, and her heart had shattered. She had sobbed all the way back to London for a man who was suffering beyond her comprehension.

She had never seen *that* Julian again.

The worst of it was that with the benefit of time, she could see that Phillip really wasn't much different from Julian. In the end, she was nothing more to him than what women were to men in general—mere objects of pleasure, fundamentally insignificant to the world.

After the sting of Phillip's death had passed, she had begun to look around her and really *see* the inequality between genders. Regardless of rank, women were chattel in English society: typically undereducated, living under a man's thumb, and completely subject to his whims. If Claudia had learned anything, it was that she wanted more from life than to be somcone's hostess, wife, or lover. Yet how did she break the bonds of society's restrictions or social mores she had never even questioned before then?

She had mulled it over for a time, feeling inadequate to the task, lacking the imagination necessary to force change. Then one day, she found the young daughter of a kitchen maid wandering about the main library. Happy to have a little company, Claudia had fetched a book her governess had read to her as a child and invited Karen to sit beside her so that they might read the book together.

But Karen did not know her letters, and she was well past the age a girl should know her letters. Worse, Karen didn't seem particularly bothered by it. Claudia had known instantly what she must do.

The very clear notion had come to her almost immediately: Women had to open their minds if they were to

gain equality and respect. Girls had to be educated
beyond rudimentary language and math so that they
might fill their heads with endless possibilities. The girls
of the lower class, who were the least likely of all to
receive an education, needed her help the most.

It was with great enthusiasm and a sense of purpose
that Claudia embraced her worthy goal, and it was one
that she had worked relentlessly toward since, her con-
viction strengthened every day by the women she met
and the many dreams and aspirations they held, regardless of rank or situation. She used her position—or rather,
her father's position as confidant to the king—to further
her cause. Her efforts, she would admit, had not always
been met with great enthusiasm. Most men and women
among the *ton* believed that the woman's place in the
home and in society was as it should be and resisted any
change. There were times that Claudia felt as if she was
trying to move a mountain, but not once did she give up.
In fact, she was enjoying a respite at Eugenie's before
tackling her largest project to date: She was determined
to garner the financial backing necessary to open a school
for girls near the London factories where many women
and children worked.

And that was what she would focus her attention on
forthwith. She would forget the Rake, forget the kiss, and
forget everything about France altogether.

So, after a hot bath, when she descended to the lower
floors for supper, she was feeling much improved, her
energy renewed and focused on the important tasks
before her. She was met at the dining room door by a footman carrying a huge bouquet of daffodils, irises, and
roses—a very unusual but pleasing hodgepodge of the
finest hothouse flowers.

"How very lovely, Jason. Did Papa have them sent?"
she asked, beaming as the footman set the monstrous
bouquet on a small console.

"No, milady," he said, and handed her a card. She
opened the card, glanced at the signature, and felt an
immediate flurry of butterflies in her stomach.

*I recall with a smile the pleasure of our
acquaintance in Dieppe, but the crossing is
remembered with even greater fondness. Please
accept this token of my thanks for your very
charming company during what could well have
been an intolerable wait.*

Yours, Kettering

The Rake had found his way home after all.

Five

WALTER TINLEY, the Kettering butler for more than forty years, opened the door of the mansion on St. James Square and immediately wrinkled his age-spotted nose. "Beggin' your pardon, my lord, but it would seem a rather pungent odor has accompanied you home."

Julian glowered at the ancient butler—the older Tinley got, the less reverent he became. Every year at Christmas, Julian offered the man a very generous pension and a lovely cottage at Kettering Hall in Northamptonshire. Every year, the old sawhorse declined, determined to serve until his dying day. "Are you going to let me in?" he growled.

Tinley stepped out of the way, drawing an audible breath when Julian passed.

Irritable and exhausted, the noise of running feet assailed his frayed nerves as Julian stepped inside. With a squeal, his youngest sister, Sophie, came flying down the marble staircase and into the foyer. "You're home!" she cried as she flung herself into his arms. He caught her about the waist, finding his balance just before they both would have landed on the floor. "I've missed you terribly, Julian! Aunt Violet said you'd be another fortnight or more— Oh, my," she said, and gingerly pulled away, nose wrinkled. "Oh, *dear*," she repeated, and took several steps backward.

With an impatient sigh, Julian tossed his gloves at a hovering footman. "It has been a rather arduous journey," he groused. "Tinley, I should very much like a bath. Have one drawn, will you?"

"Most immediately," the old man replied, and hurried as fast as his ancient legs would take him. Julian scowled at his retreating back; fortunately, Rosie, the proprietor at the Park Lane hothouse, had not been so affronted. But then, he was one of her best customers. The two gentlemen waiting to purchase fresh flowers had seemed a little offended, particularly the one who pulled out a kerchief and held it over his nose. Well, devil take them all! When he had offered that stubborn Demon's Spawn the use of the *one* coach he had been able to find for hire in Newhaven, he had fully intended to ride along. But oh no. That did not suit Lady Claudia. She wouldn't take his money, but she'd damn sure take his coach and leave him stranded in the rain with no mode of transportation. It was bloody fortunate that he had been able to find a man willing to sell an old nag to him instead of the rendering factory.

"I've so much to tell you!" Sophie said excitedly, and Julian forced a smile. Standing in the low light of the foyer, she looked pretty. Of all his sisters, Sophie was the plainest. She did not have the stunning eyes that Eugenie and Ann had, or the lovely, thick black hair Valerie had been blessed with. Her hair was a mousy color, her brown eyes small and set wide apart. Not that it mattered to him—he saw her beauty in so many other ways—but it mattered to the *ton* and Sophie had had very little success on the marriage market. That lack of success had, unfortunately, begun to erode her self-confidence. And for that reason above all else, Julian despised the *ton*.

"Have you?" he asked, and gestured for her to accompany him as he moved up the stairs.

"Lady Farnhall invited Aunt Violet and me to a tea last Tuesday while Lord Farnhall was in Edinburgh or some such place, and I didn't really want to go because I had quite a headache, but Aunt Violet persuaded me, and I am quite happy that I went!"

"Were you? And whom did you see?" he asked absently, reaching the first floor and moving down the corridor to the master suite of rooms. Sophie quickly rattled off all of the attendees, then reviewed what each was wearing as they crossed the threshold of his suite. Nodding to Bartholomew, his valet, Julian removed the grimy neckcloth and tossed it to his outstretched hand. The fastidious man instantly made a face and held the offensive garment between thumb and forefinger, away from his body, while Sophie continued her chatter about a silk or something that Miss Candace Millbrook had worn to the tea party. With an appropriate *ah* now and then, Julian disappeared into his dressing room to remove his boots and was fanning the rank odor from his nose when he heard the name Sir William Stanwood. He sat up. "Pardon?" he called through the open door.

That was followed by a moment of silence, then a faint, "Sir William called."

Julian was at once on his feet and in the main room, oblivious to his stockinged feet and dangling shirttails. "I beg your pardon?" he demanded.

The color instantly bled from Sophie's face. "He . . . he called Wednesday."

He made a supreme effort to maintain his composure, but blast her, it was difficult! Several years her senior, Sir William Stanwood was an odious man with no more interest in Sophie than her obscenely large dowry and the generous annuity her father had left her. He had a sordid reputation, was known to have one foot in and the other just out of debtors' prison, and was rumored to have something of a mean streak when it came to the baseborn women with whom he consorted. His connection to the fringes of the *ton* was tenuous at best, owing chiefly to a nebulous but apparently real blood relationship to Viscount Millbrook.

"Sophie," Julian began, but stopped as she sank into a

leather chair at the hearth, her expression both hopeful and fearful. Marvelous—he was about to crush the one true hope the girl thought she had. Oh, he had no doubt Sophie would marry one day, and when she did, it would be to a man who was not only of suitable rank, but one who could be counted on to treat her well. It most definitely would *not* be to William Stanwood.

He thrust his hand through his hair and turned to his valet. "Nothing more," he said, and waited for Bartholomew to quit the room before speaking again. "I thought we agreed during the Season that Sir William's attentions were not to be acknowledged or returned, did we not? We had an agreement, you and I."

Her gaze fell guiltily to her lap. She shrugged, studied her hands. "I merely said he called. I didn't say that I had *received* him."

Oh, no. He hadn't raised four girls without learning one or two of their tricks. "No, you didn't say . . . did you receive him?"

Another, smaller shrug. "Perhaps for a moment," she muttered, and glanced up, cringing at whatever she saw in his face. "It would have been terribly rude to turn him away! Aunt Violet chaperoned! He called as he was nearby and thought to wish us well! Where is the harm?"

The harm? The harm was that Stanwood would slither into her life like a snake, then squeeze the very breath from it! How did he tell a young woman that the *one* man in all of England she thought esteemed her above all others was a degenerate blackguard in pursuit of her money? He walked to the window, the muscle in his jaw working frenetically as he tried to think exactly how to put things so that he did not hurt her.

"I shouldn't want to seem cross, Julian, but I will be one and twenty soon. You can't tell me whom I may or may not see then."

The uncharacteristic challenge in her words shot a bolt of fear right through him. Julian whipped around, covering the ground between them in a few long strides. Sophie started badly, tried to stand up from the chair, but he caught her elbow and yanked her to her feet, holding fast. "Do not think," he said low, "that you will be allowed to see him even then, little one. You will still be in *my* house, under *my* protection, and you will never have my leave to receive him, do you understand me?"

Sophie's eyes fluttered wide; she jerked her arm from his grasp and stumbled backward. "Why shouldn't you want me to be happy?"

"Of course I want you to be happy, Sophie! But you will not find happiness with the likes of him. You must trust me—I know what is best for you."

Her bottom lip quivered. "You know *nothing!*" she cried, and rushed to the door.

"Sophie!"

She came to a dead halt, her back to him, her hand on the porcelain knob.

"Do not see him again."

She shot through the door without looking back. Hearing her muffled sobs as she fled down the corridor, Julian sighed wearily—then went in search of his bath.

When Julian's middle sister, Ann, sent a note the next day inviting him to join a few friends for the evening, Julian fairly jumped at the opportunity, anxious to escape the gloom Sophie's unhappiness had cast over the entire house. Arriving at Ann's home, Julian greeted his sister, exclaimed with horror at how fat she had gotten during his short absence, and smiled when a laughing Ann reminded him that she was five months pregnant.

Ann's "few friends" actually numbered in the dozens, and Julian made his way through the crush to join Victor, Ann's husband, at the sideboard for a sherry. A full head shorter than he, Viscount Boxworth was a quiet man who sipped his sherry while he covertly watched Ann flit about the drawing room from guest to guest. That was one thing Julian liked immensely about Victor—he adored Ann. And now that she carried his child, he could scarcely take his eyes from her. As the two stood making small talk—Julian actually doing most of the talking—he wondered what it must feel like to know one had put a life in a woman's belly, to know a quality of love that would result in an image of oneself.

Victor had just posed a question about Julian's trip to Paris when Lady Felicia Wentworth swept into the drawing room. Julian frowned; Felicia had made her desires for him known on more than one occasion and he was hardly in the mood to put off her advances. On her heels were Lord and Lady Dillbey. *Oh, splendid.* He had encountered Lady Dillbey once in a dark library; well . . . his *hand* had encountered her. Since then, she practically chased him from ballroom to ballroom, and he was hardly in a mood for *that,* either. He took his leave of Victor, and slowly worked his way to the back of the very large room, pausing often to greet acquaintances.

He was speaking to the sister of the luckless Lord Turlington—whose head, coincidentally, Julian had once shoved into a chamber pot at Eton—when he saw Claudia. In spite of Lady Elizabeth, who was leaning into him, batting her eyes and blocking his view as she rambled on about some insipid thing or another, Julian saw her. Bertie Rutherford was standing with her; the dolt was openly ogling her, his gaze dipping frequently to the décolletage of her pretty plum gown.

Julian made his excuses to a disappointed Lady Elizabeth and sauntered forward.

He smiled charmingly when Claudia's eyes rounded with evident surprise. "Good evening, Lady Claudia," he said with a gracious bow, then curtly, "Rutherford." He promptly ignored any greeting Bertie might have had the presence of mind to make, by turning the full force of his attention on Claudia.

"Ah, Lord Kettering, I see you have found your way home from France." She smiled irreverently. "I suppose the wind tossed you back to England's shores?"

Impudent little wench. "Blown in by a storm, actually, and from there I walked the length of the country, as it is quite difficult to hire a coach in Newhaven." Completely remorseless, the Demon's Spawn actually laughed at that. The foppish Bertie looked as if he was trying to think of something clever to say, so Julian moved slightly, putting himself partially between Bertie and Claudia. "I trust the flowers found you?"

Her eyes glistened with great amusement. "Why *yes!* How very kind of you to remember the men who have served our beloved England. The inmates at Chelsea Hospital are teaming together to pen you a proper thank you, as their morning room was brightened considerably by your thoughtful gesture."

Looking a bit confused as per usual, Bertie peered up at Julian. "Beg your pardon? You sent flowers to the inmates at Chelsea Hospital?"

"Not exactly," he responded smoothly.

"Oh, but he *did,*" Claudia cheerfully contradicted. "Seems he has a passion for military men."

"My passion, madam, is really—"

"—quite relentless," she blithely interrupted. "Oh! I see Lord and Lady Dillbey. Please excuse me, my lords, I should very much like to pay my respects," she said, and promptly sailed out of their midst. Bertie sighed longingly after her, then looked at Julian. "Military men, is it? I rather fancy the navy myself."

"Oh, for God's sake, Bertie!" Julian snapped irritably, and strode after the Demon's Spawn.

Dillbey lit up like a chandelier when Julian approached. "Kettering! You must come join our little debate!" he called boisterously as he extended his hand in greeting. Julian nodded to the men standing with Dillbey, then reluctantly bowed over Lady Dillbey's proffered hand. She flashed a blatantly saucy smile at him that her husband could not help but see. Claudia certainly did, judging by the way she frowned at him. "Lady Claudia, we meet again.

"Yes, astonishing how that happens, isn't it?" she muttered.

"Lady Claudia was just explaining to our great fascination that the French are debating the merits of labor organizations for women," Dillbey explained. "Apparently, she has confirmed what we have suspected all along . . . the French are imbeciles!" He laughed at his own joke, as did the two dandies beside him. Julian thought it a rather tasteless remark, and he could all but feel Claudia's discomfort. "My lady, you can be quite entertaining," Dillbey continued, smiling at Claudia. "I understand young women come away from your drawing room with any number of strange notions!" He laughed again; the two dandies chuckled along with much less enthusiasm.

"My lord!" Lady Dillbey exclaimed, obviously embarrassed. "That's simply not true!"

"Why it is!" the old fool doggedly insisted. "My dear, even *you* were quite appalled by her suggestion that women should hold seats in Parliament!" he reminded her. A memory suddenly invaded Julian's mind of Valerie, sitting on the edge of her chair, her feet swinging above the carpet. *Claudia says that Parliament should seat only women, because men argue far too much.*

"Why shouldn't women hold seats?" Claudia asked with a charming smile for the two fops. "Why should men think they are the only ones to know what is best for us all?"

"Because it is true," Dillbey responded in a surprisingly sharp tone. "Women are ignorant in matters such as affairs of state, Lady Claudia, and men do not want their wives and daughters to be unduly burdened with the hard decisions that must be made when attending to the nation's affairs. It is hardly the sort of thing one does on the basis of emotion."

The man did not care for Claudia, Julian realized, and felt a peculiar twinge of anger.

"I beg your pardon, my lord, I should not want to provoke you, but I must respectfully disagree," Claudia said carefully. "Women are not so simple that they cannot learn, or so fragile that they cannot make difficult decisions."

That caused Dillbey's face to turn quite red. Sensing

an impending explosion, Julian quickly interrupted. "You are absolutely right, Lady Claudia. In fact, I rather hoped I might entice you to help me make a difficult decision this very evening." That succeeded in gaining everyone's attention, including a murderous look from Lady Dillbey.

"What decision, my lord?" Claudia asked coolly.

"I should very much like to make a charitable donation to the Chelsea Hospital"—he glanced at Dillbey—"I've quite a passion for military men, you see." Shifting his gaze to Claudia, he grinned. "But I'm quite uncertain how to go about it. You are a benefactress of the hospital, are you not?"

"Yes."

"Splendid. Might I impose?"

She hesitated only a moment. "Of course," she said, and nodding to the little group, walked in the direction of Julian's gesture.

He nodded to the others and fell in beside her, waiting until they were out of earshot. "He's an idiot, Claudia. Pay him no heed," he muttered as they slipped through the crowd.

"But he's the leader of the moderates, and the moderates are the only ones with the clout necessary to see reforms through both houses."

Her political acumen startled Julian, and he peered down at her, wondering who had told her that. "Ah . . . I believe Lady Wentworth is asking for you," Claudia said. Julian lifted his gaze and winced. Yes, Felicia *was* asking for him, waving her fan at him like a strumpet across the crowded room. "Lady Wentworth can wait," he said curtly, and steered Claudia in the opposite direction, toward a sideboard laden with large crystal bowls of wine punch. "He may be a moderate, but he—"

"Shall Miss Early wait, too?" she interrupted. With a silent groan, Julian glanced over his shoulder—Miss Drucinda Early was advancing rapidly on the arm of her cousin, Dalton Early, who was no more than a very casual acquaintance of Julian's.

"Miss Early," he drawled.

"Lord Kettering! How do you *do*?" she squealed like a stuck pig.

"Excuse me, please," Claudia murmured, and before Julian could catch her, she had slipped through his fingers. Whatever Miss Early might have said after that, Julian had no idea. All he could see was Claudia hugging Ann, then walking out of the crowded room alone, dragging his fool heart with her.

Six

TWO DAYS LATER, Claudia had completely recovered from Kettering's uncharacteristic appearance at Ann's gathering and had chalked his attentions up to his being a Rake. Quite certain that this silly infatuation of his would soon pass, if it hadn't already, she attended church services with her father.

As she stood waiting in the narthex—her father was speaking with the vicar, waiting for the moment he could make an appearance he deemed suitable to his station—she absently admired a large bouquet of roses. As she fingered one red bloom, the blasted thing snapped off in her hand. Dismayed, she glanced covertly about hoping her father had not seen it, as this was exactly the sort of thing that could send him into a fit of apoplexy. Naturally, there was nowhere to dispose of the evidence, so Claudia hastily shoved it into her reticule.

"Tsk, tsk, tsk." She froze, recognizing the smirk in that voice, and slowly turned to cast a scathing glance across The Rake. But damn it, dressed in a coat of dark blue superfine and smiling wickedly, he looked especially beautiful this morning, and Claudia's pulse instantly leapt to a steady clip.

He looked at her little beaded reticule and sadly shook his head. "I wonder why you bother to come to church a'tall."

Of all the persons in the world to say that to her! "I beg your pardon—"

"Moppet? It is time," her father said beside her. "Good morning, Kettering. Right glad you can join us every now and then."

The libertine smiled broadly. "Lord Redbourne, it is my great pleasure to attend every now and then."

"Yes, indeed," her father said curtly, and grasping Claudia's elbow, moved her down the center aisle of the church as he nodded imperiously to acquaintances on both sides, muttering under his breath, "Must be a particularly cold day in hell if Kettering has decided to join us, hmmm?"

Yes, well, not only had he decided to "join" them, he had also decided to sit directly behind her. As a result, Claudia's skin prickled throughout the service—she could *feel* him watching her, could feel his eyes burning the skin of her neck, and in the middle of the sermon, she was quite certain she could feel his breath on her nape! His sudden fascination was making her insane, *extremely* anxious, and making her imagine she felt things she could not possibly feel. She sat rigidly, her hands clamped tightly in her lap, afraid to move even a fraction of an inch lest he think he had affected her somehow.

When the congregation rose for a doxology, his rich baritone voice slid over her like silk, and foolish as it was, she actually felt faint. As they resumed their seats, Claudia could not stand it another moment and stole a furtive look at him over her shoulder. He lifted one brow and nodded politely. *Oh!* She could hardly endure this! She would *not* endure it! Perhaps he could persuade other ladies with his charm, but not her. Oh no, not her. When the service at last ended, she marched up the aisle on her father's arm without so much as a glance in his direction, certain he was laughing, and determined more than ever to end this absurdity once and for all.

Across town, Doreen Conner, a woman with callused hands and failing eyesight, sat in her rocker as she did every day until well past midnight, doing any piecework that she could get. It was hard, tedious work, and at times her back ached more than she thought she could bear, but it was better than where she had been, and she was grateful that she could still work.

Doreen had come to London from Ireland more years ago than she could remember, before the Catholic Emancipation and before her papa discovered she was carrying Billy Conner's child. She and Billy had come so they wouldn't have to work the land like their parents, who struggled just to put food on the table. They married at a small church near the Billingsgate fish market, and with the coins they had saved—supplemented by a few from the kind vicar—they had rented a room above a cobbler in St. Giles.

Billy left every morning in search of work and came back every night, sometimes in his cups, other times just plain sullen. Doreen tidied the little room, washed their linens and took them down to the communal pump to rinse, bought their daily portion of bread and tried to make a meal of it. Sometimes, when the baker was feeling generous, he'd give her a potato for soup. By the time little Neddie was born, Doreen had figured out Billy would never find work. He had fallen in with some bad-blooded Irish lads, but it made Billy mad for her to say so, and when he had drunk a glass or two of his favorite Irish whiskey, he'd hit her if she even thought it.

Whatever those useless lads did during the day, it was not enough to feed them, let alone provide for Neddie. So Doreen began taking in piecework from the textile factories. That barely paid enough to feed them, so when a new factory opened, Doreen hired on there to be a weaver. She brought home a few shillings each week, hiding what Billy didn't drink, and it seemed to her that she worked from dawn to dusk so that Billy could have his Irish whiskey.

One night, Billy didn't come home. Doreen was frantic when one of the laddies told her he had cocked his toes up down on the banks of the Thames. In near hysterics, she rushed down to the place they buried paupers. A kind old man took pity on her, and led her around to the back where they laid them in one big hole, and she and the man had wrenched the boots off Billy's stiff feet. Clutching the boots to her chest, Doreen had headed home. In the end, she could thank Billy for two things: giving her Ned and a sturdy pair of boots.

She still had the boots.

After Billy was gone, the cobbler didn't want a woman living in a room for which he could get a pound or two more from a family man. So Fanny Kate, a woman she had met at the pumps, took her in for awhile. Doreen shared part of her weekly earnings with Fanny Kate in exchange for her watching little Ned along with her own children while Doreen worked her hands to the bone as a weaver, putting up with the overseer's roaming hands and lewd suggestions. She despised that man, with his big belly and his bad teeth, but she had no choice except to endure it, because it was the only work she could get.

One day, when Doreen returned from the factory, Ned wasn't at Fanny Kate's to greet her. Fanny Kate lifted her head from her piecework long enough to tell her that Ned had run off with some ragamuffins. For the first time in her life, Doreen had known real panic. She had set out in her dead husband's boots, walking every street in St. Giles, looking in every doorway and every alley for her six-year-old son. With each step she took, the more she realized she could not raise her son to manhood, not like this.

She found Neddie down on the docks begging fancy lords for a ha'penny as they climbed onto their fancy boats that would take them upriver to their big fancy homes. Doreen took Neddie back to Fanny Kate's and sat up all night thinking about what she had to do. The next day, she and Neddie called on the overseer at his room near the factory. Doreen offered the use of her body in exchange for a place to sleep and keep her Ned.

That arrangement worked as well as could be expected until the old goat got a child on her. He didn't care so much for her then, and when she got big, he threw her out. Doreen found her way to a workhouse, where she and Ned were allowed to stay because Ned was eight and old enough to work. The two of them worked side by side in the carding room of a factory until her water broke, and Doreen gave birth to a perfect little girl she named Lucy. It was God's will, she supposed, that she managed through those years to keep food in her children's bellies. She went to other men as necessary, but fortunately, none of them got a child on her.

When Ned grew tall and lean and handsome, he wanted nothing more than to be a sailor. He'd watch the boats come up the Thames and brag that one day he would see the world, and that he'd bring a handsome sailor home to marry Lucy and fancy dresses for his mama. Doreen wanted nothing more than for Ned to have his dream, and she worked every day, even when she was so sick with fever she barely knew her own name. She scrimped and saved and finally had enough coin to buy him a pair of fine new boots and two good woolen shirts so that he could go off and be a sailor. Her Ned left her one bright morning when he was fifteen years old, and Doreen knew as she watched him walk away with his cotton sack slung over his shoulder that she'd never see her boy again.

She and Lucy continued on at the factory as weavers. Lucy grew into a pretty girl with green eyes and yellow hair, and when she began to grow into her curves, the lads took notice of her. Doreen tried to do her best by Lucy—she warned the girl what men were about, but the lass never seemed to hear her. The girl was only thirteen when the overseer's son took her out behind the factory and showed her what a man did to a woman. She was only fourteen when another lad got a child on her. And she was all of fifteen when she and that baby died in her dirty old cot, neither of them able to separate from the other as they ought.

When Lucy died, Doreen felt as if she'd lost her right arm, but she went back to work the next day just as she always had. She let the new overseer tell her that she was late and owed a fine for it, and let the other women steal the bread from her bucket so they'd have enough to feed their children that night. She let the whole world roll over her day after day, feeling nothing. She'd smile when the fancy ladies came to do their charity work, feeling nothing at the looks of appalled revulsion as they passed by. She let the overseer maul her breast when he wanted, feeling nothing when his rank breath filled her lungs. She moved down the line when a new woman came and wanted her spot at the carding station. She just felt . . . *nothing*.

Until one cold, wintry morning. Doreen reckoned she would never know what changed between the time she went to sleep and the time she woke. But she felt different when the whistle blew and it was time to start work. She knew she was different when the new woman told her to move and she pretended not to hear her. She knew she was different when the charity ladies appeared, all shiny in their fancy clothes and jewels, and she scowled at them as they passed. And when the overseer told her she'd have to man one of the big spooling machines that caught and tore her skirts, Doreen heard herself say no. She stood up, looked the little man square in the eye, and just said no. The overseer didn't believe his ears, and he took out the stick he used when the women didn't do what he wanted, and struck her hard across the shoulders. But Doreen just said no again, only louder, and the man might have beaten her to death if the angel hadn't come and taken her away.

Of course she knew it wasn't a *real* angel. She was one of those charity ladies, with pretty grayish eyes and dark auburn hair and a gown made of fabric so fine that Doreen had never seen anything like it. She had put her hand on Doreen. None of the charity ladies ever touched her when they came to look around. But the angel put her hand on Doreen, helped her to her feet, and Doreen had walked out of that factory for the last time.

The angel had brought her to a tidy little town house on Upper Moreland Street, far from the factories. That had been a year ago, and Doreen had been at the little town house ever since, because Miss Claudia had asked her to stay and look after it. In the course of the year, several other women had come and gone, all down on their luck, some of them bruised, others just needing a place to keep their children safe for a time until they could figure out how they were going to feed them. The house was a secret for the most part because Miss Claudia said there were times a woman needed to find her bearings without her man or the magistrate or the overseer interfering. That was the one rule she had for the house: Any woman who stayed had to promise she wouldn't tell a soul about it, unless that soul was another woman in need.

Doreen kept the little house clean, made sure everyone had plenty of food and a clean bed to sleep on, and in exchange for that, Miss Claudia gave her a monthly stipend. But it was too generous to Doreen's way of thinking, so she spent her evenings doing the piecework, hoping someday she could repay Miss Claudia for all her kindness. She doubted there was enough coin in all of London to do that, but she worked at it all the same.

And she was working the afternoon she saw Miss Claudia's carriage pull up to the curb. She paused and watched her alight, taking the box the driver handed her. A frown creased Doreen's brow; something was different since Miss Claudia had come back from France. Oh, she still smiled that sweet smile of hers, but there was a distant look to her eyes and a bit of hesitation in her speech. It was almost as if her mind was in another world. It was none of Doreen's affair, but nonetheless, she had a notion of what ailed her—she hadn't worked around women all her life not to know a thing or two about them.

"Good morning, Doreen!" Miss Claudia called cheerfully as she stepped inside.

"It's afternoon. You've a fever?" Doreen asked, folding her arms across her chest.

Miss Claudia looked startled. "A fever? Of course not," she said, and laughed.

"You don't look quite right. Haven't since you come back," Doreen insisted.

"I am quite well, I assure you," she said, and swept into the parlor, where she set the box down. She removed her bonnet, let it dangle from her hand for a moment as she stared into space. "Oh my, the chair has not yet been repaired? I asked Mr. Walford to come by as soon as possible," she said, and absently dropped her bonnet. On the floor.

"Mr. Walford says he will come on the morrow—"

"He said the same on Monday—"

"He'll come when he's the time. Sit now, while I pour you some tea," Doreen insisted, but Miss Claudia ignored her. She set the broken chair upside down and attempted to screw the leg in herself. "It would seem rather easy, yet I can't seem to make the leg fit properly."

"I've already tried. That chair needs a man's hand." She glanced at Miss Claudia from the corner of her eye as she stared, hands on hips, at the chair. "Same for you, truth be told."

With a startled gasp, Miss Claudia gaped at Doreen. "I beg your pardon?"

Doreen flashed a rare, gap-toothed smile. "Ain't none of my affair, miss, but you've got that look about you if you don't mind me saying—have since you come back from France," she said, and calmly poured a cup of tea.

"That look? *What* look?" Claudia demanded as she marched across the room to accept the cup of tea Doreen offered her.

"*That* look. The one a woman gets when a man has gotten in her head and she can't shake him out." The suggestion was enough to make Miss Claudia turn a bright shade of pink, and Doreen sank into a chair, bracing her hands on her knees. "I'll be. It *is* a man!" she exclaimed, grinning.

"*No*," Miss Claudia said with an emphatic shake of her head.

"Who's the bloke?" Doreen asked, cheerfully ignoring the denial.

The pink in Miss Claudia's cheeks turned red. "There is no *man*, Doreen!"

"One of those high and mighty lords in Mayfair, ain't he? Ooh, I'll wager he's a handsome one, too. Sure, all those lords are handsome. Blimey, some dandy has set his cap on you, ain't he?"

Claudia's teacup rattled on the chipped saucer; she hastily put it down. "You've a vivid imagination, Doreen!" she said, and laughed as she self-consciously fumbled with her sleeve.

"Bloody hell, the gent has you by the tail!" Doreen exclaimed gleefully. "Well, I'm glad for it. A pretty woman like you ought to be married. Aye, a woman like you is what those dandies want in a wife."

Claudia stood, looked around the room, then suddenly sat again. "I . . . I forgot to ask. Is there anything you need?"

Doreen laughed for the first time in a long time. Miss Claudia was always so confident, so poised—exactly how Doreen imagined the queen to be. Yet at the mere mention of a chap she was a basket of nerves. "We've more than enough," she said, still chuckling, and nodded toward the box. "I reckon we fare as well as the king here. You needn't worry about us."

Claudia glanced at the box. "Yes. Well! There you have it, then!" She smiled brightly—*too* brightly—and fairly vaulted out of her chair. "I'm sorry, but I can't stay." She walked out of the parlor. Without her bonnet.

Doreen picked it up and followed her to the front door. Miss Claudia yanked it open and barely glanced at Doreen over her shoulder. "I shall call again within a few days—"

"Aye. Want your bonnet?" she asked, smiling again when Claudia flushed and snatched it from her hand. She pivoted on her heel and marched down the little stoop toward the waiting carriage, springing inside before the driver could get down to help her. Doreen smiled and waved, chuckling delightedly when the young woman refused to meet her gaze as the carriage pulled away from the curb.

Was it so bloody *obvious?* Claudia yanked her hand from her glove and pressed it to her cheek, feeling the heat of mortification seep through her skin as the carriage bounced along the pitted street. Apparently so, if Doreen Conner noticed it. This was *unbelievable!* Not a month ago, she had been very happy with her work, undaunted by society's skepticism and her father's increasing talk of marriage. She had been perfectly content, had wished only to visit Eugenie and rest for a time before she tackled the school project. And she had felt perfectly safe to do so because Eugenie said he never came to France—she had written that *explicitly* in one of her letters, said that Kettering "did not care for Frogs!"

Well, The Rake apparently did not have such a great aversion to the French, because there he had appeared next to Eugenie's fountain, as big and bold as ever. His sudden and unexpected appearance had unnerved her so badly that she could scarcely think what to do. So she had done the thing she had been taught in ballrooms across London.

She cut him.

Directly, indirectly, every way she could think of, until he had finally left Château la Claire.

Naturally, she had thought she had escaped. But oh no—the battle had only begun. It was a battle, all right. He had started it aboard the *Maiden's Heart,* proving himself a paragon of obnoxious male behavior—in spite of the fire he had lit in her belly. Thank God she had come to her senses and ended *that* for the ridiculous moment that it was! And if he had any doubts about just how absurd she found it, they should have been dispelled altogether when the very next day she took his coach and left him standing in the rain at Newhaven . . . cursing quite loudly, as she recalled.

But no! Oh no, no, no. First, he had sent that massive

bouquet of flowers, one so large and ostentatious that even her father—who usually noticed only those things that had to do with the king or his own fastidious appearance—had commented on them, taking the opportunity to remind her that at five and twenty, her opportunities for a good match were fading. As that had sufficiently humiliated her, she had sent Earl Libertine's bouquet to the inmates at Chelsea Hospital.

With any other man, that slight would have ended it. But not Kettering. Even at Ann's gathering, when she seized the opportunity to tell him openly and plainly what she had done, he had remained irritatingly unperturbed. So she had, therefore, proceeded to ignore him—not that he could possibly have noticed, what with Ladies Wentworth and Dillbey and the horrid Miss Early practically drooling all over him.

That night, naturally, had been followed by his sudden and divine appearance at Sunday service, where his inexplicable attendance was eclipsed only by the arrival of the jeweler's box later that afternoon, containing a bracelet from which a dozen or more French centimes dangled. There was no accompanying note.

The bracelet was sent to Kettering House on St. James Square early the next morning—with a note.

*Kettering, you do me a grave insult by
continuing to insist on the reimbursement of a
rather inexpensive bottle of wine and a wheel of
cheese, particularly when said wine was sour and
the cheese more aptly described as offal. Please
desist from sending any other tokens of your
appreciation, sir.*

C. Whitney

By mid-afternoon, Claudia had received two bottles of very expensive French wine and a wheel of Swiss cheese stamped with the royal order of William IV. Deciding Kettering's largesse would be much more appreciated among Doreen's charges than in her father's house, Claudia had brought it to the Upper Moreland Street house, but God in heaven, she could not escape him even there!

Well, her next note would *surely* end it. Even a ruthless charmer like Kettering would stop this game if she was unwilling to participate in it, and she would make that abundantly clear. He would stop, and Doreen would not laugh so gleefully, and she could concentrate on her school.

Feeling hardly assured, Claudia turned her attention to the window and realized they were on Regent Street. Ann had told her about a new modiste, and Claudia was suddenly of a mind to pay the shop a call. She rapped on the ceiling, instructed Harvey where to pull over, and alighted from the carriage in front of the shop. Clasping her hands behind her back, she stopped in front of the large bowed windows, closely perusing the latest fabrics newly arrived from Holland. As she studied a blue silk, a shadow filled the corner of the window. Suddenly aware of someone directly behind her, Claudia started and whirled about, almost colliding with his brick wall of a chest.

Julian grinned, leaned over her shoulder to peer in the window, and casually remarked, "The royal blue would look very well on you. It is really the only color that could do full justice to the beauty of your eyes, I think."

Clapping a gloved hand over her thundering heart, Claudia gaped at him. "Are you *following* me?" she demanded.

He laughed a rich, deep laugh as he reached for her hand, carelessly peeling it away from her heart. "My love, if I were following you, I would choose a more enticing time and place, believe me." The corner of his mouth curved upward; his gaze dropped to her lips. "But never doubt that the moment you beckon, I will follow." And then he turned her hand over, found the little circle above the buttons where the material didn't meet, and kissed her wrist. Arrogantly, openly, and very leisurely, he kissed her wrist right there in the middle of Regent Street, in front of God, England, and a curious street sweeper who happened by.

A stream of fire spread up her arm and Claudia's heart was suddenly in her throat. "Y-you may rest assured, I shall *never* beckon a rake!" she shot back, yanking her hand from his.

Still wearing that lazy grin, Julian stepped back, dipped his hat with a bow, and said, "Don't be so certain of that. Good day, madam."

And he was gone.

With a moan, Claudia sagged against the shop front. *Why wouldn't he just leave her be?* She didn't *want* his attentions! She wanted nothing to do with him, and Lord knew that Rake wanted nothing more from her than a tumble in the hay! That was, after all, the only thing Julian Dane *ever* wanted from women!

She was really almost seventy-five percent certain of it.

Seven

THIS GAME OF chase had become serious.

A bespectacled Julian stepped up into a coach emblazoned with the Kettering coat of arms and settled against the lush velvet squabs. Dressed in a coat of midnight blue and dove gray waistcoat and trousers, he felt a bit like a dandy in the middle of the afternoon—but then again, he rarely attended high teas, of all things. The invitation to this fundraising event was Ann's, really, but one he brazenly had determined extended to him. But now he was wondering why, exactly, he was doing this.

That was easy, wasn't it? For the moment, the alluring Claudia Whitney gave him something to think about other than Sophie's moping. Unfortunately for that little nitwit, Julian had learned from Aunt Violet that in his absence, Stanwood had paid not one but *three* calls, the last one more than an hour in duration. That discovery had prompted another row with Sophie that ended with her refusing to come down to supper or speak to him at all.

All right, there was that, but there was also the plain truth that he was quite intrigued by this game.

How could he not be? Claudia was such an enigma! She returned his gifts with acerbic little notes that kept him chuckling for days afterward. When he had encountered her leaving Ann's one afternoon, she pretended not to see him, practically vaulting into Redbourne's coach like a circus acrobat even though he stood almost directly in front of her and wished her a good day. And she had flushed a lovely shade of pink when he had kissed her wrist on Regent Street before snapping at him. All in all, the woman was simply refusing to succumb to his charm.

And *that* was unheard of in this town.

Julian shifted uncomfortably against the squabs. Those were the reasons he was all dressed up like a Christmas goose in broad daylight ... but there was something else, too. Something that kept him awake at night, devoured him during the day, made him mad with the absolute burning need to just *see* her. God help him, but the image of her that had lived in his mind's eye these last two years was suddenly vibrant and alive and seared into his heart with a kiss aboard the *Maiden's Heart*.

Thankfully, it was only a short drive to Redbourne House. The footman who greeted him seemed to think his name alone was sufficient grounds for entry and showed Julian to the grand salon, where two dozen guests were already gathered. Julian recognized only a handful, including his sister Ann, who smiled and nodded at him from across the room, Lords Dillbey and Cheevers, and naturally, the object of his great desire, whom his gaze found almost the moment he crossed the threshold.

She was at the other end of the exceedingly large salon speaking to old Lord Montfort. Arrested by the sight of her, Julian stepped to one side of the south doors, his gaze riveted on her. She wore a gown of royal blue trimmed in silver and worn off her shoulders in the current style. Her hair was artfully twisted, held in place by a silver ribbon. Small sapphires sparkled at her lobes, and a simple sapphire pendant rested just above the swell of her bosom.

He rather thought he could stand there all day and look at her, drink her in, and when she suddenly smiled at Montfort, Julian was amazed at how easily she seemed to illuminate everything around her. *Phillip had said that once, in the Fairchild ballroom—she illuminates everything around her.*

A sharp pain stabbed at his side.

Claudia glanced away from Montfort, her gaze scanning the crowd, passing over him . . . and then back again. Her smile faded slightly. She said something to Lord Montfort, nodded to a woman standing nearby, and started forward. Bracing himself, Julian clasped his hands behind his back, fastened the smile on his face, and tried not to enjoy so very much as he was the sight of her marching toward him.

She sailed right up and bobbed a curtsy so infinitesimal that a gnat would have taken umbrage. *He*, however, smiled and bowed low. He was, after all, a gentleman.

"And exactly how did you get in here?" she asked matter-of-factly.

With a quick, conniving glance about, he slyly beckoned her closer. She leaned forward—so close that he could smell the faint scent of her lavender perfume. "My feet," he murmured. "They come in quite handy at times such as this."

Claudia jerked backward; her brows snapped into a dark vee. "Oh, now that was highly amusing, sir. Unfortunately, an event such as this requires more than wit. It requires an invitation."

"I have one."

"Oh, *really?*"

"Yes. Ann's. I gathered it extended to me."

Claudia folded her arms across her middle, drumming slender fingers against one arm. "How very interesting. I could have sworn the invitation was addressed only to Lord and Lady Boxworth. I believe your so-called invitation is forfeit. I'm afraid you must pay for the privilege of entry now."

"Now *that* is extortion," he cheerfully informed her.

A playful smirk lifted the corners of her mouth. "And?"

Julian laughed. "All right, you have me. How much is this privilege?"

"One thousand pounds," she said, and pertly tilted her head back, waiting for him to balk.

Julian shrugged. "Very well."

Her eyes rounded with surprise. "You'll *pay?*"

"Yes, I will."

Claudia's stunned gaze burned a path from the top of his head to the tips of his patent leather shoes. "Honestly, I don't understand you," she whispered loudly. "What could you possibly hope to accomplish with such a sum?"

"I merely wanted to see you, Claudia, and I am happy to contribute to your cause. I am not an ogre."

"I never said you were an ogre," she responded, and flashed a demonic little smile. "I said you were a *rake*."

Julian chuckled, let his gaze roam her lush form, admiring the way the delectable, plump flesh of her bosom rose enticingly with every breath she took. "You took my advice, I see."

Claudia opened her mouth, then shut it. Then opened it again. "*What* advice?"

"The royal blue. You are stunningly beautiful, do you know that?"

Color instantly flagged her cheeks. She glanced nervously at her gown, awkwardly smoothing the lap of it, then looked furtively at those around them. Plastering a smile to her face, she muttered, "Now you are being ridiculous!"

"I am deadly serious."

Claudia nervously fingered the sapphire pendant as she looked around the room, smiling and nodding at others. "Do you think, perhaps, you have a fever?" she softly inquired of him. "Perhaps a brain injury of some sort? Have you perchance fallen from a tree recently and landed on your head?"

"I am quite well, thank you."

She shifted her gaze to him again. "Well then, you must simply be out of your bloody mind."

He laughed. "I take it you are not convinced of my sincerity?"

"Sincerity?" She rolled her eyes. "You would come uninvited to a benefit tea, undoubtedly for the purpose of trifling with some young innocent who has captured your fancy for the moment, and would expect me to believe you have an ounce of sincerity in you? I suppose you

expect me to believe you are a philanthropist, too!" With
a shake of her head, she stepped away, but paused and
glanced over her shoulder at him. "But the spectacles are
a nice touch." With a superior smirk, the Demon's Spawn
marched away.

An idiot grin spread Julian's lips as he watched her
glide across the room, greeting her guests, smiling that
brilliant smile of hers, and every so often—for good measure, he supposed—tossing a frown over her shoulder at
him. Clever girl that one, he thought with not a little bit
of pride.

Claudia could feel his eyes on her. Boring a hole through
her back, actually, as she explained to Lady Cheevers that
her father was at his gentlemen's club. She tried to focus
on the woman's meddling conversation, but her mind
had turned to mush the moment she had seen him standing near the door, his raven eyes locked on her. And
now, as she tried to make herself remember just what a
scoundrel he truly was, all she could seem to think was
that he had said she was stunningly beautiful. *Stunningly*
beautiful.

Yes, and what exactly did one expect a rake to say?

"Your father won't be joining us for tea, then?" Lady
Cheevers asked, bringing Claudia back to the present.
Her father's close relationship to the king was a constant
source of fascination for some. As a member of the Privy
Council, he was privileged with a wealth of information.
The one thing Claudia had learned from her father was
that William IV was not the brightest monarch to ever sit
on the throne. Apparently, his ideas could be rather inap-
propriate, and it was her father's job to make sure that
the most absurd ones didn't harm the monarchy in any
way. There were days, however, like today, when he complained that the task was too exacting. He and his friends
had repaired to the nearest gentlemen's club rather than
face her guests.

Her father was not sorry he would miss her tea.

Marshall Whitney believed Claudia's causes were a pleasant hobby for her, but they were not the sort of thing he would ever give serious consideration. That was because Marshall Whitney did not concern himself with such mundane matters as the plight of poor women and children.

"I'm afraid not, Lady Cheevers," she said, smiling apologetically. The woman's mouth puckered slightly; she was about to respond but held her tongue as Randall, the Redbourne butler, appeared. Grateful for the intrusion, Claudia excused herself so that Randall could tell her that tea was served. As everyone was directed to find a seat at one of the dozen tables set up, she moved to the center of the room. Without thinking, she looked around for Julian.

For once his dark eyes were not riveted on her. But they were riveted on Miss Harriet Reed, thank you, sitting next to him at an intimate little table for two near the hearth.

Why that should anger her, Claudia had no earthly idea, but she pivoted away from the sight of Harriet, who seemed to be practically in his lap. It made no difference to her. None whatsoever. Other than it proved her point rather neatly—Julian was a bonafide, arrogant rake. As her guests filled their cups with tea and their plates with sandwiches and pastries, Claudia refused to meet his gaze, preferring instead to study the exact cut of the crystal in the chandeliers as she began to speak.

"I should very much like to thank you all for coming today," she began. "It's heartwarming to know I can count on my friends when there is a need. You've all had an opportunity to see the drawings of a school posted on the wall?" she asked, pointing to the sketches she had done expressly for this purpose. A murmuring went up among her guests amid the clink of china on china.

There it was again, the feel of his eyes on her.

"The school doesn't yet exist, but I hope with perseverance and a bit of luck, it shall be built very soon for the benefit of girls who work in the factories." Claudia risked a glance to the back of the room; his hands were on his knees, his eyes now locked on her.

"Pray tell, how did you develop an interest in *factories?*" This from Lady Cheevers, whose only redeeming quality as far as Claudia was concerned was the fact that she was married to Lord Cheevers.

She smiled at the woman. "It's rather a long story, really, but I had the opportunity to visit some of the factories in London and Lancashire and discovered that working conditions can be quite wretched, particularly for the women and children."

"I have heard that there are all sorts of untoward things that go on in those factories," Lady Wilbarger said with a shudder. "I shouldn't like to go into one of them." Some of the other women murmured their agreement.

"You would hardly faint away, Eloise," Ann interjected from the middle of the room. "The untoward things are pitiful wages for women and children, terribly long work days, and inadequate precautions taken to ensure their safety."

"And the labor can be backbreaking," Claudia interjected. "Moreover, women are paid roughly one third what men are paid for the very same labor —yet many of them are without husbands. Their children are often forced to work, just so they can put food on their tables."

"You wouldn't advocate that an unwed woman make as much as a man, would you?" scoffed Lord Montfort, looking around to the few men in attendance for their agreement.

Oh yes, in a heartbeat she would advocate that. "I was merely explaining the conditions, my lord," she said agreeably.

"And what has all this to do with schools?" asked Lady Cheevers. "Seems to me that it's too late for the factory workers to be schooled. It would hardly be of any use to them now."

The woman's lack of compassion was astounding. "Yes, well, for many of the women that is true. But there are many young girls in the factories, Lady Cheevers, and many of them can't even read. Without a proper education, those young girls have no hope of escaping the drudgery of factory work."

"Why would we want them to escape the factories?" Lord Dillbey asked, chuckling politely as if Claudia has just uttered the most witless thing in the world. He looked around the room. "This nation relies on the goods those factories produce, and clearly we must have the bodies to work in them," he pointed out. Several nodded as Dillbey looked to Julian. "Here now, Kettering, you have a rather sizable interest in manufacturing endeavors. What would you do if you had no labor?"

Everyone looked at Julian, who dragged his gaze from Claudia and bestowed a look of pure boredom on Dillbey. "Of course we need labor in the factories, Dillbey. Yet I do not believe that obviates the need to educate our children."

"You speak as if they are *your* children, my lord," Dillbey scoffed, and sipped delicately from his teacup.

"Surely you would agree that one's occupation should be a matter of personal choice," Claudia quickly interjected. "But for many young women, the factories are the only viable option. They have few choices in the best of circumstances, but if they are unskilled and uneducated, they have even fewer choices."

"I don't agree," Dillbey said flatly, swinging his gaze back to Claudia and placing his tea on the table in front of him. "Young women don't *need* choices. Their course is preordained, and it is motherhood. If money is to be raised to build schools, those schools most surely must be built for our boys. There are just as many of them in the factories, and *they* will have a family to support one day."

Claudia clasped her hands tightly in her lap in an effort to control her soaring indignation. "That is quite true, but many of the girls will, too—"

"Precisely the problem, madam," Dillbey interrupted. "It is not a lack of education that keeps those girls in the factories all their lives. It is the lack of morals. Decent young girls will marry eventually and leave the factories to raise their legitimate children."

It was all Claudia could do to keep from lunging at the ignorant cretin. "I beg your pardon," she said softly, "but that seems rather a harsh condemnation."

The man shrugged indifferently. "It is merely a statement of fact."

"Be that as it may, would you argue that girls shouldn't even know how to read?"

"No, of course not!"

"Then it would follow that we must have schools to teach them."

"We need more schools for boys!" Dillbey insisted. "For every pound you would waste on a girl's needless education, there are two lads who could use it! If there are schools to be built, I say let them be for the boys! The only education a girl needs is how to be a proper wife and mother!"

The room grew deathly quiet; all eyes turned to Claudia. Her opportunity was slipping away, and she suddenly felt inadequate to debate the common thinking of the *ton* and searched frantically for an argument the old goat would accept.

"I beg to differ."

Twenty heads swiveled toward the sound of Julian's calm, even voice. He looked straight at Claudia . . . and her heart climbed to her throat.

"Of course we need to educate as many of our lads as we can, but we must also educate our girls. If we are to prosper as a nation, our mothers and our wives and our daughters must read and write and instill the value of knowledge and creativity in their children. I would submit that the education of our young, whether male or female, speaks volumes about the values we hold as a nation. And I, for one, do not believe we value ignorance in anyone."

"Well said!" Ann emphatically agreed.

"I am happy to donate a sum to Lady Claudia for her girls' school," Julian said.

"As will I," Lord Cheevers added, and was followed by two or three other male voices adding their support. Claudia hardly heard them—she was trying desperately to reconcile a gentleman's noble gesture with a Rake whose gaze burned her every place it touched her. As if he knew it, The Rake smiled in that lazy way of his, one brow arched as if challenging her to explain *that*.

She couldn't explain it. But she wondered if maybe, just *maybe,* she was wrong about him. Was it possible he had changed? *She* had. It was a thought that suddenly consumed her, and she pondered it for the remainder of the tea, stealing glimpses of him through the throng, feeling a jolt of lightning course along her spine every time he caught her looking at him. And she wondered about it during Miss Reed and Lord Cheevers' duet at the pianoforte.

She was still wondering about it when Randall quietly informed her that Lord Christian was in the foyer.

Claudia slipped out of the salon in the middle of Lady Cheever's solo—with a silent thanks to the Lord above for her reprieve from that awful screeching.

"How unfortunate that you couldn't come a bit earlier," she greeted Arthur, smiling warmly as she extended her hands to him. "We had quite a lively tea."

He laughed as he brought her hand to his lips. "Ah, my misfortune! Alas, I had a pressing engagement. I beg your pardon, but I agreed to fetch Kettering after he had indulged his newly found charitable streak. I couldn't even bring myself to inquire what had brought it about."

Her thoughts exactly.

"My Lord Christian, as prompt as ever." Julian sauntered into the foyer, wearing that lazy smile of his.

"Naturally. We wouldn't want to keep anyone waiting, would we?" Arthur asked, and winked slyly at Claudia. "I shouldn't want to alarm you with the sordid details, but it would seem we've some unfinished business to attend."

The image of Phillip suddenly flashed in her mind's eye. How many times had she watched him leave some engagement just like this, only to be seen at some rout much later, well into his cups, his purse empty? *I've some business to attend, my dear. I shall call in a day or two, if it pleases you.* A day or two that often turned into a week or more. A chill suddenly snaked down Claudia's spine.

Chuckling, Julian accepted his hat from the footman. "I won't deny it—I'm afraid no good will come of us tonight."

Oh yes, she could certainly believe that, and suddenly felt a bit queasy, as if she had eaten something disagreeable. "Well then," she said stiffly, refusing to meet his gaze. "Thank you kindly for your donation, my lord."

"My pleasure, madam."

"Yes, I rather imagine it was," Arthur drawled, to which Julian merely chuckled. Arthur turned to Claudia and bowed. "If you will allow me, my lady, I will take this scoundrel off your hands."

She would allow it, all right. Let Christian take The Rake far from her sight. "Yes, please do," she said curtly, and turned away, feeling like a colossal fool.

Eight

THE "UNFINISHED BUSINESS" Arthur had jokingly referred to was supper at White's with Adrian Spence. Adrian, the impossibly proud father of an infant girl, was in London for only the day and planned to return to his Longbridge estate the very next morning.

Over a steaming plate of venison stew, the three Rogues caught up on old news and the *ton*'s gossip. Over port, they argued about the exact crime Lord Turlington had committed to warrant Julian's shoving his head into a chamber pot twenty years ago, finally conceding that none of them could recall it. Well into the early hours of the morning, Adrian finally suggested it was time he returned home, as he planned an early start the next morning. But Julian was the first to rise and take his leave.

As they watched him stroll from the room, Adrian looked at Arthur. "All right, then, who is she?" he asked bluntly.

Arthur snorted. "You wouldn't believe me if I told you."

That garnered Adrian's undivided attention. "Indeed? Come on, man, out with it. Which debutante has finally snared the dashing young earl?"

Arthur slid his gaze to Adrian and smiled wolfishly. "Claudia Whitney."

For a moment of stunned silence the two men stared at each other, then simultaneously burst into raucous laughter. "Serves the old dog right" was the only remark Adrian could manage as he happily tried to catch his breath.

In a hack that smelled to high heaven, Julian was not laughing. He could not stop thinking about that impossible, frustratingly pert Demon's Spawn. One moment she was laughing with him. Or *at* him, as the case may be. The next, she was torching him with a look that suggested she thought him the lowest of all blackguards. It was precisely that look she had bestowed on him when he had left with Arthur . . . *but she had looked at him that way once before, too, when he had warned her about Phillip.*

Julian pinched the bridge of his nose between his finger and thumb, vainly trying to stave off the ache building at the base of his skull.

The ache spread to encompass his whole head by the next afternoon. Seated in his study, he peered through his spectacles at the medieval manuscript found in a wine cellar near the village of Whitten. Julian had relished history since he was a lad, particularly those tales of beautiful kingdoms and brave knights that could be reenacted in the ruins around Kettering Hall. As he grew older, he discovered in the course of his studies that he had a knack for deciphering Old English and Latin text. A boy's fascination had turned into a man's hobby, and he was now considered quite the expert—meaning, in this instance at least, that he had a commitment to Cambridge to translate the manuscript. But he hadn't deciphered a single word in two hours.

At least the manuscript gave him something to look at while his head throbbed and his mind wandered. Damn her, but he had dreamed of her overnight—a very erotic dream—and after several long months of impotence had become painfully aroused.

This morning he had debated calling on her. No, he had *warred* with himself, alternating between disbelief that he could be so bloody fascinated with a woman and indignation that she could hardly seem to abide him.

This is absurd. Julian shoved the manuscript away and rubbed the back of his neck. In the first place, he was a bloody Rogue of Regent Street and could have any woman he wanted. In the second place, she had grown up in his house, among his sisters, had known him since she was a little girl. And in the *third* place, goddammit, she had been Phillip's intended, and even if almost two years had passed, he could not betray Phillip's memory by seducing the woman he had intended to marry!

And what other man would you suggest, my lord? I know of a hostler near Redbourne Abbey. Perhaps you think he better suits? Her words from that night came back to him as clearly as if she had just spoken them. God, how he had longed to take her in his arms, kiss that lunacy from her lips. *Not a hostler, Claudia,* he had been desperate to say. *Me!* But the words had never passed his lips—he had felt the weight of his lifelong friendship with Phillip and had resisted the corporeal urges of his body in favor of loyalty.

Loyalty that still hung like a noose around his neck.

Restless, Julian came to his feet and crossed to the window. He was sick to death of moping about like some schoolboy and decided to find Sophie, perhaps accompany her to an exclusive millinery shop on Regent Street. That would surely boost her sagging spirits; hell, she might even *speak* to him again. With an uneasy shrug of his shoulders, Julian quit the study and went in search of his youngest sister.

Sophie, however, was nowhere to be found. Even her lady's maid was nowhere in sight. Julian at last found Tinley, seated at the formal dining room table, a duster resting in front of him.

"You've worn yourself out again, haven't you?" Julian admonished the old man.

"I beg your pardon, my lord, you are mistaken. I employ a variety of techniques to keep your house in superb condition," Tinley said as he reluctantly pushed himself to his feet and retrieved his duster.

"Yes, I see that you do," Julian drawled. "Have you seen Lady Sophie?"

Tinley paused, looked thoughtfully at the chandelier. "I rather think not recently," he said uncertainly.

Julian peered closely at Tinley. "No?"

"Well . . . I believe that perhaps Lady Sophie is visiting Lady Boxworth today," Tinley answered.

It was as good a guess as any, Julian supposed. To Ann's, then. "Have the phaeton brought round, will you? I'll fetch her," he said, and with a last curious look at the old man, Julian walked out of the dining room.

Sophie was not with Ann.

Ann was unconcerned. She suggested he try Aunt Violet, then smiled, patting his arm in a motherly sort of way. "You are too protective. Sophie will be one and twenty in a matter of weeks. She's grown now."

"She's an innocent," he retorted sharply.

He did not go to Aunt Violet's home at Eaton Court—his instincts told him he would not find Sophie there, either. His instincts, unfortunately, told him that she was with Stanwood, and his blood ran cold.

When he returned to St. James Square, he summoned Tinley to the library. "Think, Tinley. How long has she been gone?" he asked.

Tinley blinked, clearly confused. "Who?"

There was no point in prolonging the conversation; Tinley's memory was fading as rapidly as his eyesight. So Julian dismissed the butler with the firm instruction that Sophie was to be brought to him at once upon her return.

Fortunately, he did not have to wait long.

When Sophie entered the library a half-hour later, she could scarcely look at him. She sat gingerly on the edge of a chair, her head lowered as she fidgeted with a braid of ribbon at her waist. She was ashamed or hiding something or both, and Julian's anger soared. He paced in front of the windows, struggling to contain his anger and his fear at what could be happening with her. After several tense moments, he stopped pacing and faced his sister. "Where have you been?"

"*Ahem.* Ah, with Aunt Violet," she said meekly.

His pulse began to throb soundly in his neck. "I wouldn't make things worse by lying if I were you." She said nothing; Julian swallowed hard. "Were you with Stanwood?"

He waited a few moments, watching as Sophie seemed to shrink before his very eyes. Just when he thought he would explode, she muttered a very soft *yes*. He pivoted sharply, pacing like a madman in a furious bid to control his anger. The chit was a *fool!* That man was a wolf in sheep's clothing, a predator who would eat her up. He paused, thrust a hand through his hair as he racked his brain for the reason she would defy him so blatantly, *any* semblance of an excuse . . . but he already knew the reason. He knew instinctively that Sophie was suffering from the same quiet desperation he was.

"Sophie." His voice was hoarse with emotion. "You cannot see him." He glanced over his shoulder at her; she would not look up. "I know that you are particularly attached to him, but he is not suitable."

"How can you say that, Julian? You don't even *know* him!"

It was true that he had met Stanwood on only a handful of occasions, but Julian knew his reputation well. "I know him—much better than you believe," he said low. "I don't want to hurt you, darling, but the man wants nothing more than your money." Sophie's head jerked up; the hurt in her eyes slashed painfully at his heart. "He wants it because he has lost his in gaming hells," he doggedly continued. "His reputation is reprehensible—"

"He said you would say that!"

Julian wondered if Stanwood had told her *all* of what he might say about the bastard. For there was much more, but he was unwilling to offend her with the worst details of his reputation, which included a proclivity for inflicting pain on his bed partners.

"Please try and hear me, love. There are rumors of Sir William's cruelty . . . he will not treat you with the esteem you deserve, do you understand? He is not the sort of man who would revere a wife—"

"He has not as yet offered for me, Julian, and I dare say he won't, knowing your prejudice against him as he does," she said, lifting her chin defiantly.

Julian's hold on his temper was slipping. "You have other suitors. Aunt Violet said that young Henry Dillon has called—"

"He's a child!" she cried. "All of them! Sir William predicted this; he said you would marry me off to the suitor with the fattest purse, regardless of *my* feelings in the matter!"

The bloody bastard was pitting her against him. Fury was quickly mounting in Julian, and he fought to maintain his composure. "He is manipulating you, Sophie," he responded evenly. "I forbid you to see him, and I am not open to debate on the matter."

The hand in her lap was trembling—she was desperately trying to maintain her composure, too. "We never debate anything, Julian. You dictate, and I am expected to follow."

He ignored her remark. "Mark me, Sophie. This will be the last time I will tell you."

She came clumsily to her feet, piercing him with a dark look. "As you wish," she said bitterly, and walked unsteadily from the library, leaving Julian with the funny feeling that there would be nothing as he wished.

When Sophie did not come to supper, he sent a tray up. When Tinley returned and informed him Lady Sophie had refused the tray, Julian tossed his linen napkin aside and shoved away from the table, leaving a plate full of food himself.

He knew her misery, and God, how he wished he could change everything for her. How he wished he could make Stanwood honorable. Unfortunately for both of them, he couldn't change a bloody thing, least of all, Stanwood's rotten character. And as it stood, Julian would not change his mind in this.

He had vowed to his dying father to keep his sisters safe and well. He had failed miserably with Valerie. He would not fail with Sophie.

God, he had to get out of this house. What was once a spacious mansion was beginning to feel like a closet where he and Sophie were forced to co-exist. Harrison Green, he had learned from Arthur just last evening, was having another of his bawdy routs in celebration of All Saints' Day. The nephew of an influential earl, Harrison Green had more money than brains, and his single purpose in life was to provide the town's entertainment. A rout at Harrison Green's was guaranteed to be crowded with London's elite, unfettered by convention or propriety—exactly the sort of mindless entertainment Julian needed at the moment.

Julian was not disappointed. Arriving at Green's, he could scarcely squeeze past a harried footman, wig askew, to gain entry. Once inside the foyer, he was immediately accosted by Lady Phillipot, a very tall and rather large woman squeezed into a gown so tight that he could see the stays of her corset straining against the satin. Her ample bosom was dangerously close to spilling over when she latched on to his arm with a bright smile. Julian had heard that Lord Phillipot was abroad, and thought that rather explained the woman's overly bright smile.

"Kettering!" she chirped loudly, beaming at him. "Ooh, what good fortune that a *Rogue* has joined us!"

"Lady Phillipot, how do you do?"

"Did you come alone?" she asked eagerly, peering around him. "Shall I show you around? Oh, say that I shall! I should very much like a few dear friends to see a man as handsome as *you* on my arm!" she declared, and burst into a loud, piercing laugh.

"Earl Kettering? Good God, didn't think to see *you*

tonight!" Harrison Green, a short, round man who still dressed in the bright colors of a past era stuffed his monocle in his eye and peered closely at Julian. "Didn't think to see you *any* night, truth be told."

"What, and pass up what promises to be such a lively event?" Julian asked, smiling at Lady Phillipot as he peeled her fingers from his arm. "Don't mind, do you old chap?" he asked Green.

"Lord no! Just leave some of our fair damsels to frolic with the rest of us, will you?"

Lady Phillipot howled at that. "Harrison, you devil," she cried, slapping him on the shoulder with her fan.

"I shall endeavor to do just that, but I shan't make any promises," Julian said, and smiling, smoothly stepped away from Lady Phillipot before she could latch on to him again. "I assume the game room is in the usual location?" he asked, not waiting for the answer as he quickly gained the stairs.

The size of the crowd surprised him but then again, the late fall meant fewer soirees as the gentry slowly returned to their country homes for the winter. He pushed his way through the throng of men and women in various stages of flirtation along the stairs, drinking liberally from a flute of champagne someone had pressed into his hand.

On the first floor, the drove was even thicker. A waltz was in full swing in a small ballroom. Across the hall, a long sideboard was set with food; several small tables were scattered about and filled with Green's hungry guests. Just down from there was the main salon, where several men were engaged in card games on which hundreds of pounds were wagered. Julian picked up another flute of champagne from a passing footman and made his way to the ballroom, preferring the scenery of dancing women to the smoke-filled gaming room. That was one thing he truly enjoyed about Green's affairs—innocent young debutantes, fearful of ruining their pristine reputations, would never darken his door. The sort of women who attended a Harrison Green affair were either married—and therefore past the age of worrying about their chastity—or uncaring of society's regard for them.

Those were the women he enjoyed the most.

Like Lady Prather, who was making her way toward him. Julian smiled as she covertly brushed her hand across his thigh. "My lord, you've been gone so long," she pouted prettily.

"Not so very long," he said, surreptitiously running a hand around her waist and over her hip. "Where is Lord Prather?"

"The game room, as always," she said, deliberately brushing her breast against his arm. "Will you dance with me?"

He was only human. He led the pretty blonde onto the dance floor and waltzed her into the thick of the crowd, smiling as she murmured all the things she would like to do to his body. The end of the dance found them near the string quartet and partially secluded from the crowd. Julian could not help himself—he kissed the temptress, hungrily and long—until reason caught hold of him, and he begged his escape before he found himself in deep trouble with another husband. Leaving a sulking Lady Prather behind, he worked his way to the far end of the ballroom and the doors opened onto the terrace to draw breath into the house. He leaned against the wall and sipped his champagne, watching the dancers twirl by him, smiling suggestively at a group of young women who were eyeing him over the tops of their fans.

A movement just outside his peripheral vision caused him to turn his head toward the terrace—and Julian caught his breath.

Claudia.

He had not expected to see her here tonight—Harrison Green seemed so . . . *inadequate* for her, if not a little risqué. But there she was, alone on the terrace, standing beneath the overhang of the porch above. Her gaze was locked on a rather garish painting of the sun and moon and stars above her head. In the shallow light of a pair of rush torches, she turned a slow pirouette, thoughtfully tilting her head from one side to the other as she studied the painting.

She looked magnificent. The pewter satin gown she wore was the exact color of her eyes. The bodice of the gown dipped enticingly low; the sleeves, fitting tight around her upper arms, left her shoulders gleaming white and smooth. In one hand a half-empty flute of champagne dangled. The other hand fingered the triple strand of pearls at her neck that matched those strung loosely through her coiffure. A thick tress of hair was carelessly pushed behind her ear, tangling with the pearl drop earrings she wore.

He was reminded of the night two years past, when she had appeared at the Wilmington Ball on her father's arm, snatching the breath from his lungs.

She slowly came to a halt, her head bent backward, exposing her slender neck. Julian swallowed a lump of strong desire as he gazed unabashedly at that neck, the slope of it into her shoulders, the rise of a generous bosom—

Her unexpected laughter startled him, a joyous laugh that spilled over the terrace and into the night. She stumbled backward a step or two, smiling as she lowered her head. Bowled over by her brilliance, Julian felt his heart suddenly hammering against his chest, his blood coursing hot through his veins. She sipped from the flute, then turned toward him, her eyes registering her surprise when she saw him standing there, watching her.

And God help him, she smiled. She *smiled* at him, freely and honestly. Swaying a bit on her feet, she lifted the flute to her lips and drained it, then pointed the empty glass at him with a playful frown. "Really, one shouldn't spy. It's quite rude."

"Was I spying?"

"You were," she said, and absently twirled the flute between slender fingers.

"No. Not spying. Merely enjoying the air."

"Mmm . . . it is wonderful, isn't it?" she asked, sighing, and glanced at her empty flute. Then at him. "Are you going to drink that?" she asked, and pointed to the flute he had forgotten he held.

"Not presently." He walked out onto the terrace, handing her the champagne. With another gorgeous smile, Claudia drank, her lips touching the crystal where his had been. In the dim light, her eyes fairly shone, as if lit from somewhere deep within. There was no loathing in her expression as there was last evening, but . . . curiosity? Amusement? He bent his head to one side, considering her. "I must be dreaming," he said flatly.

Claudia arched her brows and handed him her empty flute. "What an odd thing to say. You aren't dreaming, my lord."

He shook his head and carelessly set the empty flute on the edge of a planter. "I *must* be dreaming because I think you are actually being rather . . . civil. Dare I say pleasant? Am I dreaming?"

A luscious grin spread across her lips. "Oh no, you are not dreaming. Merely delusional," she said, and laughed lightly. "However, I must thank you for your generosity—"

"Ah!" he exclaimed, and nodded knowingly. He had sent the bank draft for her girls' school early that afternoon. "There *is* a reason for your kindness."

Claudia smiled coyly. "Yes, well, you *were* quite generous." The creamy skin of her neck began to flush. "I am in your debt."

For the amount he had given her? That caused him to grin broadly. "I rather like the sound of that," he said, laughing. "But you should know that your indebtedness comes for a paltry sum."

"Really?"

He nodded.

She rose up on her tiptoes and whispered, "Five *thousand* pounds?" And slipped down again. "But that is quite a lot of money! It should take me *weeks* to raise such a sum. But you . . . you just *gave* it to me!" she exclaimed, casting one arm wide. "Just gave it to me . . ."

And it was worth every bloody shilling, too, just to see

her smile—even if it was one helped along by a flute of champagne. "Claudia?" he drawled, "how much champagne have you drunk?"

She laughed again, cast a beaming grin to the sun and the moon above her head. "Harrison has such fine champagne, has he not?"

"Yes, and quite a lot of it, apparently."

She turned her beatific smile to him; he felt it shimmer down his spine and land firmly in his groin. "*Quite* a lot," she agreed with an emphatic nod.

It was also a contagious smile—it spread to his own lips as he moved closer to her. "You are a bit into your cups, my dear, and I'm afraid there is only one thing to be done for it."

Claudia immediately stepped back, and laughing, he caught her elbow. "Don't fret—I am hardly going to accost you." *No matter how badly I want to.* "I had in mind a dance or two . . . just until you are feeling your old, demon self."

Claudia laughed as he slowly pulled her toward him. "You taught me how to waltz, do you remember?"

"I remember."

Her smile faded; she peered up at him, as if seeing something in the distance. "I was a demon then, too. And you . . . oh, you were *terribly* handsome."

If she hadn't been quite so far in her cups, Julian might have read more into that throaty whisper. But he merely chuckled. "As opposed to now?"

She flashed another, terribly alluring smile. With the tip of her finger she touched the knot of his neckcloth. "*Now* I think you are devastatingly handsome." Those words banished every gentlemanly instinct from his head. But before he could even react, she added lightly, "for a *rake,*" and giggled devilishly.

"Demon's Spawn," he muttered, straining to hold himself from kissing the smirk from her lips.

"Libertine," she shot back, and suddenly leaned into him, asking breathlessly, "Dance with me?"

Nine

CLAUDIA WANTED TO dance under the moon and the stars, even if they were rather crude renditions, just as they had years ago at Kettering Hall. Julian didn't think that such a grand idea and muttered something about stars and demons and trouble. But when the strains of the string quartet's waltz drifted out onto the terrace, he very gallantly bowed, smiling when she managed a clumsy curtsy. She slipped one hand into his and placed the other on his shoulder.

"Hmm . . . it appears I might have to count the steps for you."

She snorted. "Dance, will you?"

With a chuckle, he pressed his hand against the small of her back and swept her into the rhythm of the waltz. He moved as gracefully as she remembered, leading her easily, twirling her one way and then the other so effortlessly that Claudia had the sensation of floating. She smiled up at the moon and the sun and the stars painted above her head, watching the bright colors blur into a kaleidoscope. The champagne had muddled her mind a bit, making her feel all woozy and shiny and wondering if perhaps he wasn't such a *very* bad rake. And she *liked* dancing with him; she liked the way his arms felt like iron beneath her fingers, the way his hand rode the small of her back. She just wasn't quite sure why that made her giggle.

"I don't think I've ever seen you so relaxed," Julian remarked.

Oh, she was relaxed, all right. Practically weightless.

"I had rather thought you might never grace me with your smile again."

That was ridiculous and made her laugh as she lowered her gaze from the ceiling to look at him. His dark eyes were fixed on her lips; a strong shiver ran down Claudia's spine. "Why, I smile all the time, sir. From sunup to sundown practically, and particularly in the mornings when Randall brings me tarts."

A corner of Julian's mouth tipped upward. "Tarts, is it? I would have thought you learned your lesson. You recall, don't you, that you once ate your weight in them? You had a bellyache so ferocious that I had to send for Dr. Dudley. I should hope at the very least you learned to pace yourself."

She laughed gaily; what an absurdly faulty memory he had! "You have us all smashed together in your head, don't you? Can't remember one from the other. *That* was Eugenie."

"I don't have you all smashed together, I assure you," he said, his smile fading softly. "There is one that stands out from all the others—one that I can't seem to get out of my head."

Her initial assumption was that he meant Valerie by that, but his black eyes seemed to pierce her, boring down, down, down, into her very heart, and she realized that he was speaking of *her*. She missed a step—something she hadn't done in years—and Julian expertly righted her without missing a beat or taking his eyes from her. Heat and an odd sense of fear rumbled like thunder into her core. He was toying with her, seducing her for the sake of the chase, wanting to use her for God knew what purpose. *"Why?"* she suddenly blurted. "Why are you doing this to me? Why are you suddenly everywhere that I am?"

His response was to pull her closer so that their bodies touched—his thigh pressed to hers, her breasts to his chest. His hand curled around her fingers, gripping them tightly. "Because I can't get you out of my *mind*, Claudia! I haven't in a very long time and I am sick to death of pretending you aren't there."

All right, she was suddenly having trouble breathing. He was lying! Julian Dane thought of no one but himself—he certainly didn't moon over women! Oh *God!* This was too confusing! She couldn't *think* now, and curse Mary Whitehurst for so relentlessly begging her to come along tonight while her husband was away! She should have *known* this was the sort of affair he would attend!

"Are you all right?"

No, she was not all right. She forced herself to look at him. "Do you remember the night of Eugenie's wedding ball?" she suddenly asked. Julian's brows dipped into a confused frown, but he nodded. "You asked me to stand up with you for the first waltz." A moment passed; he blinked. There was no recognition in his eyes, nothing in his expression that suggested he remembered it at all. Claudia felt her heart begin to sink a little. "You . . . you asked me to stand up, and when it was over, you asked me to save another dance for you." There. It was out, one of the tentacles in the root of her distrust. But Julian only looked puzzled, and the heat quickly spread to her face and neck.

"I don't understand. Do you mean to say that I requested a second dance but did not claim it?"

Heat that was turning to fire—he looked appalled. "You . . . you just . . . yes. That is what happened." Her face was flaming. Really, she could use a bit of champagne just now!

"It *is?*"

Perhaps the earth would open up and swallow her whole. Having stated his horrid perfidy aloud she felt completely ridiculous. Ridiculous and pathetically silly. "You wouldn't understand," she muttered miserably.

"You are quite serious, aren't you?" he asked, his voice incredulous.

Claudia realized they had come to a halt at the edge of the terrace. "What I am trying to say"—she closed her eyes for a moment, tried to concentrate—"is that I have known what you are for years now."

He dropped her hand, folded his arms across his chest as his eyes narrowed with obvious displeasure. "You have known what I am for years now." It was a statement of incredulity, not a question.

"Ah . . . yes," she said, sounding terribly unsure.

"And that would be?"

Now was hardly the time to dissemble, she thought wildly and muttered, "A rake."

The expression in his eyes darkened. An absurd sense of panic welled up in her.

"A word, madam," he growled, and snatched her wrist, dragging her across the terrace, down into the garden, marching along at quite a clip toward the hothouse in the corner of the grounds. Claudia moved almost unconsciously, her thoughts a whirlwind of confusion, her heart warring mightily with what was left of her good sense.

Halfway there, he seemed to think better of dragging her and hauled her into his side, clamping an iron arm around her waist and steering her onward. "I've come to the conclusion that you are not only the Demon's Spawn, you are also woefully ignorant of men. And let me just add that this discovery is rather astonishing, what with the way you topple men over like chess pieces everywhere you go."

"What?" she gasped as he reached for the door of the hothouse and pushed it open. "I don't *topple* them!"

"The bloody hell you don't," he said, and pushed her across the threshold of the hothouse, following right behind. "I could list them all if you'd like," he continued sharply as he rooted around a table, producing a candle. Lighting it, he swung the door shut with his foot and held the candle high. "Benjamin Sommer, Daniel Brantley, Maurice Terling, Colin Enderby—"

"Oh!" she fairly shrieked, insulted that among the list

of suitors was the invidious Baron Enderby. "Colin Enderby has *never* darkened my door, and if he ever does, Randall is quite clear that he is to shoot upon sight!"

Julian paused to place the candle on a workbench. "I beg your pardon, Lady Claudia," he said, dipping into a mocking bow, "I surely meant to say the Duke of Gillingham. Or the Marquess of Braybrook. Or the Marquess of—"

"All *right!*" Claudia snapped, and pressed her forehead into her palm. "Honestly, I don't know the point of all this!"

"The point," he said, his voice noticeably softer, "is that I confess that I can't get you out of my mind, and you respond with some perceived cut from a half dozen years ago. You think that makes me a rake, and I think you haven't the slightest idea of what a rake is."

"I know what a rake is," she said slowly. "I know what you and Phillip used to do. I know where you went. . . ." Her throat felt thick; she didn't want to think of Phillip now.

Julian said nothing for a long moment. "I hope to God that isn't entirely true," he muttered.

So did she.

"But it doesn't change anything," he said, the gravel crunching beneath his shoes as he moved toward her. She looked up when he reached her; he took her hand and folded it into his. "It surely doesn't change the fact that I can't get you out of my mind," he said, reaching for her temple to brush his knuckles into her hair. "When the sun comes up, I think of you. When it sets, I think of you, and every moment in between, it seems."

Even though his words were absurdly sentimental, they made her heart race erratically. It was racing so badly that she feared it would fail her. His fingers twined in a strand of lose hair, untangled it from her earring, then trailed down her neck, to her shoulder, gently caressing her skin. "When you walk into a room, everything else ceases to exist for me. I think about how you would feel in my arms or lying beneath me," he added quietly. "I think about how you would feel if I were deep inside you and your body surrounded me."

She was going to faint. "I d-don't believe you," she stammered.

He said nothing, let his gaze scorch her with its intensity. His hand slipped around the nape of her neck and he gently pulled her forward. *Oh no.* He was going to kiss her and make her mad with longing all over again. She didn't want that . . . *oh yes, she did!* She wanted it with every fiber of her being; wanted it as badly as if it were the air she needed to breathe.

"You are afraid to believe me," he softly corrected her, and his other hand slipped around her back, urging her into his chest. Julian trailed the pad of his thumb across her lips. "You are afraid of *me.*"

She was afraid, all right. Of the dark glint in his eyes, the seductive set of his mouth. Of the whispered words that captivated her, suspending her between wild desire and reality. Something in her womb fluttered, a rush of breath escaped her. Julian ran a thumb across her lips, and as if in a dream, she watched as he lowered his head to hers, quailing only when his lips brushed softly across hers. Her lids fluttered shut, and she at once felt outside of herself, almost as if someone else was experiencing the tender pressure of his mouth and tongue.

What was she doing? Her mind screamed to stop, knowing that his kiss could melt all of her defenses, *knowing* that it was nothing more than play to him. Yet her heart had raced too far ahead, her body simmered beneath his hands, and she instinctively feared that it would take a team of four to pull her away from him now.

His hands came up and cupped her face, barely touching her, yet sending a thousand tiny bolts of electricity through her. He drew her lips between his teeth one at a time, tasting and shaping them to his will. With his tongue, he probed deeply, while his hands trailed to her ears, her neck, and her shoulders. She had the strong sensation of drifting, and he must have thought so, too, because he slipped one arm around her waist, anchoring her to him.

This was insanity! It was *madness* that allowed him to use her, madness that allowed him to charm her into this! But when he deepened the kiss, Claudia boldly pushed her tongue forward to explore his mouth. It was wonderfully erotic, the taste of champagne on his breath, the feel of his tongue twining with hers. With the tips of her fingers, she felt the cut of his thick sideburns against his skin, the tender spot of his temple, the satin feel of his hair. She had never kissed like this, never experienced such a swell of pleasure as this. . . .

Julian suddenly wrapped his arms around her and hauled her into his chest, pressing her tightly against him as he surged into her mouth. His arousal pressed hard and long against her belly, and when he lifted her onto the workbench, against the apex of her thighs. Fascinated—*provoked*—she moved against the hardness, wanting to feel it through her skirts.

With a moan deep in his throat, Julian suddenly toppled her onto her back on top of the workbench and covered her.

One hand spanned the whole of her rib cage, moving upward until it rested against the side of her breast. With the heel of his hand, he pressed against it while his mouth moved over hers, filling her with his tongue and his breath and his passion.

The prurient sensations unfurling in her body numbed her mind to everything, including her conscience. Claudia's hands tangled urgently in his hair, then fell to his shoulders to feel the muscles there and in his back contract with his movement. His hand pressed more firmly against her breast; his thumb flicked across the hardened peak pressing against her gown, and another violent shudder rifled through her.

Julian lifted his head, sucking in his breath. "You are right to fear me," he gasped. "I fear myself—I want to touch all of you, every inch of you." His lips skimmed the column of her neck as his hand cupped her breast, squeezing gently, fitting it to his palm.

She wanted him to touch every inch of her, and it scared her. "I fear myself more," she exclaimed hoarsely, and pushed against his chest. "I don't know why I allow you to seduce me like this!"

"Seduce you? Darling, you seduce *me,* with your eyes and your mouth and your voice," he murmured hoarsely. "Can't you believe that I want you? Can't you *feel* that I do?"

Oh, she could feel it, deep inside her, tingling in the pit of her belly. "I know what you are doing, Julian. You are toying with me—"

"Not with you, Claudia. Never with you," he whispered earnestly, and continued his gentle assault of all her senses. Her body was giving way to him even though her heart knew it was a tryst, a meaningless dalliance. She closed her eyes, allowing herself to drift even further down this course with him, instinctively knowing she had passed the point of return and that she couldn't stop this now, that she didn't want it to stop. Her body burned everywhere he touched her—and when he reached inside her gown and freed her breast from her camisole and bodice, she felt herself slide even deeper into a fog of pure, undiluted pleasure. Her breast swelled in his hand; his fingers massaged the tender flesh that had never been touched by another living soul, sending waves of desire crashing through her.

But when his lips closed around her, the desire spiraled out of control, drawing from a well between her legs and pulsing to the breast that he suckled. He snaked one arm behind her back and lifted her to his mouth. Claudia's arms entwined above her head; pots and trowels crashed to the gravel below them. She felt herself surging upward as the desire she was feeling built to an intolerable pitch, its pressure both sharp and pleasurable—

"Oh my God!"

A woman's voice, an intruder, shattered the passion that surrounded them and Claudia suddenly could not breathe. She struggled to sit up, but Julian shoved her off the side of the bench, away from the door. She landed hard on the gravel; pebbles embedded in the palms of her hands. Her first thought was that he had shoved her away in shame, but she realized he had come to his feet, was standing between her and whoever had found them.

"Good God, is that *you,* Kettering?" The voice belonged to Harrison Green. Now on all fours, Claudia crawled to safety behind the bench and several potted plants. "I saw a light and I thought—"

"Who *is* that?" the woman's voice whispered audibly. "Claudia *Whitney?*"

"I beg your pardon, Mrs. Frankton, you are mistaken," Julian said sharply. Behind the bench, Claudia wrapped her arms around her knees and buried her face on the top of them. "Sorry about the light, Green . . . you understand?" Julian continued.

Harrison nervously cleared his throat. "Yes, yes. We two were just wandering about. So sorry to have disturbed you. Mrs. Frankton? Shall we rejoin the others?"

The woman made a sound of disapproval, and then Claudia heard the rustle of her petticoats. There was some flurry of movement at the door, and after what seemed like minutes, it closed.

"Claudia."

There was regret in Julian's voice, but not nearly as much as was in her heart at that moment.

She was ruined.

"Claudia," he said again, and his hands were on her arms, pulling her to her feet. She stumbled upward, realized she was still in a shocking state of undress, and quickly turned away to arrange herself as her mind rifled through all the horrible possibilities—of which there were an alarming number.

"What . . ." Her voice was shaking; she could not bring herself to speak.

Julian moved, slipping his arm around her abdomen and pulling her into his chest, and Claudia realized she was trembling uncontrollably. "It's all right," he whispered into her hair. "Everything will be all right."

That was a lie, and well she knew it. "No it won't," she hoarsely disagreed. "Mrs. Frankton knows it was me . . . with you . . . *like that.* You know her as well as I . . . it shall be all over town on the morrow!" *Her father. He would expire with shame.*

"Then marry me."

Claudia froze. Neither one of them moved for a moment until she suddenly began to slap his arm away from her waist as if it were a snake and staggered free of him. She was frightened now, truly frightened—for a man like Julian to offer marriage . . . "You are insane!" she said harshly, and pressed her hands to her abdomen to keep the tremors from erupting into illness.

"Claudia, listen to me! I have compromised you irrevocably. I should not be able to live with myself if I did not set the matter to rights, and I daresay you will suffer the most from it. Think about it—it's a good match, you and I. We know each other quite well—what more could we ask?"

"You can't be serious!" she cried, and moved unsteadily, frantically into the shadows. What did he think, that after all he had done she would waltz to the altar with him? So what if he had been seen latched to her naked breast? Such things happened all the time among the *ton,* and everyone knew it! It was a meaningless dalliance, nothing more!

"Listen to me, Claudia. This will ruin your reputation—"

"Oh God, don't try and convince me that you would save my reputation!" Hysteria was rising in her throat, choking her. She pressed her hands to her cheeks—they were blazing. *Her father would kill her, or at the very least, lock her away. How many times had he told her? Everything she did reflected on him, and therefore, the king . . .*

Julian was suddenly beside her, his hand anxiously on her arm. "What options do you have? You must consider your reputation, and there is your father's position with the king—at the very least I owe you the protection of my name. It's not a bad solution, Claudia, and really, it's the best one."

Lord God, she couldn't breathe, much less think. It was all so fantastic, so very absurd! She would *not* marry for the mistake of sampling carnal pleasure! Men did it all the time—why couldn't she? Why should her reputation suffer for it? *His* certainly wouldn't! "I will not bend to the outdated expectations of the *ton* in this!" she exclaimed wildly. "I will not be forced into marriage because of some ridiculous fear for my reputation. *Your* reputation won't suffer as a result!"

"But yours will, Claudia. They will cut you directly, refer to you in reprehensible terms in their parlors, and by all means, keep their children from you for fear your behavior will infect them. You know it is true. It is the way of our world."

Our world. It had happened to Sarah Cafferty. Seduced into a lord's bed, disgraced and banished to the country, unmarriageable, untouchable. God help her, it had happened to Sarah Cafferty, the daughter of a marquis, and it could happen to *her.* Oh Lord, oh Lord, why had she succumbed to the temptation of passion with *him?* To be brought down by him, just as Phillip had been, all because she desired his kiss!

Claudia had never felt so despicably low in all her life.

"You know I'm right. Look, let me go out and bring a carriage around. Let's quit this place—we'll go some place private and talk. But we can't stay here—"

"There is nothing to talk about," she bit out. "I won't marry you, Julian. Not ever."

Silence.

She glanced at him from the corner of her eye and cringed—his eyes were blazing. "Indeed it is not the ideal circumstance, but I cannot think of what you could possibly—"

"I will not marry you over such a silly, meaningless

mistake, but moreover, I will not marry you because I honor Phillip!"

"What has Phillip to do with any of it?" he snapped. "I don't think he is coming to your rescue, Claudia! Mother of God, what can I say to make you understand? *You*, Lady Claudia, the daughter of the very powerful Earl of Redbourne, were seen on this bench, beneath a man—"

"Beneath a man who prides himself on being a *rake!* Beneath a man who led another man to his death! I will not forget what you did to Phillip, and I will not fetter myself to you for all eternity because of it. I shall face ruination before I dishonor his memory!"

Stunned, Julian took a step backward as if she had slapped him. "What in God's name are you talking about?" he asked roughly.

"You kept him from me!" she cried hysterically. "You kept him from me and coerced him into accompanying you to all those places that ruined him! Albright may have shot him, Julian, but *you* put him in that field!"

Raw pain hardened his features; he glared at her, his black eyes gleaming with the fire of abomination, his lips pressed tightly together. He finally looked away, clearly disgusted, and shoved a hand through his hair as Claudia caught a ragged breath in her throat.

"No one believes that more than I do," he muttered angrily. "God knows, when Phillip was on top of a whore at Farantino's or putting himself further into debt he was not with you. You are right—I killed him. I, Julian Dane, led him to his demise, and tonight I almost met my own. Thank you, Lady Claudia, for stopping me from making the biggest mistake of my life."

Claudia gaped at him, unable to speak.

"Good luck—you are going to need all that you can get," he said bitterly, and quit the hothouse, leaving her to find her own way out of this mess.

Ten

THE EARL OF REDBOURNE heard the first
ugly rumor concerning his daughter not two days after
the alleged incident had occurred. He was seated in a
chair turned toward the great hearth at his club, sipping
his usual port and languidly puffing on a cigar when he
had the grave misfortune to overhear a snippet of what
Sir Robert Clyde was loudly bragging. Having indulged
in a half dozen too many brandies, Sir Clyde apparently
did not know that Redbourne was sitting where he was,
or else he would never have said what he did—that he,
too, had once tasted the lips of Lady Claudia, and would
have tasted all of her had they had but a moment more in
the coach.

Shocked, Redbourne did not even realize he had
dropped his port and come to his feet—his only thought
was that Sir Clyde had just uttered the grounds of his
own death warrant. And Redbourne would have called
him out then and there, but his old friend Lord Hatfield
intercepted him, pulled him away, and quietly told him of
the tale that was circulating freely among the *ton.*

The news that Claudia had been caught in flagrante
delicto at a Harrison Green affair had rendered
Redbourne speechless. Staring at Hatfield, he slowly sank
into the leather wingback chair, shaking like a leaf.

It was inconceivable—his daughter would never do
such a thing! He frantically reminded himself that
Claudia had been raised in the best of circumstances, had

been perfectly trained for her role as a peer's wife and hostess. It simply was not possible that she would allow herself to be pawed by a despicable Rogue of Regent Street, and especially *not* Julian Dane!

It was incomprehensible.

And he repeated that over and over as he hurried home, intent on hearing what had transpired at that rout from his daughter's own lips. He would hear it all, then think what to do to keep the ugly rumors from spreading too far—to the *king,* for godsakes!

He arrived home at the same time Lord Montfort's footman was leaving. Standing in the foyer, Redbourne gestured for the note the man had brought. It was addressed to Claudia. Redbourne opened it, feeling not one scintilla of guilt—she was still his daughter and his responsibility, and as such, her mail was open to his inspection. He quickly scanned the vellum and felt his pulse begin to quicken with dread. The note very politely conveyed that, due to unforeseen circumstances, Lord Montfort would not be making a donation to Claudia's charitable project. No other explanation was given, nor was one needed.

Redbourne's pulse jumped erratically.

Montfort was a wealthy man. The unforeseen circumstances he referred to were the rumors of Claudia's hideous display of loose morals. Frankly, Redbourne would have done the same in Montfort's shoes—if Claudia couldn't be trusted with her own chastity, she could hardly be trusted with the man's money. What frightened Redbourne most was the unanswered question of just how many people knew.

He found her in her sitting room with a servant's daughter—Redbourne couldn't remember precisely which servant—in whom Claudia had taken a particular interest. He had chalked it up to her being five and twenty and still unmarried, and wished she would just agree to marry one of the half dozen suitors who regularly sought him out and bear her own child. Claudia and the girl were sitting side by side on a lawn green couch, an atlas spread across their laps.

Surprise flit across Claudia's face as he entered, turning into a beatific smile. "Papa! How wonderful that you should join us!"

Redbourne glanced at the girl. "Run along and find your mama."

The girl looked hesitantly at Claudia, whose smile slowly faded. She nodded to the girl. "Let's continue tomorrow, shall we? There now, off you go—your mother is in the kitchen with Mr. Randall." The girl slid off the couch, peering intently at Redbourne as if she had never seen a grown man before, walked slowly to the door, then reluctantly slipped out.

He waited until the door had shut behind her before turning to look at Claudia. Her lovely face tilted up to him, and he was struck with the disappointing notion that it was such a waste of beauty. "I understand you had a rather fine time of it at Green's latest soiree."

All of the color suddenly drained from her face. "W-what?"

Deny it. Tell me it is an abominable lie. Redbourne walked farther into the room, crumpling the note from Montfort. "Rumors apparently abound that you were discovered alone with a man in a rather . . . *compromising* position. Is that true?"

For a moment, Redbourne feared she might actually be ill. She could not possibly have done this—her reaction was one of shock and dismay that such horrid things would be said about her. When she found her breath, she would beg him to bring all his power to bear on whomever had started this despicable lie.

"It is true," she murmured. "I am so very sorry, Papa."

Marshall Whitney's world tilted. Staring at his flesh and blood, he refused to accept that this child of his could have slandered his name with such careless depravity. It could not be true! "With Kettering?" he heard himself ask with great disbelief. "On a bench beneath him, your breasts exposed?"

Wincing painfully, Claudia shamefully averted her gaze from him.

Redbourne stumbled to a chair, his mind racing. If the king heard of this disgrace, he might very well have him removed from the Privy Council. Worse yet, he would be the laughingstock of every club in London—his daughter, a whore!

"Papa, I—"

"No!" he said sharply, throwing up a hand. "Do not *speak!"* Taking several deep breaths, he fought for composure. He had never lifted a hand to Claudia, but if the gel ever deserved a sound thrashing, it was now. "Why?" he finally managed. "Why would you *degrade* yourself?"

"I don't know," she muttered miserably.

Furious, Redbourne jerked his head up and glared at her. "You don't *know?"*

Claudia remained silent.

"I have given you all that I can, raised you in the best of circumstances. How could you throw it all away? And for . . . for the sake of *lust?* What kind of woman *are* you? Why in God's name did you do it?"

A sob caught in her throat as she glanced heavenward. "I don't know! I thought . . . I mean to say I *wanted* to know—"

"I don't want to hear it!" He suddenly vaulted from the chair and began pacing furiously. "I don't want to know what madness overcame you! I never saw such lascivious behavior in your mother! *God,* Claudia, have you any idea what you've done? You've ruined everything! Do you think any of your suitors will call again? Believe me, they will not—no one will make a match with a woman disgraced by her own lust! Look at this!" He lifted Montfort's crumpled note for her to see. "You have already put your charitable endeavors in jeopardy!" He tossed the note at her, hitting her squarely in the chest.

She did not pick it up from her lap. "I am not disgraced! Kettering is not disgraced, so why—"

"Kettering will pay the piper, you may depend on it! I

won't allow him to succeed in bringing this humiliation upon my house!"

"What do you mean?" Claudia asked breathlessly. "W-what do you intend to do?"

Redbourne scowled at her. "He shall marry you," he said low. "I will see to it that he makes a legitimate whore of you!"

She recoiled physically, and for a scant moment, Redbourne almost regretted his words. *Almost.* But her ungodly lust had brought scandal to his pristine name, and by God, she would know the consequence of her folly!

"I won't marry him, Papa."

After what she had done, she would *defy* him? For the first time in his life, Redbourne could hardly stand to look at his daughter. "You will do as I tell you," he said in a voice trembling with rage, and started for the door.

"You can try and force me to your will"—she spoke so softly he had to strain to hear her—"God knows, as a woman, I have no rights in such matters as this. But you will not impose your will on him, I assure you."

Redbourne twisted sharply around and leveled a lethal gaze at her. "You had best worry less about your *rights* and pray that he doesn't hide you away in some remote corner of the world for the rest of your life. The bastard certainly has the means and the reason to do so."

Her eyes widened with mortification. *"Papa—"*

"Save your breath—you should have considered the consequence of lying under that bastard like a whore at the appropriate time." And with that, he walked away.

A steady rain was falling on the little town house on Upper Moreland Street, crowding the inhabitants into the house from the small but cheerful garden in back. Three of Doreen's charges—women ranging in age from twenty to almost five and sixty—were gathered in the basement kitchen, baking the last of the teacakes. Two more women were gathered around sewing baskets in the parlor, chattering gaily over their darning while three young children played at their feet. Doreen sat at the front window, rocking back and forth as she labored over the piecework in her lap, looking up and out the window occasionally when a carriage or pedestrian passed.

Claudia stood at the bay window, staring blindly into space as she had been doing for the better part of an hour since delivering fresh fruit for the children. This house was the only place she felt like herself now. Her life had been turned upside down and everything she thought she knew was suddenly open to debate—and God knew she had done enough of that. Word of her carnal experience had spread like fire through the *ton,* thanks to Mrs. Frankton, the story becoming more outrageous with each telling. It was humiliating to learn from Brenda, her maid, that some unscrupulous men—men she had known for years and had hosted in her home—were fanning the flames by claiming to know Claudia Whitney's person, having been associated with her in *that* capacity.

It was even more humiliating to learn that she had not, apparently, been The Rake's only conquest at Harrison Green's that night—Brenda had also heard about a rather tawdry kiss Julian had shared with Lady Prather in the ballroom.

Claudia folded her arms across her abdomen, seeing Julian's dark face above her again, his black eyes shining. *You are right to fear me . . .*

She shook her head, tried to clear her vision, but it was blurred by a thin sheen of tears she could scarcely keep at bay. She had finally come to realize . . . or admit . . . that her folly had cost her much. It didn't matter that certain factions of the *ton* judged her unfairly—Julian Dane was just as guilty as she was, yet she had not heard a word spoken against him. Nor did it matter that she was a grown woman, capable of making her own decisions and mistakes—the error in her judgment was adversely affecting her father's reputation. Her argument that she was a thinking adult with free will who should be allowed to enjoy the same pleasures in life as a man was met with an icy reproach. The essence of it, really, was that she was a woman, and therefore, her will was supplanted by that of her father, or a brother, or a husband.

Her reputation was annihilated beyond repair, apparently—the donations to her school project had dwindled to almost nothing. In the last few days, she had received a half dozen notes in which offers so generously made two weeks ago were withdrawn. Worse, when she had called on kindly Lord Cheevers to discuss the withdrawal of his pledge, he had refused to see her. His butler had turned her away at the door.

It was that for which she could not forgive herself. Above all else, her folly had affected children like the three little girls playing behind her now. Because she had allowed her desires to emerge unchecked, those girls might not receive the education they needed and deserved. The tears began to well again.

"I reckon there ain't much to be done for it," Doreen said, startling Claudia from her ruminations. She glanced at the woman who had been forced to trade her body to keep food in her children's bellies and felt a wave of self-loathing.

"I don't suppose," she muttered wearily.

"They've got you over a barrel. Only one thing to do, it would seem."

Claudia turned toward Doreen, staring at her as she calmly rocked, her needle flying in and out of the fabric. "What?"

Doreen shrugged lightly. "Marry him."

Dear God! "No," Claudia responded flatly.

Doreen did not look up. "It won't get any easier, not for you. I know this bloke has made you all sad and nervous of late, but he also made you moon-eyed—"

"I have *never* been moon-eyed!" Claudia protested as she sank onto a stool next to Doreen.

Doreen glanced up briefly from her piecework, but her skepticism was clearly evident. "You know that ain't so.

You were moon-eyed as a cow, right here in this parlor. Marry him. Won't do you any harm."

"Doreen!" Claudia exclaimed. "You vowed never to allow a man to rule your life again! Why should *I* do so?"

Doreen lowered her sewing and fixed Claudia with a stern gaze. "There's a difference between you and me, miss. You're one of them, the Quality. You *must* marry if you are to live. You can't work if you are of a mind to, and even if could, you'd not last a day in the factories. You're too fine for that. What else can you do? That father of yours won't keep you forever. Seems to me there ain't really no choice, not for a woman like you."

Claudia opened her mouth to protest, but Doreen shook her head. "It ain't worth your breath to argue. Besides, you've naught to fear from men, not like we do," she continued, gesturing toward the other women in the room. "Once that dandy marries you and has you, he'll leave you to your own. He won't need you to feed him and clothe him or bring him coin. God's teeth, I reckon he won't need you a'tall 'cept to be on his arm when the occasion warrants it. A woman couldn't ask for a better arrangement in this world, and it ain't like you got any choice in the end, is it? It's our lot in life, and ain't nothing any of us can do about it."

Having said it, Doreen calmly returned to her sewing. Claudia stared at her for a long moment, then shifted her gaze to the rain-slicked windowpane.

There was no argument she could offer that even she would believe.

Julian held Sophie's crumpled note in his hand, his jaw clenched tightly shut. It was directed to Stanwood, but had been delivered to him by the mistake of an old butler. Would he be forced to *physically* stuff some common sense into Sophie's empty little head? Did she think she could continue to defy him without consequence?

His hand went to the back of his neck, rubbing hard to erase the feeling of discomfort. She had quite lost her mind. When he had confronted her, she had blanched, but then had quickly regained her courage. *"You can't stop me from loving him!"*

Lord, he was weary of this! Sophie had never been so stubborn and the change in her was more than he could bear—not now, *especially* now—he could hardly care for himself, much less her. Julian rubbed his neck harder. He had told her, calmly and simply, that if she tried to contact Stanwood again, he would pack her off to Kettering Hall forthwith. And he had meant every word of it.

He looked at the vellum in his hand again. Addressed to Stanwood, Sophie's handwriting flourished in great sweeping strokes, promising—amid some choice complaints about an overbearing older brother—to find a way to meet him. For the life of him, it seemed quite beyond his ability to understand why she could not see his point in this.

It was beyond his ability to understand anything these last few days. He was at a loss—his body ached in every joint, bothered by the vague but pervasive sense of disquiet. It certainly didn't help that he hadn't slept in days, thanks to Phillip. Ah yes, Phillip's ghost came to him every night, just as he had in those long nights immediately following his death, invading his dreams. Everything came back, old wounds opened anew: the disbelief, the guilt, the voice of the vicar and the empty words, *know ye the quality of love . . .* It all came to him in fragmented dreams, memories startled out of a deep slumber after many long months by her single remark, spoken in a voice still coarse with desire.

Albright may have shot him, Julian, but you put him in that field . . .

Lord *God,* how he despised her! And it absolutely mortified him to think he had been lured to her by some adolescent adoration. Bloody hell, he had reacted like a puppy to her, licking her skin, inhaling her scent. He would have gotten down on his knees and begged her to let him make love to her, he was quite certain. But her rejection had cleaved him in two, left him feeling rudderless.

Julian dropped his forehead to his arms on top of his desk and closed his eyes. *If only he could sleep for an hour or two without thinking of her. Or Phillip. Or Sophie and, dear God, Valerie, too—all the ugly testaments to the quality of love in his life.*

The feel of a cold, clammy hand on his skin startled Julian. He shot upright, blinking rapidly against the light, trying to focus on the watery image of Tinley, whose stooped frame waited patiently, regarding him with a rather bored expression on his face. "*Jesus,* Tinley, might you have knocked?" he snapped.

"I did rap, my lord, but there was no response save a bit of snoring. Nor did you respond when I rapped on the edge of the desk."

Julian glowered at the old man. "What do you want?"

"Lord Redbourne to see you, my lord."

Bloody grand. "Then I suppose you had better show him in," he muttered, and shoved to his feet, making a feeble attempt to straighten his clothing.

"Shall I serve brandy?"

Julian chuckled in spite of himself. It was so like London—civility above all else, even when one man likely wanted to kill another. "By all means, serve brandy. Ask him to supper, why don't you?"

Tinley neither responded nor smiled as he shuffled out of the room.

Julian was at the hearth when Redbourne stormed in. He hadn't actually seen the earl in many months, and was struck by how much Claudia resembled her father. He was stately in stature, rather tall. His graying hair was perfectly arranged in the wispy Greek style favored by men of fashion. His handsome face showed signs of strain—telltale signs around the eyes, between the brows. His blue-gray eyes—Claudia's eyes—swept Julian from top to bottom.

Redbourne's lips curled into a sneer. "Well, Kettering, you don't *look* like a bastard. But you are that and more, you blackguard. I have every right to demand satisfaction for what you've done!"

All right then, they would dispense with the civilities. "Then do it, Redbourne," Julian responded evenly. "I'm not of a mind to putter around the issue."

With a shout of contemptuous laughter, Redbourne strode decisively into the room. "You are awfully cocksure, my lord! You have disgraced me! Trust me, if I were to put a bullet through that rotten heart of yours, no one in London would fault me for it!"

"I did not disgrace you, Redbourne," Julian said calmly. "Your daughter did that to you."

The color drained from the earl's face. "Don't push me, Kettering."

"And don't threaten me," he responded low. "If you want something of me, ask it."

Redbourne pressed his lips so tightly together that they all but disappeared. "I have come to *ask* you to be a gentleman. You've known my daughter since she was a girl—you were once a brother to her," he said, his eyes reflecting his disgust as he spoke, "and I should hope you would be man enough to do the right thing. I am asking you—*begging* you—don't allow my daughter's ruin at your hand."

Julian's gaze locked on Redbourne as he slowly shoved his hands into his pockets and leaned against the mantel. "I offered marriage, but your daughter refused me. It seems she rather despises me."

That was obviously news to Redbourne. "She has a rather unique way of showing it," he muttered. He moved to the desk, absently shoving a hand through his perfectly arranged hair. "She is ruined, Kettering. *You* ruined her. The rumors that circulate are devastating—I know you will understand the import when I tell you the rumors have even reached the king's ear." He glanced at Julian from the corner of his eye.

Julian lifted a hand to rub the juncture of his neck and shoulder.

"I am appealing to you to behave as a peer, as a gentleman. As a man who has proudly raised four sisters. You'd ask what I am asking if the woman in question were young Sofia."

"Her name is Sophie." The ache in Julian's shoulder spread into his chest, and he restlessly shoved away from the mantel. "I understand your position, Redbourne, but you must consider mine. She has refused my offer and I am therefore hardly inclined to force her to accept it against her will."

"You would if it were Sophie," Redbourne quickly shot back. "If this . . . *abominable* thing had happened to your sister, you would seek every means available to avoid scandal. I know that about you."

True. He would do whatever he must to protect any one of his sisters—it was an instinct in him as natural as breathing. He shrugged. "Even if I agreed, Claudia would not."

Redbourne snorted disdainfully. "What option does she have? Her folly has made her a virtual prisoner in my home. She rarely goes out, her friends cut her, she is not invited anywhere—she has no choice, unless she relishes living her life as a spinster."

Julian tried to picture Claudia in Redbourne's stuffy house, alone . . . her sparkle smothered by scandal.

"It's not as if you must unite with her, you know."

That brought Julian's head up; he glanced curiously at Redbourne. "Pardon?"

Redbourne shrugged lightly. "Yours certainly would not be the first marriage among the *ton* in which the happy couple chooses to lead separate lives . . . in all things."

Julian blinked. It had never occurred to him to marry before that night at Harrison Green's. It had certainly never occurred to him to do it in name only. But then, these circumstances were atrocious. He had compromised Claudia irrevocably and had learned that she despised him completely—he couldn't imagine being married at all, much less to a woman who despised him. Nevertheless, he felt keenly the weight of his responsibility for this mess.

Perhaps Redbourne was right. Perhaps they could co-exist in the same house peacefully enough; both the St. James house and Kettering Hall were large enough that they could go for several days, even weeks, without having to see or speak to one another. It *could* work.

He turned his head, looked at Redbourne. "If I should agree, would you be able to obtain a special license?"

Relief washed over Redbourne's face. "Of course," he said quickly. "Then you'll do it?"

Swallowing past the lump of uncertainty lodged in his throat, Julian nodded.

Redbourne turned on his heel and strode to the door. "You are doing the honorable thing, Kettering. No one can fault you for it."

Perhaps . . . but Julian had the uneasy feeling that there was one person who could and would.

Eleven

SHE WOULD, APPARENTLY, be forced into marrying The Rake.

Through her lashes, Claudia looked at the man who would be her husband as he spoke casually to Louis Renault—as if this sort of family gathering happened all the time.

It had only happened because her father had insisted upon it after coercing her into agreeing to marry Kettering. Oh, he had been truly magnificent in that— first sweetly cajoling, then threatening her, then swearing on her mother's grave to make her life a virtual hell if she did not agree to Kettering's offer. He had thrown everything at her he could think of, but she had resisted valiantly, certain she could weather the storm and determined not to lose everything to The Rake. The earl probably had no idea which threat in particular had finally swayed her. It was not the threat of spinsterhood, or the rabid vow to closet her away. It was the moment he had declared her poverty-stricken, stripped of her annuity and her allowance—and therefore, stripped of the means to support the town house on Upper Moreland Street.

Battered down, Claudia had tearfully agreed then, and the moment the words slipped from her mouth, her father had forcibly sat her at his desk to pen a note to Kettering. Under his watchful eye—he had literally hung over her shoulder—her tears blinding her, Claudia had written a terse note accepting his supposed offer.

Kettering had come round to see her the next day, but she had made Brenda beg off for her, unable to look at him just yet. He had sent his regrets up with Brenda, and Claudia had not seen or heard from him again.

Until her father had forced her to come to this so-called family supper.

Julian had been politely reserved since their arrival, greeting her distantly, his lips barely grazing her knuckles. But his obsidian eyes had pierced her with a look; a probing, questioning look that brought a heat to her neck. Then Eugenie had rushed to greet her, alternately sobbing with joy and regret and joy again, and his eyes had shuttered.

They had not spoken since.

Not during the round of whiskey for the men before supper, not on the promenade to the dining room, and not over wine before the meal was served. Eugenie and Ann had seen to it that she survived the supper, speaking very carefully of the wedding, treading softly around the affair as if they had not been surprised out of their wits by it all. In the gold salon after supper, when the men remained in the dining room for a glass of port, Eugenie had quietly discussed the details of the wedding breakfast with her, as if mentioning it would cause her to burst into tears— Eugenie had always been perceptive that way. And when the men rejoined the ladies, Claudia had deftly avoided any conversation with him at all by focusing intently on Ann's complaints of swollen ankles and a strange craving for broad beans.

But she had felt his eyes on her, surreptitiously watching her every move. *Oh, God, how would she ever survive this? How could she possibly walk down the aisle to him? Lie in his bed?*

A shudder ran through her, chilling her to the bone. For the thousandth time, she thought of Eugenie's wedding and the way she had glided down the aisle on Julian's arm to a beaming Louis. She thought of how proud and handsome Julian had looked that day, how desperately in love she had been with him, how she had stood at Eugenie's side and imagined that the vicar was speaking to her and Julian—

Stop! Claudia squeezed her eyes shut for a moment to regain her balance. She was not that silly girl any longer! Seven years had passed and with them, her doe-eyed innocence. Seven years in which she had learned what men were, what they *truly* wanted from women, and how easily they could dismiss women from their lives if it suited them. She understood that women were the vessels upon which they satisfied their desire, chattel to command in marriage. And looking across the room at him, Claudia believed her future husband was the epitome of the worst of them. Because he was the sort of man who could bring a woman to a state of blind devotion without so much as flexing his heart.

Worse, Claudia knew she was the sort of woman who succumbed easily to his charm. She certainly had at Harrison Green's, somehow believing herself above propriety and chastity. Her mistake was one of monumental consequence, one she would regret the rest of her days. But the damage was done; her only hope now was to beg him for a few concessions that would enable her to survive this loveless marriage, a few ground rules they could both agree upon that would make it less hurtful. *Please God.*

She could not avoid him forever, no matter how much she wanted to. Julian glanced at her from the corner of his eye, nodded at something Louis said, and tried not to squirm with impatience. He felt as if he was about to crawl out of his skin, a feeling that had only gotten worse since she had arrived. God, but her smile, that devastating flash of brilliance was gone, and in its place a look so sullen that it made him wince. Her dismay was palpable; he felt it so keenly that he wondered if he had confused it with his own. It was clear she was averse to this marriage, but what was done was done—there was nothing either of them could do now, for to call off the wedding would plunge them into a scandal so deep neither of them could escape. He was, therefore, of the firm opinion that they should simply make the best of it. It was not the end of the world . . . not yet, anyway.

And as he excused himself from Louis's company, he was bound and determined that she would see his reasoning and come to the very same conclusion.

He strolled casually across the room, cognizant that they all strained not to watch the exchange. His sisters, naturally, were beside themselves with glee that he would finally marry—their dearest friend, no less. Oh, they knew very well what had happened to bring this marriage about, but they did not allow a lurid little scandal to stand in the way of their happiness. Frankly, he had the sense all day that they had been gamely struggling not to burst into wedding song. It was a supreme sacrifice for them, he knew, to remain subdued because of the somber reasons behind the pending nuptials.

It did not, however, keep them from grinning widely when Claudia came to her feet as he approached. Surprised, Julian halted, clasping his hands awkwardly behind his back. "A word, madam?" he asked quietly.

"Yes, please," she responded, and calmly walked out of the room. With a glance at the others, Julian followed her, motioning for the footman posted just outside the salon to follow them. Claudia started to the east; Julian reached for the small of her back and felt the muscles stiffen beneath his palm as she stopped and turned halfway toward him.

He let his hand drop. "I suggest the library. Unless, of course, you prefer the breakfast room?"

"Um, no. Excuse me," she muttered, and walked stiffly in the opposite direction, her dark gold and green skirts floating behind her. Julian could not help but think of that afternoon at Château la Claire when she had glided across the grass, barefoot, the sun bringing out the bits of gold shimmering in her hair. That day seemed like years ago now, he thought, reaching to open the door of the library.

Claudia squeezed past him, carefully putting as much distance between them as possible, then fairly sprinting to the far side of the room where she took refuge near a globe. As they waited for a footman to light several candelabras about the room, Julian beheld his bride-to-be, thinking that with her hands clasped tightly together and her chin held high, she looked very much like the defiant little girl who had stood so often in his study at Kettering.

He couldn't help but smile. "Relax, Claudia."

She did not relax, but shifted uncomfortably from one foot to the other. Julian glanced at the footman hovering near the door and dismissed him with a nod.

"I . . . I don't want to do this," she said when the door shut.

The troubled sound of her voice pierced his soul; he sobered instantly. "Why don't you sit down? You'll be more comfortable."

"Isn't there some other way? I mean, there must be *something* you can do!" she blurted anxiously.

God, if he could fix this for her, he would. "Unfortunately, the only thing I can do is marry you."

A bit of color crept into her cheeks, and Claudia folded her arms tightly about her waist, and looked at the ground. "There *must* be another way!"

"There is not," he said curtly. He had no desire to belabor that painful point, and strode aimlessly across the room. There was nothing more he could say. He was sorry she was so against it . . . *against him,* but what could he do? He could hardly—

Julian heard a sound and jerked around; Claudia's fist was pressed against her mouth in her struggle not to cry. She whirled away from him, but Julian was quickly at her side, trying to hold her, although she shoved away from him. "Don't cry, Claudia," he uttered helplessly. "It will be all right."

"I feel so *helpless!*"

"I know you do."

"I have no voice, no say! I am *nothing!* Cheevers

won't receive me, they say horrid things about me, and my father barely speaks to me!"

He winced, truly sorry for the indignities she was undoubtedly suffering. She suddenly lifted her head and swiped angrily at the tears on her cheeks. "But there is no going back, is there?"

"No," he said.

"All right, well then, I . . . I will not cry. I only . . . I've some questions."

"About?"

"I am rather curious how it will be after we, ah . . . after Saturday."

"How what will be?"

"You know . . . *us*. I mean, this," she quickly corrected, gesturing wildly about the room. "Will I be placed under any restrictions?"

"Restrictions?" he echoed dumbly, uncertain as to what she might be thinking.

Claudia glanced heavenward with a sigh and wiped the wetness from beneath her eyes. "You are not making this very easy, Julian."

"I beg your pardon for that, but what sort of restrictions were you expecting?"

"Will you restrict my freedom in any way?" she asked, gesturing irritably. "Tell me where I can go and where I cannot? Whom I may see or not see?"

Now wasn't this just bloody grand? She not only thought him a murderer of sorts, but also a man who would imprison his wife. "That's ridiculous, Claudia. Why would I restrict you in any way? You may come and go as you like."

"Will I be allowed to remain in London, then?" she asked skeptically.

"I rather assume you will remain with *me*, wherever that might be. Do I presume too much?"

She blinked, her gray eyes clouded with confusion. "So . . . so you don't intend to send me to Kettering?"

Where in God's name did she get these absurd notions? "Claudia," he said impatiently, "I intend to live as any man and wife would, wherever it suits us, whenever it suits us, in London or at Kettering. I am certainly not going to imprison you, and I am not going to banish you."

She glanced down. The soft light of a candelabrum framed her profile as she scuffed the toe of her slipper into the carpet. The slipper had a tiny little bow on it, so light and fragile. Something in Julian reacted violently to that bow. As absurd as it was, it reminded him of Valerie, of another time he had felt the need to make everything all right and had failed. He had failed with Phillip, too. Claudia despised him for that failure, and Julian suddenly did not want to be responsible for another person's well being. No. He could not *bear* the responsibility.

God Almighty, he did not want to *feel* anything for an alluring little wench who could seduce him with nothing more than a smile and in the next breath cut him to the bone. And she had a dozen smiles at least, smiles that captured him, tugged at his heart, held him hostage . . . *When she looked at him, did she think of Phillip?*

"Well then, there is one other thing," she said softly.

"Yes?" he asked curtly.

"Will I . . . will you grant me an allowance?"

He snorted. "No. I intend for you to be penniless, too." That sarcastic response seemed to confuse her again, and Julian motioned impatiently toward the door. "Of *course* you will have an allowance, Claudia. I will provide for whatever your heart desires and deny you nothing. Good God, do you recall *nothing* from the summers you spent at Kettering? You may name your own allowance—"

"Thirty pounds?" she quickly interjected.

"Per annum?" he asked sharply.

"Per month?" she asked meekly.

Extravagant, but what did he care? He could certainly afford it. If it kept her occupied, separate from him . . . "Done. And let us further agree to peacefully coexist, all right? You shall go about your business, and I shall go about mine. There is no reason for either of us to suffer unduly for our folly," he said, halting abruptly in front of her. "I don't intend to punish myself forever for this colossal mistake." Claudia blinked, lifted an uncertain gaze to him, searching his face, silently questioning the sudden change in him, and Julian cursed her for the unwelcome pull of his heart. "You can do that, can't you, Claudia?" he demanded snidely. "Ignore the presence of another? I know I certainly can."

The harsh words seemed to fill the room until she quietly responded, "Better than you, my lord, I assure you."

"Marvelous," Julian drawled, and pivoted on his heel, moving quickly for the door before he did something very foolish, like begging her to love him. "Shall we return to our guests? No doubt they are wondering if I've got you on a bench again," he said, and refused to acknowledge the burn in his gut when he heard her pained gasp of astonishment. Why should he? Her dismay was no different from his own. Ah yes, a crushing dismay that the wheels were turning, wheels he could not possibly stop, wheels that would run them over if he allowed it. There was no way out of this catastrophe for either of them.

A hard, steady rain was falling in London on her wedding day. In the barouche, Claudia sat across from her father, avoiding his gaze. Her stomach lurched with every swerve of the coach; she had been sick with regret for days now.

She glanced up at the patch of dull gray sky above the rooftops that slowly slipped past, wondering for the thousandth time why she had ever allowed herself to be coerced into this. *Unfortunately, the only thing I can do is marry you. But I don't intend to punish myself forever for this colossal mistake.* She would never endure it! Abruptly squeezing her eyes shut, Claudia fought off the tears she had managed to keep at bay for the last forty-eight hours.

The coach slowed, rounded a corner. "Buck up now. We've arrived," her father said sharply.

Claudia winced at the sight of the cathedral. Several

men milled on the top step of entry, just beneath an overhang. The earl had, naturally, insisted on two dozen or more prominent guests to witness what had been billed as a small, family wedding. He thought that would make it seem almost planned, but it was absurd—the whole of London knew she was being forced into this, her public and everlasting penitence for her indiscretion.

"Come on, then, you look rather weepy. Enough of that now."

She slid her gaze to her father's impassive face. What did he expect her to do, titter gaily like a blushing maid? Honestly, she had never thought him a particularly sentimental man, but his indifference this past week had bordered on heartless. Could he not understand, not even a little bit, how very difficult this was for her? How very *humiliating* it was to be dragged into a union with a man of Kettering's character?

"Did you love Mama?" Claudia suddenly asked.

She might as well have asked him if he was a traitor to the crown. "I beg your pardon?" he gasped.

"Did you love Mama?" she asked again, marveling that she had never before asked him that simple, fundamental question.

Oblivious to the door swinging open, the earl gaped at her as if she had lost her mind. *"Love?"* he repeated, as if the word pained him. "What are you doing, Claudia? This is hardly the time—"

"Papa, please! Just tell me—did you love her?"

He frowned darkly, ran his thumb and finger down the sides of his mouth, then mindlessly smoothed his neckcloth. He glanced at the footman standing at attention next to the open door. "A moment, Stringfellow," he said, and gestured for the door to be shut.

It was a long moment before he spoke. "As with most marriages within our rank, ours was arranged through our families. We hardly knew one another," he said circumspectly. "However, I quite respected your mother. I suppose I even grew rather adoring of her after the first year of marriage when she was with child. But it would be untruthful of me to say I loved her—and neither should you trouble yourself with such sentiment, Claudia. It is hardly necessary to a successful marriage, and I rather think such a notion can be disruptive after a time. Love is like a fine wine—it eventually turns to vinegar. You would do best to strive for a healthy respect for your husband. If you give him your obedience, an amicable companionship will see you through."

Claudia gaped at her father, both fascinated and appalled. Was it possible that he could have shared the greatest of intimacies with a woman—the conception of a child—and thought it nothing more than amicable companionship?

"Now. We've only a minute or two before you are due at the altar." With that, he flicked the door open and exited quickly.

Claudia did not move—*could* not move. Through the open door, she stared at the church and the men gathered on the stoop staring curiously at the barouche. Her stomach moved again and she wondered madly what the scandalmongers would make of it if she was actually sick at the altar. There was no time to contemplate it, however, because her father's gray head appeared in the opening, and his expression clearly relayed that he was quite beyond exasperation. "Enough of this, Claudia!" he whispered hoarsely. "You have made your bed and now you shall lie in it—come along now!"

If that wasn't the greatest understatement of the decade—oh yes, she had made her bed, all right. Numb with fright, she slowly, deliberately, pulled the hood of her cloak over her bonnet, adjusted the cloak about her shoulders, and extended her hand to her father.

The small crowd gathered on the top step of the church parted to let her pass, all of them staring as if she was some sort of oddity as they murmured faint congratulations, to which her father naturally responded. In the narthex, Eugenie, Ann, and Sophie were anxiously waiting. Claudia had not taken much interest in the planning of this wedding, listlessly deferring to Eugenie's relentless enthusiasm and Ann's eye for details. She glanced at Sophie as she removed her cloak and handed it to an attendant—her eyes were red-rimmed, as if she had been crying, and her mouth was set in a frown. Eugenie fairly danced at her side, whispering excitedly about who had come. Ann flitted around like a bumblebee, tending to her gown.

Self-conscious, Claudia looked down. Her gown was a silver velvet with an overskirt of a very fine, transparent chiffon intermittently decorated with tiny little crystals that reflected the soft candlelight in the church. It was a little tight through the fitted bodice and the waist; she supposed she had gained a bit of weight since she last wore it. It was really a rather old gown, one she had worn a few years ago when she attended a very important ball with her father—the very same ball at which Phillip had waltzed her into a heady state of adoration. She had not worn the gown since, but now the silver velvet seemed a good, somber color for the occasion.

"It's time," her father muttered, and grasped her elbow tightly as if he was afraid she might bolt. Ann was suddenly bustling around them, arranging everyone in a line, whispering last minute, frantic instructions into Sophie's ear before fairly shoving her from behind the screen that separated the narthex from the nave.

Eugenie followed, grabbing Claudia in something of a bear hug before stepping into the aisle. The earl silently grasped her hand and clamped it down upon his forearm, then pulled her forward. The panic in Claudia's chest rose to her throat; she stumbled beside her father, righting herself just as he stepped into the aisle leading up to the altar.

A sea of people swelled to their feet; heads swiveled until all eyes were on her. Claudia's vision suddenly blurred—with tears or fright, she wasn't certain—and she frantically searched for something to focus on, something that would keep her from seeing their faces. Her lashes fluttered wildly, she looked toward the vicar—

Julian.

Oh, God. *Oh, God!*

Her stomach listed violently. Standing next to Arthur Christian, he wore a dark gray frock coat and trousers, a navy waistcoat intricately embroidered with silver thread. Taller than everyone else, his black hair—still too long, she thought madly—gleamed in the light of the dozens of candles at the altar, contrasting vividly with the white of his collar. Although his round spectacles made him appear less predatory than normal, they did not hide the glint in his raven eyes, or the fact that they were riveted on her.

Heaven above, he was *magnificent.*

Her heart was hammering furiously now, gathering momentum with each step that drew her closer to him. Claudia could not tear her gaze from his. Mesmerized, she did not hear the vicar ask who gave her to him, or her father's answer as he put her hand into Julian's. His fingers closed around hers; the earl stepped away, and there was nothing between them, nothing but the ugly truth. But still, Claudia gazed up at him, still disbelieving, caught on the edge of a waking nightmare. Julian smiled reassuringly, leaning into her as they turned toward the vicar. *"It's all right."* He whispered it so softly that she thought for a moment she had imagined it, but the gentle squeeze of her fingers assured her she hadn't.

And there she stood beside him, murmuring mindless responses to the vicar, staring helplessly at the stained glass window of the Virgin Mary. She was shivering; it was so cold in the cavernous cathedral, the only spot of warmth his hand, wrapped firmly around hers. It was odd, she thought dreamily as he pushed a plain gold band on her finger, that a single hand could hold her up, buoy her during the most extraordinary moment of her life. The hand of a man who had ruined her life not once, but twice now.

"I now pronounce you man and wife . . ."

She heard nothing else, just felt his hand on her cheek, the brush of his lips against hers, his soft sigh on her lips. And when he raised his head, Claudia saw the glimmer of something deep in his black eyes, *too* deep—for a moment, he seemed almost vulnerable. He took her hand in his, put it in the crook of his arm and covered it protectively with his own, and led her down the aisle as music lifted from the strings of the quartet.

Oh, Lord.

It was done.

But it was only beginning.

Twelve

Dᴜʀɪɴɢ ᴛʜᴇ ᴡᴇᴅᴅɪɴɢ breakfast, the weight of reality began to seep into Claudia's marrow. It wasn't just the gold band that felt foreign and unnatural on her finger. Nor was it the guests who politely acknowledged her new status by addressing her as Lady Kettering.

It was *him*.

Not that Julian had uttered a word to her, other than to tell her that Sophie would be staying with Ann and Victor for a fortnight. He had offered this in the course of the carriage ride to her father's house on Berkeley Street and had waited patiently for her response. But Claudia had not found her voice quite yet, and he had at last turned his attention to the window.

He had hardly spoken to her since, but it didn't matter. His mere presence was overpowering. He chatted easily and gaily to the many people who congratulated him, acting as if this had been an event they had *wanted* to occur. Perfectly charming, relaxed and witty, his presence filled the space around her, pushing her into a corner. As the afternoon wore on, the consequence of her folly weighed heavier and heavier. She belonged to *him* now.

And he touched her. Since the moment they had been pronounced married, he had touched her freely—her hand, her elbow, the small of her back. This was not something she was accustomed to—her father had never been one for displays of affection and what little she got, she had forced. But the feel of *his* fingers on her elbow, *his* hand riding her waist, was too . . . comforting. It frightened her. If she allowed him to lull her into a false sense of security, he would wound her in the end, she was certain of it. He would eventually tire of her, eventually seek his pleasure elsewhere, just as he always did.

And there were words. *"To the health and happiness of my young bride,"* he had toasted, *"I pledge my undying respect and honor."* A woman sighed; Arthur Christian applauded the earl poet, and Julian smiled into her eyes as he touched the rim of his flute to her own. She had to remind herself that they were just words, said to please the guests. Yet her stomach had fluttered wildly.

And now they were alone.

Alone and apart in the massive Kettering House on St. James Square. When they arrived, old Tinley showed her to her new suite of rooms, and there she had remained, staring out the window at the gray day, the rain-soaked courtyard gardens, and the wisps of smoke rising from chimneys across the London skyline.

Having paced restlessly in front of the hearth of the master suite, Julian stopped and glared at the clock on the mantel. Eight o'clock. Four hours now since she had followed Tinley up without a word, presumably to change and join him. He had not actually *said* that to her, but he thought she would have understood it. Like it or not, it was their wedding day. What did she intend, to mope about in her rooms until the bitter end?

He pivoted on his heel, strode toward a small brass cart, and helped himself to a whiskey from the crystal decanter there. He wasn't exactly new to feminine moping. With four sisters—any one of whom may have locked herself in her room at any given time—he was quite accustomed to waiting out such episodes. But not this time—he was too impatient, too unsettled by the rapid succession of recent events.

He should have kept her longer at Redbourne's, kept her occupied, he thought wryly as he sipped the whiskey.

But he had been anxious to be away from the prying eyes watching closely for any tear in the façade or any other sign that the scandal had not quite ended. And he had actually felt sorry for Claudia—she had been a bundle of nerves all morning, a shadow of her usual self, starting at the slightest touch and shrinking from the good wishes of Redbourne's fifty or more guests.

Redbourne, that idiot! The man held his position with the king in higher regard than he did his daughter! For the sake of appearances he had invited fifty guests to what should have been a quiet ceremony for the immediate family and hosted a wedding breakfast to rival that of any wedding in the *best* of circumstance! Not once, not *once,* had he heard Redbourne say a kind word to Claudia or show her even a modicum of sympathy. No, he had been too concerned that the wedding seem as planned and proper as was possible and that not one untoward piece of gossip reach the king's ear.

Well, Julian had done his part all right, and it had been one of the hardest things he had ever done in his life.

It was unnerving, to say the least, to utter the words that bound him to a woman for the rest of his life, particularly when that woman detested him. But that rather uncomfortable sensation was nothing compared to the raw emotion at seeing her on her father's arm in that silver gown—exactly as she had appeared that night almost two years ago.

It had rocked him to his core, thrown him off balance, made his insufferable desire for her surge to the surface. It was all he could do to keep from gaping in wonder as he had watched her glide down that aisle, her large blue-gray eyes fixed on him. When Redbourne handed his daughter over to him for all eternity, he had seen the bewilderment in her eyes . . . and his heart had ached for her.

It *still* ached, he thought, and downed the rest of the whiskey. The ache was different now, however, having spread through him like a cancer and making him want to claw his way out of his skin. Seeing her so subdued, he had longed for the old Claudia, the bright star in the *ton*'s galaxy. The woman who could rattle a man with a mere smile, the woman who had captivated him in France. But that Claudia was gone, perhaps forever destroyed by this marriage. There was no idea he could conjure that he thought would entice his bride into this marriage.

But he owed it to her to make the best of this predicament—it was the least he could do for having ruined her life. That meant ignoring the reasons why she despised him, pushing Phillip as far from his thoughts as possible. He had to show her that they *could* live peacefully with one another.

Starting with a quiet supper on this, their blasted wedding day.

He knocked on her door an hour later, having sent for wine and a light supper. There was no answer; Julian opened the door and walked into her rooms. The only light came from a small fire in the hearth that cast huge shadows on the walls. On a table set directly in front of the fire were several covered dishes, a bottle of wine and two wine goblets. Claudia stood in the shadows with her hands clasped behind her back, leaning against one wall. She had not changed; the crystals embedded in the folds of her gown twinkled like tiny little stars around her.

She was so beautiful.

He stepped across the threshold and shut the door behind him, shoved his hands in his pockets, regarding her just as warily as she regarded him. "That's a beautiful gown. I remember the first time you wore it."

Claudia's expression did not change. "Yes, well, there was no time to commission another one."

"It was a compliment. You were as beautiful then as you are today," he said, watching her breast rise with a very deep breath. "I believe it was the night of the Wilmington Ball."

"Yes," she murmured faintly, "the Wilmington Ball. Papa was quite perturbed that night because I danced with one gentleman three times. He was positively apoplectic."

Redbourne hadn't been the only one. Phillip had monopolized her all evening, evoking a rare envy in him. "It was a long time ago," he said, and inclined his head toward the table. "I thought you might be hungry. Shall we dine?"

Claudia glanced at the covered platters. "Oh." She pushed away from the wall and moved slowly to the table, perching stiffly on the edge of a chair. "I . . . I don't know what you like," she muttered, lifting a cover.

"It doesn't matter," he said, and moved to take the other seat. He reached for the wine, filled her glass, then his. Claudia did not look at him; she forked some roast beef from one platter onto a gold-rimmed china plate, and followed it with a helping of boiled potatoes. With a shy glance beneath her lashes, she handed him the plate.

He took it, watched her fork two potatoes onto another plate, then suddenly set it down. "I can't do this."

Julian paused, lowering the goblet from which he was about to drink. "You are not hungry?"

"No, I can't do *this*!" she cried, gesturing at the table and the room. "I can't pretend, Julian!"

"No one is asking you to," he said evenly, placing his goblet on the table.

She dropped her gaze to her lap. "Tell me, please, what do you want from me?"

What did he *want* from her? To look at her one day and not feel such insane longing. "I grant you our marriage is not ideal, but it is hardly hell, Claudia. I understand how distressing today's ceremony must have been for you—"

"Humiliating," she suddenly interjected, and came abruptly to her feet. "You cannot imagine how humiliating!"

And perhaps he could imagine it very well, he thought, watching her pace in front of the hearth. "I am terribly sorry this has been so humiliating for you, but unfortunately there was nothing I could do."

"Yes, so you have said, Julian. Believe me, you have made it *quite* clear how unfortunate this is for you."

He had no idea what she meant by that but did not like the tone of her voice. "I don't like this any more than you do—"

"But it's not the same for you! *You* weren't forced into this, *I* was! I am *your* chattel now—I might as well be a fat old cow!"

"Don't be ridiculous!" he snapped, and stood abruptly, raking a hand through his hair in exasperation. "You are not my *chattel,* Claudia—ah, to hell with it. I won't argue something so foolish. Look here, what is done is done, and I do not intend to dwell on it."

"Meaning?" she asked, folding her arms defensively across her middle.

"Meaning," he said, planting one elbow on the mantel and peering sharply into her face, "we are quite married now, and you might as well accept that fact, because God knows, it will go easier on us both once you do!"

"Oh, I've accepted it, my lord," she said low. "Just as my father said—I have made my bed, and now I am lying in it. How could I possibly accept this folly any better than that?"

"I would suggest, madam, that your petulance is not helping matters in the least," he muttered irritably.

"My *petulance?*" she exclaimed indignantly. "Pray tell, Julian, what would you like me to do? Pretend this is all quite all right? That I somehow *wanted* this to happen?"

Yet another reminder that she despised him and one he certainly did not need. "Do us both an enormous favor and don't make this any worse than it already is!" he said hotly.

"I could not possibly make it any worse than it is!" she exclaimed. "And don't expect me to make it better for you!"

Cold anger shot through him. Unthinkingly, he grabbed her elbow and yanked her to him. "Don't push me, Claudia," he warned her. "There were two of us in that hothouse, and as I recall, you were enjoying it as much as I was!"

Her eyes were suddenly glittering with fury. "How *dare* you! Let go of me," she muttered angrily, squirming in his grasp.

"Not until I am damn good and ready," he responded through clenched teeth, and jerked her hard into his chest, crushing her in his arms as he quickly descended to devour her luscious mouth. She struggled fiercely, tried to push his arms away. But then something happened—her struggle was suddenly filled with an urgency he fully understood. She opened her mouth beneath his, and he thrust eagerly into the warm recess, mimicking another, earthier motion. He drew her lip between his teeth, savoring every nip of her plump flesh. And then her hands were around his neck, pulling his head down to hers as she pressed her lithe body to his, against the hard shaft of an arousal he had not felt in months—*years*.

Then suddenly she stopped, tried to turn her head away from his, and he felt the tears on her cheeks. He dragged his mouth across her cheek, to one blue-gray eye, then pressed his forehead against hers. "It doesn't have to be so hard, sweetheart," he murmured raggedly. "Don't . . . don't make this so hard for us. It's our wedding day, and I want to make love to you. I want to bury myself deep inside you and feel you wrap yourself around me. I want to give you pleasure you have dared not dream of and I would that you want the same. Let me love you, Claudia."

With a soft whimper, she closed her eyes. *"No,"* she whispered helplessly, and her hands began to slide from his shoulders. "It will only hurt us in the end, don't you see?"

Julian caught her wrists. *"Yes.* I won't let it hurt us," he insisted. "Just let me love you." He lowered his head again, before she could protest, brushing her lips gently, touching her with the tip of his tongue, skimming the seam of her lips. He let go of her wrists, sliding his hands to her back and the tiny row of buttons there. She didn't resist him; she grasped the lapels of his waistcoat and clung to him. And when his hands slipped underneath her gown to touch her back, her lips parted with a soft sigh and she met his tongue with her own, thrusting boldly into his mouth.

Mother of God.

Her tongue was like a flame, licking and tantalizing him beyond reason. The fire ran like a river to his groin, building to an unimaginable heat. He pushed the gown from her shoulders, his fingers gliding over her satin skin, down to her waist as he kissed her more deeply.

He abruptly lifted his head; her eyes were glittering like gems, their color almost deep water blue. Her lips, swollen from his kiss, were as red and as plump as summer berries. He dropped his gaze to her breasts, drew an uneven breath. They were partially covered by a chemise that clung to her; hardened nipples jutting against silk from two perfect globes. Brushing the pad of his thumbs across them, he felt them stiffen even more as her fingers curled tightly into his arms, and he hoped to high heaven he would have the strength to hold himself until it was right for her.

"You make me feel so . . . so *helpless,*" she whispered. As beautiful as she was, as *alluring* as she was, she was an innocent. But her eyes . . . the bewildered hunger in her eyes penetrated his consciousness, sent a heat swirling through him, pushing down to the fire already flaming out of control in his groin.

Julian gritted his teeth and wrapped his arms around her, holding her tightly to him in a fierce embrace. "I am helpless too, Claudia. I want to make love to you so badly I may very well expire with it," he murmured thickly, and buried his face in her neck, drawing the pearl dangling from her lobe into his mouth. It was impossible to let go of her, and damned near impossible to think of her innocence above his own raging need. He grazed his cheek against hers, fully intending to end this now, fully intending to wait until Claudia was ready—however long it took.

But as his hands slid to her shoulders and he began to lift his head, she turned her face into him, dragged her lips across his cheek, searching for his mouth. Surprised, he was motionless for a moment, long enough for Claudia to slip her tongue between his lips and kiss him with an ardor that matched his own and quickly driving him to the brink of madness. Without thinking, Julian lifted her into his arms and carried her into the adjoining bedroom.

He had no idea when or how her gown came off. He only knew that she was almost naked in his arms—he ripped the neckcloth from his neck, clawed at his shirt until it was gone as he gazed ravenously at her body. When he tugged gently at the drawstring of her petticoats, they fell away, pooling at her feet. *She was resplendent, radiant.* Julian slowly sank to his haunches, trailing his hands down her side, over her hips and thighs. Carefully, he lifted one foot, then the other, until she was free of the garment, and steadied her when she started to sway. She wore just a light silk chemise and a thin pair of drawers.

He looked up, caught her gaze as he slowly slid the drawers over the gentle flair of her hips. She steadied herself with a hand on his shoulder as he lifted her feet to free her of the fabric. His hands glided up her legs, around to her bottom, and he impulsively buried his face in the gentle swell of her belly, calling on everything he had to respect her innocence, to take his time to show her the many ways a man could love a woman. He had wanted her for so long, just like this, in his arms . . . it was torture not to take her with the full force of the fire coursing through him. But Julian forced himself to rise, sliding his hands over the thin silk chemise that barely covered her, up her rib cage, over her breasts, hardly touching her at all.

"You are beautiful," he murmured, and reached for the pins in her hair, releasing one thick tress at a time. *A goddess,* he thought, and kissed her lightly, toying with her lips as he reached for the thin straps of her chemise and pushed them off her shoulders.

The chemise slipped away, baring what were exquisite breasts. He lowered his head, flicked his tongue across one tip. Claudia swayed into him, bracing herself against his arms. His body, throbbing with painful anticipation, strained impatiently against his trousers. He cupped her breasts gingerly, almost reverently, felt them swell in his palms as Claudia drew another ragged breath. Her eyes were unfocused; a dark blush had flooded her cheeks. With the back of his hand, Julian brushed her brow. *"Claudia,"* he whispered, and kissed her forehead before stepping away to sit on the edge of the bed.

As he feasted his gaze on her body, she shyly dropped her head, folded her arms across her bare stomach. He had thought her beautiful for years, but he had never understood *how* beautiful. Her body was not of this earth—legs long and shapely, hips flaring delicately from a slender waist. A dark patch of curls at the apex of her thighs, delectable breasts. *He didn't deserve this.* She wrapped her arms even tighter about her middle, unconsciously lifting her breasts.

"Come here, sweetheart," he said softly, and extended his hand. Claudia glanced at it, almost reluctantly put her hand in his. Julian pulled her into his lap, wrapped her in a warm embrace, gliding his lips across her neck, her cheeks and mouth, until she was responding to him, her hands seeking his chest and shoulders. He slowly leaned backward, taking her with him, then rolled her onto her back. "Don't think," he murmured. "Don't do anything but lie there and let me make love to you." And silencing any protest, he trailed a row of kisses from her lips, down her chin, to her breasts. As he laved one hard peak, Claudia squirmed beneath him; Julian slipped an arm beneath her, catching her to him. He took her fully into his mouth, nipping the rigid peak with his teeth, swirling his tongue around it. He massaged her other breast until the pliant flesh grew firm in his hand, then shifted to give it equal homage with his mouth. Above him, Claudia made a sound in her throat; a half moan, half cry. Julian tightened his grip on her, drew her farther into his mouth

and mercilessly laved her while his hand floated down
her belly and over her thighs.

She moaned then, a deep, aching moan, and Julian
lifted his head to look at the face that had haunted him
these last two years. One hand rested carelessly over her
heart, the other was twined in the mess of dark hair
above her head. Her eyes glittered in the near darkness—
she said nothing, just gazed at him.

Merciful God, he would never survive this—he was
perilously close to exploding as it was. A wave of unbearable lust suddenly moved him forward and he kissed her
roughly, devouring her small sigh as his fingers skimmed
her inner thighs, tangled in the dark curls between her
legs. Claudia lurched at his touch; but Julian caught her
shoulders and hugged her tightly to him as he began a
deliberate exploration.

She began to writhe beneath him, arching into his
hand, moaning against his neck. It was almost more than
Julian could bear, but he kept his pace, exploring her with
gentle insistence, probing deeper with his fingers, stretching her, preparing her for him, until he felt the thin mem-
brane that sealed her chastity.

He withdrew, kissed her passionately before rolling
onto his back to remove his trousers, and quickly came
over her again, reveling in the feel of the silken skin of her
belly against his erection. Claudia reacted as if she had
been singed. Whimpering softly, she flinched where he
touched her; her hands clenched fitfully in his hair. The
sound of her breath, he noticed, was as deep and desperate as his own.

He wedged one knee between her thighs, grazing his
erection over the soft patch of curls. A sharp gasp and her
hand found his wrist and clung to it, her nails digging
into his skin when he moved to her entrance and pushed
gently. He gritted his teeth in a supreme act of self control. *"Shh . . ."* he whispered, more to himself than to her,
and pushed a little more, slipping into the tight, wet heat
of her. He lowered his head, touched his forehead to hers,
and pushed a little farther, clenching his jaw harder as

her body tightly surrounded him, pulling him deeper into her and squeezing the passion from him. His hips pushed forward again, a little at a time, stretching her open, until he felt the barrier of her maidenhead.

He paused, lowered himself to her. She was panting now, her eyes wide with apprehension, a thin sheen of perspiration covering her skin. Julian licked the salty hollow of her neck. "Hold on to me, sweetheart," he murmured. Her arms obediently slid around his neck, and Julian lowered his head to kiss her, thrusting his tongue deep into her mouth at the same moment he lifted his hips and drove past her barrier.

Her body seized tightly; she went rigid in his arms, but she made no sound. Julian panicked a little; he kissed her gently, tenderly, stroked her neck and shoulders until she at last released a long sigh. Slowly, her body began to relax, and very timidly, she began to respond to his kiss— and Julian began to move. Gingerly at first, sliding gently in and out of her in long, patient strokes that almost killed him. Moaning softly, Claudia's knees came up around his waist, and Julian's desire began to boil in his groin.

He shifted his weight to better reach the core of her, and began to move with urgency, thrusting deep inside her, reaching for her womb, wanting her to feel the same, incredible passion that swirled through him. He wanted her to feel the same intensity of anticipation he felt now, his body dormant for so long, filled and straining to the point of bursting. She threw one arm above her head, grasping at pillows and bed hangings as her hips began to rise to meet him. Julian groaned deep—he was past the point of tender lovemaking, had fallen into a sea of desire that pulled him under with its current. The sea swept him forward then pulled him back, sweeping forward again, farther still, harder and deeper. She rose to meet each onslaught, swirling her hips in an ancient lover's dance. Julian was fast losing control as the desire spiraled tighter and tighter in him, and reaching between their joined bodies, he urgently stroked her as he plunged deeper into her warmth, oblivious to all else . . .

Until he heard the sound of her tears.

That sound splintered like glass into his consciousness at the moment she climaxed. But he was already lost. Her body was convulsing hard around him, gripping him tightly, and drawing his own, violent climax. He fairly exploded; the life drained from him like a break in a dam, rushing furiously into her depths.

And Julian felt the faint stirrings of love deep in his soul.

With a final thrust, he lowered himself to her, resting his forehead against her shoulder as he sought to drag air into his lungs. She shivered beneath him, the aftermath of her passion and her tears. He blindly felt her face, his fingers dragging across the path of wetness on her cheeks, and his heart wrenched painfully in his chest.

He had *hurt* her.

And she had destroyed him.

The wind had picked up, was howling outside and rattling the windowpanes. Claudia lay entwined in Julian's arms, entranced by the feel of the heavy breath of his sleep on her neck as she tried desperately to deny what had happened between them.

Oh, but it *had* happened . . . the most extraordinary experience of her life, the most intense, physical release, running the gamut from great pain to exquisite pleasure. He was right—it was a pleasure she had dared not dream, a freedom of spirit that she had not even thought possible for a woman. The intimacy of that act was extraordinary, the trust it demanded, the strength it required, together building to the most unbelievable experience a man and woman could share. Somehow, he had released her soul to the heavens.

But not without taking a little piece of her heart in exchange.

The experience had been so moving on so many different levels that she had not been able to stop the tears. Tears of joy, of frustration, of fear, of *wonder*—all of it, everything she had experienced in the last two weeks had finally culminated in one explosive moment, and in the course of it, she had lost a little of herself to him.

So soon!

There had been no words between them when it was over, nothing but a gentle kiss to her teary eyes, and then he had slipped out of her, rolled over onto his back, and thrown one arm over his eyes as his fingers twined with hers. He had not touched her again, not until he was deep in the clutches of sleep and unconsciously gathered her close, making her feel safe and secure and wanted.

Claudia gingerly pushed his arm from her belly and inched her way to the edge of the bed. Wrapping the thin, cotton coverlet around her, she stood slowly, careful not to wake him. The only light came from the dying fire in the adjoining room, but it was enough for her to make out his naked form. His chest was broad and muscled, the expanse of it covered with a fine layer of down that tapered to a line running to the nest at his groin. She shivered, pulled the coverlet tightly about her, and gazed in wonder at his body. It fascinated her—she cocked her head to one side, considering the size and weight of his sex, wondering how he managed to walk about with that hanging between his legs. Or *ride,* for goodness sake! And how it had ever fit inside her . . .

Her face flamed; Julian suddenly rolled over in his sleep, onto his stomach. Claudia's eyes widened slightly at the sight of firm, muscular buttocks—the flame in her face was spreading rapidly down her neck, and she quickly turned away, fairly certain she should not be gaping at a man like that, even if he was asleep.

Even if he was her husband.

Oh, God.

She hurried into the outer room and sat heavily at the table, staring morosely at the uneaten food. The wine Julian had poured had been left untouched; she lifted the goblet to her lips and drank thirstily, hoping it would numb her. Her body still tingled, still ached from that incredible experience.

How could she have let it happen?

Of course she *knew* she would have to lie with him, but she had never thought she would like it so very much! How was it that he could do such incredible things to her body? *I want to bury myself deep inside you, feel you wrap yourself around me . . . let me love you, Claudia.* Every time she thought of it, she felt the queer tingle in the pit of her stomach. Trembling, she put the goblet down and buried her face in her hands. She possessed some sort of character defect, surely—what else could explain the physical desire—the *lust*—she felt for that Rake? What, must she recount his many misdeeds against her every time he so much as looked at her? This was a disaster! She would give him her heart, she *knew* she would, and he would crush it, toss it aside like so much rubbish in favor of a new attraction. He had done it before to her. He had done it to many other women.

Had Phillip?

She lifted her head, stared into the fire.

Had Phillip titillated women so easily? Would he have lifted her to the heavens as Julian had tonight? Would he have—

"Can't you sleep?"

With a startled gasp, Claudia looked over her shoulder. Leaning against the doorframe, Julian stood barechested, his trousers pulled up loosely around his hips, unbuttoned. She gripped the edge of the coverlet a little tighter. "Ah, no. Yes." She winced lightly. "I was hungry."

Julian smiled at that, padded across the carpet to her, and kissed the top of her head before sprawling onto a chair next to her. He reached out, laid his hand on her thigh—unconsciously, she thought—and made a face as he looked at the food. "Dear God, I hope you haven't been eating *that*."

With a shake of her head, she reached for her wine. Julian resumed a slouch against the chair, regarding her beneath hooded eyes as she sipped. "Terribly seductive of you to look like that," he said after a moment. "All wildly mussed and naked beneath that coverlet."

Claudia's face flamed.

He abruptly leaned forward and reached for a strand of her hair, twining it lazily in his fingers. "I didn't mean to hurt you," he muttered softly. "I would take my own life before I would willingly hurt you."

Another piece of her heart gone, just like that. She shifted uncomfortably. "It . . . it didn't hurt so terribly much," she lied.

"Come back to bed with me, Claudia. I won't hurt you again, I swear it."

Ah, but you will. She glanced warily at his handsome face, remembered the storm in his expression as he drove deep inside her. "Now?" she asked stupidly.

He considered her for a moment, then let go of her hair and leaned back. "Would you prefer I return to my own rooms?"

No, no, stay and hold me. "Yes. Yes, I . . . I think I would, please," she said, and looked to the fire so he would not see her lie. "I . . . I need to be alone." Julian said nothing, but she could feel him staring at her, trying to penetrate her thoughts. After a long moment, he stood up. As he walked by her, he ran his palm tenderly over her crown. "I am sorry I hurt you," he said again, and leaned down, his mouth in her hair. "It will be all right, Claudia. Everything will be all right." And with that, he disappeared into the adjoining bedroom.

When she heard a door shut a few moments later, she laid her head on her arms and let the torrent of tears come until there was nothing left in her.

Thirteen

THREE DAYS LATER, Julian was rather relieved when Arthur Christian called unexpectedly, full of apologies for disturbing him so shortly after the wedding, but in desperate need of his signature on some papers having to do with the iron factory in which the Rogues were partners. Arthur's arrival couldn't have been timelier, as Julian was just beginning to panic. And he was *not* a man given to panic.

Much less a man who knew what to *do* if he should panic.

It was that explosive, mind-shattering experience in her bed on their wedding night that had undone him. *Really* undone him, made a lovesick fool out of him and a miserable one at that, as he was trying very hard to give Claudia a bit of space until she was ready to accept that they were, for better or worse, quite inextricably married.

But unfortunately—for him, anyway—all the good intentions in the world hadn't prevented him from slipping into her bed in the middle of the night last evening, or from pressing his throbbing arousal into her hips, or from caressing her breasts as she lay on her side. Claudia never uttered a word, nothing more than a wistful sigh when he found his way under the bed linens and felt her heat. She had squirmed, moving her hips seductively against his hardness until he could stand no more. In silence, he had slipped into her warmth from behind, driving deep into her until she cried out in pleasure, then releasing himself into her.

Panting, they lay spoon-fashion afterward, his arm draped over her belly. At some point, he had slipped into a deep, comfortable sleep. But something had awakened him, and he had found himself alone in her bed. Again.

She was in the room adjoining the bedchamber, staring at the glowing embers in the hearth, a sheet wrapped tightly around her. There was something about the way she held herself close and tight, something in the purse of her lips that made him believe she was even more vulnerable than he had thought. She looked so forlorn sitting there, so miserable—it was not the Claudia he knew, and he had suddenly felt the sick dread of something gone terribly wrong. He had backed away, slipping out of her room just as quietly as he had come. And then he had tossed and turned the rest of the night, madly wondering what she was thinking, what caused her to rise in the middle of the night and stare so sadly into the dying embers. Did she despise him so completely? *Did she think of Phillip?*

That was the question that drove him mad. He could cope with anything else, but the ghost of Phillip haunted him in a way Julian could not comprehend. It was ridiculous, not to mention bordering on insanity! Yet he could not seem to stop himself. Nothing could shake that awful, uncomfortable feeling that Phillip was watching him— that he *knew* Julian had let him fall into his grave so that he might have Claudia. It was absurd! *Phillip was dead!*

Nonetheless, he had closeted himself in his study all day, had tried to work on the medieval manuscript in preparation for a lecture he was due to deliver at Cambridge soon. He had tried to do *anything* but think of her, or Phillip, or this bizarre circumstance of marriage he found himself in.

Nothing worked.

In the middle of the afternoon, in spite of himself, he had asked Tinley about her. The old man had thought hard about that, declared he was rather certain she had not appeared today. So Julian had very nonchalantly strolled into the kitchen—a room he had visited twice, perhaps three times since he had inherited this house—and had asked a very shocked cook if her ladyship had sent for anything.

She had not.

So he had returned to his study, wrestling with the urge to go up and see about her, panicking a little because he feared he just *might* go up and do Lord knew what when, thankfully, Tinley announced Arthur.

Julian could tell from the way Arthur peered at him that he found his near glee upon seeing him a little odd. Julian adjusted his spectacles and tried to look quite relaxed, but after a moment, Arthur sighed, shook his head, and tossed back the brandy Julian had thrust into his hand with an insistence that he stay a bit. "I *knew* this would happen."

"What?"

"What!" Arthur snorted. "Look at you, three days after taking your marriage vows, and already chafing to get out."

Out. Julian seized on that—yes, *out* is where he needed to be. *Anywhere* but in this room, thinking of her. Was it possible? Could he leave his bride? Yes! Distance was the one thing she seemed to want from him, wasn't it? So let him give her distance, if even for a short time. He looked at the papers Arthur had brought, shuffled them into a neat stack. "Well, now that you've discovered my tragic secret," he said casually, "was there something you had in mind?"

Arthur laughed. "You'd like that, wouldn't you?" he asked, and nodded politely at Tinley as he walked in, carrying a silver tea service. Julian had not sent for tea—it was almost the supper hour. Tinley was losing what was left of his feeble old mind. "I confess, Kettering, I'm not sure it's safe to cavort about town with a newlywed," Arthur cheerfully continued. "Makes any contemplation I might have had of calling on Madame Farantino's rather difficult."

Julian snorted at that. "I was hardly suggesting a night out on the town, Christian," he said, watching Tinley shuffle to the door and pause, leaning against the brass knob as he took a deep breath. "I was merely suggesting that marital bliss might go down a bit easier with a good port."

"Indeed?" Arthur drawled as Tinley shut the door behind him.

"You wouldn't deny an old chum a bit of escape, would you?"

Grinning, Arthur shook his head again and drained his snifter. Setting it aside, he came to his feet. "As the last *free* Rogue of Regent Street, I suppose I am honor-bound to help you." He strolled to the door and glanced over his shoulder, waiting for Julian to stuff his spectacles in his coat pocket and join him. "And what of your bride?"

She'll be grateful to be rid of me. Julian shrugged, avoiding Arthur's steady gaze. "She ought to be getting accustomed to it, don't you think?" he answered vaguely.

With a skeptical shake of his head, Arthur walked out the door. "I *knew* it," he said again.

Claudia stood at the full-length mirror of her dressing room, turning slowly from side to side, critically eyeing the gown she had chosen to wear to supper. It was a dark plum brocade with a low square neck, and without petticoats, it draped very prettily. She worried a moment about her hair—It wasn't dressed, but pulled back to fall freely down her back. From across the room, Brenda made a sound of approval. "Lovely, mum," she said admiringly, and came across the room to hand her a pair of amethyst earrings. Claudia fastened one on her lobe, recalling with a slight flutter in her belly how Julian had taken the pearl earring in his mouth. She fastened the other one, and gave herself one final inspection.

What was she doing?

Accepting her marriage, that was what. How many times did she have to tell herself that? She had decided this morning—having awakened still wrapped in the coverlet—that it was the only sensible, *practical* thing to do. Now if she could only convince herself that accepting this marriage didn't mean that she was giving up any part of herself. No, she was not surrendering anything, so there was really nothing to mope about . . . although she had practically perfected the art in the last several days.

Enough of that. He had said they would find a way to peacefully co-exist. Entirely possible—he was a gentleman. She was a lady. They could certainly live in the same house and be civil. Perhaps they'd even be friendly! Julian was, after all, ruthlessly charming, as she very well knew. What harm was there in an occasional supper together? It didn't *mean* anything!

And the fact that she had dragged out a *new* gown for the occasion meant even less. It was part of her trousseau—she was *supposed* to wear the clothes in her trousseau. It certainly was *not* to impress him. Yes, and what a pathetic liar she made! Claudia frowned at her reflection. The truth, should she care to admit it—which she did not—was that he had touched her in a way she did not believe she could be touched. Last night had been magical, the pleasure he gave her washing over her in some sort of waking dream. It had been magic and exotic and gentle and rough . . . he had lifted her to the height of sensuality, then had let her drift back to earth in a dream.

It was so earthy, so primitive, that it had scared her. So much that she had slipped from his arms again, certain that what she was feeling, what she was *doing* with him was a weakness he would eventually exploit. In the morning's light, however, that seemed awfully severe, if not childish. He had shown her nothing but pleasure, taking care to bring her incredible fulfillment before taking any pleasure for himself. There was nothing to suggest he had been insincere, or that he was merely using her. For heaven's sake, she had been married three days now, and had yet to leave her rooms! She was pouting like a spoiled child who had been denied her way. But she was not a spoiled child, she was a grown woman, and it was time she acted like one.

She found Tinley in the salon, polishing the top of a brass torchère, which she thought rather odd given the hour. "Good evening, Tinley!" she said cheerfully.

"Good evening," he responded, sounding a bit distracted as he stared at the torchère.

Claudia moved farther into the room, admiring the furnishings and paintings. Thick Oriental carpet, furniture made of English walnut and marble, two very large paintings of country life by Hans Holbein the Younger amid several smaller paintings, and a gilded ceiling that was an exact replica of one she had seen at St. James's Palace. Kettering had good taste, she would give him that—and apparently as much wealth as she had heard rumored.

"Is my Lord Kettering about?" she asked, tracing her finger around the rim of a French vase made of fine bone china.

"No, milady. He's gone out."

Claudia glanced at the ancient butler. "Out?"

"Yes, milady," he said, leaning very close to the torchère to polish a very tiny little spot. It was hardly in need of polishing; the thing was polished to such a sheen that there was really no need to even place candles on it. "Has he gone out for the evening?" she persisted.

Tinley paused, looked at something over her shoulder, then resumed his work. "I can't recall, really."

Frowning lightly, Claudia asked, "Do you know *where* he went?"

"Yes, milady. Madame Farantino's," he casually informed her.

Her breath caught in her throat. "Madame Farantino's?" she choked out.

Tinley nodded, never looking up. "Aye. Marital bliss might go down easier with a good sport," he blithely repeated.

The breath in her throat dislodged with a gasp. Claudia gaped at the old butler, disbelieving her own ears. A million thoughts sped through her mind, not the least of which was that Julian Dane was, as she had so often reminded herself, a despicable *rake!*

She whirled away from Tinley, stared blindly about the grand room. All right, all right, she had not expected him to be faithful, not for a moment—*but in just three days?* How could he make love to her, then seek another woman . . . good *God*, was she doing something wrong?

No! No, no, no, she would *not* assume responsibility for his lack of character! Oh, but he was a contemptible, *vile* human being! A man with no conscience, and the sooner she remembered that, the better she might adapt to this private little hell she had created for herself!

Claudia suddenly marched out of the salon without another word to Tinley, bound for her rooms, feeling the wall start to come up and surround her foolish heart . . . a heart she had so very nearly surrendered to him! Well, The Rake could have her body as was his right, but he would never have her heart and soul. She had fallen victim to his charms once, twice—but never again! Oh no. Never again.

And she'd be damned if she was going to waste a new gown on the likes of him!

They had each consumed one glass of port when Julian surged to his feet, shrugged into a cloak, and patted himself down in search of his spectacles. Seated in a comfortable leather armchair, Arthur watched him with great amusement. "Off so soon, Kettering?" he drawled. "Thought you were anxious to be away from all that marital bliss."

Julian dug his eyeglasses from his coat pocket and put them on, regarding Arthur nonchalantly. "You are to be commended for your generous rescue, Christian. Seems to be your forte."

"I beg your pardon, sir, but my forte is predicting your

future. Been doing it all my life, you know," Arthur responded, and lifted his port in a mock toast to himself.

"Indeed?" Julian smiled, pulled on the leather gloves a footman hurried to hand him.

"Care to know my latest prediction?"

Julian laughed as he took his hat from the footman. "Go on, then. Amuse me."

His hazel eyes gleaming with mirth, Arthur smiled at Julian. "I predict," he said, pausing dramatically to sip his port, "that you will fall madly in love with your wife."

Julian started inwardly, but caught himself and laughed roundly at his old friend. "Always the sentimental fool, Arthur," he said, and still laughing, turned away, suddenly desperate to be gone.

"Don't *you* be the fool, Kettering," Arthur called after him, and Julian kept walking, feeling all at once very uncomfortable.

At St. James Square, he bounded up the steps to his house and burst inside, tossing his cloak and gloves to a footman just as Tinley came dragging into the foyer.

"Ah, Tinley. Where might I find Lady Kettering?" he asked, fully expecting to be told she had not come down.

"Couldn't say, milord," Tinley said, earning a strange look from the footman. The butler never saw it, however—he continued along his path, disappearing into the north hall.

"Beggin' your pardon, milord, but her ladyship is in the blue drawing room," the footman offered.

With great surprise, Julian looked at the footman. "The blue drawing room?" The footman noded. Aha, so she had come out of her self-imposed prison. "Very well," he said curtly, and headed for the blue drawing room.

The door was open; he could see Claudia sitting at a card table near the hearth as he drew near, playing a solitary game. She was wearing a plain seagreen gown, her hair tied simply at her nape, no adornments of any kind. No matter—even plainly dressed, she was still quite alluring. It amazed him how the woman could take his breath away just by *being*.

She glanced up briefly as he crossed the threshold, but quickly focused again on her cards. "Wasn't there enough amusement in the streets of London to keep you occupied, my lord?" she asked pleasantly.

Interesting; the despair he had heard in her voice the last few days had vanished. "What could possibly occupy me there when I have the such a fascinating creature in my very own house?" he asked as he crossed the room.

Claudia snorted. "Full of piss and wind again, I see," she retorted cheerfully.

Julian laughed. He leaned over her, intending to kiss her cheek, but Claudia coyly ducked her head. All right, he would settle for the top of her head, which earned him only a bit of a squirm. Smiling to himself, he took the seat directly across the table from her and watched her play her game. Her brow wrinkled in thought; she chewed on her bottom lip as she studied the cards. Ignoring him completely, she tapped a manicured nail against her cheek, considering her next move. When she finally laid the card, she glanced up at him and smiled brightly. "Care for some good sport?"

He smiled. "Always."

"Yes, so I've heard," she said, and leaned back in her chair. One foot swung freely under the table, kicking her skirts up; a devilish little glimmer appeared in her eye. "Do you know the game of commerce?"

"Naturally," he responded, although a card game was definitely *not* what he had in mind.

"Would you care to play with perhaps a bit of wagering to liven up the game?" she asked sweetly.

Oh, now this would prove amusing. He chuckled, quite certain she didn't know the first thing about wagering—it was hardly the sort of thing that tutors taught earls' daughters. "It would delight me enormously, madam. Have you any coin?"

"Have you?" she shot back, and smiling wickedly, gathered up the cards. She dealt the first round, which

Julian easily won, as well as the second. In fact, he won the first four games so easily that he felt a bit guilty—it felt almost as loathsome as stealing from the blind. After the fifth round, Claudia got up, sailed to the desk across the room, and returned with a sheet of paper on which she scratched out a voucher for two whole pounds. Julian had to bite his tongue to keep from laughing, and deliberately threw the round so she would not lose her measly two pounds. The poor girl knew nothing about wagering, but she seemed to be enjoying herself, and Julian was enjoying himself just watching her, so he continued to play, throwing an occasional game to her when her stack of vouchers got too high.

The night had passed well into the early morning hours when Claudia picked up the deck and shuffled, eyeing her vouchers stacked neatly at Julian's elbow. "I've a new wager," she said, peeking up at him through her thick, dark brown lashes.

"Yes?"

"My allowance next month. Double if I should win."

Was he imagining things, or were those tiny demon fires suddenly shining in her eyes? Intrigued, he asked, "And if you should lose? What would be my prize?"

Claudia flashed a languid, lazy smile at him as she laid the cards down and motioned for him to cut the deck. "If I lose, my lord," she said softly, "you may have the prize of your choosing."

And her smile turned so seductive that Julian's groin lurched in protest. He leaned across the table. "Anything?"

With a throaty chuckle, she moved forward, propping herself on her elbows so that her breasts threatened to spill right out of her gown, just under his nose. She ran her knuckles over the bare skin of her bosom, absently tracing a path down the cleft between her breasts. *"Anything,"* she murmured huskily.

Hell yes, he'd take that bet, and eagerly cut the cards. "I believe the deal is yours, my darling," he said, and settled back, cheerfully thinking of exactly how he might claim his prize. In front of this very fire, so that he could watch her blue-gray eyes darken with desire—

"Another card?" she asked politely.

Julia glanced at his hand. Two jacks and a ten. "No, thank you." The demon fires in her eyes were blazing very brightly now, and he imagined them as she reached her fulfillment—

"Then shall we draw?"

Poor girl. Lucky boy. Julian laid his hand down and smiled. "Two jacks are rather hard to beat, love," he said apologetically.

Her smile faded. "Oh my. Two jacks *are* hard to beat, aren't they?" With a heavy sigh, she laid one king down. And then another. The heat began to rise under Julian's collar, and he fairly choked when she laid her last card. *Three kings!* Disbelieving his own eyes, he jerked his gaze up to Claudia.

She grinned like a cat. "But I suppose three kings are even harder to beat, aren't they?" She leaned across the table again, to where her mouth was only inches from his. "Now *that* is what I call good sport," she said, and stood gracefully, as if she duped men at cards as a matter of course. Incredulous, Julian looked at the cards again.

Claudia burst into a fit of laughter and instantly covered her mouth with her hand. She was *laughing* at him! "Oh, and a bank draft will do nicely, thank you," she added, and still laughing, sailed from the drawing room. Julian stared after her—the Demon's Spawn had just *duped* him! Expertly, too, and without the least bit of compunction! He hadn't been outplayed like that in years. *Damn* her!

Damn her twice—he had *really* wanted his prize!

In a tearoom nestled among the shops of a quaint little lane far from Mayfair, Sophie Dane nervously adjusted her gloves, taking great care to make sure there were no wrinkles in them. William did not approve of droopy gloves.

Nervously, she looked down, fingered the lace that edged the neck of her new gown, then adjusted her gloves again.

William was late.

He had said to meet him at precisely three o'clock with a stern warning not to be tardy. It was now half past three, and she was expected at Ann's for tea at five. Sophie sighed, glanced at the tea service again. This was becoming so difficult! She hated lying to her sisters most of all, but William had insisted they not be told of their secret meetings, as they would only take Julian's side in this. She had a hunch he was right about that, so she had told Ann and Eugenie she was paying a call to Aunt Violet this afternoon. Hopefully, if William wasn't too terribly late, she could hurry by Aunt Violet's so it wouldn't be a *complete* lie.

A tap on the window caused her to turn slightly; William frowned at her through the glass, then disappeared, reappearing inside seconds later. He looked terribly dashing in his dark brown frock coat. His blond hair was perfectly dressed; his moustache impeccably trimmed. As he walked to her table, Sophie thanked God one more time that William was in love with *her*. She beamed at him as he fell into a small wooden chair across from her and helped himself to a biscuit.

"I thought you'd never arrive," she said, smiling eagerly.

William shrugged. "I said I'd arrive by half past three."

Actually, he had said three o'clock, but William was under an awful lot of pressure.

"A plate of biscuits? Nothing more?" he inquired.

"I'm sorry," she said, and hastily poured him a cup of tea as he reached for another biscuit. "Did you, perchance, call on your acquaintance at the bank today?" she asked.

He frowned, sipped at the tea. "Yes, I called on him. He was not inclined to entertain my request for a short-term loan," he said, and looked glumly at the bud vase in the middle of the table. "Kettering is doing this to us, you know."

At the mere mention of her brother's name, Sophie's breathing constricted. "J-Julian? Whatever do you mean?"

William lifted his deep brown gaze to her, filled with dismay. "What I mean, Sophie, is that your brother is so dead set against us he has used his considerable influence to keep me from a small loan! He's out to see me ruined, I tell you, all for the crime of loving you."

"But . . . but he doesn't even *know* about us!"

William grasped her hand and tenderly stroked her palm. "Believe me, love, your brother *knows*."

"I don't believe it! How could he . . . it's so unfair!" Sophie exclaimed.

Gripping her hand tightly, William looked imploringly into her eyes. "I know, my darling, yet I have tried to tell you what sort of man he is! I cannot fathom it myself, but apparently he would rather keep you from your heart's desire than part with a single shilling!" he exclaimed, and let go of her hand. "God knows he can afford to!" he added irritably.

Anger soared in Sophie's heart. As much as she didn't want to believe it, she had seen the evidence of just how close-fisted Julian could be. She was still miffed at how suspiciously he had looked at her a few days ago when she had asked for a little more than her usual allowance. As William had pointed out to her, she *never* asked for more than her allowance, yet he had wanted to begrudge her a few trifling pounds! He had quizzed her, finally accepting her explanation of wanting some new, rather expensive hats. William was right—she was fortunate to have such a generous dowry and annuity so that she would not always have to rely on Julian. If only she had permission to marry so she could *have* her annuity! Honestly, the whole situation seemed so terribly hopeless. "Oh, William!" she exclaimed. "What will we do?"

"There now, Sophie," he murmured. "I will think of something. I've an appointment with another banker on

Thursday. Surely Kettering can't extend his influence to *every* financial institution in this town!" He smiled, picked up the remainder of his biscuit and popped it into his mouth. "In the meantime, have you a few pounds to spare, love?"

Of course she did—she *always* did. She reached into her beaded reticule and pulled out a thick roll of bills. William promptly stuffed them in his coat pocket without bothering to count them. He then fished in his pocket for a couple of crowns and tossed them onto the table. "Come on then, let's be gone from this place," he said, and stood, motioning Sophie to her feet.

She quickly gained her feet and straightened her bonnet.

"Your gloves, Sophie."

Horrified, Sophie hastily straightened her gloves so that they didn't sag around her wrists. When he seemed satisfied, he extended his arm to her and led her outside.

As they strolled down the street, William smiled charmingly at her. "Is that a new gown?"

Sophie's hand immediately went to her collar. "It is one of Ann's. She gave it to me. Do you like it?"

"It's very nice," he said, and Sophie smiled with relief and pleasure. "But it's not a particularly flattering color for you, is it?" he added thoughtfully.

Ann had said the apple green went very well with her complexion. "It's not?"

"No, I rather think not. A nice blue would be a much more appealing color for you, wouldn't it?" He chuckled, shook his head. "Really, my dear, sometimes I think you rush out of the house without regard for your appearance a'tall." Patting her hand, he proceeded to lead her down the street as Sophie forced down her humiliation at being unable to do something as simple as dress.

Fourteen

Apparently, Claudia delighted in torturing Julian.

There could be no other explanation for the fact that her behavior had done a complete turnabout in the few weeks since their wedding. She had gone from a stunned and saddened young woman to one who was, amazingly, suddenly brimming with life. She seemed to enjoy every moment of every busy day—and Lord *God,* they were busy—the bustling activity that filled her days spread light from one end of Julian's St. James mansion to the other.

Therein lay the torture.

That light did not include Julian. Not that Claudia *excluded* him, exactly—but there was a distance between them, a chasm he could not seem to bridge. When he got too close, something in his wife shut down, boarded up, refused to let him in. Sometimes he felt as if she was almost blind to him and wholly focused on something that only she could see.

Julian grew increasingly uncomfortable with the arrangement. A rash had spread inside him, driving him mad like an itch he could not reach. It did not take him long to comprehend that he could not live with his wife in this way, not with walls between them that he could not see, much less scale.

The extraordinary lovemaking they had enjoyed was only a memory now. Not that Claudia ever refused him;

she was nothing if not a dutiful wife. But with the exception of that first week when her natural warmth and desire had shone through, she seemed to barely tolerate his presence in her bed, subduing her response altogether, determined to take no pleasure in his touch. And when his passion consumed itself, she would turn away from him or find an excuse to get out of bed.

Predictably, the next day's light would bring the walls up around her again, and acting as if nothing happened, Claudia would spill into her day, retreating behind a whirlwind of activity that left *him* breathless.

To be with a woman who was not infatuated with him was new and perplexing to Julian. And as he had raised four girls into four perfect women, he was hardly inexperienced in the ways women thought and behaved. But Claudia was a very different experience. In addition to the walls she put up, she also had some rather unconventional ideas in that pretty head of hers. And she was quite fearless, too, having lost, apparently, any feelings of helplessness she might have had in the beginning.

First of all, there was the matter of her afternoon teas. Once a week, a parade of twenty women, including his three sisters, would converge on Kettering House and crowd into the main sitting room. In the course of what should have been a refined gathering of ladies, one would hear shouts of laughter, shrieks of excitement, and the emphatic voices of debate quite plainly from behind the closed doors. After a couple of hours of that, the doors would suddenly swing open, and the ladies would march out, all sporting a gleam in their eyes that made grown men shudder.

Julian had discovered the teas quite by accident, when one day he happened to catch two young footmen snickering outside the doors. Once he understood what they were about he chastised them, sent them on their way . . . then lingered to listen. Yet in the space of a week or two, several male servants gathered around those doors—along with Julian—their eyes often rounding with shock or their faces blanching at the things being said. And they scattered like chicks whenever they heard anything that even remotely sounded as if the ladies were coming near the door. The last straw for the house servants was the day that, in spite of their dire warnings, Tinley entered the inner sanctum with a fresh pot of tea . . . *and did not come out.*

If Julian harbored any notion that he might keep the teas his little secret, he was quickly corrected one afternoon at White's. Adrian Spence, Alex Christian, the Duke of Sutherland, along with Victor and Louis, descended on him like an attacking horde of geese, demanding that he stop the teas at once. They insisted his wife was perhaps a bit deranged and definitely in need of a strong hand. Because, in addition to smoking his cheroots made of a special American tobacco and drinking his port—which the duke claimed was a bit like kissing a chap who had just come from White's—Claudia and her ladies were exploring new concepts in women's equality that had every man feeling embattled in his home. It seemed that the ladies were insisting on some rather intolerable changes, including learning about the parliamentary process and the system of suffrage in England, the very absurd notion being that women should very well vote one day. *Heaven forfend.*

What the men did not know, thank God, was that the teas were not the only furious activity that had servants scrambling in his house. Someone was always rushing somewhere; Claudia seemed constantly gone off in pursuit of something to do with girls and schools, almshouses, hospitals, and a half dozen other charitable endeavors that she fancied. And when she wasn't engaged with her friends or her charities, his little nieces, Jeannine and Dierdre, were frequent visitors to Kettering House. Claudia read them stories, or marched them off to the kitchens where they painted little clay pots and planted little sprigs of violets in them. The results of their labors covered every conceivable surface in her sitting room.

More often than not, however, the girls arrived in frilly little gowns, then emerged from Claudia's rooms dressed in play costumes—as knights, or sea captains, or highwaymen. They did not aspire, apparently, to queenly thrones or other maidenly pursuits. Julian had no idea where his wife found the capes and wooden swords and red coats that transformed his nieces into little men— although he *did* recognize that their highwaymen masks were his neckcloths—but he assumed their play was innocent enough.

Until he discovered that Claudia fancied the girls little jockeys.

It had astounded him to discover the two little girls on Ladies Mile in Hyde Park one afternoon, riding an old mare bareback—wearing boy's short pants, no less, and oh yes, riding astride. After sending the three of them home, Julian decided not to mention the incident to Louis, who had some rather fastidious ideas about what girls should like and do. Nor did he think it necessary to mention that his footman, Robert, was overseeing their wooden swordplay on a fairly regular basis . . . or that Eugenie seemed to think all of these antics perfectly all right.

He rather believed Louis would appreciate his great discretion and perhaps might even return the favor one day.

All in all, living in Claudia's sphere was a little unnerving.

On one particularly crisp afternoon, Julian ventured out on the back terrace to enjoy the change in seasons and a cheroot. The crystal clear air was filled with the scent of fall, and as he wandered across the flagstones, languidly perusing fallen leaves, he spotted Claudia, all three of his sisters, Mary Whitehurst, and another young woman he did not recognize on a grassy lawn below.

Tables were set up on the outer edge of the lawn and covered with tablecloths, small vases of roses, and a variety of plates that looked to be luncheon fare. Two footmen stood nearby, ready to serve. But the women were not seated for luncheon—they were gathered about in a tight little circle, examining what looked to be a rather crudely stuffed scarecrow. Where they had found *that* thing was a mystery, and intrigued by it, Julian paused to see what they were about.

Claudia and Eugenie were engaged in a rather animated discussion. Nothing new in that, certainly, but as the ladies abruptly turned away from the scarecrow and started fanning out in something of a half circle, Julian realized with a shock that they were all holding pistols. *Real* pistols.

They took care to put an arm's length between each other, twenty paces or so back from the scarecrow. Julian watched in stunned terror as Claudia abruptly lifted her pistol and fired at the scarecrow—missing completely, of course, the bullet landing God knew where. Panic and fear seized him at once. *"Claudia!"* he roared, and tossing aside the cheroot, rushed down the terrace steps. Eugenie saw him first. Smiling, she waved to him as she carelessly set her pistol on the edge of a luncheon table. To Julian's horror, the thing discharged. A collective screech went up from the women and in a sudden flurry of skirts and petticoats, all six of them flung themselves down on the grass.

So did the footmen.

Claudia was the first to push herself up on her elbows and glance around at the other women as they slowly lifted their heads. "There we are! No one appears to be hurt," she announced rather cheerfully.

Julian stormed into their midst, arms akimbo. "It's a miracle none of you are hurt!" he angrily chastened them. "Ladies, come to your feet if you can, but do *not* touch the pistols!" he ordered, and leveled a fierce look on Claudia. The Demon's Spawn smiled. A radiant, self-satisfied smile.

And she kept smiling as Julian ascertained that no one and nothing was hurt but an old birdbath. His heart was still pounding mercilessly, and with the help of the two stunned footmen, he quickly gathered up the pistols as the ladies brushed themselves off, chattering excitedly about Eugenie's mishap. When he flashed a dark look at Ann, she proudly reported that *her* gun was not loaded.

Eugenie mumbled that perhaps Louis did not need to know the exact details of their luncheon, to which Julian hastily and quietly agreed, and Sophie only glared at him, which he thought rather fortunate, given that she had a gun in her hand.

By the time he came to his wife, he was of a strong inclination to drag her over his knee for having scared the wits from him. He recognized the gun she held as one of his own, had the rather sinking suspicion that the ladies were all carrying their husbands' guns, and realized they had been driving about town with loaded pistols in their reticules. *Good God!* "What in the hell do you think you are doing?" he demanded, very gingerly taking the gun from her hand.

"Teaching them how to shoot." She said it as if it was the most natural thing in the world to say. Or *do*.

Julian's frown deepened. "Claudia? Do you even *know* how to shoot?"

"Honestly, I *thought* I did," she said, glancing thoughtfully at the scarecrow. "Papa showed me once."

That response only made his heart pound harder. "Someone could have been seriously harmed," he admonished her. "Why in God's name would you think to teach them to shoot?"

That earned him a dark look that suggested he was an imbecile for even asking. "Why *not* teach them?" she demanded. "Don't women have the right to protect themselves?"

"This has nothing to do with *rights,* Claudia, this has to do with keeping six women from harming themselves!"

"Then you think us too simple!"

"No," he growled, raking a menacing gaze across her.

"Then *what?*"

"Claudia!" he fairly bellowed. "Women have fathers and husbands to protect them, and therefore, it is not really necessary that they—"

"That's ridiculous," she interrupted, flicking her wrist disdainfully.

"No, it is not *ridiculous*," he insisted. "There is a

reason for physical differences between the sexes, my
dear. Men guard and protect their families, women nur-
ture their young and keep the home fires burning, and
that's all there is to it. Now, if you want to learn to shoot,
I will teach you. But I will not have you endanger the
lives of others because of some misguided notion of
women's *rights!*"

That was received with dead silence. From the corner
of her eye, Claudia stole a glance at her guests standing
about, mouths open, enthralled by the exchange between
them. She mumbled something under her breath that
sounded very much like "blockhead," and looked up at
him, her eyes shimmering with her fury.

He responded by bestowing the fiercest look in his
arsenal on her. "Do not, under *any* circumstance, think to
show these women how to shoot again unless I am with
you, or Louis or Victor is. Do I make myself perfectly
clear, madam?"

Her blue-gray eyes darkened. "*Perfectly* clear," she
muttered, and Julian actually feared whatever the hell
that tone of voice meant. Feared it so much that he
turned and abruptly marched from the lawn with his
cache of pistols, forcing himself with each step to remember that his wife was rather unconventional, and in
calmer moments, he actually adored that about her.

Days after the shooting accident, Claudia was still working doubly hard to push all thoughts of her arrogant husband from her mind. Actually, she did not allow herself to
think of *anything* but the activities she had carefully
planned for each day, because that was the only way she
could keep hold of her sanity. Every moment of every day
was filled with trips to her charities, or Upper Moreland
Street when she could get away, impromptu invitations to
friends, and even a trip or two to the textile factories in
search of a site for her school. If she could find nothing
else to occupy her time or her thoughts or her vision, she
made sketches of the girls' school she would build one

day, forcing herself to mentally count desks and chairs and slates and primers so that she would not think of him.

That usually did the trick, as funding for her school was uppermost in her thoughts these days. Unfortunately, donations promised to her before The Disaster were now, for all intents and purposes, nonexistent. What few she had received—those from Lady Violet, Ann and Eugenie, and of course, the bank draft she had received from Julian the day after her tea—were hardly enough to meet her need. Claudia had figured, based on the allowance she had negotiated from Julian, that it would take her twenty years to save the funds necessary to build a quality school—and that was assuming she never spent another farthing.

So she doggedly continued to call on old acquaintances in her quest for donations, and in the course of it, learned to accept the refusals that came with thinly veiled censure because of her scandal. She developed a humble appreciation for the few donations that were made.

Lord Dillbey didn't help matters, either. It seemed the old goat enjoyed deriding her efforts in various public places. She knew that he had taken to calling her planned school the *Whitney School of Morals, Loose though They Are*. Apparently, Dillbey made a joke of her everywhere he went, and she feared that those who might have contributed were loath to do so now, not when they faced certain ridicule by a powerful statesman.

It was the dilemma of the lack of donations for her school that she was *trying* to contemplate one afternoon in her sitting room, but her usual attempts to fill her thoughts had failed her, and it was Julian's fault. Punching her fists to her hips, she glared at her latest rendition of the school she had hung on the wall, then at the books spread across her desk. She tried, Lord God she *tried* to push him from her mind, put him at a safe distance, pretend he wasn't significant. As if it were humanly possible to do that! No, it was not possible, not when he came to her as he had last night, touching her in

ways that made her shiver, lifting her into ethereal worlds
where her body and his were indistinguishable from one
another. And it seemed the harder she tried not to *feel* it,
the more she did. Deeper and fuller and more profoundly
each time. *Damn him!*

She abruptly lifted her hands to her face; her fingers
felt cool against her heated skin as she recalled a conversation she had overheard once in the ladies' retiring room
at some rout. Lady Crittendon, a beautiful woman married to a man as wealthy as Midas and as old as Father
Time, was in conversation with a friend when Claudia
entered the room, and proceeded to relate a chance
encounter with Lord Kettering in a low, silky tone.
Insisting that neither had intended anything to happen,
she had implied rather boldly that they had exchanged
more than a greeting. When her friend asked her if she
was concerned that the Rogue might brag of his conquest,
Lady Crittendon had laughed and confided that
Kettering was a man who could hold his tongue very well
indeed—and in all the right places. The two women had
tittered gleefully, and Claudia had wondered what they
meant.

Oh, what ignorance! Not once had she ever imagined,
not even in her wildest dreams, what a man might do to
a woman with his hands and his tongue and his— She
suddenly sprawled onto a chair, her legs stretched in front
of her, her arms draped over the sides, and took several
deep breaths.

At first she had resisted him, quite certain no self-
respecting woman would allow *that* to happen. But her
resistance was awfully weak and very short-lived—
astounded as she was by the incredible sensation of his
touch, quickly swept away by the sheer pleasure of it, she
had writhed uncontrollably, shamelessly seeking more.
He had held her firmly, sucking and nipping and laving
her languidly, driving her to the edge of a desperation so
deep that she had, at last, exploded into a thousand little
pieces of herself and scattered all over the place.

Claudia closed her eyes and drew a very deep breath

in an attempt to steady her breathing, which was, all of a sudden, rather shallow.

She had always understood, of course, why women flocked to him, only now, she understood it better than ever.

But it was really the little things that made him so completely irresistible. Like the way he was constantly touching her. Affectionately, without thinking, as if it was second nature. He touched her hand, her waist, the wisps of hair around her forehead. Little, comforting touches that could soothe the most troubled of souls. Ooh, and there were the things he said to her at the height of passion; praising her beauty, whispering how ravenous with desire she made him.

With a moan, Claudia pressed her forehead against the palm of her hand, wincing as another swell of longing swept over her, unwelcome and uninvited. *He touched her,* and then he would leave in the company of Arthur Christian, sometimes with Adrian Spence, too, the three of them laughing at some private jest as they sauntered down the curving steps to St. James Square. No one had to tell her what they did or where they went, and certainly Julian never offered. It wasn't necessary. She recognized the pattern because it had been the same with Phillip: Rogues leaving in the company of one another, laughing gaily, attracting the attention of men and women alike as they climbed into their expensive carriages and set off for a night of carousing with drink and women from Madame Farantino's.

She could never seem to quite fully reconcile the Rogue who set off for an evening of carousing with the husband who treated her so tenderly. When she tried, she was filled with doubt about her perceptions of him, inevitably debating herself until she was exhausted.

Yes, well, this was the sort of uncertain marriage a woman made when she betrayed everything she had ever known and allowed herself to be seduced. Her punishment for giving in to her basest desires was her own private little hell where she was tortured by his touch, *craved* it, and wished every day of her life that he would love her, *truly* love her.

Claudia's hands fell to her lap and she slowly opened her eyes, forced herself to swallow past the dull pain in the pit of her belly, and focus on the sketch of her school. The school was her only answer. She had to focus on something, push her feelings down, bury them, ignore them completely. It was the only way she might survive.

The rap at the door was a welcome intrusion. "Am I interrupting?" Sophie asked as she closed the door softly behind her.

"Of course not!" Claudia quickly came to her feet, smiling. She had been quite relieved when Sophie finally returned from Ann's to live at Kettering House—another, pleasant diversion from her thoughts. "Come, I've something to show you," she said, gesturing Sophie forward.

Sophie hurried across the room. "Oh, Claudia, there is something I absolutely must discuss with you."

"Me too. Look at my sketch, would you? I think this version might be too big, do you think?" she asked, peering closely at her drawing.

Sophie looked at the sketch, then at Claudia. "But it's exactly the same as the others."

"They are not *exactly* the same," Claudia muttered, and yanked the sketch down. "What is it you wanted to discuss?" she asked, tossing the sketch on a table with several others.

With a groan, Sophie fell dramatically onto a settee. "Oh, Claudia, I am quite desperate! I swore I wouldn't burden you, but my brother is so mean-spirited, I simply cannot abide living in this house a moment longer, I swear it!"

That surprised Claudia—for all his faults, Julian doted on his sisters and always had. "Sophie!" she exclaimed, smiling. "What on earth are you talking about?"

"You must *promise* not to take his side in this! I can't

speak of it to anyone except you," she said, anxiously propping her weight on one elbow.

Now she had Claudia's undivided attention. "I promise," she said, and sat on the edge of an embroidered chair next to the settee.

Sophie pushed herself into a sitting position and looked forlornly at the carpet. "I've a beau," she muttered.

Claudia laughed. "Oh, Sophie, is *that* all? Who is he?"

"Sir William Stanwood. He's a baronet—do you know him?" she asked, a twinge of anxiousness in her voice.

The name was only vaguely familiar to Claudia and she shook her head.

"Oh, he's *wonderful!*" exclaimed Sophie, suddenly beaming. "You will *adore* him! He's quite handsome, and he's very tall, and blond, and he is so very determined to make a good life, you know. He's not at all like the dandies Aunt Violet brings around, but very conservative in his manner. A gentleman—"

Claudia squeezed Sophie's knee. "He sounds divine! So what is the trouble?"

"Julian won't allow me to see him," Sophie said, sniffing indignantly.

Something rumbled in the back of her mind, and Claudia's smile faded. "Why on earth not?"

"He believes William is not sincere in his esteem."

As your friend, I am honor-bound to say that Phillip is not the sort of man for you, Claudia. The old wound split open with Sophie's words. "Is that so?" she asked icily. "And pray tell, what gives Kettering such superior insight?"

Sophie shook her head. "He doesn't really even *know* him! William holds me in the highest regard, yet Julian forbids me to see him under any circumstances, and if I should try he has threatened to send me to Kettering Hall for good!"

"But *why?*" Claudia insisted. "What could he possibly have against Sir William?"

Sophie dropped her gaze and fidgeted with the

polished oak arm of the settee. "Well . . . he has said many hateful things, but I rather think he believes William is not of suitable circumstance to marry me."

Oh, now *that* was just grand! Naturally, *he* could share his favors with just about any female who crossed his path, but dear Sophie was not allowed to follow her heart because of her bloody *situation.* "Are you quite certain? He refuses Stanwood's suit because he is only a *baronet?*"

"Oh yes, I am certain that is the root of it! Claudia, what am I to *do?* To be without William is not to be borne!" she cried.

Claudia was at once on her feet, marching to the sideboard. "I'll tell you what you do. You follow your heart!" she exclaimed. "You can't allow Kettering's lack of sentiment to guide what may be the most important decision of your life!"

"But *how?* Julian is so very stubborn in this!"

The indisputable gulf between his own behavior and what he expected of Sophie was simply intolerable. But it was so typical, so very *male,* and it infuriated Claudia. "I don't know," she admitted truthfully. "But I do know this: You will regret it all your days if you give up your heart's desire for the sake of his ridiculous notion of propriety!"

"Then you'll help me?" Sophie asked desperately.

"Of course I will, if I can. What of Eugenie and Ann? We could—"

"No!" Sophie quickly and violently shook her head. "They know nothing—William warned me that they might very well take Julian's side in this."

Keep it from Eugenie and Ann? They both were aware of the inequalities women faced in the course of their everyday lives—they would understand. But neither was as anxious to correct the world as Claudia, and the two of them absolutely adored their pig-headed brother. Stanwood was probably right. "Yes, well, I'll help you if I can," she said at last. "But I am not sure what I can do—"

"You can talk to him!"

Claudia glanced at Sophie—how could she explain that *she* had married for the sake of propriety? That she and Julian were caught in some make-believe world of marriage where they didn't really speak to one another? Without thinking, she ruefully shook her head, and Sophie suddenly sprang to her feet and rushed to the sideboard. "Then help me *see* him," she said, grabbing Claudia's shoulders. "I should very much like to meet William in the park tomorrow at noon—"

"Alone?" Claudia heard herself ask.

"Claudia! I am almost one and twenty—I *must* see him! You can help me! You can tell him that we are off to call on Mary Whitehurst! Then you go round to see her, and I shall meet William!"

Lie to him? "Oh no. No, Sophie, I am a horrid liar, really I am, and honestly, I don't think I could actually *lie*—"

"Not *lie*," Sophie hastily reassured her. "I *shall* pay a call to Mary Whitehurst, I shall meet you there! Only later, after I've seen William. You see? It's not a lie."

Hardly convinced, Claudia frowned skeptically. "And what of Tinley? He will ask where you go."

Sophie rolled her eyes. "Tinley can't remember his name most days! *Please,* Claudia! You are the only hope that I have! I shall *never* see William if you won't help me and I can't very well follow my heart if I can never see him, can I?"

But to lie! Still, Julian was being entirely unreason able about this. Perhaps she could just avoid the subject altogether . . . "All *right,*" she said, shrugging out of Sophie's grip.

"Oh, *thank* you, Claudia!" Sophie cried, throwing her arms around Claudia's neck.

"Thank Claudia for what?"

Both women started at the sound of Julian's voice. Sophie quickly dropped her arms from Claudia's shoulders. "Um . . . for, ah, for helping me with a problem," she muttered awkwardly, and looked anxiously to Claudia.

That only caused Julian to walk farther into the room. "A problem? Is there anything I can do?"

"No!" Sophie responded a bit too sharply, then smiled nervously. "It's ah . . . it's a female matter, really, and I—"

Julian quickly lifted his hand in supplication. "My apologies."

"Not at all." She cast a meaningful look at Claudia. "If you will excuse me, then," she muttered, and hurried from the room, hardly sparing her brother a glance as she passed.

Julian sighed wearily as he watched her disappear into the corridor, but when he turned to face Claudia again, he was smiling warmly. "I'm sorry if I interrupted."

"Ah, no. No!" Claudia tried to reassure him, and feeling the lie on her face, walked quickly to the desk, where her school ledger was lying open.

Julian strolled up behind her; his arm slipped around her waist. "It's awfully quiet this afternoon," he said, nuzzling her neck, making her shiver with that strange, cool heat only he could invoke.

"Rather thought you'd have planned a tea or some such thing," he murmured against her skin. His lips grazed her earlobe; a thousand white-hot tingles ran down her back and arm.

"Ah . . . the, ah, teas . . . are Thursday," she stammered. Julian kissed her ear; Claudia turned her head slightly, so that his next kiss caught the corner of her mouth, enticing all of her senses, and she felt herself on dangerous ground. One more kiss, one more moment in his arms, and she would succumb to his touch. When he lifted his hand to her face, she ducked abruptly out of his embrace, walked unsteadily to the other side of the desk, and sat heavily in the chair.

Julian regarded her warily. Claudia pretended not to notice, but bent over her book as if she studied it intently. He moved to the corner of the desk, absently fingered the violet blooms in a little pot there. "What are you about?"

"I am, ah, reviewing the ledger in which I record the donations to my school project," she replied.

"Is something amiss?" he asked, walking around the desk to stand behind her.

"Oh no. No, I'm just balancing the latest entries, that's all."

He leaned over her shoulder, the spicy scent of his cologne wafted across her, and from the corner of her eye, she could see his clean-shaven chin. With his finger, he quickly ran down the column of figures she had carefully recorded. "Why don't you leave it? I'll do it for you," he said, and turned into her, kissing her temple.

Claudia squirmed. "That's really not necessary. I don't mind—"

"You shouldn't have to worry about financial matters, love. I'll take care of it."

Shouldn't *worry* about financial matters? What, did he think her too ignorant to balance her own blasted books? "Thank you, but I am really quite capable of doing the calculations. I *did* learn to add and subtract."

Julian laughed, stroked her cheek with one finger as if she was a precocious child, and pulled the open ledger across the desk so that he could peruse it. "Don't be ridiculous, love. Of course you are capable. But it . . ." His voice trailed off; he straightened, retrieved his spectacles from his coat pocket and donned them, then leaned over again, peering intently at the open book. "What have we here?"

Claudia glanced at the ledger page and knew instantly what he saw; the withdrawal of Lord Cheevers' donation. "Oh, that. Lord Cheevers withdrew his donation—"

"Why should he withdraw his donation?" Julian interrupted, yanking the spectacles from his nose.

Claudia felt the warmth of humiliation creep into her cheeks. "Because . . . because of the scandal," she muttered.

He looked at her, seemingly confused for a moment, then glanced again at the ledger. "And Montfort, the same thing?" he asked, not really needing an answer. "Nothing from Belton, either?"

"I never received many of the pledges that were made to me."

Julian said nothing as he stared down at her ledger. After a long moment he suddenly moved, strode around the desk to fetch a chair, and carried it around the desk, placing it next to Claudia with a decisive *thump*. He sat down, shoved his eyeglasses on his face and picked up the pen.

"Julian, please," Claudia implored him. "I can balance—"

He abruptly covered her hand with his. "Claudia. I *know* you can balance your ledgers and I rather imagine you could do it standing on your head. I only want a list of names."

"But why? What are you doing?" she asked, confused.

He smiled thinly. "I think that perhaps Lord Cheevers has forgotten a little debt owed to the Duke of Sutherland during a particularly nasty parliamentary debate. I rather imagine Alex might persuade Cheevers to reconsider his donation. As for Montfort, well, I shall spare you the ugly details of *that* debt, but rest assured, he should make a very generous donation once I have spoken to him."

"Do you mean to say that you would speak to them on behalf of the school?" she asked, incredulous.

Julian lifted one brow in puzzled amusement. "Of course I would speak to them! Claudia, if this school is something you want, then I shall gladly bring all my influence to bear on it. You need only ask me."

She blinked; Julian smiled, brought her hand to his lips, and kissed her knuckles. "I want to help you in any small way that you will allow me." With that, he turned his attention back to the ledger. "Belton," he mumbled, and idly scratched his chin. "Nothing to be said for him really, except that he is a consummate idiot." Julian continued to squint at the ledger, his brow creased with the frown of concentration as he mumbled similar sentiments about several of the other patrons listed.

Claudia watched him, surprised, fascinated, and even a bit heartened. Her father had never shown any interest in her charities, and neither had Julian, really, other than to inquire politely about her activities from time to time. It was not her experience that men were ever particularly interested in what they deemed a lady's pastime, and they most certainly were content to leave the charitable functions to the women. It had never occurred to her, not once, to ask her father or Julian for help. That he would offer, would take such an interest—and such detailed notes!—both confused and touched her and made her question for the thousandth time if perhaps she had misjudged this Rake, her husband.

Fifteen

Fortunately, Claudia didn't have to lie to anyone when Sophie slipped out to meet Sir William the next day, as she discovered Julian had left early for Cambridge. Nor did she have to lie the day after that, when Sophie came home more in love than ever and peppered her with a hundred questions about men and love and the universe. As the weather was starting to turn, Claudia used that as an excuse to escape Sophie's delirious state and paid a call to the house on Upper Moreland Street before the rains came.

And as she stood in the small parlor on Upper Moreland Street, she felt the cold seep through her bones to her very marrow. Doreen Conner stood in front of the small fire, her bony hands on her hips, impassively watching Claudia, having just given her the news.

Ellie was dead, strangled by her lover.

Claudia had met Ellie only a handful of times. The young woman had worked as a "daily" servant until a few weeks ago, when some incident involving her current beau had gotten her ejected from her employment and her living situation. With no money and no family to whom she could turn, she had been brought to Upper Moreland Street by a woman who had once stayed at the little town house. Ellie was there only a few days before her beau discovered where she was and began to make himself known. Doreen said that Nigel Mansfield often came around after he'd been in the public houses, quite late at night, and far into his cups. On one occasion, he was so intoxicated and angry with Ellie over some slight that he had tried to break down the locked door. But the barrel of Doreen's gun, a rather huge thing Claudia had appropriated from her father's gun cabinet, had properly cowed him.

Ellie was trouble, everyone thought so, but Claudia had genuinely liked her nonetheless. Plump and cheerful and pretty, she was so very thankful that she had been given a place in the town house that she was eager to contribute in any way she could, most notably by doing a great amount of work around the place. "There must be something we can do," Claudia muttered helplessly, heartsick at the news of her death.

"There ain't nothing to be done for her now, miss," Doreen said stoically. "All of us, we tried to tell her that Nigel was a mean one, but she wouldn't listen."

"He must be brought to justice!" Claudia insisted, shivering unconsciously at the memory of Doreen's description of how they found Ellie—lying on the back stoop, her own scarf bound so tightly around her neck that it had cut the skin.

Doreen resolutely shook her head. "We've no evidence it was him. For all we know, Ellie found herself another bloke last night that done this to her. And besides, there ain't a magistrate who'd care enough about poor Ellie to go after the man. No, miss—he'd take one look where she come from, her lot in life, and he wouldn't waste one moment on her. No one gives a damn about our Ellie, save us."

Despair sank in around Claudia at the naked truth in Doreen's matter-of-fact reasoning. The injustice done to women was the very reason she had found this house, wasn't it? To protect them when the world turned a blind eye? Yet in spite of this house, she hadn't helped Ellie at all. She might have had a place to sleep, but nothing else had changed. In the end, she'd had nothing to fall back on but a drunk. "There is *nothing* we can do?"

"Ellie's in a better place now, miss. You done your best."

Then her best wasn't good enough.

Riding home, Claudia realized just how little the house on Upper Moreland Street really meant. Now, more than ever, she understood how important it was to build her school so that young women like Ellie would have *some* choices in life and not end up strangled on a stoop. But even the school hardly seemed enough—it certainly did not change the way the world thought, or how the law treated women. And it certainly didn't change *men,* for heaven's sake.

Claudia closed her eyes, laid a hand across her lower abdomen, cramping with the pain of her monthly cycle. Saddened by Ellie's death and feeling ill, she felt alone and vulnerable, wishing there was someone to whom she could turn for comfort.

She missed Julian.

The sentiment crept into her mind, surprising her. Gone to Cambridge, or so his terse note had said. She suddenly pressed her fist to her temple, trying to clear the ugly thought from her mind, not wanting to pursue the dull suspicion that he might have a mistress in town. He certainly wouldn't be the first man to take one and would hardly be the last. Claudia had reminded herself at least a dozen times that it was quite common among the *ton*; she could easily think of a half-dozen men rumored to have mistresses, kept in relative splendor. And those half-dozen men had a half-dozen wives who did not seem to care particularly. She told herself she didn't care, either.

Oh, but she did.

As hard as she had tried to be indifferent to him, unwelcome emotions kept bubbling to the surface and she just couldn't force them down any longer. She cared, Lord God, she *cared!* She wanted him all to herself, wanted his smile to be for her alone, his hands and his mouth . . .

Claudia closed her eyes, leaned her head against the

squabs. Everything about her life was a mess, a vast jumble of confused emotions and longings and bitterness. One day she would think she had everything sorted out, had discovered that place inside her where she could survive. And in the very next breath she'd find herself rearranging her day just to catch a glimpse of him as he strode into his study or laughing with Arthur on his way out. As hard as she had fought it, she could not help herself—she loved him still, as much as she had as a girl and in spite of everything that had happened between them.

It was bewildering to be so smitten with The Rake. He confused her. There were moments he seemingly adored her, was interested in what she was about, eager to be helpful. But then there were the moments he would go off with Arthur and leave her to daily activities in which he appeared to have no interest. In those moments, she felt as if she did not quite succeed in measuring up to the expectations of a man like Julian, and that as there was nothing particularly unique or special about her, he apparently thought nothing of seeking his satisfaction in other quarters.

The irony of her situation was not lost on Claudia— she had long forgotten her indignation over Julian's advice that she wasn't good enough for Phillip.

Because it was *Julian* she wanted to love her.

It had always been him.

The rain came in the afternoon as expected, and Julian was chilled through to the bone by the time he reached St. James Square. Kettering House was awfully quiet, he thought, as he paused in the entry to hand his things to Tinley. "All is well, I trust?" he asked the old butler.

"There aren't any ladies about, if that is what you mean, my lord," he said wearily, and Julian gathered the old man was just as harassed by Claudia's activities as all the other men he knew.

"Where is her ladyship?" he asked.

Tinley missed the coat stand, dropping Julian's great-coat onto the floor. "In her rooms, my lord."

"And Sophie?" Julian persisted, stooping to pick up the overcoat and hang it for the butler.

Tinley paused, looked at the mirror above the entry console, obviously thinking. "I wouldn't know, my lord," he said at last.

That hardly surprised him, but sick of the suspicions, he refused to allow himself to wonder exactly where his sister was.

Julian sighed wearily as he mounted the stairs, wondering if Claudia had even noticed he was gone this time. As he moved down the wide corridor of the first floor, he paused at the door leading to her rooms and stared at the brass knob, overwhelmed by the urge to see her. Hell, he *always* wanted to see her gorgeous face. Yet a few weeks of this forced marriage had trained him to leave her be, to ignore his gut instincts and pass her door when he wanted to go in. It was the way she wanted it.

But it was not the way *he* wanted it, and it never would be. A man ought to be allowed the company of his wife on occasion without feeling as if he were intruding. He had been gone two days, had thought of little else but her, and did not think it so very unreasonable to expect his wife to greet him.

Julian put his hand on the knob and turned it, pushing open the door before he allowed himself to change his mind.

"Good afternoon, my lord," said Brenda, looking up from her task of folding linens.

Blast it, but he felt like an awkward schoolboy, and quickly glanced about the small sitting room. "Good afternoon," he responded tightly. "Ah, where is your lady?"

The maid began folding a towel. "She's resting, my lord. Feeling a bit under the weather," she said, nodding toward the door of the bedchamber.

She was ill? An ancient fear rushed through his veins,

and Julian forgot his clumsiness, walking quickly to her bedchamber and closed the door behind him.

Weak gray light filtered in from the window, filling the room with shadows. Fully clothed, Claudia was lying on her side, her back to him and her face to the windows, her knees curled to her chest. Her hair, unbound, spilled like dark ribbons behind her. Her gown, a deep rich blue, draped her body, and her stockinged feet peeked out from beneath the hem. Cautiously, he approached the side of the bed.

"Julian?"

Her soft voice curled around his heart, surprising him with the strength of its hold. "Yes," he responded quietly, and sat gingerly on the edge of her bed. "You are not well, sweetheart?"

She did not roll over, but shrugged her slender shoulders. "I'm all right. Just a bit of a stomachache," she murmured.

A stomachache. Living with four young women had taught Julian a thing or two about the root of such maladies—Claudia was suffering from her menses. Relieved, he quietly expelled his breath as he stroked her hair. "Let me rub your back," he murmured, and balancing himself with one arm across her body, began to massage her lower back. "Shall I fetch you some laudanum?" he asked after a moment. "It would help ease the pain."

Claudia tensed. "I, ah . . . Brenda gave me some."

"It hasn't helped?"

"Not terribly much," she admitted shyly.

The light behind a spindly tree outside cast shadows across her face; she was pale, her eyes red-rimmed as if she had been crying. Julian felt a tightness in his chest and despised his inability to make her better. He stroked a finger across her silken cheek, drawing a deep but silent breath when Claudia closed her eyes at his touch.

He resumed rubbing her back. "Is there nothing I can do for you?" he asked earnestly.

"Yes . . . talk to me," she murmured.

That startled him—Claudia never wanted conversation from him—if anything, she seemed to abhor it. What in God's name should he say? "All right," he said slowly. "I went to Cambridge, and while I was there, I visited the King's College Chapel. Have you ever been? It's magnificent," he continued at the small shake of her head. "The ceiling must arch three stories above one's head. A boys' choir was singing, and you can't imagine how the sound of it is lifted up before it settles down around the listener, as if it is actually coming from the heavens." He spoke softly, rhythmically rubbing the small of her back. Claudia's lashes fluttered against her pale skin, and she pillowed her head on her hands beneath her cheeks.

"There are tens, perhaps dozens of candles lit in the cathedral, and when the light flickers, it makes the figures in the stained glass look as if they are alive," he soothingly continued, and leaned over her. "There is much pageantry when the gnomes appear and dance along the top of the organ pipes; first on the bass, then the treble, then the highest tenor," he whispered.

He had no idea where that came from, other than an ancient habit of lulling little girls to sleep with fairy tales. But a faint smile appeared on Claudia's lips, so he continued. "After the gnomes, the priest begins his ballet with the fairies. He is quite large, mind you, but I vow that I have never seen one so light on his feet as he. He dances a particularly lovely ballet on the very tips of his toes. One would swear he was actually tripping through a meadow in pursuit of butterflies."

Claudia's faint smile broadened. "And what do the students do while the priest performs his ballet?"

"Ah, the students," he murmured. "They are generally quite appalled, you see, because the ballet interferes with their picnic." He smiled; but a shadow scudded across her face, and her smile faded in it. He started to move away, but Claudia suddenly rolled over and threw her arms around his neck, burying her face in his shoulder. Astonished, Julian quickly put his arms around her, held her close. She said nothing, just clung to him, hiding her face in his shoulder . . . *crying?*

His chin on top of her head, Julian soothed the loose curls of her hair, wincing with the sound of each muffled gasp into his coat. "What is it, my love? What is wrong?"

She shook her head, tightened her grip around his neck. "Nothing . . . I'm sorry. I don't know what is wrong with me. It's so unlike me to *cry*," she gasped, and another sob escaped her.

"It's all right," he said, stroking her hair.

"I was thinking how precious life is," she continued raggedly, "and how quickly and easily it can be ended. One moment someone is here and then the next they are gone, just like that."

Everything in Julian convulsed; the feeling of discomfort washed over him so quickly that he actually felt faint for a brief moment. How was it possible that Phillip could find him even now, in this single moment with Claudia? "Why would you be thinking such a thing?" he demanded, a little more roughly than he would have liked.

"I . . . I know someone who died, a woman, a young woman . . . she died so unexpectedly, and it's so unfair! I keep asking myself, why her and not me? Why should she be taken in her prime? What was the purpose of her life, then, if she was to die so young? It . . . it frightens me."

It sickened him. Phillip would never be gone from him.

"I'm sorry," she said again, her arms sliding from his neck. "I suppose I'm being ridiculously sentimental."

Silent, Julian let her pull away, fearful of what he might say if he opened his mouth. This . . . this marriage was his hell. He had known it for weeks now. Claudia leaned back, looked up at him with luminous blue-gray eyes shimmering with tears. His arms fell away from her, and he stood from the bed. "You aren't feeling well, that's all. Why don't you rest?" he said blandly, and turned toward the door, hardly thinking or feeling anything but the pain of his despair and guilt.

"Julian—"

"I'll have Tinley send up a tray, all right?"

That suggestion was met with a moment of silence, but Julian dared not turn back and look at her again for fear that he might shatter. "Yes. Thank you," she murmured, and he heard the creak of the bed as she lay down.

He walked blindly down the corridor, simply moving away from her, away from his fantasy that one day Phillip would be gone and Claudia would love him. He kept walking, down the great curving staircase, until he was standing in the foyer. "Have a mount saddled," he said to a footman, and still continued on, until he was standing out in the stone portico of his home, feeling the wet and cold seep into him, waking him from the slumber of his hell.

It occurred to him, as he stood there staring out at nothing, that perhaps he should maintain his distance from Claudia not because *she* wanted it so much, but because it was the only method of self-preservation he had left to him. If he wasn't near her, she couldn't make him feel the monster of guilt and regret that seemed to destroy everything in his path while vicars sang about the quality of love.

He moved to the corner of the portico, withdrawing one of his American cheroots from his pocket, and struck a match. Cupping his hand around the flame, he lit the cigar. When he lifted his head, he noticed a plain black gig on the curb just beyond the gates of his house.

That was curious. Julian leaned to one side to have a better look at it. It was a gig, all right, a two-wheeled, one-horse carriage—not something one saw very often in Mayfair or St. James, where phaetons and barouches and landaus symbolized the elite status of the residents there. A man and a woman were in the gig; he fumbled in his pocket for his spectacles and looked again.

His heart started badly—it was Sophie, engaged in a rather torrid kiss.

Julian inadvertently dropped the cheroot.

His first inclination was to yank her from that gig and throttle her then and there for such unseemly behavior. His second inclination was to wait and confirm his worst fear—that the man kissing her was Stanwood. Before he was forced to decide, however, Sophie stumbled out of the gig, awkwardly pushing her gloves up as she simultaneously tried to attach her bonnet to her head. Stanwood was talking to her; Sophie was nodding enthusiastically. She took several steps backward, bumped into the gate.

"Your mount, my lord," a young groom called.

Perfect timing. He would have his talk with Stanwood somewhere other than the front of his house, as he would hate to see the bastard's blood all over the walk. He marched to where the lad was holding his mount and vaulted up onto the roan's back. As he gathered the reins, Sophie walked through the gate, clearly entranced. *"Sophie!"*

The girl started so badly that she stumbled. "Julian!" The blood drained rapidly from her face. "I—I didn't know you had returned," she stammered.

"Where have you been?" he asked, dispensing with any greeting as he tightened his hold on the anxious roan.

"Ah, I . . . where have *I* been? Why, ah, with Aunt Violet."

Oh God, Sophie! "Go inside and wait for me," he snapped, and signaled the roan forward, riding through the gate the groom opened, veering sharply to the right in pursuit of the goddam gig.

It wasn't hard to find Stanwood; the gig was in front of a Piccadilly public house. Julian tethered his horse and strode inside, ignoring the barmaid who tried to greet him. He scanned the crowded room and spotted Stanwood as he sauntered toward a table in the back where two barmaids were entertaining a patron. Julian started after him, roughly pushing past one man who made the mistake of stepping into his path.

Stanwood turned just as Julian reached him. Surprise flitted across the blackguard's face just before Julian shoved him into the wall. "I told you in May, and I'll tell you once more, Stanwood. Stay away from my sister. Next time, I'll kill you for it," he said low.

Fear flashed briefly in Stanwood's eyes before he

clawed at Julian's hands. "Unhand me, Kettering!" he spat. "You've no right to treat me in such a manner!"

"I've *every* right," he breathed angrily, and shoved him hard against the wall again, knocking from their mountings two porcelain plates that shattered on the wood floor. "Don't think I don't know about your debts, sir, or that no bank will lend to you. Don't think I don't know about your inquiries into my sister's annuity. You want nothing more than her bloody dowry!"

Stanwood shoved back, unbalancing Julian. "What of it? I'm not so different from you! Rumor has it Redbourne settled quite a sum on you to take that harlot off his hands!"

Julian's heart stopped cold; the room suddenly seemed to shrink. His hands curled into fists, and he saw nothing but the whites of Stanwood's eyes as he lunged at him. The barmaid's shriek was lost in the thud of his fist against Stanwood's face. The two of them crashed to the floor, Julian's fist finding purchase twice more before shoving Stanwood's head into the floor and scrambling to his feet. "You *son of a bitch,*" he snarled, "stay away from my sister, do you hear me?"

Touching his split lip gingerly, Stanwood looked at the blood on his fingers. He smirked at it, then at Julian. "How will you stop me?" he asked mockingly. "Sophie will be one and twenty in less than a month's time. You can't hold her prisoner."

It took every ounce of strength Julian had to keep from killing the man right there, in that crowded room, with his bare hands. "If you come near her, I will use every ounce of my influence to ruin you, Stanwood. There is not a bank in Europe that will lend you a single shilling. Your debts will be called in. You won't be able to find employment with a reputable establishment. You can't hide from me," he said evenly, "so you had best heed me." And with that, he turned on his heel and walked from the room with Stanwood's biting laughter pounding in his ears.

Sixteen

Sophie's heart would not stop pounding from her near-disastrous encounter with Julian and the sheer terror of imagining what he might have done had he seen William's carriage in front of the house.

On the couch in her rooms, she frantically assessed her situation as impossible and completely hopeless. How long could she continue to steal out of the house to meet William in obscure places with a desperate hope that no one saw them? Was she to avoid her own brother for the rest of her life? She *wanted* to tell Julian the truth, but William said that if they went to him now, he would only be angered because she had disobeyed him. They needed to allow some time to pass, William said, so that Julian would come to see how he truly adored her and did not care a whit for her fortune.

But she'd never be able to endure the wait!

The door banged open; with a start, Sophie jerked around—and she knew the moment she saw Julian's face. He *knew!* Her stomach plummeted instantly; she felt as if she had just been rammed against the wall, the breath knocked clean from her lungs. The room seemed to spin as a million thoughts roared through her mind, centering quickly on one—William. He meant to take her from William, banish her just as Sarah Cafferty had been banished from London, to deny her the one man who would make her happy.

Unable to speak, unable to breathe, Sophie gripped

the arm of the couch and tried to catch her breath. *Claudia. She had to speak with Claudia.*

"A word, Sophie." His voice filled the room, reverberating against the walls, the furniture, the ceiling. Sophie squeezed her eyes shut; cold fear pricked at every fiber in her. Desperate, she turned her back to the door and to her brother, frantically seeking to put the pieces of her shattered composure back together.

"Where did you go this afternoon?"

The fear paralyzed her tongue. Stumbling to her feet, she moved awkwardly to her bed and clutched at the hangings.

"Answer me!" he demanded, and she realized he had moved closer. Her grip tightened on the hangings, and she desperately sought a way out, a plausible lie—

"You were with Stanwood. In spite of the fact that you have been forbidden to see him, you were with him, in front of my house."

He had seen them. The floor seemed to shift under her feet and Sophie's grip on the bed hangings slipped. She stumbled, landing on the edge of the bed. Julian was suddenly towering over her, glaring down at her with eyes as black and as hard as coal. "You have disobeyed me one time too many, Sophie," he breathed angrily. "You and I leave for Kettering Hall at once."

That single pronouncement verbalized her worst nightmare. "*No,* Julian!" she cried frantically. "You don't understand! William *loves* me!"

Something flared in his eyes, and he roughly grabbed her shoulders. "Stanwood does not *love* you, Sophie! He loves your bloody *fortune!*" he roared.

Hot tears spilled from her eyes, blinding her, and Sophie shoved helplessly against his chest. "Yes, he *does* love me! Why won't you believe a man like William could love me?"

Julian stilled; his grip on her arm slackened. "My God, Sophie," he muttered hoarsely. "Have you no more esteem for yourself than that?"

Esteem for herself? With a groan of pain, Sophie

struggled out of his grip and stumbled away from the bed. Julian had no idea what her life was like. He was a man, he was handsome, he was a wealthy earl to whom women flocked like geese. He had no idea what it was to be the youngest sister of such an earl, the plainest and dullest of them all, the one who had to be sent to finishing school if there was to be any hope of a decent offer for her. She knew that the men Aunt Violet brought around to court her were appropriately pedigreed, but were not considered prize catches among the *ton*. But William— *William* made her feel desirable and alive. He loved her! And Julian would deny her love for the sake of a proper pedigree!

His hand was on her shoulder. "Sophie, darling, there are many other lads who—"

"No!" she cried, shrugging his hand off. "No, Julian! I love William!"

"Be that as it may," he said hoarsely, "I cannot sit by and allow that blackguard to ruin you. I have no choice— I forbade you and you expressly defied me. I gave you my trust and you betrayed me. I have no choice but to take you away from here before you are ruined."

The fear was suddenly strangling her. *"No!"* she sobbed, and whirled around to face him. "You *can't* send me away! I shall die there! Oh, Julian, I beg of you, do not send me away—I swear I won't see him again, I swear it on Valerie's grave!" she begged hysterically. "Just don't send me to Kettering Hall!"

Julian hesitated only a moment before he shook his head. "You leave me no choice, Sophie. I cannot trust you, and as I am responsible for your health and safety, I will do what I must. There will be no more discussion of it. Get ready to leave," he said tightly, and turned on his heel, striding for the door.

Terrified, Sophie watched his retreat. *"Julian, please!"* she screamed.

He paused at the door; through the blur of her tears, she saw his shoulders sag and for one insane moment, she hoped. "We depart in an hour," he muttered, and walked out of her room, ignoring her as she collapsed on the floor in despair, sobbing uncontrollably.

The laudanum had helped Claudia to sleep, and when she awoke, she felt much improved—enough to contemplate joining Julian for supper. Perhaps she was feeling altogether a bit too sentimental, but when he had wrapped his arms around her this afternoon, she had felt secure, almost as if nothing could touch her there—*death* could not touch her in his arms. But the glimmer of comfort, both physical and emotional, had ended so soon. *Too* soon. Yes, well, if it hadn't been for her little display of tears and self-pity, he might have stayed.

Claudia paused in the brushing of her hair to frown at her reflection. No doubt he thought her very silly, crying and carrying on like that. In truth, she hardly knew Ellie at all, but she had grieved as if the woman was her very own sister. Slowly, she resumed the brushing of her hair, swearing that she would not be so sullen, when Sophie burst into her suite, her face streaked with tears. Claudia started with great surprise. "Oh, *Claudia!*" Sophie wailed, and hurled herself across the room, landing at Claudia's feet to bury her face in her lap.

Tendrils of dread coiled around Claudia's heart. "Dear God, what has *happened?*"

"Mercy save me, it's *Julian!*" the girl cried into her lap.

The tendrils were suddenly squeezing the very life from her. Panicked, she roughly forced Sophie's head up. "*What* of Julian? What has happened to him?"

Sophie gave a feeble shake of her head. "*Nothing* has happened to him—he is a *beast!*"

A strong wave of relief flooded her. She realized she was clutching the sides of Sophie's head in something of a death grip. "Calm yourself, Sophie. Take a deep breath and tell me what has happened," she said evenly, lowering her hands.

"I *hate* him, I swear I do! He's *horrid*—he says . . . he

says I must go to Kettering Hall! He would banish me before he would see me happy!" Sophie cried hysterically. "He knows about William, and he means to *banish* me!"

So Julian had at last discovered his sister's affections for a mere baronet. It seemed terribly harsh of him to react in such a way—how could he make Sophie cry so wretchedly?

"You promised you would help me if you could," Sophie continued raggedly. "You are the only one to whom I can turn now! *Please* speak with him, Claudia! He won't listen to me! You *must* speak with him! I . . . I cannot go to Kettering, I will *perish* there, I swear it!"

"Is his objection Stanwood's rank? Is it nothing more than that?"

Sniffing loudly, Sophie nodded, and Claudia felt the old burn of indignation in her. It was perfectly all right for a *man* to take whomever he wanted to his bed or the altar, but the moment a *woman* thought to look past her narrow little world, the entire British aristocracy was suddenly shaking at its very foundation! Stanwood was a *baronet,* for God's sake, not a murderer or a highwayman, and Julian would deny his sister the chance to marry the man she adored for the sake of his bloody propriety! "I will speak with him," she assured Sophie.

"I *knew* you would! You can make him change his mind!"

Claudia wasn't so certain about that. As furious as she was for Sophie, English law made Julian's word final. If she could not persuade him to let Sophie follow her heart, there were few options available to Sophie to fight him, much less any that would not embroil her deeply in scandal. Having been in a similarly precarious situation, Claudia's heart went out to her sister-in-law, and she gingerly laid a hand against her wet cheek. "I will talk to him, Sophie. I will do everything in my power to persuade him that he cannot dismiss your feelings in this. I shall speak to him tonight—"

"*Now!*" Sophie shrieked, clearly on the verge of crumbling with anxiety.

Claudia eased Sophie back so that she could stand. "Very well, I shall speak with him now."

With a great sigh of relief, Sophie threw her head back and closed her eyes. "Thank you, Claudia! I know you will convince him—you *must* convince him!"

God in heaven, she hoped that she could—she could not bear to think what Sophie might do if she failed.

She found Julian in the small blue drawing room on the third floor, poring over one of several musty leather-bound books stacked around him, so engrossed in the tome that he did not hear her enter. Claudia paused at the threshold, gazing at him. His round, wire-rimmed spectacles were perched precariously on his nose; a thick strand of ink black hair swept across his brow, dipping over his eye. The faint shadow of a beard covered his jaw . . . which was bulging with the angry clench of his teeth.

She must have moved, because he suddenly looked up, and for one brief, fleeting moment, his heart shone in his eyes. But he quickly dropped his gaze to the book again. "You are feeling much improved, I see."

"Yes, I . . . thank you." She faltered, feeling suddenly awkward, as if she was indeed intruding. She took several steps forward and clasped her hands behind her back. "If I may . . . might I have a word?"

Julian glanced up again, his black gaze swiftly running over her. "Yes?"

"It's about Sophie," she began, and Julian surprised her by slamming shut the book he held in his lap.

"Save your breath, Claudia. I am ill-disposed to discuss that little half-wit at the moment." With a scowl, he tossed the leather-bound volume onto the stack with the others.

"All right," she said carefully, and walked to the hearth where she pretended to look at a china vase.

"All right? That's it? Surely there was more you wanted to say," he snapped irritably.

Claudia stole a glance at him—he had folded his arms tightly across his chest. She had never seen him so angry and swallowed past a lump of sudden nerves. "Yes, there is more."

He snorted disdainfully. "Naturally there is. Well, then? Let's have this over with, shall we? Plead Sophie's case. Go on, then, Claudia—you wanted to tell me what a heartless cad I am, how it is her *right* to foolishly do as she pleases!"

Short-tempered and sarcastic, too, she thought uneasily. If there was one thing consistent about her husband, it was that he was always pleasant—roguish, but charmingly pleasant all the same. She took a steadying breath. "I merely wanted to inquire . . ."

"Yes?" he snapped impatiently.

". . . if you had ever had the pleasure of being in love."

That clearly stunned him, and good God, she had *no* idea where it had come from, no comprehension of how those words had found their way to her tongue. A palpable tension suddenly filled the room and Claudia cringed inwardly as the full weight of that tension pressed down on them. His gaze still locked on her, he removed his spectacles, carefully folded them, and deliberately stuffed them into a coat pocket. The only thing that belied his calm was the erratic leap of a muscle in his jaw.

"I have been foolish enough to love," he admitted quietly, "but I would hardly term it a pleasure."

Insane as it was, Claudia was suddenly wild to know just *whom* he had loved. A dozen names or more popped into her mind—debutantes, married ladies, widows, a host of names that had, at one time or another, been linked with his. But she bit her tongue, forced the thousand questions down, and nervously running the palms of her hands over the fabric of her gown, cleared her throat. "So . . . was there not a time you thought you might simply perish without her? Can you not understand, perhaps a little, how Sophie feels?"

Raw emotion glanced his hard features. Claudia's breath caught in her throat; she could swear it was pain that clouded his eyes. With some effort, he shoved to his

feet. The look on his face, the expression of contempt—
Lord God, how he despised her at this moment.

Alarm quickened her pulse as he strolled toward her.
"What about you, Claudia? Was there ever a time you
thought you might *simply perish* for want of a lover?" he
mocked her. "Have you ever lain awake at night because
his image haunts your sleep or been quite incapable of
breathing because his mere *presence* has snatched the
very air from your lungs?" He paused in front of her; heat
flooded her, and she took an involuntary step backward.

"Well, Claudia? Do *you* understand how she feels?"

Staring at his glittering obsidian eyes, Claudia could
not think clearly. "I . . . I understand . . ." Incredibly, the
expression in his eyes hardened even more. "I understand
that Sophie is in love, and to banish her now is unthinkable—"

"Let me tell you what is *unthinkable*," he interjected,
his voice impossibly bitter. "It is unthinkable to believe
that she may find some sort of salvation in *love*," he spat
acidly. "It is unthinkable to believe that she may somehow *improve* her life by marrying for love! And madam,
it is absurd to believe that such feelings are *ever* mutual,
or that they elevate her situation to some loftier plane, or
that they change one bloody thing about the goddam
world! Trust me, the sooner the little nitwit realizes that
her so-called *love* is an illusion, unrequited and unwanted, the better off she shall be!"

His voice carried such furious despair that Claudia
could scarcely breathe. He *had* loved and lost, but before
she could even grasp that thought, Julian seemed to read
her mind, and with a smirk, turned away, strolling casually to the sideboard where he lifted a crystal decanter. "I
rather imagine you believe in fairy tales, too," he drawled
in a strangely hollow voice.

"You don't believe what you are saying, Julian. You
don't believe that Sophie would be better off having
never loved at all."

He chuckled darkly as he poured a sherry. "Ah, but I
do, Claudia. The fallacy of love is that there are *two* who

experience it, when in reality, it is rarely the case that even one is so inclined. And, I daresay, if one should feel . . . *love* . . . so strongly, one might very well smother the both of them with it." He paused, looked toward the window for a moment. "Or suffer from the want of it," he added roughly, and quickly downed the sherry.

The depth of emotion in that statement stunned her; she had the strong urge to wrap her arms around him and hold him tightly against her heart. It was impossible to believe—unfathomable, really—that Julian might have experienced heartbreak. She knew very well what it was to love someone and never have the affection returned, how lonely it was, how devastating. Incredibly, the expression on Julian's face reflected just that.

"Stanwood doesn't love her and he never will, Claudia," he said, still staring out the window.

"Is that not for Sophie to decide?" she asked gently.

"Absolutely not," he snapped, turning to face her. "He is a blackguard, a man of despicable morals, questionable tastes, and violent temperament! He is known to treat women cruelly, he hasn't a shilling to his name, and he wants her fortune, nothing else."

"But how would you truly *know* that?" she tried to reason.

"I know of his reputation, Claudia—"

"Reputation!" she exclaimed, shaking her head. "Do you know the horrible things that have been said of me? Lies and untruths! You can't possibly form your bad opinion of a man on the basis of gossip!"

His eyes narrowed dangerously. "Don't think to lecture me, madam."

"She *loves* him, Julian. If you banish her—"

"I am not *banishing* her!"

"Then what would you call it, sending her to Kettering Hall?"

Angrily, he stalked toward her. "I am keeping her safe and well! It is my responsibility to do so, and I will thank you not to interfere!"

"I am only trying to have a rational discussion—"

"I did not *invite* discussion. This is not another of your social debates, Claudia, it is my duty as her guardian and protector to decide what is best for my sister! Hell, it is my moral obligation! And it has *nothing* to do with you, so you might as well run along and find another charity to promote!"

He might as well have punched her in the gut. She leveled a heated gaze on her husband. "You do not value my opinion in this."

"Good *God!* Not only do I not value it, I couldn't possibly care less what it is!"

Her sympathy had quickly given away to furious indignation. "You promised to treat this marriage with respect—"

"I promised to save your reputation! Do not romanticize it," he said with a dismissive flick of his wrist.

Oh, God, there was no danger of that! With an angry toss of her head, she marched to the door. "Thank you, my lord, for your audience. I know it was quite an imposition on your time," she said. "I shall tell Sophie that she was right—you *are* a pig-headed beast! But I shall also tell her not to lose hope. We will find a way!"

"Splendid," he drawled, and gestured for her to leave. "Scheme away, why don't you. But she goes to Kettering Hall *tonight.*" With that, he seated himself and picked up the book he had been studying and opened it.

He was dismissing her, just as her father had done all her life, insinuating that she was more irritant than anything else. How the devil had she ever thought she cared for him? She turned sharply and sailed through the door, slamming it shut behind her and determined that Sophie would follow her heart in spite of his tyranny.

Julian felt the violent slam of the door as well as he heard it. He stared blankly at the pages in front of him, and after a moment, turned the book around so that it was right side up.

I just wanted to ask if you ever had the pleasure of being in love.

His chest constricted painfully with the discomfort; he

closed his eyes, pressed his fingers into them. *Was there never a time you thought you might simply perish without her?*

Oh, yes, Claudia. Each and every day.

Damn her, he knew *exactly* how Sophie felt—it was one of the many reasons he wanted her away from London and Stanwood. She did not deserve to know the pain he felt, but deserved so much better than that, than *Stanwood*—except that the idiot girl thought so little of herself that she believed he was her best chance at happiness.

And how exactly did he dispute her? It wasn't as if *he* could point to a marriage built on mutual respect and esteem. His only option was to protect her from herself.

The trip to Kettering was more unbearable than he had imagined, beginning with the ugly departure from St. James Square. Claudia would not even look at him. Pale, she clung to Sophie, whispering in her ear as Sophie sobbed against her shoulder. They clung to one another so fiercely that Julian seriously contemplated forcing Claudia along just to get Sophie into the chaise. But at last Sophie let go, apparently giving in to defeat, and Julian had fairly stuffed her into the chaise. As they pulled away from the small courtyard onto St. James Square, Claudia called out to Sophie, reassuring her that Eugenie and Ann would never stand for this injustice, either. Worse, old Tinley stood beside her, hunched at the shoulders and shaking a liver-spotted fist in the air at his wicked employer.

Things went steadily downhill from there. Sophie sobbed uncontrollably as the chaise weaved slowly through the narrow streets of London. Just when Julian thought she couldn't possibly shed another tear, the wailing would begin all over again. When they reached the outskirts of London—and he was fairly confident she would not bolt from the chaise—he made the driver stop so that he could climb up on the seat with him, much to that man's surprise. Julian perched beside him, wincing and pulling his hat lower and lower with every wail that drifted up to them, until the brim of his beaver hat practically covered his ears and eyes.

Fortunately, they were treated to a full moon, which made their travel easier, but Julian imagined every village through which they passed must have believed a madwoman was escaping, so loud was Sophie's fury.

They reached the mammoth Georgian house that served as the Kettering seat by dawn's first light. Sophie had long since sobbed herself to sleep, and as Julian lifted her in his arms, he was reminded of the many nights he had carried her to her own bed after she had crawled into his, having been frightened by thunder or something under her bed.

How extraordinary that little girl had become the woman in his arms.

He hated Kettering Hall.

So much did he despise his country house that he left before the sun was directly overhead, with very little sleep and what little breakfast he was able to choke down. He took a horse from the stables instead of the chaise so that he might quickly escape this tomb of memories, and left a wretched, sobbing Sophie in the foyer, held firmly in the thick arms of Miss Brillhart, Kettering Hall's housekeeper. Miss Brillhart, bless her, understood the situation quite clearly, and had urged him on. Julian tried desperately to close his ears to Sophie's plaintive wail, had even tried to reason with her one last time, but she wouldn't listen to him. She called him a beast and a few other choice names, and in the end, he had been forced to walk out the door without looking back. *He was doing the right thing!*

Perhaps, but he avoided the family cemetery all the same, riding around the north side of the estate so he would not have to see the remnants of another time he had supposedly done the right thing. The elaborate headstone at Valerie's grave—an angel, rising high above all other markers—was the constant and stark reminder of his attempts to protect another sister. Or rather, his bloody failure to save her life.

A cold shiver ran through him; with a hard spur to the flanks of his mount, Julian tried to push the memory of the unhappiest event of his life from his mind by pushing his mount. In truth, Valerie had always been sickly, although she had seemed to improve in the last two years of her life. At the prime age of eighteen, a year or so after Eugenie married, Julian had taken her to London for the Season, squiring her to all the best soirees and balls. She had loved the whirl of activity, and though she was pale and a little too thin, she had captured the attention of more than one young fop.

It was in the course of that spring that she contracted the fever that decimated her.

After a fortnight, she had not improved, and Julian could recall even now that dull, aching fear that had lodged in his heart. Instinctively, he had sent to France for Louis and Eugenie and at the same time brought the finest doctors to Valerie's bedside, insisting they try every remedy, even those they claimed experimental. Nothing seemed to work; Valerie's illness dragged on, weakening her. In complete desperation, he had brought her to Kettering and the long-time family doctor who had nursed her since she was a baby.

He had been, Julian bleakly recalled, quite convinced Dr. Dudley could cure her one last time. To that man's credit, Dr. Dudley had tried everything he could. Nonetheless, Julian had almost strangled the kindly doctor when he at last said aloud what Julian already knew deep in his soul.

Nothing could save Valerie.

It was only a matter of time.

Except that Julian refused to accept it, railing violently at anyone who dared try to console him. So Dr. Dudley had reluctantly sent to Bath for a colleague who had experimented with some promising new medicinal combinations. Dr. Moore came at once, examined a delirious Valerie, then very clearly warned Julian that his new elixir was highly experimental and perhaps even deadly. But there had been no other option—both doctors agreed she surely would die without it.

Julian ordered she be given the elixir. He had done what was best for her.

But the poor girl reacted badly to the potion, and was too frail to withstand the ravages of the prolonged fever. He did not leave her side, even when exhaustion pushed him to the brink of collapse, but within days, she slipped quietly into eternal sleep while he held her in his arms and begged her to live.

The pain, dull astonishment, and fury with God had almost destroyed him. He had loved his sister with all his heart and could not bear to think he had helped to kill her, had broken his vow to his father to keep her safe and well.

His mount crashed through a grove of trees, but heedless of the low-hanging branches that slashed at his arms and legs, Julian drove the horse forward.

He had loved Phillip, too, like a brother. Phillip, who had been his constant companion since they were lads, inseparable into adulthood. Smaller than the other Rogues, Phillip had always been something of a ruffian, always pushing the very boundaries of propriety and societal acceptance. Julian had long thought his behavior was a sort of unconscious effort to make up for the lack of physical stature. But after Valerie's death, he began to view Phillip's conduct with increasing apprehension. It seemed *too* ribald, even for Phillip. Nothing seemed to satisfy him; not copious amounts of whiskey, not gaming, not his pick of Madame Farantino's women—even two of them at once.

The horse burst through the tree line and into an open meadow, and Julian bent low over the steed's neck, urging him faster.

He had tried to save Phillip, too. At first, he had offered enough money to clear the enormous debts in exchange for Phillip's sobriety, if only for a time. Anything would have been an improvement. But Phillip had scoffed at his offer, thanked him for his needless pity with not a little sarcasm, then heatedly swore that if Julian ever called his character into question again, he would gladly shoot him without a single thought.

Having throughly wounded Phillip's pride, Julian could do nothing but keep a silent vigil, choosing to accompany his friend on lewd excursions that repulsed him, convinced that if he was with Phillip, he could at least keep him from harm.

And then came Claudia.

Julian slowed the roan, released his grip of the reins and straightened, rubbing the nape of his neck to erase the familiar despair that was suddenly raging through him.

Claudia Whitney had walked into that ballroom and had turned everything upside down. He had known, of course, that Phillip had set his blurred sights on her. It had actually amused him until that night, until he saw her again for the first time since Valerie's funeral. Nothing was ever the same again. Oh, he continued to accompany Phillip along his path of debauchery, and on the rare occasions Phillip was sober, he even attempted to persuade him to change his conduct—but not nearly enough or as strongly as he should have. No, no, no, not enough at all, and he and the Lord above knew very well why he had not. Because, thank you, he was hopelessly besotted with the Demon's Spawn.

He had loved Phillip, truly loved him like his very own brother . . . but Claudia was right. He had killed him; at least helped his death along.

Rather a dangerous pattern you have established, old boy. A wild shout of laughter tore from Julian's throat, reverberating against the low gray sky.

Was there ever a time you thought you might simply perish without her? For two years, he had adored her from a distance, thinking he might simply perish every time he saw her. Then he had seen her at Château la Claire and something deep inside had broken free, rising like Lazarus from the ashes of his soul. It was plain,

Julian thought hopelessly, that he had thought he might simply perish without her for a very long time. And what had he done? Ruined her.

Ah yes, Julian, know ye in his death the quality of love . . .

He knew it. He knew it like an arrow that pierced his heart and twisted about, up and down and around, torturing him unto death.

That arrow would not harm Sophie. God save him, if there was one thing he *must* do right, it was Sophie. That wretched girl needed him, whether she realized it or not, and he would gladly commend himself to hell if he could not keep her from harm.

Seventeen

CLAUDIA FOUND IT impossible to eat or sleep after Julian had dragged Sophie away. Alone in the dining room the following evening, she frowned at the thick slice of cake the footman Robert had served her, from which she had removed all the raisins and arranged them into a frowning face—with spectacles—on the edge of her plate.

She toyed with the notion of summoning Ann and Eugenie to tell them what Julian had done, but thought better of it. Such news was best delivered by The Rake himself. But *banishment?* It was so primitive! Sarah Cafferty had been banished to Cornwall amidst a highly publicized scandal—it was an abominable practice, demeaning to women everywhere. And as hard as she tried, Claudia just could not reconcile the man who had coldly forced Sophie into that chaise with the man whose eyes had betrayed the ravages of a loss so deep it pained him still.

Their argument yesterday had enlightened her to a side of Julian she had never seen before, and damn him if it wasn't a vulnerable side. Claudia never would have believed that Julian Dane had a vulnerable bone in his body, not in a thousand years.

She suddenly dropped her fork and buried her face in her hands, miserably confused. There she was, about to feel sympathy for a tyrant again. What difference did it make that he had been hurt by one of his many paramours? It certainly didn't give him the right to whisk Sophie away like a mere piece of property. Nor did it excuse the fact that he obviously placed Sophie's happiness lower than propriety. It was so very arrogant of him to believe that some people were better than others by virtue of their birth or gender!

Claudia lifted her head and pushed the plate aside, her gaze fixing on the candelabrum in the center of the table. Last night, she had lain in bed trying to make sense of a situation that seemed increasingly complex. As the days passed, she was having a harder and harder time reconciling the arrogant, superior, vainglorious man with the one who showed streaks of kindness. It was impossible to ignore the nights that he and Arthur Christian left together, undoubtedly bound for Madame Farantino's. It was impossible to believe *that* man was the same man who would gently rub her back when her courses pained her, or send bouquets of fresh hothouse flowers to her teas when the other husbands derided their wives for attending, or get down on his hands and knees to frolic with Jeannine and Dierdre.

Yet he was the same man who seemed uninterested in her cause, with the exception of having made a list of names he would persuade to fulfill their pledge. Sometimes she felt as if he was managing her like one of his holdings, leaving her unchecked, unfettered, as long as she did not suddenly twist off wildly in a direction he did not expect.

But there *was* evidence of a softer, unguarded side of him she could not deny, as the argument yesterday had so poignantly pointed up to her. Nor could she deny that the kindness and patience he showed Eugenie's daughters often made her ache with a longing for something more between them, a distant hope that perhaps *they* might produce children one day. And what of Tinley? How could she ignore the fact that the doddering old man could scarcely lift a feather duster anymore, yet Julian ignored his senility, sparing the man's pride and allowing him to feel needed?

All right, but how, then, could he ignore Sophie's heartache, decide what she should feel and whom she should feel it for? Sophie's devastation meant nothing to him, and Claudia could not bear that. *I am honor bound as your friend to tell you that Phillip is not the sort of man for you.*

No! She did not want to relive that, not again, but Mother of God, how could she not? How could she ignore his callousness, once to her and now to Sophie, as if they were inanimate objects, incapable of thinking or feeling for themselves?

"Madam? Shall I remove the cake?"

With a thin smile, Claudia responded politely, "Please, Robert. And pour a spot of port, would you?"

Robert blinked, hesitated for a fraction of a second, but quickly recovered and returned with the port a few moments later. Claudia thanked him, sliding her gaze to the long green velvet drapes as she sipped the heavy wine. *Banished.*

The more she dwelled on it, the more incensed she became.

His ghosts and Sophie's sobs chased Julian all the way back to London, reverberating in his head until he was quite sure he was deaf.

Surely there was *something* he could do short of locking her away at Kettering Hall, although he was damned if he could think of what. By the time he reached the outskirts of London, he was physically and mentally numb, propelled forward by the simple but overpowering desire to see Claudia's brilliant smile, perhaps even feel her arms around him. An insane hope, he knew, particularly after their argument, yet part of him stubbornly hoped that she had come to see his reasoning.

At St. James Square, he handed the reins of his mount to a young groom and wearily dragged himself into the foyer. Handing his leather gloves to Tinley, he said, "Have a bath drawn at once and inform Lady Kettering I have returned. I should like it very much if she would join me for supper."

"Might like it very well, my lord, but she's already dining," Tinley casually informed him, and hobbled off. A footman stepped forward to receive his cloak.

Julian sliced an impatient look across the footman. "See to it that he at least remembers the bath, would you?" he asked tersely, and strode across the foyer, headed for the dining room, trying hard to crush the adolescent excitement the mere mention of her name always sparked in him.

That he missed Claudia so badly in the space of twenty-four hours was unnerving as hell, made him feel silly and weak and quite awkward in his skin. Even as a young lad, he'd never been so bloody infatuated with anyone. It outraged him that his body seemed to think she was the only cure to the infernal rash in his heart. Yet when he turned the corner and neared the dining room, he had to force himself to walk and not sprint to her side.

A footman attending the dining room door opened it for him; as he came across the threshold, a startled Claudia came hastily to her feet, clutching a linen napkin. She wore a satin gown fitted tightly to her, the color of a cloudless blue sky trimmed in white. Around her slender neck was a triple strand of pearls, matching the large tear-drop pearls that dangled from her earlobes. Her hair had been piled carelessly on top of her head; little wisps of curls draped her neck.

Arrested, Julian paused, staring at one long curl that spiraled down to her shoulder. It amazed him that his mind's eye never seemed to capture her true beauty. "You look . . . lovely," he remarked, well aware that the words hardly did her justice.

One delicate hand came up and fidgeted with a tear-drop earring. "Thank you. Did you just return? I thought you would remain at Kettering Hall for a time," she said quietly.

"I thought it best that I leave at once."

Her hand stilled and she looked at him. "You are very good at doing what you think is best, aren't you?"

The rash flared in his stomach; all at once he felt a fool. What exactly had he thought would happen? That Claudia would rush into his open arms, as anxious to see him as he was her? *The hell she would.* The woman despised him; it hardly mattered to her that he had just endured one of the worst days of his life, and he felt the pain of raw anger rumble through him. "You have already made your opinion known to me. I see no reason to go over it again," he said tightly.

She cocked her head to one side as if to assess just how beastly he was, and folded her arms defensively across her middle. "Yes, well, you have made it quite clear that my opinion is so meaningless to you that you will not even do me the courtesy of listening."

God in heaven, not this, not now! He had only wanted to look at her, just hold her, not argue! *Not speak.* "Your opinion," he drawled, sauntering to the table, "is inconsequential. I have made my decision, and that is the end of it."

"No," she said simply.

"No?" he echoed, incredulously.

"I will not be dismissed, Julian—"

"And I will not be pushed into discussing this further—"

"I shan't leave this room until I have said what I must, whether you want to hear it or not! It is cruel of you to treat Sophie so abominably! She *loves* Sir William, yet you would apparently rather see her miserable before you would allow her to follow her heart!"

God grant him patience. "Claudia," he began, "Stanwood is—"

"A baronet!" she exclaimed hotly. "But that's not good enough for *you,* not with your ridiculous ideas of who is proper for whom! Can't you see that you are playing God with people's lives? This is *exactly* the same as what you did to me, do you even understand that?"

What he had done to her? Confusion clouded Julian's

brain for a moment—he knew very well what he had done to her, he had *ruined* her for chrissakes, but for the life of him, he could not understand how that related to Sophie. "Pardon?" he asked stupidly.

Claudia made a sound of exasperation. "You tried to banish me, too, in a way. You never thought I was good enough for Phillip, which is why you strove to keep him from me. When that didn't work, you took it upon yourself to try to convince me that I was not good enough for him, hoping that I might slip away! As *if* . . ." she choked on a strangled cry and tightened her arms about her. "As if it was *any* consequence to you at all! But he was your friend, and apparently you would rather he had courted Madame Farantino than me! You never thought I was good enough for him, you don't think Stanwood is good enough for Sophie, and you don't care *who* you hurt! But Sophie loves Stanwood, just as I loved Phillip!"

Her words stabbed clean through his heart like a knife, and he suddenly could not seem to catch his breath. It was impossible . . . *impossible* that she could have misinterpreted his warning so badly! He opened his mouth, but he was too stunned to think, much less speak. *She had loved Phillip . . .*

"No! No, no. Let us be *completely* honest," she continued, almost hysterically, and behind her, the two footmen exchanged uneasy glances. "You never thought I was good enough for *you!* From the time I was a little girl, you made that *very* clear, but I was just a *girl,* Julian, barely old enough to know what I was doing! Yet you let me know then that I was somehow inferior, not quite up to your standards, and you *still* do! You think it perfectly all right to have your paramours, but you've no idea how *painful* it is," she said, her voice breaking, "so painful that when Sophie told me you objected to Stanwood because of his *rank,* I urged her, unequivocally, to follow her heart at all costs and *defy* your blasted convention—"

Fury exploded hot inside of him. "You did *what?*" he roared, unnoticing of the footmen slipping out of the room.

The sound of his voice shook Claudia from her tirade;

her eyes widened. "I . . . I told her to follow her heart, not some silly rule about who is good enough for whom," she said with much less confidence.

He would strangle her. In the morning, the authorities would find the body of his wife with those words strangled from her lips. Julian leaned over, grasped the edge of the table tightly as he fought to keep his rage in check. The ignorant chit had no idea what she had done, no concept of the peril she had put Sophie in! "William Stanwood," he said, struggling to keep his voice even, "does not love Sophie. He is a profligate. He wants nothing more than her goddam fortune. His debts are staggering and it is a bloody miracle he has not as yet landed in debtors' prison. His solicitor has inquired into every one of my accounts in an effort to ascertain the exact sum of Sophie's dowry and the annuity our father left her." He lifted his gaze and glared at her. "And furthermore, *wife,* it is widely known among the men of the *ton* that Stanwood delights in beating the whores he lies with, apparently deriving some sort of sick satisfaction from it!"

Color rapidly drained from Claudia's face. She moved awkwardly forward, catching herself on the back of a dining chair. "W-what?" she whispered hoarsely. "Sophie said—"

"Oh, for God's sake, Claudia! Sophie would have said anything! She is terribly unsure of herself and quite certain she is in love with that degenerate!"

With a blink of her eyes, Julian could see the truth sink in. "Oh no. Oh *no*—"

"Lord *God,* what a tremendous mistake I made in trusting you and Sophie!" he continued hotly. "I had no idea that she was sneaking around behind my back, much *less* that my wife knew of it and condoned it! Had you told me, I surely would have given you every vile reason to be alarmed! But as it was, I found no reason to repeat such obscene things to the women I would protect!" he fairly shouted.

"My God," she whispered, her eyes roaming wildly

about the room. "Oh my *God!* I am so sorry, Julian. I didn't know—"

"That's rather the problem, isn't it, Claudia?" he spat contemptuously. "You are so caught up in your dema-goguery that you are blind to the truth—blind to *everything!* The walls you have erected prevent us from speaking about anything of import! I confess I am quite at a loss as to how to bring them down, and I daresay I am sick to death of trying!"

She said nothing; just bit her lip and lowered her gaze.

It was the same as always; she closed herself off to him, the doors between them slamming shut and locking. His discomfort was suddenly suffocating. He jerked around, wanting her gone from his sight. "Leave me," he said curtly, and stalked to the sideboard, prepared to drink every drop of liquor he could find.

"Julian, I—"

"Go!" he bellowed, and heard the rustle of her satin skirts, her ragged breathing as she moved to the door.

"Claudia!" he said sharply. He glanced over his shoulder, watched her head bow as if she prayed for strength before she turned to face him.

"One more thing." *God, Kettering, don't do this.* He was a fool, a goddamned fool, he thought as he glared at her stricken face, on the verge of laying his heart bare to her. "You have misjudged me from the beginning. That night I called on you before Phillip died . . ."—he saw the hurt flash in her eyes—"I did not mean to imply that you were not good enough for Phillip. I meant to convey that *he* was not good enough for *you*."

She gasped in disbelief, her hand fluttering to her throat.

"When the rumors began to circulate that he meant to offer for you, I could not bear to think that *you,* of all people, the one bright light in the whole bloody *ton,* would innocently marry a drunkard facing ruin. I could not bear to ever see you unhappy, and frankly, I could not bear to see another man have you. If you intend to crucify me all our days, at least do it for the right reason." He paused, summoning every ounce of his courage. "I . . . I *loved* you. I loved you from the moment I saw you at the Wilmington Ball and every moment of these last two years. There never were any paramours, Claudia. There never was anyone but you."

Her other hand covered the one at her throat, and Julian wondered if she meant to be ill. Whatever she thought, he stopped there, acutely aware that she stared at him as if he had lost his bloody mind. Perhaps he had, at long last. His little confession now seemed absurdly insipid, and embarrassed, he turned back to the sideboard. "There is nothing more, no more startling revelations," he said sarcastically. "You've nothing to fear from me. I am quite recovered from it now."

"*Julian . . .*"

The soft whisper of his name sounded exactly as he had heard it in so many dreams. But it was too late. "*Leave me!*" he said roughly, and closed his eyes. After what seemed like minutes, he heard the door shut softly. He picked up the bottle of wine and walked unsteadily to the table, falling heavily into a chair. And there he remained for several hours, attempting to drown the image of her that bobbed about in his mind's eye.

If Claudia had had a bottle of wine at her disposal, she, too, would have attempted to drown herself. As it was, she was pacing her rooms wildly, unable to believe— to *accept*—how very wrong she might have been. Was she truly such a *fool?* She pressed her fists against her temples, trying to stave off the piercing headache that descended on her the moment she left the dining room.

How could she possibly have been so bloody stupid? Disgust filled her—disgust with herself, for so boldly advising Sophie to defy him without fully knowing the facts, even after Julian had tried to tell her. She had let her indignation guide her and was as ashamed as she was mortified—oh, *Lord,* the note she had slipped into

Sophie's valise, urging her to follow love! Claudia choked on a sob, sickened by her impetuosity.

But what truly made her heart ache was that she had, apparently, misinterpreted his call two long years ago.

So convinced she knew his character, she had twisted his words around, inventing her own story to fit what she believed of him. He had meant to help her. But no, she could not see that then, would not listen to a Rake who made her heart soar with longing. She had believed the worst of him for two years more, wanting to blame him for Phillip's death. It had been easier that way, easier to believe Julian had led Phillip to his demise than to believe the worst of Phillip.

But she had known.

She could no longer deny that she had known of Phillip's increasing debilitation, or that he was losing sight of himself and his position in society. She had known that behind the smiles he reserved for her, the gifts he gave her, the whispers of steadfast esteem, something wasn't quite right. And she had stubbornly insisted it was Julian's fault.

It was easy to blame Julian for everything. His reprimand for a girl's foolish kiss, his slight at the wedding ball seven years ago—what on earth had made her think a man of his stature would have been infatuated with a seventeen-year-old girl? But it was a fantasy she had built, one she had carried forward, allowing it to color everything around her. Her adolescent crush and subsequent hurt had influenced her long after it should have. How it mortified her now to know she had been so shallow as to judge him on the basis of those meaningless, innocent encounters! It was exactly the sort of thing she fought every day—the blind acceptance of who and what women are supposed to be, based on outdated, stereotypical, uninformed thinking.

She paused in her pacing to press the heel of her hands into her eyes. She had never been more contemptible than she was at this moment . . . *and he had loved her!* The little things Julian had done over the last weeks, things that had seemed meaningless, but spoke volumes, now assailed her. The way he touched her wrist, her temple, her waist. The way he possessively took his hand in hers when they attended Sunday services. His constant smile, his indulgence of her every wish. *When the sun comes up I think of you, when it sets I think of you, and every moment in between, it seems.*

With an anguished cry, Claudia squeezed her eyes tightly shut and felt the hot tears slide from the corners of her eyes. She had deigned him indifferent when he had shown tolerance of an impossible situation, of her thrashing about, of trying to find her own way in this marriage. He had given her the freedom to do it her way, deferring to her wishes.

Why was everything so bloody *complicated?*

She dropped her hands, stared blindly into space. Was it true? Had she really been so ridiculous? Had he never been unfaithful? She was not a wife to him, not really. Even on those increasingly rare occasions he would come to her bed, she turned her heart away from him, allowing him her body, but not her soul. Cringing, Claudia sank onto a chair feeling sick with regret. She had done everything she could to push him away, to shove him into some corner. How could she blame him for seeking his satisfaction elsewhere? The most absurd thing of all was that she *wanted* to share his bed! Mother of God, how she wanted to share his bed . . . but pride, her foolish, useless pride, had gotten in her way.

A bitter laugh lodged in Claudia's throat—the irony of it was that she thought she was being so strong, so independent, striking a victory for women everywhere when all she had done was shove a marriage already teetering to the brink of collapse.

How exactly did she repair the awful rift between them now?

She wasn't confident at all that it *could* be repaired.

She slept fitfully as doubts about everything she had ever known grew to monstrous proportions. It was almost noon before she descended to the breakfast room. Tinley informed her that Julian had left very early, shortly after dawn. "Did he say where he was going?" she asked.

Tinley pondered that. "Don't believe so, ma'am," he said, and a footman carefully shook his head behind Tinley to confirm it.

After what she had done to him and Sophie, he undoubtedly wanted to go as far away from her as he could get, had probably sought refuge among the Rogues. Which was why she was surprised to see Arthur Christian shortly after the luncheon hour.

Tinley brought him into the sunroom where she was, and Claudia could tell from the expression on his face that he had been expecting Julian. She paused in the course of her correspondence and rose to greet him. "Arthur."

"Claudia, how splendid to find you well. I, ah . . . is Julian about?"

She shook her head. "I'm afraid he has gone out," she said with an apologetic smile. "I rather think we'll have to resort to drawing pictures for Tinley, so that he'll know precisely who among us is about and who is not."

Arthur chuckled. "Yes, well, I shouldn't want to bother you. I'll just leave a card—"

"Umm . . . Arthur?" she said hastily, "might I ask you something?"

"Of course!"

Claudia blanched, appalled at what she thought to ask. No, no, she couldn't ask a man *that*.

"Something on your mind?"

"I beg your pardon, never mind," she said, and quickly resumed her seat, busying herself with her letters.

Regarding her curiously, Arthur walked farther into the room. "Go on, I won't laugh," he promised her, and flashed a charming smile.

Well then, it was now or never, because she could never find the courage again. She had to ask—she had to know if there was any hope of sorting it all out. Unable to look Arthur in the eye, she shuffled her papers, sucked in her breath, and blurted, "When . . . when you and Julian go out at night, where do you go?" *There. It was out.*

Arthur made a small sound of surprise. The papers stilled in her hand and she unthinkingly closed her eyes, afraid of what he might say. He cleared his throat. "I . . . we typically visit a club. White's, usually. The Tam O'Shanter, although we have not enjoyed it so much since Phillip . . . that is to say, we prefer White's."

Slowly, she opened her eyes and stared straight ahead. "Just the club? Nothing more?"

Another hesitation. "What exactly are you asking?"

"Do you go to Madame Farantino's?" she blurted, wincing.

Arthur made a choking sound. "Dear God, Claudia, that is hardly the sort of thing—"

She swung her gaze to him. "Please, Arthur," she implored him. "I . . . I really must know."

That seemed to take him aback. He stared at her for a moment, rubbing his jaw between finger and thumb. "Julian has not been inside the establishment in more months than I can remember," he said flatly.

The floor felt as if it was sinking beneath her. "Is there . . . is there any place else?" she asked anxiously.

Arthur frowned. "Claudia, listen to me. Julian Dane is so hopelessly besotted with his wife that he hasn't so much as glanced at a barmaid. There is only you."

There never were any paramours, Claudia. There never was anyone but you.

Her heart fluttered oddly in her chest, and she slumped against the chair, staring blindly at the correspondence. *How badly she had misjudged him!*

"I beg your pardon, I thought that would please you," Arthur said coolly.

"Oh, but it does," she murmured. "You've no idea."

"Yes. Well, then. If you would be so kind as to tell the chap I've been round, I would greatly appreciate it," he said, and quickly quit the room.

Claudia didn't hear him—the silent scream of her deep regret was roaring too loudly in her ears.

Eighteen

SOPHIE WAS RUNNING AWAY—just as soon as she figured out where she was going and how to escape Miss Brillhart.

Miserable, she sat in a window seat of the main drawing room on the ground floor, her forehead pressed against the cool glass. It was a dreary day, raining since the early morning hours, perfectly befitting of her mood. It had been three days since Julian abandoned her here, three days without a word.

Sophie glanced at the crumpled note Claudia had slipped into her valise. She opened it and read it once more.

> *Never despair! Follow your heart, no matter how difficult it may seem, and love will prevail.*
>
> *Always, C.*

How could she help but despair? William was no doubt wondering what had happened to her, and dear heavens, she had not seen him in three whole days! She missed him terribly—if she didn't return to London soon, he might forget all about her. Somehow, someway, she had to get to London before that happened.

But how? She couldn't ride alone—she had never been terribly good with a horse, and she was certain the mount must be changed along the way. How on earth would she accomplish *that?* There was the chaise. Julian had left it, and the stable master said someone would come for it in a day or two. She had considered the idea of hiding inside—but surely someone would notice her before they reached London and would take her to Julian straightaway.

There *had* to be a way!

A movement caught her eye as she sat brooding; in the distance was a lone horseman, riding hard up the oak-lined drive. As he drew closer, Sophie's heart started—*it was William!* He had come for her! Her heart fluttered wildly in her chest, and her spirits suddenly soaring, she flung herself from the window seat, burst from the drawing room, and ran down the corridor to the front entry, reaching the massive oak doors well before the footman. She rushed eagerly onto the circle of marble that marked the mansion's entry and watched the rider approach.

He came to an abrupt halt, threw himself off the mount, and stalked toward her, his face grim.

"William!" she cried.

He grabbed her around the waist and hauled her into his chest, crushing her mouth beneath his in a bruising welcome. Oblivious to the servants gathering in the door behind them, Sophie squealed with delight when he finally released her.

William scowled at her. "Why did you not send a note? I've been sick with worry! I had to learn what had happened to you from that fool Tinley!"

Sophie's grin broadened. "Oh, William, I *would* have, but I could not! Julian . . . he *saw* us, and he was so very angry. He forced me to come here right away and before I could send word." She smiled up at him, noticed the cut on his lip, and gingerly touched a finger to it. "What happened?"

He pushed her hand away; his gaze shifted over her shoulder. "Who is here with you?"

"No one. Miss Brillhart, the housekeeper. She was our governess—"

"Where is she?" he interrupted.

"I . . . I don't know—"

William pierced her with a dark look as he clasped her shoulder and gave her a little shake. "Sophie, *think!* I must speak with you—take me somewhere we can be private."

Of course! Sophie glanced nervously over her shoulder; the footmen were eyeing William curiously. Two parlor maids behind them were whispering furiously, and one cast a disapproving look at William. "This way," she muttered, and clutching his hand, ran around the side of the house to a door that led into a small sunroom at the end of the east wing.

Once inside, Sophie started for the door leading to the main corridor, but William grabbed her from behind and jerked her into his chest, almost knocking the breath from her as he nuzzled her neck. "You know what he has done, don't you? He has announced to the world that he will not sanction your happiness. He has humiliated us, Sophie, in front of all of England," he muttered, and bit her earlobe. Sophie shrieked softly, but William seemed not to hear her.

"There is only one thing left for us to do, only one way for us to be together," he said against her skin. His breath excited her; she leaned her head against his shoulder, her eyes closed, exposing more of her flesh to him. "You know what we must do, don't you, Sophie?"

"Mmm. . . . what?"

William suddenly turned her around to face him. "I've missed you terribly," he said, and thrust his hips forward. Sophie gasped with surprise and titillation. William caught the back of her head, covered her mouth with his and devoured her hungrily. Sophie felt herself melting into a molten pool of desire.

Without warning, he abruptly lifted his head, leaving her dizzy. "I can't live without you, my sweet, for I swear I'll perish! There is only one way for us," he murmured between a rain of kisses to her face. "You know what it is." When she didn't immediately respond, his fingers curled painfully into her shoulder. "Don't disappoint me,

Sophie, not after I have ridden like a madman to fetch you. You know what we must do!"

"But . . . but I *don't*," she whispered hoarsely.

William suddenly let go of her. "*Think,* Sophie! Kettering will never give his consent . . . but *you* can."

"*Me?*" she squeaked.

"You'll be one and twenty shortly. . . ."

Her heart climbed to her throat. "William, I *can't,* not without—"

"I thought you loved me," he said flatly, and shaking his head, turned away. "You lied to me."

"No! No, William, I *do* love you!" she said desperately. "But I cannot defy Julian in such a way!"

"I see. You would defy *me,* but not him? I mean nothing to you!"

"Please don't say that," she cried, feeling suddenly weak with confusion and frustration. "I love you, William! But I don't know what to do!"

He whirled around, grabbed her arm. "Come to Gretna Green with me. Now. Right away. We don't *need* his permission! You are of age; if you sign this," he said, pulling a folded paper from his coat, "there is nothing he can do! If you love me, Sophie, you will marry me now. I swear to God he will come to accept it much quicker if the deed is already done!"

Stunned, she stared at the papers he held. It was enticing and exciting to think she could marry William now, without delay. Yet something in her warned that to do so—to *elope*—would be disastrous. Julian would kill her. "I . . . I don't know," she said uncertainly.

In a flurry of black, William was suddenly on his knees before her, his hands clutching the side of her skirts as he pressed his face into her gown. "*Please,* Sophie! I love you! I cannot live without you, don't you understand? I shall do something desperate, I swear to God I shall if I am forced to live without you even one more day!"

Sophie's heart took wing of her senses. Tears slipped from her eyes as she bent over his head. "Oh, *William,*" she sobbed. "Yes, yes, I will do it!"

"Hurry, love," he urged her, coming to his feet. "Don't speak to anyone. Just run and gather a few things. Be *quick*. If they know what you are about, they will try and stop you. I will wait for you outside. *Hurry!*"

He shoved her forward.

Sophie slipped into the corridor, almost colliding with Miss Brillhart. The housekeeper was deathly pale. "Lady Sophie? Who is the gentleman caller?" she asked, looking anxiously at the door Sophie had just come through.

"Um . . . an old friend. Please excuse me, I've a terrible headache," she lied, and pushed past, unable to look her old governess in the eye.

"Lady Sophie!" Miss Brillhart called after her, but Sophie was already sprinting down the corridor. In her rooms, she grabbed a small bag and stuffed two gowns into it, a cotton night shift, and two pairs of drawers. Frantic, she glanced around the room. *What did one take when one eloped?* There was no time for it! Miss Brillhart appeared in the doorway, her chest heaving with the exertion of having run up two flights of stairs. "My lady, please!" she rasped. "What are you doing?"

Wild with excitement, Sophie shoved Miss Brillhart aside and ran. In the foyer, she paused only long enough to grab a cloak and throw it about her shoulders.

"My lady!" Miss Brillhart shrieked.

With a start, Sophie whirled around, clutching her valise in both hands.

Flanked by two footmen, Miss Brillhart held her hands out to Sophie. "My lady, *think* of what you are doing!" she begged, taking one tentative step. "Think of the shame you will bring to your brother's good name! You can't do this!"

"I *can* do this!" Sophie shouted, feeling strangely victorious. "I will follow my heart and *not* his convention! Love will prevail, Miss Brillhart!" The housekeeper made a sudden move, and in a moment of terror, Sophie threw the valise at her as she whirled and dashed through the door. William was mounted and waiting for her; he yanked her up behind him and sent the horse galloping down the drive. Clinging tightly to him, Sophie glanced over her shoulder to see a handful of bewildered servants and a very pale Miss Brillhart watching them flee.

In London, the rash was festering in Julian, slowly destroying him. He stared blindly at the document in front of him, unable to read it. Claudia had rent him in two, cruelly dividing him between betrayal and longing. Part of him hated her for misjudging him so completely and without cause. Another part despised her for making him mad with desire every time he looked at her. But there wasn't any part of him that could forget what she had done to Sophie—it was the final blow to his battered heart.

He had sworn to his dying father that he would keep the girls safe, and having failed miserably with Valerie, he'd be damned if he would fail with Sophie. Claudia had betrayed him in the most heinous way imaginable by trespassing onto ground she had no right to enter. Her meddling had forced him to take drastic measures he had not wanted to take, and for all he knew, thanks to her, Sophie's reputation was already in tatters.

It was not something he could easily forgive.

This marriage, he thought bitterly, had come to an inevitable end. It was only a question of how.

When Tinley showed a bedraggled footman from Kettering Hall into his library, Julian could see that he had ridden like a desperate man and immediately expected the worst—she was dead, just like Valerie and Phillip. Somehow, he forced himself to take the note from the footman. Somehow, he calmly retrieved his spectacles from his coat pocket, and carefully placed them on the bridge of his nose before he opened the note. A crumpled piece of paper fluttered to the floor but he ignored it, scanning Miss Brillhart's neat handwriting. He did not hear Claudia come in, heard nothing but the rush of blood in his head.

She might as well be dead.

He stooped to pick up the piece of paper that had fallen and recognized Claudia's handwriting.

"Dear God, what is it?"

Slowly, Julian lifted his head and turned to look at her angelic face. The note was the thing that would at last drive him into the den of madness, consume his soul . . . break his heart. It was far worse than he could have imagined, the absolute living death of his sweet, sweet Sophie. Never, not once, had he believed she would do this.

He extended his arm, both of the damning notes in his hand. Claudia's eyes, shimmering with fear, flicked to the notes, then back to him. When he made no move, she slowly came forward and took the papers from him. Impassive, he watched her read them, watched her hand press against her abdomen as she looked at the note penned in her own hand, and the other—still clutching Miss Brillhart's note—cover her mouth and her silent scream.

He turned away and strolled to the window, looked out over St. James Square. He had failed Sophie, miserably and irrevocably. By law, she probably already belonged to Stanwood, and there was nothing he could do for her. *Nothing.* Never in his life had he felt so bloody powerless or alone. And while he stood gazing thoughtfully out the window, the discomfort quietly began to choke the life from him. *Let it.*

It was Claudia's sobs that filtered through his consciousness; he turned to look at her standing in the middle of the room, crying silently into her hand. And he calmly walked out of the library, away from the sound of her guilt.

Nineteen

JULIAN WENT IN search of Sophie, ignoring Victor and Louis's advice against it and their warnings that it was too late. He returned to London more than a week after he left, arriving at sunset. The family was waiting for him, gathered in the gold salon as they had done every night since receiving the news of Sophie's elopement. Claudia hardly noticed them—she had been too consumed with guilt and frantic with worry for Julian. Never had she seen a man look so haunted or despondent as he had when he left.

When the footman opened the door to the salon to give Julian entry, everyone came anxiously to their feet. Only Tinley seemed not to notice, doing something at the sideboard that obviously fascinated him far more than his master's arrival. Behind them all, Claudia rose slowly from her seat at the writing table.

Julian strolled into the room, loosening his neckcloth. His gaze swept over them all, passing her as if she did not exist. His nieces, oblivious to the tension in the room, jumped from the settee and rushed forward to greet him.

"Jeannine, my love, what a beautiful frock!" he exclaimed, picking her up to place a kiss on her cheek.

"Mine is new, too!" complained Dierdre.

"And how terribly elegant you look!" he said, as if he had just come down for supper, and lifted Dierdre for a kiss. He put the girl down, absently ran his hand over the crowns of their heads. "I did not find her," he announced flatly, and looked up at his sisters. Claudia's heart sank; wordlessly, she lowered herself onto her chair and looked to the window. *God,* how the guilt gnawed at her.

"Julian," Louis said quietly. "Sophie is in London. Stanwood sent word, requesting an audience on the morrow."

A glimmer of hope scudded across Julian's rugged face. "They are in London? Are they—"

"Oui," Louis quickly answered, knowing full well what he was about to ask.

For a moment, Julian looked almost nauseated, but quickly turned away from them. "Then it is over. There is nothing we can do."

"No, nothing," Victor muttered.

He moved to the sideboard, his shoulders stooped with fatigue as if he carried some enormous burden. "A whiskey, Tinley," he said tightly, "and a strong one at that." He glanced over his shoulder at Louis. "Did he say *where* in London?" he asked, his voice biting.

"Non, rien."

"Of course not," he muttered angrily. "The bastard knows too well that I would come for him if only I knew *where!"* His jaw clenched, and he jerked his head toward Tinley, who had made no move to pour him a drink. "A bloody *whiskey,* Tinley! Can't your addled brain comprehend even that?" he bellowed.

Claudia gasped softly; the girls stopped fidgeting and looked at their uncle in horror. *"Julian!"* Eugenie whispered anxiously, but Tinley merely looked at him. "It can, my lord," he said indifferently, and reached for the decanter.

"My apologies, old chap," Julian muttered, and stalked away from the sideboard, inadvertently catching Claudia's gaze. His black eyes suddenly riveted on her, the hatred in them boring a hole right through her. He abruptly looked away, falling gracelessly into an armchair, his legs sprawled in front of him. Tinley appeared at his side, offering the whiskey on a small silver tray. Julian took the little glass and tossed the contents down his throat. "Again," he said hoarsely, handing the glass to Tinley.

As the butler shuffled away, Julian motioned for them all to be seated. "I looked everywhere, in every village between Kettering and Scotland, it seems."

"Oh, Julian," said Eugenie, "you mustn't blame yourself. It was Sophie's doing."

He sliced an impatient glance across his sister before shifting his gaze to Claudia. "I don't blame myself," he said meaningfully.

Oh no, he blamed her, and she deserved his disdain.

"We had no idea she was so headstrong—she was always so very shy!" Ann exclaimed helplessly.

"She is not headstrong, she lacks confidence. When one lacks confidence, one is easy to exploit," Julian corrected her.

"What will you do?" Louis asked.

Julian snorted, rubbed the back of his neck. "What the hell *can* I do? Once she took her vows and signed the betrothal papers, she became his. I rather doubt an annulment can be obtained now"—he paused to bestow an impatient frown on Eugenie for her demure gasp—"I know of no other course open to me."

"Divorce," Claudia mumbled, and blanched, shocked that she had actually said it aloud.

Eugenie closed her eyes; Ann sucked in a sharp breath and whipped around to her. "Absolutely *not!*" she exclaimed heatedly. "She is already ruined by this scandal, and we cannot allow the rest of us to be ruined along with her! Divorce is out of the question!"

"Yes, out of the question," Eugenie echoed, rubbing her fingers into her temples. "It would scandalize the Kettering name across all of Britain! Besides, Sophie has no grounds for it. She must prove cruelty or insanity or something equally ridiculous."

Frustrated, Claudia looked to Julian. He glared at her as he took the second whiskey Tinley brought and nodded the butler's dismissal.

"You can refuse to dower her," Victor suggested.

Julian nodded. "I will not dower her. But as you and Louis know, Victor, my father's will provides the girls an annuity. Sophie's annuity begins on her twenty-first birthday. In a matter of days, Stanwood will have it. And I am loath to fight it, even if I could. The scoundrel is penniless, and that annuity is the only means he will have of providing for her."

A silence descended over the room, save for the two little girls squirming restlessly on the settee. Louis stood up. "Then there is no more to be said today. Come, *chérie*, we take our leave," he said, gesturing to Eugenie. "We shall meet this blackguard on the morrow."

Eugenie rose obediently, ushering her daughters along ahead of her. Ann and Victor followed suit. Julian made no move to stop them. Eugenie paused to place her hand on his shoulder. "I am so sorry, Julian, but you must know that you couldn't have done anything to prevent this from happening."

He shrugged indifferently and sipped at his whiskey. Claudia's heart went out to him—he looked so tired, so ill. She could almost feel his agony emanating from him, radiating to everything around him. Ann leaned down to kiss the stubble on his cheek, and Victor murmured something Claudia could not hear. "See them out, Tinley," he said wearily, and tossed back the last bit of whiskey as the door shut behind them.

They were alone.

Julian refused to look at her, and Claudia felt as loathsome as she ever had in her life. After a moment he came to his feet and walked across the room to pour yet another whiskey to the rim of the glass. He calmly returned to his seat, took a large sip of the liquid, and with a heavy sigh, leaned his head against the chair and closed his eyes.

It seemed to Claudia that hours passed as she watched him, feeling invisible, before she finally spoke in a voice cracking with tension. "How far did you travel?"

He slowly opened his eyes and stared at the whiskey in his glass. "To Lancaster."

"I'm sorry you had to go so far," she murmured, nervously fingering the small gold cross around her neck.

He glanced at her then, his gaze cold and hard. "I would have ridden to the ends of the earth if I could have stopped her," he said sharply, and turned away again, as if she disgusted him. He was angry, that much was clear. But there was more, she thought as he closed his eyes once more. There was devastation.

She could see it in the weary lines around his eyes, the clench of his fist against his thigh. She had seen him look this way once before, long ago, when Valerie had died. Despite his fury with her, Claudia could not help feeling an overwhelming anguish for him, a deep, heartfelt sorrow.

That sorrow moved her to stand and walk to where he sat and kneel by his knee. His eyes remained closed, but he winced slightly when her hand glided over his and turned it over. When she pressed her lips very softly against his palm, he flinched, opened his eyes, and gazed down at her as she pressed her cheek into his palm. A lone tear slipped from the corner of her eye, coursed softly down her face—and Julian pulled his hand away from her cheek. He turned away, drank from his glass. "Your sympathy is touching, Claudia," he said, his voice hoarse. "But you are too late with it."

No, she wasn't too late, she could *not* be too late! *"Julian,"* she whispered faintly, words failing her, "I am so sorry. I am so very *sorry* for what has happened." Another tear slipped from her eye—her words sounded so empty, so inadequate, and she all at once felt very fragile, as if she was on the verge of shattering.

"If you want to help me, Claudia, you will leave me be," he said impassively, and stood, his knee brushing her shoulder as he stepped away. "I've much greater things to contend with at the moment than your sudden attack of conscience."

That remark stabbed at her heart. "Please, Julian, don't do this. Let me help you!" she insisted.

Julian responded by walking out the door without looking back.

The family gathered beneath a pall of gloom the next afternoon, not unlike the one that had settled over Kettering Hall five years ago with Valerie's death. The similarities between the two somber occasions were not lost on Julian, God, no—he felt both catastrophes keenly, felt the same burning pressure in his head. He anxiously rubbed the nape of his neck as he stood beneath a portrait of his father, staring up at dark eyes that mirrored his own and wondering if the old man somehow knew what a mess Julian had made of things.

It was that which he was contemplating when he heard Claudia join him. He knew it was her by the familiar sound of her footfall, but he did not look up, sparing himself the humiliation of seeing the pity in her eyes again, as he had when she had knelt beside him last evening. Fortunately, she did not beg him sweetly to let her help as she had then. In fact, Julian had no idea what she did—he did not turn around and she remained silent until Louis and Eugenie joined them a few minutes later. When he finally turned to face the room, Eugenie was with Claudia on the settee, their dark heads bowed together as they whispered fervently to one another.

"I accompanied Boxworth to White's last evening," Louis remarked quietly, stirring Julian from his brooding. "Unfortunately, this scandal goes very rapidly among your society, *mon ami*. You should distance yourself before it ruins your name."

Julian slowly turned his head to look at Louis. The Frog steadily returned his gaze; he was quite serious. Hardly surprising—any self-respecting man in Julian's position would disown Sophie, and frankly, that thought had certainly crossed his mind. Not because the *ton* would expect it of him, although God knew they would— a woman did not defy authority and propriety in such an appalling manner without risking complete censure. But

Julian didn't give a damn what the *ton* thought. It was just that there were times, like now, that he wanted Sophie gone, because he was quite certain he could not bear to ever look at her again. He was that angry with her—*violently* angry with her. "You are not me, Renault," he responded with a shrug of his shoulders.

"Thank God for this small favor," the Frog muttered, and strolled away.

Frowning, Julian swung his gaze to his father's portrait again. His limbs felt like lead, his mind churned with anger and desperation and, yes, even humiliation. It had been many years, decades even . . . perhaps never . . . that a person had trumped him so greatly. Particularly one of Stanwood's ilk.

When Victor and Ann arrived a few moments later, Julian noticed Ann had been crying. She muttered some apology, blaming it on her condition. Julian despised her tears all the same, felt himself sinking under the weight of them as Ann stared morosely at the floor, Victor behind her with a comforting hand on her shoulder.

They waited.

Restless, Julian looked at the door, the window casements, his father's portrait—anywhere but at Ann or Eugenie. Hell, he was hardly able to look himself in the eye, much less his sisters. What sort of man did they think their brother now? He hated all of them for looking at him as if they expected him to fall to pieces, shatter into a million fragments, explode with remorse and frustration and the overwhelming sense of powerlessness.

But not as badly as he hated himself for teetering on the brink of doing just that.

As the clock struck three, his heart began to slip in his chest, sliding down to his gut. At a quarter past, he impatiently stalked to the window, peering out across St. James Square, half expecting to see Stanwood down there, surrounded by those who would welcome this scandal, laughing at him.

The unexpected, gentle pressure of a hand on his arm startled him so badly that he almost came out of his skin.

Julian jerked around, sliced a scathing look across Claudia. She instantly removed her hand from his arm. "Tinley," she murmured.

He looked up; the butler was not two feet away, bowing crookedly like an old circus performer. "Lady Sophie has come home, my lord."

God help him, he would squeeze the bloody life from someone. With a quick glance at the others, Julian nodded curtly. "Show them in." He was suddenly aware of Claudia again, at his side. She was too close to him, too close, her presence suffocating. He moved abruptly to the middle of the room, braced his legs apart, and clasped his hands tightly behind his back. *God give me strength . . .*

Stanwood entered first, exaggerating the hitch in his gait like a bloody cock as he sailed into the green salon. Smiling broadly, he bowed with a flourish to Ann and Eugenie. "Ah, my dear sisters," he crowed with delight. "How *well* you look."

Julian opened his mouth, but whatever he might have said to the bastard died on his tongue as Sophie walked sluggishly into the room, her head bowed. His gaze narrowed on his little sister as the million things he would say warred for a place on his tongue. But before he could speak, she lifted her head and pierced him with a look so forlorn that he all at once felt submerged, as if he floated somewhere just beneath the surface—voices were suddenly muted in his ear, his vision of everything around him blurred. Sophie's chin began to tremble as she looked at him, and Julian saw the perfect despair swimming in her brown eyes. He was not even aware he moved—he only knew he was suddenly halfway across the room, his arms held out to her.

Her tears erupted like a dam burst; she flung herself into his arms and buried her face in his coat, sobbing uncontrollably. Julian held her tightly to him, caressed her back. "*Shhh,*" he whispered in her ear, "*don't cry, pumpkin. Everything will be all right.*"

"Oh, *come* now!" Stanwood scoffed, and grabbed Sophie's hand, dragging her from Julian's embrace. He wrapped his arms around her shoulders and squeezed tightly. "That's hardly necessary, my love. You'll cause him to think you regret what you've done!"

"No, of course not," she muttered, and shakily wiped the tears from her flushed cheeks.

"Well, then, Kettering," Stanwood continued with a smirk. "You heard her—can't ignore me any longer, can you? Might as well introduce the family to me."

"You know them," Julian responded low, fighting the deep urge to strangle the smirk from Stanwood's lips.

"Indeed I do." With a chuckle, Stanwood turned to face the rest of them, a sneer of pure contempt on his lips. "But they do not know *me*, do they? Take the venerable Madame Renault, for example, and her renowned French husband. I never traveled in their circles, so how could they know me? But you know me now, do you not, Genie?" he asked casually, clearly shocking Eugenie with his familiar address. "And Ann, of course," he said, shifting his sneer to her. "We encountered one another once before—you probably don't recall it. You were leaving St. George Cathedral and I tipped my hat to you, wished you a good day. Unfortunately, you did not deign to acknowledge it."

Ann looked uneasily at Sophie. "William," Sophie said weakly, "please allow me to introduce you properly—"

"For goodness sakes, Sophie!" he exclaimed laughingly, and tightened his hold on her to such a degree that Sophie looked almost pained. "You make it sound as if I am an outsider! Ah, but I am a part of the family now." He glanced at Claudia, cocking his head to one side. "You understand, surely, Lady Kettering. You know very well what it is to join this esteemed family under the cloud of a bit of scandal—"

"That's enough!" Julian roared.

Stanwood laughed gaily, released Sophie, and took several steps toward him, his arms outstretched. "Julian! We are brothers! What, you would debate it? Of *course* I am part of your family now!" He smiled, casually straightened his neckcloth, and without looking at his wife, said, "Tell him why we've come, dear."

With a small shake of her head, Sophie looked help-lessly at Eugenie.

"*Tell* him!" he said more forcefully, his derisive smile deepening.

Behind him, Sophie began to wring her hands. She looked to Eugenie again, then at Julian's boots, seemingly unable to look him in the eye. "We, ah . . . we have no place to live. William and I thought . . . w-we thought . . ." She paused, cleared her throat. "We thought that perhaps you would agree to lease a house near the park—"

He had not thought the extortion would come so soon. "Am I to understand that, having ruined my sister, you would now attempt to extort money from me?" Julian interjected, yanking a lethal gaze to Stanwood.

"No!" Sophie exclaimed, but her protest was silenced by one look from Stanwood, and the resentment began to pound in Julian's chest like a drum.

"I would prefer to call it a loan," Stanwood said, turn-ing back to Julian. "Don't look so chagrined, Kettering. We require it only a fortnight or two—just until Sophie's twenty-first birthday. Then we shall have funds sufficient to last us all our days." He flashed a sickening smile; behind him, Sophie bowed her head and closed her eyes.

"Call it a loan if you will," Julian said with deadly calm. "It is extortion all the same."

Stanwood's face darkened. "We require a residence, Kettering. Should you like to see where I could afford to keep my wife? It is small by your standards, and I dare-say too far south of the Thames. It is, however, margin-ally clean, and I think the rats are not quite so thick there as—"

"*Oh my God!*" Eugenie cried out in horror.

"We take your point, Stanwood!" Victor angrily inter-jected.

"Good," he drawled.

That was enough. If Stanwood wanted to extort

money from him, he could damn well do it without frightening his sisters half to death. Julian started toward Stanwood; the bastard stepped backward like the coward that he was, and Julian sneered as he brushed past him and reached for the handle of the door. "Rest assured, sir, I shall endeavor to find you suitable lodgings . . ." —he glanced at Sophie, who had yet to look up—"near the park if you like." He opened the door and held it open. "I thank you for bringing Sophie to us. We are most grateful to see she is safe and well."

A small sound escaped Sophie. "You . . . you are most generous," she murmured, risking a shy glance at him.

"It has nothing to do with generosity, love," he drawled, and pierced Stanwood with a look so hard that the man visibly flinched. "Was there more, Sir William?"

For the first time since he had entered the salon, Stanwood looked disconcerted. He glanced uneasily at the rest of them, seemed to think for a moment, then quickly shook his head. "For the moment, no," he said tightly, and motioned impatiently to Sophie, who hurried to his side. "We are temporarily at the Savoy. Wish them all a good day, Sophie."

"Good day," she mumbled, and gazed longingly over her shoulder at her sisters.

"Come on, then," Stanwood said, and scowling at Julian as he passed, dragged Sophie behind him as he quit the room. Julian watched until they were far down the corridor before closing the door.

"Outrageous!" a frustrated Louis bellowed as Julian turned to face them. "Who is this . . . this *bastard?*"

"He is, unfortunately, Sophie's husband," Julian said wearily, and walked to the sideboard in search of something to dull his fury.

"Did you see her?" Ann cried. "Dear God, did you *see* how she looked?"

"He would rob us! We cannot allow it!" Victor heatedly exclaimed, looking to Louis for confirmation and receiving a firm nod in response.

"But we can, Victor," Julian said. He suddenly felt

extremely fatigued. "We must think of Sophie. If he wants his revenge on me, I intend to let him have it."

"You do not mean this!" Louis burst forth. "You cannot surrender to blackmail! What, do you think he stops with lodgings? He will demand all from you before he is through!"

"What are a few hundred pounds compared to her happiness?" Julian shot back, frowning darkly at Louis. "I don't give a damn about the money!"

"But this is *blackmail*, Julian!" Victor insisted. "He would use Sophie to hold your coffers ransom to him!"

"Exactly!" Julian bellowed. "He would *use* Sophie! I have no doubt whatsoever that he would use her in the cruelest way possible against me. He wants money, and money is nothing to me, not when I see her as she was here! I *cannot* knowingly do anything that might lead to her harm!" He jerked up a bottle of port from the rest and eyed it menacingly. "I *cannot*," he insisted more to himself than to the rest of them, and poured the port into a glass.

"He's right," Ann said frantically, her eyes beseeching Victor. "We must think of Sophie!"

"Yes, we *must*," Eugenie agreed, and hastily crossed to Louis, standing in front of him, her hand on his arms folded implacably across his chest. "Louis, darling, I cannot bear to think of her residing in one of those wretched neighborhoods! You heard him! *Rats*, Louis!"

Victor and Louis exchanged black looks; Louis looked down at Eugenie's upturned face, the muscles in his jaw bulging as he bit back his protest. After a moment, he glanced at Julian and sighed. "This is a mistake, *mon ami*," he said, his voice considerably softer. "You must accept that Sophie made her choice when she eloped—you owe her nothing."

"Louis!" Eugenie cried. Louis suddenly wrapped his arms around her and roughly kissed the top of her head. "You must accept it, too, *ma chérie*," he said gently. "She has done this to herself."

But she was an innocent. Julian took a healthy gulp of the port. And then another. "You may think what you like, Renault, but she is my responsibility, and I will do everything within my power to keep her from harm. For the moment, it would seem a house near the park is the asking price for that."

"It will be a king's ransom in the end," Victor added stubbornly, to which Julian shrugged indifferently before downing the rest of his port.

There was little discussion after that, with the exception of Eugenie and Ann's suggestions for exactly where Julian ought to find a home for Sophie, Eugenie being of the firm opinion it should be as close to St. James Square as possible. Julian kept silent, but he did not like the sound of that too terribly much. He rather doubted that he could bear seeing Sophie, if only occasionally. If only across the Square.

As the debate continued, his gut churned with anxiety, and he stalked restlessly from the windows to the hearth and back again, moving aimlessly, pausing every now and again to look up at a portrait of his father.

He was vastly relieved when at last Louis stood and helped Eugenie to her feet, signaling the end to the somber occasion. Numb, he watched Claudia bid them all a good day and walk them to the door of the salon.

He was leaning against the window casement, holding the bottle of port loosely in one hand when Claudia at last turned to face him. Her blue-gray eyes were full of sadness, and he brought the bottle to his lips and swigged a mouthful. He did not want her here, not now—he was too spent to endure a traitorous wife. "You are undoubtedly fatigued after the encounter with Sir William. Perhaps you would like to nap before supper," he said indifferently, and took another drink of port.

"Wouldn't you like some company?"

Julian smirked, disregarding the hurtful look in her eye. "No, Claudia. And even if I did, I should think I'd like it from Tinley before you."

It was obvious that stung her sharply; Claudia glanced uneasily at the carpet. "I know you are hurt—"

"I am sick unto death of your perceptions," he bit out,

and stood abruptly, crossing quickly to the sideboard, where he put the bottle of port down so hard that the crystal decanters rattled against one another.

"Yes, so it would seem," she uttered softly. "I can't seem to apologize to you in a way that seems appropriate—"

"In that, madam, you are correct," he snapped, and swung around from the sideboard, bracing himself against it with his hands as he fixed a cold glare on her. "There is nothing you can do that would be appropriate, not now, not ever. So please do me a simple courtesy and just . . . go *on*."

"Julian, I want to help you."

What madness had invaded her he could not say, but the woman refused to surrender, almost provoking him to a fit of rage. "You have helped me quite enough, haven't you, Claudia? I could not possibly endure any more of it! So if you please, *good afternoon*," he snapped, motioning angrily toward the door.

Her shoulders sagged, her courage apparently failing her. Looking terribly dejected, if not confused, she turned toward the door.

Except Julian was not quite through with her. "Before you go—"

She pivoted sharply, her lovely face radiating hope, and Julian realized he felt nothing. The feelings for her, feelings he had carried inside him for two long years, were gone. Smashed, beaten down, obliterated by her indifference to him and her callous disregard for Sophie. He didn't want her help, he didn't want her hope—he didn't want anything from her at all. *God, how he despised her now!* "I would greatly appreciate it if you would allow me to walk through my own house without forcing your helpfulness on me again. Hear me well, Claudia. I do not want your help. I scarcely want anything to do with you at all."

She blinked, then merely nodded, as if he had informed her of something as mundane as the time tea would be served, and turned away, walking out of the salon, her head held high and her spine ramrod stiff.

How she managed to walk out so calmly was beyond Claudia, especially since her legs threatened to buckle beneath her at any moment. Yet the next thing she knew, she was in her suite, having sent Brenda off to prepare a bath she hoped was so scalding hot that it might actually wash away her remorse. And as she calmly undressed, she realized why she was able to bear his disdain.

Something had happened that had inexplicably changed her. Something that forced a mellowing of the indignation from which she had suffered for many years and roused her from the deep hurt that had defined her.

Oh, she knew very well what had *happened*—she had seen his heartache, as plainly as if he wore it draped like a sash of honor across his chest. And the moment she saw it in his ravaged face, she had at once and with clarion vision understood how wrong she had been. As she sank into the hot, fragrant waters of her bath, she thought of the way Julian had once looked at her . . . that strange, warm way he had of making her tingle inside.

Yet she had ignored him completely, had run from his efforts to make their marriage bearable. She had tried to escape him in every instance—in her bed, at his table, among his family—she had been too afraid of her feelings for him, too afraid of being hurt. She had made him out to be indifferent, a ruthless charmer with little else on his mind than carnal pleasure. She had convinced herself that her causes were more important than anything else, pretended that everything else faded in comparison. Nothing mattered, and therefore, nothing could hurt her . . . including her husband.

Lord God, she had been deluded all right. Nothing had pointed that up more than Sophie's return. Of all the things she expected to happen when Sophie walked through that door, his embrace was not one of them. Not in a thousand years would she have expected him to embrace his fallen sister so firmly, folding her in the protective, forgiving circle of his arms. She had expected him to rail at Sophie, perhaps even disown her, but *never* to comfort her, not after the dishonor she had brought him.

It was not a simple act of kindness, but a gesture worthy of kings.

And now? Yes, what *now*, Claudia? *Oh God, what now?*

She languidly finished her bath, mulling over the awareness that had finally battered through her thick head, pondering what she must do. When she came to the inevitable conclusion, she rose from her bath and dressed. Her conclusion was hardly profound—it was merely instinctive.

She had to fight.

If she wanted his love, she would have to fight to earn it. She needed her courage now as she never had before, because this would be the most difficult battle of her life. She had to fight not only for herself but for Julian, too. For them.

Because he needed her more than ever, whether he wanted to accept it or not.

Twenty

JULIAN IMPATIENTLY SWIPED at the lock of his hair that fell again across his brow, tickling him, reminding him that he was, indeed, quite alive, and not suffering from some horrid dream. He glanced at the little pot of violets next to his elbow and scowled. The damn things were everywhere and he was bloody tired of looking at them. With a heave to, he managed to get his arms and legs to move together to push himself up from the leather chair he had sunk into, then staggered across the carpet to the sideboard.

There were several bottles there, some he recalled sampling earlier. Squinting, he selected a bright blue bottle, smiling when he saw the bottle was full. "What have we here?" he mumbled, and, tipping his head back, let a stream of gin burn the back of his throat and his gullet. "Ah," he muttered, wiping the back of his hand across his mouth. "Good ol' bloody gin."

"Julian?"

Her voice was like drums banging in his ears and sent his heart reeling in a strange but familiar sense of confusion. He awkwardly turned and looked over his shoulder.

His grip slipped; the gin bottle clanked against the glassware on the sideboard.

Damn her. *Damn her!* Wearing a gown of shimmering lilac satin, the witch looked every inch an angel. Her beauty was extraordinary and it angered Julian that he was, once again, struck hard by the magnificence, the sheer perfection of her.

He *hated* her, hated her for making him weak with wanting and enslaving him to her! "Get *out,*" he snapped, jerked around, grabbed the bottle of gin, and reeled toward the leather chair he had vacated in front of the hearth, as far away from her as he could possibly get under the circumstance. He fell into it, drank from the bottle he clutched in one hand, staring blindly at the violets as he strained to hear any sound of her. There was nothing. The discomfort rolled over him in a sickening wave, and faltering, he risked another glimpse of her.

She was still standing at the door, her long, slender fingers on the door handle. Julian scowled; she quietly shut the door. *"No,"* he said, shaking his head so violently that nausea burned his throat. "Don't want you here. Just *go.*"

But she was moving toward him, seemingly gliding on air. In a moment of sheer madness, Julian believed it was an apparition advancing on him, the image from his dreams. His scowl turned into a confused frown, and he sat up, watching the gossamer silk skirt float out from her body as she flowed toward him, smiling. *Smiling.* A soft, compassionate smile that sent a shiver down his spine. He watched her, wishing to God in heaven that she had come to him before now.

Before he had stopped loving her.

"God!" he suddenly roared, and sagged in the chair, bracing his forehead against his hand, tenting his eyes. Who *was* she? Who was this creature who tormented his dreams and his days and his heart? "What do you want? What in God's name do you *want* of me?" he cried out.

"To love you," the apparition whispered in a velvet voice.

Julian's heart slammed hard against his ribs; her scent wafted over him, lavender filling his senses. He made no objection when the bottle of gin slid carefully from his fingers. His heart and lungs labored with her nearness, but he made no sound at all, did not open his eyes. He felt her fingers moving beneath his chin and jerked away, catching her wrist in a firm grip as he opened his eyes. Her face was just above his; he could see the flush of her pristine skin. Her blue-gray gaze penetrated the fog around his brain, gaining entry into his depths, scoring his very soul. A man could drown in her eyes, wander straight into them and slip beneath the surface, lost forever.

That was the sum of it, wasn't it? He had been lost in her for so long, lost a little more of himself each time he was with her. And now he was hopelessly trying to kick his way free of her depths, but she had ensnared him, pulling him deeper still. He abruptly shoved her away; Claudia gracefully stepped back, moved from his reach, and knelt at his feet in a soft *swoosh* of lilac satin. "What do you think you are doing?" he demanded roughly.

She didn't answer, but took his foot and put it in her lap, running one hand up his calf. Even through the leather of his boot he could feel the sensation of her touch and recoiled fiercely. But she held on, carefully working the boot from his leg until it was loose, then lifting his heel and pulling the boot from his leg.

Oh God, he did not have the strength to fight her. Indistinct little tingles ran up his leg and straight to his groin as she removed the other boot. "Why do you do this?" he demanded angrily. Bracing her hands on his thighs, she pulled herself up to her knees, then moved so that she was on the floor before him, between his legs, her hands moving along the tops of his thighs. She pinned him with a clear, steady gaze. "I know you despise me, Julian—"

"No. No, I do not despise you. I feel *nothing* for you," he interjected, unwavering in the face of that enormous lie.

"All right then, you feel nothing. But I do. I would give my heart to you on a platter if that is what you wanted."

"What I *want*," he spat, "is for you to leave me be. Just leave me be!"

She shook her head; a wisp of dark hair came loose from her coiffure and floated to her shoulder. "That is the one thing I will not do," she murmured silkily. "I will not leave you, not like this, not when you are hurting so."

Something in him went wild with fury and despair, consuming all reason and torching every wicked desire, every carnal hunger within him. He pitched forward, hardly noticing Claudia's small cry of alarm as he came out of the chair and toppled her onto her back in front of the hearth. Coming over her, he pinned her wrists on either side of her head. She lay beneath him, her breast rising and falling rapidly with the earnestness of her breath, her gaze steady on him, calm and sorrowful . . .

Julian squeezed his eyes shut. "You want me now, Claudia? After all these weeks of pushing me away, you want me *now?*" he breathed.

"Yes."

The softly whispered response sent a wave of raw hunger crashing through him and obliterating everything in its wake. He was suddenly crushing his lips to hers, probing deeply between them with his tongue, savoring the sweetness of her breath. At some point he had let go of her, because her delicate hands were holding him tightly to her as she had never held him before, possessively, her hands searching his back, his shoulders, his neck, tangling in his hair, pushing the coat from his shoulders and arms.

She wanted him . . . for a moment? A day? A year? Did he bloody well care at the moment? He dragged his mouth across her chin to the swell of her breasts rising above the neckline of her gown and mouthed the succulent flesh. Her fingers raked through his hair, behind his ears, tracing tantalizing little paths to his shoulders. When he slipped his hands behind her back to unfasten her gown, she arched into him, pressing her breasts against him, burning him with a look of unadulterated sensual ardor. "Do you want me Claudia?" he asked, roughly shoving the gown from her shoulders to her waist.

"Yes," she whispered again, gasping softly when he covered her breast with his mouth, nipping at the tip with his teeth.

Her hands drifted inside his shirt, to his bare chest, where her fingers danced lightly across his nipples, drawing them to a peak and churning the desire in his loins. He groaned, laved the other breast as his hands fought the satin of her skirts, dragging them up, his fingers skirting across the inside of her thighs where her smooth skin was moist and warm. He touched his lips to the column of her throat as his fingers trailed down to the apex of her thighs.

Her response was a low groan, the ragged drawing of breath into her lungs as he slipped a finger inside her, his thumb brushing the tiny pinnacle of her desire. Claudia clutched frantically at his arms, her fingernails digging into his skin beneath the wide sleeves of his shirt. Julian hardly noticed; he was bewitched by her eyes, captivated by the dark pools of longing beneath heavy lids. "Do you want me like this?" he asked hoarsely, and she sighed, biting her lower lip. The dam broke in him then; weeks of longing, of holding himself back, of denying his feelings for her crumbled into nothing. He moved swiftly, yanking her drawers from her hips so that he could bury his face between her legs and inhale the musky scent of woman. His tongue slipped between the folds, circling around and over the pinnacle that made her writhe beneath him, then down, deep inside her and back again. The scent and the feel of her filled his body through every pore, swirling around and around and pooling in his groin, burgeoning in his sex, straining to be free, to be *in* her.

The crescendo of her gasps turned to cries of pleasure as he sustained his desire on her body, licking and nipping and sucking her until he felt the violent shudder deep inside her, felt her thighs contract around his head, heard her cry out. He was throbbing painfully now, but still he lapped at her, fervently kissing the evidence of her passion from her thighs. When she at last stopped moving beneath him, he lifted his head. "Do you want me like this?" he uttered, his voice hoarse with passion.

Claudia came up, cupped his face in her hands and kissed him hard, her mouth searing him, drinking the remnants of her own flesh from his lips. Julian struggled with his trousers, at last freeing his aching erection, and fell to his side, taking Claudia with him, lifting her leg over his hip. She kissed him; Julian slid easily into her heat, too easily, his body yearning for instant gratification. Gritting his teeth, Julian tilted his head back, unwilling to spill his seed into her just yet, clinging to a thin thread of control left in him. He forced himself to go slowly, wanting to savor the moment, the moment she had at last come to *him* and said she wanted him. He would remember it all and forever, and deliberately kept his pace slow, prolonging his own agony.

Claudia's breath and tongue flitted across his neck, inside his ear, along the crease of his lobe. "Is this what you wanted?" he asked her again, wanting to hear her say it, and drove into her. Claudia closed her eyes, lost in the throes of passion. "Is this why you have come?" he asked, thrusting hard.

"Oh, Julian," she exhaled into his shoulder. "I have come because I love you!" she murmured, and tenderly kissed his cheek.

That simple utterance shattered his heart into a million shards. How he had longed to hear her say that, how he had dreamed of it, had wished for it a million times or more. He pushed her onto her back, lifted her leg and thrust harder, his blood raging with desire and confusion that those words would come *now*, when he was at his weakest, when she had hurt him so. He lengthened his strokes, bearing into her all the bewilderment and passion and hope he had carried inside these two long years. She moved beneath him, panting, her body tightening around him, and when she cried out, his passion exploded furiously within her.

He collapsed on top of her, his mind awash in disbelief. He felt himself sliding out of her, the hardness of him deflated by his confused passion. In sheer frustration he shoved her away and rolled onto his back.

Claudia came up, bracing herself against the floor with one arm. "Julian! What is wrong?"

He looked to the fire and pushed himself up. "You may want me now, Claudia, but it is too late. Far too late." The sound of her dismay only served to irritate him—he stumbled to his feet and clumsily fastened his trousers.

"How . . . how could you say that?" she asked as Julian stooped to retrieve his clothing. "You don't believe me. You don't believe that I love you!"

Those words burned. *Why now?* What did he do with those words now? Did he ignore the doubts in his heart? Did he allow wild hope to build again? How could she say that *now,* how could she ruin it all by declaring something he so desperately craved after he had depleted all he had to give?

Julian looked down at his wife. Her hair spilled wildly about her shoulders and she seemed unconscious of her nakedness. Her breasts, pale as the moon in the light from the hearth, rose softly with a breath that seemed to catch in her throat as she gazed up at him. *Damn her allure all to hell.* "Frankly, Claudia, I don't know what to believe anymore," he muttered helplessly, and stepped over her, pausing only to fetch his boots as he walked out of the salon.

In his rooms, he quickly dressed. He had to get out. He could not stay here with her, not like this. What a goddam fool he had been to think they could co-exist in one house! He stalked to the foyer and commanded a footman to fetch him a hack. As he waited, he realized with painful acuity that he had finally hit rock-bottom in his life, bouncing like an India rubber ball to be hit again and again. Ah, God, such was the quality of love!

It was hours later that he found himself standing across the way from Madame Farantino's, leaning against the streetlamp with a cheroot dangling from his mouth. He really had no idea how he had come to be here. After leaving Kettering House, his head still fogged from the liquor, he had made the hack circle Hyde Park, and finally tiring of that, he had gotten off at Regent Street, wandering aimlessly about until he had, somehow, ended up here.

A footman across the way motioned him to come inside. Julian tipped his hat in acknowledgment, but settled against the lamppost and dragged on his cheroot. Certainly it had occurred to him to go inside; she had left him feeling a bit like a caged animal, anxious, strangely ravenous. Part of him was tempted to go inside and expend that anxiety on a woman who would demand nothing more than his sex and leave his heart and soul intact.

Julian flicked the cheroot to the cobblestone and ground it out with the heel of his boot. Shoving his hands in his pockets, he took one last look at Madame Farantino's before turning toward the Tam O'Shanter. He never had any intention of crossing the threshold of Farantino's, no matter what his body wanted to believe. Whatever he thought of Claudia, one thing remained, unfortunately for him, quite unchanged.

He still loved her.

Desperately so.

Twenty-One

JULIAN LEASED A small but well-appointed town house on South Audley Street for Sophie that was only a short walk to Hyde Park. Stanwood took residence there on a cold morning, but left early that afternoon to call upon a notoriously expensive haberdashery. Apparently, his wardrobe was not befitting his new residence, and he insisted Sophie accompany him, more, Julian thought, to keep her at a safe distance from her family than to seek her help.

That was one thing Stanwood did quite well. Julian faithfully called three times a week—more than that he believed made him seem desperate. Less than that made him quite desperate. He worried constantly about her; she had lost quite bit of weight since her elopement, perhaps as much as a stone. Dark circles shadowed her brown eyes, and although she smiled and spoke cheerfully when he called, he thought her cheerfulness forced, her smile painted on for his benefit. Sophie was miserable.

So was Julian. He was absolutely powerless to do anything for her within the confines of the law. There was nothing he could do, not one goddam thing to change this tragedy for her. Sophie's loss of innocence weighed heavily on his heart; nothing could ever give that back to her. The only thing Julian seemed capable of doing at all was enduring his hatred for Stanwood, and that took every ounce of strength he had.

Even his attempts to at least set the bastard up in

respectable employment had failed. Having convinced Arthur to take Stanwood on as a clerk in the Christian family law offices—no easy feat, that—Stanwood had declined with a sneer, saying that morning hours were not to his liking. That was plainly true—on more occasions than not, the toad met Julian in the afternoons still in his dressing gown. He drank heavily, too; the smell of liquor permeated the house.

But what infuriated Julian most was the way Stanwood spoke to Sophie, as if she was a child or a servant to be commanded to sit, to stand, to fetch for him. It seemed he treated everything she said as ridiculous, laughing in that condescending way of his. It was all Julian could do to keep from wringing his neck—and when Stanwood sensed that Julian was about to lose his temper, he would put his arm around Sophie with a sneer and remark upon the privileges of married life. The scoundrel knew exactly how powerless Julian was, and he delighted in it.

Worse, Stanwood began to borrow heavily against Sophie's impending annuity. Julian had anticipated it, had advanced him one thousand pounds shortly after the couple's return to London—but that sum was now twenty-five hundred pounds and growing weekly. It puzzled Julian—having arranged for the house, he knew the cost of letting it. He knew the approximate cost of the many new clothes Stanwood seemed to possess, and the few Sophie had been treated to. None of it added up to as much as even five hundred pounds. He strongly suspected Stanwood had begun to gamble away Sophie's fortune, but as he was reportedly never seen at any reputable gaming hell, Julian wondered exactly *where* he was gambling so unsuccessfully. He would have a deuce of a time finding out.

Stanwood could not abide for her sisters to be alone with Sophie, and made it quite clear that he could scarcely tolerate even Julian's presence. Unfortunately, Julian was his only means of income, and he could ill afford to ban him from his house. So Julian called three

times a week, quite happy to let his mere presence perturb Stanwood, and hoped it would perturb him right to
death.

But Julian could not accept how powerless he was.
Worse yet, at the end of every day when he faced the fact
that another twenty-four hours had passed in impotence,
he was forced to endure the torment Claudia was putting
him through.

Torment. Hell, yes, it was torment on every level, open
and deep, and penetrating the darkest depths of his soul.
It was nothing overt, really, but a million little things
piled upon one another that threatened to smother him.
As ludicrous as it seemed, Julian was convinced Claudia
was attempting to kill him with kindness—and if he ever
uttered that to another living soul, he was quite certain
they would cart him off to Bedlam.

Nonetheless, the evidence certainly supported it. It
was an unspoken fact that the two of them had called an
uneasy truce. He supposed they had settled into the disquiet of their marriage, neither of them willing to push
any farther. He had thought her reserved politeness a
symbol of that truce . . . until her kindness began to affect
him, little things designed—he *thought*—to comfort him.

For example, one evening Claudia surprised him by
announcing Eugenie and Louis would join them for supper. That was odd; he was not in the habit of dining with
Claudia of late—he could hardly look at her seated at his
table, knowing what she had done to Sophie. *Had done to
him.* So he therefore spent the unusual supper engaged in
argument with Louis, first over the insidious little
LeBeau—who apparently was still threatening to have
Julian's head—then over exactly when the Renaults
would return to France.

The tactic worked. He and Louis were quite oblivious
to the ladies, hardly noticing when Claudia rose from her
chair and went to the sideboard. But Julian *did* notice the
frantic whispers with the footman and then the appearance of a silver tray on which sat four small wineglasses
and a bottle of wine. Not just any wine, mind you—

imported Madeira wine, sent for and received all the way from Portugal.

He would have thought nothing of it under normal circumstances. He certainly was not the only peer to have a special liking for the wine, and he certainly wasn't the only one to have ordered it specially from Portugal on occasion. What was unusual was that he had depleted his stock, and had remarked one night—long before Sophie had run away—that he had been remiss in ordering the wine, and therefore, would be forced to wait months for it. He had not as yet put in his order.

When the footman served the wine, Claudia beamed at him as if she had just snared the fattest fish in the river. Julian looked at her with all due suspicion, but she very happily turned her attention to Eugenie. It was obvious the Demon's Spawn had recalled his remark from weeks ago and had found the blasted wine somewhere. *For him.* She had actually *thought* of him, before Sophie had even gone, and nothing could convince him otherwise.

And if *that* wasn't enough to convince him, the incident of the silk neckcloths certainly did. Tinley, damn him, had somehow managed to ruin a handful of fine silk neckcloths Julian had had tailored in Paris. They were scorched, as if someone had attempted to iron them. Bartholomew wailed his innocence. Not Tinley—he stated he was quite clearly at fault, but for the life of him, could not remember what he had thought to do with the neckcloths. Nor had he been particularly contrite about it. After some railing on Julian's part, the expensive neckcloths had been discarded.

Yet one by one, reasonable copies of them began to appear in his wardrobe. One day there were two of them; a fine silver silk, another gold and black pattern. The next day, the burgundy, followed by the forest green the next. Bartholomew was as perplexed as Julian was. When Tinley was questioned, the old man readily assured his lord that he had lost most of his mind, but not *that* much of it.

It was her. Claudia was the only other person who

could possibly know which ones had been lost, and as the daughter of a fastidious earl—one far too concerned with his appearance in Julian's humble estimation—she knew very well where and how to replace them. He did not ask her, but every time he wore one of the resurrected neckcloths, he watched her closely, looking for any sign that she had done it. The little devil pretended to never notice.

There was more. Her teas had suddenly stopped, as had the bizarre events for ladies she had often staged. There was no explanation for it, but it seemed to Julian that instead of her teas, she was waiting for *him* every evening. She seemed always nearby, engaged in some quiet activity. Just *being*. And he noticed that when Claudia was just being, his snifter was filled with fine brandy, his cheroots were neatly trimmed and handy, the newspaper folded to the financial pages as he liked it.

She was driving him mad, all right, because he was actually beginning to look forward to her presence, to feel a curious sense of peace when she was near. No one needed to tell him how preposterous that was. Everyone knew that Claudia Whitney was a woman who laughed at men and filled her days as she pleased. She was the sort of woman for whom a man would do just about anything—God save all of the poor bastards—but she was *not* the sort of woman who would actually dote on a man. Yet she *was* doting on him! The question was, why?

It honestly frightened him on a level he could not quite comprehend. If everything had been normal, he might have become completely besotted with her . . . if he wasn't already. But Julian was not going to allow that to happen. He was not going to fall any more in love with her than he already had the misfortune to have done. He was not going to believe her utterance of love that night in the library. He was not going to let the woman touch him in any way, because the *next* time she turned away from him, he was quite certain it would kill him.

Julian was up earlier and earlier each morning, his sleep growing more fitful. On one particular morning, he allowed Tinley to serve him a steaming plate of eggs and tomatoes—then proceeded to do a full inspection, as there was no telling what Tinley might think were eggs these days. Satisfied everything was in order, he dined at leisure, perusing yesterday's newspaper, until Claudia startled him by breezing into the breakfast room at an ungodly early hour, a gorgeous smile on her face.

He extended a curt nod before jerking the paper up so that he could not see her. He could hear her, however, and heard her rummaging around the room before seating herself at the table. He waited, expecting some sort of cheerful quip to start his dismal day . . . but he heard nothing even as benign as a small sip of tea. Against his better judgment, he lowered his paper.

Seated directly across from him, Claudia flashed a brilliant smile that dimpled her cheeks. He lowered the paper farther, frowning mightily at her, because the Demon's Spawn looked as if she had just swallowed one very fat canary. "Well? What are you about?" he gruffly demanded.

Still beaming, she nodded to the table between them. Julian looked down; there between them was a small pot of violets, its purple flowers a showy contrast to the dark mahogany wood. A pot like a dozen or more now scattered about the house. He stared at the little pot, and kept staring as Tinley wandered to the sideboard and helped himself to tea. "I don't understand," he said at last. "What is the significance?"

Claudia's grin widened impossibly, and Julian was quite certain he did not want to know the significance. "Don't you remember?" she asked gaily. "You had them on your table every morning at Kettering Hall—you said you liked to look at your favorite color because it helped you eat Mrs. Darnhill's dreadful porridge."

The Demon's Spawn had lost her mind. "I never said any such thing," he protested.

"Naturally you did," Tinley interjected, and sipped casually from his teacup.

Julian cast an impatient glance at him. "Shouldn't you be polishing something somewhere?"

"It's *Wednesday,* my lord."

That signified only in Tinley's decrepit mind, and Julian was about to tell him so when Claudia insisted, "You *did,* Julian. The violets grew almost wild around Kettering, and there were fresh cuttings of them every morning. Jeannine and Dierdre and I have been potting them for weeks now. They've decided violet is their favorite color, too."

Merriment danced in Claudia's eyes; he felt a hard pull in his chest. *Marvelous. Fall victim to her charms again if you think your fool heart can take it.* "I did not ask for violets, Claudia. The stuff grew like weeds and the gardeners had to do *something* with it so we would not be overtaken. The servants put the violets on the morning table, not I. I merely said what came to mind to persuade four young girls to eat their porridge instead of the ghastly tarts Cook made for them."

Her smile faded completely, and Julian had the curious sensation that a light had gone out in the room. "Oh," she said quietly. "I thought you would be pleased."

Yes, undoubtedly she had hoped he would be so pleased that he would return to his old habit of chasing after her like a puppy. He resented the hell out of it, particularly because he was so dangerously close to doing just that. He folded his paper and stood. "I am not particularly pleased. I have no great love of violets," he said, and shoving his hands in his pockets, walked out of the dining room, leaving his breakfast unfinished.

And leaving Claudia absolutely fuming.

What in God's name was the *matter* with him? Had every shred of human decency taken leave of him? She looked at Tinley; the old man shrugged, sipped his tea, then put the cup down. "His lordship is a bit testy this morning, it would seem," he remarked.

"And *rude,*" she added irritably. She looked at the

little pot of violets, frowning. "I was so certain he *liked* violets!"

Tinley eased himself into a chair at the table. "There hardly seems much his lordship cares for of late. I find him rather dreary all in all."

Yes. Impossibly so. Claudia stood and picked up the violets. "We *will* change that, Tinley." Shoving the little pot in the crook of her arm, she smiled at the old butler. "Or die trying," she chirped, and marched out of the breakfast room.

After much internal debate, she decided against putting the pot with all the others, as this one had been especially decorated for Julian. The girls had spent what seemed hours laboring over the pot for their uncle, so Claudia at last entered his dark study to put the forlorn little plant in a prominent position on his desk. He could not possibly miss it—she just hoped he didn't toss it aside as he had every other gesture she had made to reach out to him. Particularly since violets were so bloody difficult to come by this time of year.

She folded her arms across her middle as she considered her placement of the little pot, trying very hard not to give in to the despair that had plagued her these last weeks. Yesterday, Doreen had cautioned her to be patient, reminding her that what she had done was not easy to forgive. Rocking in that chair of hers, she calmly informed Claudia that it might take months, if not years, for Julian to forgive her, then had tactfully pointed out that he might *never* forgive her.

What if he never forgave her? Claudia shifted her gaze to the drawn curtains, great swaths of heavy velvet that shut the world out from this room, just as Julian had shut the world out of his heart. How would she possibly exist in darkness like this? How would she survive the sunrise every morning, the sunset every evening, and all the lonely hours in between? God, how would *Julian* survive? He was despairing, drowning in it. It was painfully obvious—he wasn't sleeping, hardly eating, and the dark shadow of worry grew deeper under his eyes each day.

She had helped to do it to him, she knew, but she could change it only if he would let her. Yet he stubbornly shut her out as he did the rest of the world, refusing to let her in. And that was killing them both.

With a firm shake of her head, Claudia pivoted on her heel and marched out of the study. One thing was certain—she would never survive if she dwelled on it every waking hour. Her best course was the same that had always sustained her—to stay frightfully busy. All those years waiting for her father to notice her, she had stayed busy. Waiting for Phillip to call, she had stayed busy. And when she had been forced into this marriage, she had done the same, not letting a single moment of unplanned space exist, not one bit of time in which she might think or feel or hope.

It was not easy—the guilt and loneliness she felt in this house was only made worse by the scandal Sophie's elopement had visited upon this family. Lord Dillbey had delighted in it, using it as a platform to warn everyone at supper parties across all of Mayfair that Claudia Dane's ideas would lead to ruination for women everywhere. There was no doubt that the entire Kettering family was suffering from their scandals, and as for her, no one would come to a tea now if her life depended on it.

So she spent her time with Jeannine and Dierdre, Ann and Eugenie, Doreen, and her weekly call to Sophie.

When she arrived at the Stanwood home later that afternoon, another new and harried footman greeted her—servants never seemed to last more than a day in this house. Apparently, the poor man had not received the proper instruction in being a footman as of yet, because he left her in the vestibule while he went off to find Sophie. That was why Claudia had the misfortune to encounter Stanwood. He strode into the vestibule as if he was the king himself, another footman on his heels.

A lecherous grin spread his lips the moment he saw her. "My, my, look who has come to call, Grimes. Lady Kettering." He extended his hand, palm up. Reluctantly, Claudia put her hand in it, repulsed when his lips moved over her gloved knuckles. He took his time in releasing her hand, his grin widening.

She resisted the urge to wipe her hand on her cloak.

"My wife did not mention she was expecting you. I wonder why not? Perhaps she is sensitive to your unfortunate reputation? Hmmm? Do you suppose?" he asked as he casually fit a leather glove onto his hand.

The man was an ass. Conscious of the footman, Claudia merely smiled. "I can't imagine why she didn't mention it. I call every Wednesday afternoon."

"I usually don't allow Sophie to have callers unless I am present," he continued, meticulously fitting the second glove. "But I rather suppose I might make an exception in your case. I am certain that your visit will be quite circumspect, given your own dilemma."

All right, she had gone past being sickened to being quite infuriated. "I beg your pardon, sir, but what *dilemma* would that be?"

With a dark chuckle, Stanwood had the audacity to chuck her under the chin as if she were a child. "My hat, Grimes," he said to the footman, then smiled again at Claudia. "Forgive me for attempting to be gentle. I was referring, Lady Kettering, to your ruination. They say he had you on a table—is that true?"

Lord above, what she wouldn't give to strangle the breath from his throat! "Actually, it was a workbench," she politely corrected him, acutely aware of the dark color flooding the poor footman's face.

Stanwood laughed roundly and moved toward her until he was standing very near, towering over her, his eyes stone cold. Claudia's stomach did a nauseating little flip; a kernel of fear rooted in her and began to grow rapidly. Miraculously, she held her ground, meeting his gaze head on. "I assume that you work hard to repair your tattered reputation, madam. And I further assume that in doing so, you would not wish to embroil yourself in more scandal, and therefore, would not advise Sophie to any foolishness. I will allow you to call." His gaze fell to her mouth; his tongue flicked slowly across his bottom lip.

"However, I shall quite definitely be in residence when you grace us with your presence Wednesday next."

Claudia could not help herself; the man revolted her, and she awkwardly stepped back, bumping into the door. Stanwood chuckled. "Go on, then," he said patronizingly. "Go find our Sophie." Claudia did not wait—she was suddenly desperate to be away from him. How in God's name had Sophie ever found him desirable?

She heard him laugh, speak low to the footman as she hurried out of the vestibule, and her stomach twisted again.

Fortunately, the other footman found her in a narrow corridor. "Beggin' your pardon, milady. Lady Stanwood is in her sitting room just now. If you will follow me." Claudia nodded, and followed the footman through a small maze of doors and hallways and staircases. On the second floor, he paused in front of a green door and rapped. From the other side, Claudia heard Sophie's muffled reply.

As the door swung open, she spied Sophie sitting with her back to the door, slightly hunched over. Thanking the footman, Claudia anxiously stepped inside and shut the door behind her. "Sophie! Are you well?"

With a thin smile, Sophie turned slightly; Claudia's breath caught in her throat at the sight of her sister-in-law. It had been only a week since Claudia had last seen her, but the change was remarkable. She was still in her dressing gown, although it was nearly three o'clock. The girl was gaunt, as if she hadn't eaten in days. Dark skin ringed her bloodshot eyes, and the natural luster was gone from her hair. "Sophie! What has happened to you?" Claudia exclaimed, feeling a rise of panic.

"Happened?" Sophie choked on a laugh. "Nothing has happened! I've been a bit under the weather, that's all."

It was a lie. "Have you sent for a physician? You should be—"

"No, of course not," she said. "I am quite all right. Now come and please sit down—I'm so glad you've come! Shall I ring for tea?"

Claudia tossed her cloak to a chair and sat nervously on the edge of an ottoman near Sophie. "Now I see why Eugenie and Ann were so concerned yesterday—Ann says she never has the opportunity to speak with you alone—"

"What is their concern?" Sophie asked, a little impatiently. "I can take care of myself!"

"Of course you can," Claudia hastily reassured her, and leaned forward, settling her hand on Sophie's knee. "It's just that you don't *look* very well. Has Sir William said anything at all? Surely he has noticed—"

Sophie surprised her with a bitter laugh. "He's hardly here enough to notice much of anything," she said, glancing at her hands. "Really, Claudia, I am quite fine. I've had an ague, I suppose, but I am well down the road to recovery."

But she wasn't fine. "Why isn't he here?" Claudia asked bluntly. The cretin ought to be fetching a physician, if nothing else!

Sophie shrugged. "I don't know, precisely. But in truth . . . in truth,"—her voice fell to a whisper—"I am *glad* for it."

Claudia blinked, surprised. This was hardly the same woman who had made such emotional declarations of undying love for him. "Oh, Sophie, darling . . . what is wrong?" she asked, wincing when a single tear slipped from Sophie's eye.

"He's . . . he's not at all the man I thought," she said, and suddenly looked frantically over her shoulder— rather odd, seeing as how they were alone in the room, and giving Claudia the very distinct impression that she was afraid. "Promise me you won't tell a soul what I've said!" she whispered anxiously as she jerked her gaze back to Claudia.

"Sophie—"

"*Promise* me, Claudia! If Julian knew . . . if *any* of them knew, they would be so very angry with me!"

She *was* panic-stricken, and Claudia grasped her

hands, holding them firmly between her own. "No one will be angry with you."

"They *will!* They will because there is nothing they can do! I *married* him for God's sake, and now I am his for all eternity!"

Claudia could not dispute that—the moment Sophie said her vows and signed the betrothal papers, there was nothing short of an act of God or Parliament that would set her free. Much to Claudia's chagrin, her eyes began to water, brought on by the never-ending sense of guilt. She looked at Sophie through a haze of tears—stooped over as she was with her hair falling limply about her—looking as if she carried the weight of the world on her thin shoulder. "Oh, Sophie, what can I do?" she blurted. "Tell me how I can help you!"

Shaking her head, Sophie pulled her hands from Claudia's grasp and unsteadily wiped her own tears away. "Nothing. There is nothing you can do, Claudia." She glanced up and attempted a weak smile. "I suppose we all pay the consequences of our actions, don't we?"

Ah, God.

Ashamed, Claudia stared at the carpet, unable to conjure anything comforting to say to Sophie, other than she was so very, very sorry. Lord help her, she was forever sorry these days, but it was never enough. If she could, she would trade herself for Sophie, put her own life in this predicament so that Sophie would be free.

"I'll ring for tea," Sophie muttered, and pushed herself from the chair. As she moved sluggishly toward the bell pull, Claudia lifted her head.

What she saw froze the blood in her veins.

A myriad of images suddenly deluged her mind's eye: images of Phillip holding her, Phillip crushing her to the wall, crushing her breast, crushing her lips, crushing her throat with his hand. Drunk out of his mind, he had attacked her the last night she had seen him alive, his hands everywhere, hurting her. Terrified, she had struggled, finally stopping the assault with a slap that reverberated up her arm. Never in her life would she forget the fear and revulsion and the feeling of utter helplessness the moment she realized she could not possibly stop him from raping her.

All of that came rushing back to her, pounding dangerously at her temple as she stared at the multi-colored bruise on Sophie's shoulder where her dressing gown had slipped away. It frightened her, made her belly roil with nausea and her heart hammer hard against her chest. Without thinking, she surged to her feet and rushed toward Sophie, startling her badly.

"*Claudia!* What are you doing!" she shrieked as Claudia reached for her dressing gown.

"He did that to you, didn't he?" she demanded, her voice shrill with fear.

Sophie's face went ghostly white; she clutched at the thin dressing gown and wrapped it tightly around her.

A silent scream of terror and remorse lifted from her heart to God, and Claudia lashed out at Sophie's hands, pulling them off the dressing gown. Shrieking, Sophie tried to fight her, but Claudia was too determined—she had to know, had to see it with her own eyes, know the full extent of Stanwood's depravity. When at last she freed Sophie's hands and yanked the dressing gown open, she stepped back in horror, covering her mouth with a badly trembling hand.

There were bruises everywhere—up and down her ribs, in varying shades of purple and yellow and green. On the underside of her breast, across her abdomen. The clear mark of fingers on the inside of her thighs. Sophie stood rigidly, her head bowed meekly as Claudia gaped at her with tears spilling from her eyes. "Oh, God. Oh, God. *Sophie . . .*"

Sophie carefully pushed a strand of hair behind her ear, then slowly wrapped the ends of the dressing gown around her before calmly tying the sash. "He is very careful to hit me where no one can see," she murmured. "Except for my maid Stella, that is, but he has threatened her life should anyone find out."

Sophie had to leave. At once, without delay. All the

bloody consequences in the world be damned, Sophie had to leave this house at once. "You must leave here," Claudia said quietly.

"No!" Sophie responded sharply. "I *cannot* leave! What respectability my family has left will be destroyed if I—"

"You cannot stay here!" Claudia cried, gesturing wildly at her body. "The next time he may very well *kill* you, Sophie!"

Sophie laughed, a strange, high-pitched laugh that pierced Claudia's heart. "He won't kill me! He *needs* me! Without me, he hasn't any income!" she shouted hysterically, and whirled toward the wall, banging her fists against the paneling. "Christ *God,* what a fool I am!"

Frightened, Claudia lurched forward, wrapping her arms around Sophie and pressing her cheek to her hair. "You *must* leave him! You have grounds for divorce, don't you see? Extreme cruelty—"

"And who will file on my behalf? Julian? No, he won't do it. Firstly, because I will *kill* you if you ever tell him! And . . . and secondly, he won't risk all that he has to the scandal! Even if he did, Claudia, there's no guarantee that I would be granted a divorce! William could fight it . . . he could stop it from happening! Julian knows that!"

Claudia didn't know if that was true or not, and she was too frantic to care. "I don't know what he'll do, but I do know that this . . . this *violence* will not improve with time. I fear for your life, Sophie! You must go from here!"

Choking on a desolate sob, Sophie slapped at Claudia's hands until she let go and twisted out of her embrace. "Even if the family could withstand the scandal, just where do you think I would go, Claudia? If I go to Julian, William will call him out, and I cannot *bear* that! Tell me, where in God's name would I *go?*" she cried helplessly, and covered her face with her hands.

"I know a place," Claudia breathlessly answered. "I know a place where you will be safe, a place he will never find you. Never!"

Sophie lowered her hands. "*What* place? What place could you possibly know besides your father's house or Kettering Hall?"

"It is a place," she frantically continued, "where women can be safe. A place for women just like you, Sophie. No one knows of it, and it is nowhere near here. He can't find you there, I swear it! Come on, then, gather your things. We can go today!"

Sophie gaped at her. A whirlwind of emotions clouded her eyes—despair, disbelief, hope—after a moment, she shook her head and looked furtively at the door. "No, not today. He'll return soon, and he'll know it was you who helped me."

In great frustration, Claudia threw her hands up. "Can you not *see* the bruises on your body? Are you not the least afraid of what he is capable of doing?"

"I know *exactly* what he is capable of doing, believe me," Sophie answered low, and a chill coursed Claudia's spine. "Tomorrow. He is attending the market fair in Huntley and will be gone overnight."

"A market fair?" Claudia asked, confused.

Sophie frowned, flicking her wrist in a show of disgust. "Racing. He has lost quite a lot of Julian's money recently, and he thinks to make it up with a few wagers."

"All right. Tomorrow, then. Julian will help us—"

"*No!*" Sophie shrieked. "You can't tell him! You must *swear* you will not tell him!"

"He must know where you are, Sophie! I cannot keep this from him!"

"If you tell him, I will not go! I would die before I let him see my shame, Claudia! I would take my own life first!" she cried hysterically.

Claudia frantically thought what to do. She could not keep something like this from her husband—Sophie's own brother! But then, she could sense Sophie's deep shame, unfounded though it was. "All right, all right!" she conceded, "I won't tell him now. But he will be frantic with worry when he discovers you are gone!"

"He won't come until Saturday. He won't know for

two days," Sophie said, her eyes beseeching Claudia. She told herself to calm down, told herself that the most important thing was to remove Sophie from harm. As for Julian—*God, she couldn't keep this from him!* But she couldn't *think* now, and for the moment, Sophie had her word.

When she was certain Sophie was safe, then she would figure out how to tell Julian.

Twenty-Two

ONE OF THE most difficult things Claudia
had ever done—ranking right up there with facing Julian
after Sophie's elopement—was to keep the latest news of
Sophie from him. Throughout supper and well into the
late evening hours her mind warred with it. Every time
she looked at him, she felt the crush of guilt and uncertainty. In the drawing room, she sat staring blindly at the
pages of a book in her lap, preoccupied to such a degree
that Julian actually asked if something was wrong. That
startled her; she turned her head to look at him, unsure if
he had actually inquired after her.

"I beg your pardon?" she asked.

Miracle of miracles, a faint smile turned the corners of
his mouth up. "I asked if you were quite all right. This is
usually the point in the evening when you try and impress
upon me how very pleased you are to have made my
acquaintance. As you have not offered any evidence of it
tonight, I cannot help but wonder if you are perhaps
unwell."

Good God, he was *jesting* with her! Stunned, Claudia
shook her head. "I beg your pardon, sir. I never meant to
imply I was *that* pleased to have made your acquaintance."

Julian chuckled softly at her quip. His eyes quickly
flicked the length of her before he returned his attention
to the manuscript he was reviewing. A faint yearning
swept her as she shifted her gaze to the book again, but

she pushed it aside, spending the next several moments anxiously reviewing the escape plan she and Sophie had devised. Stanwood planned to leave midday on the morrow. Claudia would meet Sophie and her maid, Stella, at the corner of Park Lane and Oxford Street, where they could easily slip into an unmarked hack, unnoticed.

"All right, what are you thinking? You look positively frightening with your face all scrunched up like that."

Startled again, Claudia's gaze flew to Julian. "Scrunched up?"

He smiled. "You seem lost in thought."

"Ah," she said, confused by his companionable demeanor. "Well, yes. Yes, I was thinking. About Sophie. I called on her today." The pleasant atmosphere between them suddenly dissipated, and Claudia regretted her words at once.

Frowning, Julian glanced at his manuscript. "Oh? And how did you find her?"

Having already trod upon forbidden ground, she had nothing to lose now. "Wretchedly unhappy," she said softly.

Julian's frown deepened; he removed his eyeglasses, and closing his eyes, pinched the bridge of his nose between his thumb and finger. "Yes, well, unfortunately, that is her own doing."

"There must be something we can do," Claudia continued carefully. "Surely there must be grounds for a separation of some sort."

Julian gave her a piercing look. "You know as well as I that their union is impossible to dissolve if Stanwood is unwilling."

"But he is cruel to her. He corrects her constantly and keeps her confined in that house."

"All rights afforded to him by the law!" Julian responded sharply, growing visibly angry.

Deep breaths, she reminded herself. "She could sue for divorce. It's been done before."

"On what grounds?" He came abruptly out of his chair, stalked to the hearth. "Insanity? Impotence?

Sodomy?" Claudia gasped, but Julian continued, "Do you honestly think I haven't considered it before now? There is no *reason!* She chose him! She cannot *unchoose* him because she has discovered they do not suit, and I, for one, hardly know if that is true! Perhaps she has confided in you, Claudia, but she tells me very little other than she is getting along *swimmingly.*"

The raw anger unnerved her, and gripping the arms of the chair in which she sat to keep from shaking like a coward, Claudia stubbornly continued. "There is cruelty. She could sue on the grounds of cruelty."

Julian suddenly braced his arms against the mantel and dropped his head between his shoulders. "Do you even know what that means?" he asked hoarsely. "It would require evidence of physical violence to her person. I'll grant you that Stanwood is a cur, but there is no evidence he hits her. And if he does, there is no evidence that it is any more than routine discipline."

"Routine *discipline?*" she gasped, wildly affronted by the implication it was all right to beat a wife into submission.

With a groan, Julian tossed his head back and stared at the ceiling. "I do not *condone* it, Claudia! It is an ugly truth, but hitting one's wife does not constitute violence in the eyes of the law!"

Dear God, if only she could tell him the truth. Claudia bowed her head, struggling to keep Sophie's confidence, remembering her frantic promise to her. When she lifted her head, she flinched—Julian was staring hard at her, trying to read her thoughts. "There is no evidence of violence . . . is there, Claudia?" he asked quietly.

A million thoughts crowded her mind. "No." *Dear God, how easily the lie rolled off her tongue.* She instantly dropped her gaze to the arm of the chair, fidgeting with the embroidery of the upholstery. "But if there were, would you do it? I mean, would you help her to seek a divorce?"

Rubbing the back of his neck, Julian moved restlessly

to the window. "Divorce," he said simply, as if testing the word in his mouth.

"Is it the scandal that gives you pause?" she anxiously interjected—too anxiously—he shot her a curious glance over his shoulder.

"I would not *welcome* scandal, by any means," he said. "My father's good name has withstood enough in the last six months. Have you any idea what would befall Sophie if she sought divorce? Even if she had legal reason to seek it, her life would be ruined. No gentleman would have her—*no* gentleman. She would be forced to live tucked away in my house like a diseased relative. No children. No friends to speak of, as no lady would consort with a divorcée. She would not be able to go out into society a'tall. What sort of life is that?"

"A far cry better than what she has now," Claudia muttered.

"God help her, then, Claudia," he said, his voice dangerously low. "God help us all, because that girl knew what she was doing the moment she rode off with him. She made her choice, good or bad, and now she must live with the consequence." With that, he moved restlessly to the door. "I've some work to do," he mumbled, and quit the room before she could say more.

But his words remained with her. Staring into the flames of the fire, unseeing, Claudia struggled with her decision. He would not help Sophie; he had resigned himself to her fate, perhaps thought she was getting what she deserved for her impetuosity. It was galling that if Sophie had been a young man and made this very same mistake, everything would be different. The whole ugly matter would be neatly resolved with separate houses and perhaps the occasional joint appearance at holidays for the sake of propriety. But as a woman, she would give her life for it, and there was nothing in between. The world would not forgive Sophie Dane her mistake.

———

William was irate.

Sophie watched him from beneath half-closed lids as he ranted about the missing purse and the forty pounds that were in it. Forty pounds that he would lose at the horse races on the morrow. "I haven't time to go to the bank now!" he shouted at her. "The mail coach departs at one o'clock!"

"You had best hurry along, then," Sophie suggested.

"Don't tell me what to do!" he snapped. "What of that maid of yours? Where was *she* last evening?"

Her heart skipped a beat. "She had a free day, my lord. Her mother is quite ill, and she was caring for her," she lied.

"The kitchen boy, then. He looks like a little thief!"

"I think you have simply misplaced it—"

William spun around, his hand lashing out and catching her squarely in the jaw. The impact of the blow knocked Sophie backward and crashing into a wardrobe. "Do not speak to me as if I am stupid!"

Unable to speak, Sophie slowly raised her hand to the burning pain in her jaw. The darkness suddenly faded from William's face and he reached for her. Frightened, she flailed her arms at him, but as usual, she was helpless against him—he pinned her arms to her sides in a tight embrace. After several moments, he raised a trembling hand to her face and gingerly touched the spot where he had struck her. "I'm sorry, darling, I'm so sorry," he pleaded. "But I'm under quite a lot of pressure—you *know* that! Why do you say things to upset me?"

She merely shook her head.

"God, does it hurt terribly?" he asked softly, wincing sympathetically. He gently pressed his lips to the swelling. "It won't leave a mark, I am certain of it." He smiled tenderly, brushed her hair from her forehead, then kissed her. "I'd best be along now if I'm to make the bank *and* that coach." He walked over to the bed and picked up his coat. "Mind you, look very hard for that purse," he said amicably. "I'll want to know you have found the culprit when I return Saturday."

Swallowing past the nausea in her throat, Sophie asked, "You'll not return until Saturday, then?"

William stopped mid-way to the door and looked heavenward with a weary sigh. "I've asked you not to henpeck me, Sophie! I'll be home when I have finished my business. Perhaps Saturday. Perhaps later." He extended his hand, gestured her to him. Somehow, Sophie made her legs move, made herself go to him and stand still as he kissed her. "Take care, my dear," he said, and walked out the door, as if it was perfectly natural to strike one's wife, then trot off to the races.

She stood in the middle of his room for what seemed an eternity, unmoving, straining for any sound to suggest he might be returning. When she was at last convinced he had gone, she walked to his wardrobe, rummaged among his many new coats, and pulled his purse from the pocket in which she had hidden it. She opened it, checked to make sure the forty pounds were still there. *Forty pounds*. In a matter of hours, that would be her entire fortune.

The escape was much easier than Claudia had imagined. It was quite cold and wintry, but Sophie and Stella appeared at the appointed time, looking for all the world as if they were out for a casual stroll. Claudia instantly found a hack and the three women climbed inside, feeling as nervous as if they were stealing the crown jewels.

By the time they reached the house on Upper Moreland Street, their respective nerves were frayed to the very ends. Each time the hack shuddered to a halt because of heavy traffic, they flattened themselves against the grimy squabs, fearing that someone might recognize them. That seemed highly unlikely the farther from Mayfair they rode, but Stella frequently imagined she saw someone she knew through the dingy window, and their hearts would pound mercilessly all over again.

At Upper Moreland Street, Claudia gave the driver a gold crown for his excellent driving and another to wait for her, which he happily agreed to do. As they climbed out of the hack, Doreen appeared on the stoop, her hands planted firmly on her hips, stoically watching as Sophie and Stella trudged up the steps with the two small bags they had dared to take away. She took one look at Sophie and shook her head. "Poor dear. You'll be wanting some tea," she said, motioning them inside. Sophie hesitated and looked over her shoulder at Claudia, her eyes full of trepidation. Claudia understood—they were in a part of town Sophie had never seen before, one of decidedly lower class than that to which she was accustomed. And in spite of having a heart as large as the moon, Doreen's stern demeanor hardly instilled a sense of warmth in strangers. Claudia tried to assure Sophie with a nod—which apparently worked for the moment, because Sophie very cautiously crossed the threshold.

Inside, a woman took Sophie and Stella's cloaks, then ushered them into the parlor with cheerful chatter, insisting that they warm up by the fire. As the woman helped Stella drag another chair to the hearth, Sophie leaned toward Claudia and whispered, "What is this place?"

Doreen overheard her and flashed one of her rare smiles as she patted Sophie's arm. "Let's have us a tea. We'll have us a tea we will, and then we'll talk all night if you like." With a furtive look at Claudia, Sophie nodded uncertainly, and took a seat in the chair nearest the small fire. It was then that Claudia saw the bruise on her jaw.

Astonished that she had not noticed it before now— the ribbon of her bonnet had covered it, she supposed— Claudia tried very hard not to stare at Sophie. It was a new mark, one that Stanwood had put there sometime between her call yesterday afternoon and their escape. It made Claudia's stomach churn with revulsion; she could not conceive of the beast that would beat someone so much smaller than he. He was a coward, a bloody coward, and as she tried to put Sophie at ease by pointing out interesting things—some children's watercolors, the women's needlework scattered on pillows about the room, the piecework piled next to Doreen's rocking chair—she wished someone bigger and stronger than Stanwood would beat *him* into submission.

Her attempts to calm Sophie were not having the desired affect—the poor dear's eyes were growing wider and wider with consternation. It had to be very difficult for her—Sophie was a lady, the daughter and sister of an earldom that had its roots in centuries of English monarchy. She had been raised in luxury, had never been exposed to the working class except to receive their services. Never like this, certainly, and it was all quite foreign to her. Claudia began to worry that she might not stay, might feel as uncomfortable here as she did in Stanwood's house.

A woman appeared in the door carrying an old tarnished tea service. As she moved into the room, Sophie's eyes rounded impossibly with what seemed like sheer terror. She fixated on the woman, staring intently at her as she placed the service down and poured a cup of tea. As the woman offered the cup to Sophie, Claudia saw what she saw—the white of the woman's left eye was bloody red, the skin around it black and blue.

Sophie lifted her hand to the bruise on her chin. The woman slowly lowered the proffered tea to the table and sank into a chair, folding her hands tightly in her lap. The two women stared at each other until the woman muttered softly. "You ain't alone, miss."

And Sophie began to sob.

Claudia stayed an hour, until the snow began to fall. Sophie had calmed considerably, but nonetheless clung to her tightly as she took her leave. "It will be all right, Sophie," Claudia whispered fervently.

Sophie nodded, trying hard to believe it, and the truth was that Claudia could only hope it would be all right. As the hack pulled away from the curb, a sick feeling of dread filled her to the back of her throat. As powerful as she knew Julian to be, he could not single-handedly change the laws of Great Britain to accommodate Sophie. Worse, there was the little matter of telling Julian what she had done.

That engendered an entirely different sort of panic in her.

Twenty-Three

JULIAN'S EYES STRAINED to make out the meticulously scripted letters of the ancient manuscript; his brain labored to translate the text into English. In two hours of work he had succeeded with one stanza. Just one four-line stanza. He removed his spectacles and restlessly ground the heels of his hands into his eyes. *How long could he continue like this?*

His hands slid from his eyes to the back of his neck, and hanging his head, he rubbed the taut muscles, feeling the shaft of tension down his spine and into his legs. This constant anxiety was killing him, this wild discomfort with everything and everyone around him. It was her fault, he thought bitterly, her fault because he could not stop loving her, no matter how hard he tried. No matter how hard he fought to put a steel cage around his heart, she just kept squeezing in.

He dropped his hands and slowly lifted his head, his gaze inevitably landing on the little pot of violets that sat on the corner of his desk. He leaned back, templing his fingers, studying the silly little thing. Someone tended the pot every day, watering it faithfully, pruning the dead blooms. Every day, more blooms appeared, their numbers now practically bursting from the confines of the little porcelain pot. Even *that* was different—it was painted with sunshine and trees and flowers, and if he wasn't mistaken, a godawful rendition of the front façade of Kettering House.

The roots of those violets had, miraculously, twined around his dead heart, had squeezed a little more life into it each day, forcing him to remember that he loved her, that for all her peculiarities and crimes of passion, she was what he wanted in this life. It was the blasted blue and purple blooms that caught his eye every morning, dragging his attention to them, drawing him closer to their beauty . . . just as he was drawn to Claudia. And it was the crude little paintings on the porcelain pot, all things warm and bright, carefree and indifferent, but beautiful all the same.

Just like Claudia.

Julian abruptly shoved the old manuscript away from him and stood, moving unsteadily away from the desk and the violets. He *did* love her. Certainly he was angry with her for having so thoughtlessly influenced Sophie's decision to elope. Yet he knew that the bad advice had not been given malevolently; Claudia had done it out of a passionate belief she was right. No, he no longer held Claudia responsible for Sophie's misfortune.

So what exactly, then, did he continue to fight? What made him struggle to avoid her, labor to keep her from his every waking thought? Julian paused in front of the windows, staring blindly at the snow that covered St. James Square.

Perhaps if he were honest with himself—an endeavor in and of itself—he would acknowledge that there was a part of him that simply could not bear to know that she did not return his deep affection. He suspected her recent and sudden declarations of love to be the product of her guilt. She was blaming herself for Sophie's tragedy, and her sudden attention was her way of atoning. Eventually, she would tire of her self-imposed penance, and when she did, he was certain things would return to the way they had been. She would despise her circumstance, think of Phillip often, and flit through Julian's life and his heart like a butterfly, taunting him with her prettiness while she eluded capture. When that happened, he was quite certain he would crumble like earth between his fingers, disappearing into the tall weed-infested grass that had become their life.

So he clung to his survival instincts and held her at arm's length.

Which was just as well, because there was another, equally desperate part of him that remained certain he would, eventually, ruin her, too. The dark forces of nature that seemed to govern his life would find a way to harm Claudia, just like others he had loved. He had been pushed to the limits of his sanity when Valerie died, shoved over the edge into the black abyss with Phillip's death, and was now spiraling down into darkness with Sophie's ruin. When misfortune at last found Claudia—and it would, if he loved her—his soul would surely burn in hell for it.

It was better, he had concluded, to keep her out of his mind and his heart. It was better to bury himself in ancient tomes, never lifting his head, blocking out all sound and light.

He turned away from the window and glanced at the clock on the mantel, then scowled deeply. Unfortunately, in a lighter moment, he had felt compelled to accept an invitation to join the Albrights and guests this evening for supper and cards. As much as it repulsed him, it was a fact that appearances among the *ton* were everything. Because of Sophie, he had accepted the invitation, knowing that if he were to keep up the pretense of her marriage, it had to seem as if everything was fine with the Kettering family.

Twenty-four hours had done nothing to bring about a brilliant idea, nor had the passage of time done anything to ease Claudia's panic, which was now a full-blown raging hysteria. Jesus, Mary, and Joseph, she had committed a *crime* by taking Sophie away from her home! An unpardonable crime, and worse yet, under English law, her crime was *Julian's* crime. He was guilty for stealing his own sister, for which he could lose his lands or his liberty or maybe even his head, and he didn't even *know* it!

Several times Claudia almost left her rooms in search of Julian, prepared to confess all and beg his help. Cold, hard fear had stopped her each time—fear that he would ultimately force Sophie home after he had throttled his wife. Claudia could bear his wrath and whatever punishment he might mete out, but she could not bear to see Sophie's return to Stanwood. No, she would die first before she allowed that to happen.

Her indecisiveness had kept her in a state of agitation all day, and she dressed thoughtlessly for the Albright supper party. She hardly noticed the elegant hairstyle Brenda gave her, weaving strands of silver ribbon through her dark hair that picked up the embroidery of her bodice. When she fastened the aquamarine and diamond earrings to her lobes that matched the necklace she wore, she at last forced herself to look in the mirror. The rose-colored velvet and brocade gown went well with her complexion, she supposed, but nothing could erase the lines of worry around her eyes, the pale skin, the guilty set of her mouth. Other than that, she did not think she looked particularly like a criminal.

With a weary sigh, she pushed a curl from her temple and slipped lackadaisically into her pale rose slippers, then reluctantly made her way downstairs as if practicing her walk to the gallows.

In the blue drawing room, Julian paced impatiently as he waited for Claudia, his apprehension growing with each step. This was a bad idea, he thought, a very bad idea. How would he endure her at his elbow all evening? What had made him think he could act as if all was well in front of two of the most meddling men in Europe? If there was any one thing that he despised about Adrian Spence and Arthur Christian, it was their uncanny ability to read him like a goddam book.

"Oh, my. You are . . . *beautiful.*"

Her hushed voice startled Julian; he had not heard her enter and turned awkwardly, feeling his breath rush from his lungs as he did so.

Oh, God. She appeared before him like a princess. Very deliberately, he turned to face her fully, unable to look away from the stunning sight of her.

She blushed; smiling faintly, she self-consciously pushed a dark curl behind her ear. "Do I offend? I apologize. It's just that you look so . . . *well,*" she said, and laughed uncertainly.

He could feel the heat of her simple compliment spreading through his body. Still, he could only stare, marveling at how she had managed to captivate him yet again, knock him off-center and send him into a tailspin of desire.

Her fair cheeks began to glow with her flush. "I sincerely *hope* I didn't offend."

"No," he said, finding his voice. *It's just that I was thinking the same thing of you.* "Please," he added like a simpleton, and motioned toward one of two leather wing-back chairs directly in front of the fireplace. Her tremulous smile deepened. "It's early yet," he said gruffly. "Would you like some wine?" He flicked a gaze to the footman at the door and nodded curtly, then somehow managed to command his legs to move from the windows to the fireplace.

She hesitated, peering at him warily before following his gesture to sit, fussing with the loose curls of her hair as she glided across the carpet. She sat lightly on the edge of the chair facing the one he had taken, and as she arranged her skirts just so, he admired the ripe fullness of her intricately embroidered bodice—what there was of it, anyway—rising softly with each breath.

The footman appeared on her left, bowing with his silver tray. With a sweet smile, Claudia took a glass of wine, waiting until Julian was served before sipping daintily. He did not drink, but continued to gaze at her over the rim of the crystal glass, feeling the familiar sense of discomfort, the old fright that he might never hold such beauty in his arms.

Claudia lowered her wineglass and fidgeted with the jeweled necklace that rested against her throat. After a moment, she peeked up at him through her thick, dark lashes. "It's almost a year now since I saw you at the Farnsworths' Christmas Ball," she said, dropping her gaze to the wineglass for a moment. "I remember it because you wore all black then, too. Black coat and trousers. Black waistcoat and neckcloth. You looked very much like a dangerous highwayman." She paused; when he said nothing, she nervously cleared her throat. One finger traced the rim of the wineglass, round and round and round.

Julian remembered that ball very clearly. He had arrived at the tail end of some insane excursion, one that had taken him past Dunwoody, where Phillip was buried. What had possessed him to stop at Phillip's grave he would never know, but he had, taking a handful of hothouse flowers. And he had left Phillip's grave, his head aching to the point of bursting—the result, he had told himself, of no sleep and too much drinking. *Not guilt.*

"And you were still wearing your spurs," she added. "Miss Chatham remarked upon them, too—she rather fancied you had ridden all the way from Kettering Hall just for the Farnsworth Ball."

Julian arched a quizzical brow. "And what did you think?" he asked quietly.

"That you were the most handsome man in all of London," she answered instantly.

He felt the first crack in the ice around his heart. Very calmly, he put the wine aside and asked, "Why do you flatter me so?"

"I do not flatter you, Julian. I admire you—I can't seem to help myself," she said, and drank hastily from the wineglass. "You simply reminded me of that night. I'm sorry."

"I remember you, too," he heard himself respond. "You wore a ribbon of dried hollyberries in your hair."

A smile of genuine surprise swept her lips, one of her many smiles that could lighten his soul in the blink of an eye. "You remember *that?*" she asked, clearly pleased.

"As well as the hollyberries on your shoes."

Claudia smiled fully then, and Julian could feel the warmth and brilliance of it on his heart, thawing the ice. She laughed gaily, a melodious sound he had not heard in weeks. "Papa was quite displeased with me, I'll have you know. Swore I ruined a perfectly good pair of slippers."

"I thought it rather festive," he said, and realized that he was smiling, too.

"I don't know how you managed to see all that," she continued laughingly. "You were clear across the ballroom, surrounded by your many female admirers. I think they were four or five deep. And as I recall, Miss Chatham was among the most ardent."

He remembered, all right. Even remembered kissing a panting Miss Chatham in the vestibule and wishing it had been Claudia. "A pity you weren't among them," he said.

Claudia's smile slowly faded; her blue-gray eyes locked with his for a long moment, and Julian had the sensation that she could see past his protective armor, past the ice. "I was among them," she said at last. "I have always been among them—you just couldn't see me. And I shall always be among them, regardless of what may come."

Speech eluded him. He suddenly moved forward, wanting to touch her, wanting to demand the truth from her. Reaching across the gap between them, he tenderly ran his hand over her elbow, down to her wrist, wrapping his fingers firmly around it. "Claudia," he said low, "never tell me something like that if only to appease your troubled conscience. Never tell me that unless you mean it with all your heart—"

"My lord, the coach is ready," intoned Tinley from the doorway. Startled, Julian turned toward the old man as he hobbled into the room to rest against a chair. "In the drive, nice and warm for milady," he added with a self-satisfied grin.

The old man's timing was incredible. "Thank you," Julian uttered with only a modicum of civility, and looked again at Claudia. She was smiling, her eyes were sparkling, and slowly, uncertainly, he stood, his hand floating up her arm to her elbow to help her to her feet.

She rose gracefully, hesitating slightly as she stood before him. "I *do* mean it, Julian, with all my heart," she murmured, and rocked up to the tips of her little rose slippers to shyly kiss the corner of his mouth.

Before he could recover from the extraordinary sensation of that simple kiss, she was walking toward Tinley, putting out a hand to steady the old man as he hobbled to the door. Dumbly, Julian followed her to the foyer, staring hard at her as she donned her cloak and bonnet, struggling into his gloves as he struggled to believe her. He followed her just as dumbly out onto the hard, crusty snow, feeling her gay laughter invade his very marrow when she slipped and knocked against him.

And when the coach lurched forward, jostling them as the driver searched for the smoothest stretch of road, he regarded her suspiciously, afraid to believe her. She responded with a soft smile, her eyes sparkling as brilliantly as the jewels at her throat. "You don't believe me," she said at last.

"Not entirely," he admitted cautiously. *But God knows I want to.*

The coach lurched sharply to one side Claudia tried to brace herself, but began to slip from the velvet squabs. Julian instantly reached for her, catching her under her arms, and without thinking, dragged her into his lap. "I *want* to believe you."

Something flashed in her eyes; she abruptly grabbed his head, holding him with surprising strength as she kissed him, sliding her lush lips across his, nipping at the flesh along the edge of his mouth. She crushed her lithesome body to him while he carefully, almost unwilling, moved his hand delicately along her shoulder and neck, to her cheek, cautiously cupping her face.

The coach lurched again, and just as suddenly as it had begun, it was over. Claudia lifted her head, gazing down at him as she took several deep breaths. "I don't know how to convince you," she said. "I don't even know if I should." She moved off his lap to sit beside him. Julian did not respond, fearing that he might show her how desperate he was to be convinced, how dangerously close he had come to it by virtue of one smoldering kiss. Artlessly, she leaned against him as if they were old lovers, staring thoughtfully out the window as the coach bounced along. He quietly curled his hand around hers, and Claudia responded by squeezing his fingers.

Julian felt the reassuring little squeeze all the way to his heart, and wondered if he was perfectly mad to believe it could be right between the two of them, that they *could* be old lovers one day.

The Earl of Albright had, against his better judgment, brought his wife along on what was intended to be a very short trip to London. He had fully intended to return to Longbridge, his country estate, by the end of the week. Certainly, he had not meant to stay so long, much less host a supper party. But his wife, Lilliana, had insisted upon it, reminding him that she had been stuck at Longbridge for weeks without so much as a single guest and no one to talk to but him and the baby and various and sundry cows. And then she had shoved him flat on his back so that she might guarantee the answer she wanted by making passionate love to him. He was, as usual, quite helpless.

Therefore, he and Arthur stood at the sideboard, surveying the roomful of guests. Lilliana and Claudia were laughing gaily with the Duchess of Sutherland, Lauren. There was Arthur's brother Alex, the Duke of Sutherland, seated on a settee with Louis Renault and Lord Boxworth, engaged in heated conversation about the latest spate of parliamentary reforms. Ladies Boxworth and Renault were in attendance, and naturally, Julian Dane, who stood to one side quietly sipping from a glass of port and watching his wife like a hawk.

Adrian slid his gaze from Julian to Arthur with a smirk. "I'd say the old chap has it rather bad."

"Right awful," Arthur replied immediately, "although I'd venture to guess he doesn't yet know it. He was never very astute in matters of the heart."

"What, you would judge the man by the number of broken hearts left in his wake over the years?" Adrian asked laughingly.

"Did you see him at supper? Gazing like a lovesick lad when she spoke of organizing women's labor. He's gone round the bend, if you ask me—smitten with a woman born to trouble," Arthur observed, clearly amused.

"I'll say," Adrian muttered as he slipped his gaze to Claudia. "Do you know she actually had Lilliana convinced that the daughters of my tenants would do well with a summer in London at our considerable expense? Lilliana had drafted a rather complicated schedule for it, and was about to go and explain it all at a tenants' meeting before I caught her."

"A summer in London? What on earth for?" Arthur asked, clearly confused.

Adrian frowned. "Culture and education."

Arthur looked at Adrian; the two men simultaneously broke into laughter.

If Julian had heard the exchange, he might have laughed, too. But he hadn't heard a bloody thing all night—Claudia had consumed him. If he wasn't simply gazing at her, he was thinking about that ride in the coach. And if he wasn't thinking about that, he was feeling rather proud of her eloquent argument to organize women's labor.

Now, in the red drawing room, he was impatiently biding his time until he could make a proper escape, take his wife home, and continue the discussion begun in the coach. Having had the intervening hours to reflect, he was more than happy to let Claudia convince him that she adored him. He had even gone so far as to allow himself the fantasy that they might put the awful past behind them and begin fresh—starting with his making love to her. Over and over again, if he was so fortunate.

But then Max, Adrian's butler, caught his eye. The diminutive little man appeared in the door, hopping nervously from one foot to the other as Adrian sauntered forward. Julian knew Max, knew he tended toward the dramatic, but he nonetheless had a terrible sense of foreboding when Max motioned wildly in the direction of the vestibule and a frown creased Adrian's brow.

The sudden commotion in the corridor startled Julian; he moved to the center of the room as Adrian stepped across the threshold. "Ho there!" he called gruffly. "What do you think you are doing?"

Before anyone could react, Stanwood suddenly appeared at the threshold, looking wildly furious. Julian's stomach dropped; he quickly stepped around the settee as Stanwood barreled past Adrian and into the room. *"Halt there, Stanwood!"* he bellowed, ignoring the cry of alarm that came from one of the women. "I will thank you to leave Lord Albright's home at once—"

"Not before you tell me where she is! What have you done with my wife?!"

"Oh, dear God! What has happened to Sophie?" Eugenie shrieked.

Julian lurched forward as Stanwood, practically foaming at the mouth, whirled toward Eugenie. "She's *gone!* You have taken her from me, but it won't do you any good! That slut belongs to *me* now!"

Julian did not realize that the roar of indignation was his own. It hardly registered on him that Sophie was missing—his rage made him too deaf, too blind to anything but Stanwood and his own firm intent to kill him this time. He lunged, shoving Stanwood into the wall with a hard blow to the bastard's eye. Quickly regaining his balance, Julian raised his arm again, but someone restrained him as three footmen rushed to subdue

Stanwood. Furious, Julian struggled against the restraint; Adrian said heatedly, "Don't, Kettering! He's not worth it!"

"Did you think you could hide her from me forever?" Stanwood gasped, struggling against the hold of the three men. "You *can't,* Kettering. She belongs to *me* now, every inch of her *and* her bloody fortune! I will do with that whore what I like—"

"Stop it!" Claudia shrieked. *"I* took her!"

A stunned hush fell across the room; Julian felt as if the floor had shifted beneath his feet. *She* had taken Sophie? His mind could not absorb that, or the implications of it. He shrugged out of Arthur and Louis's grasp, mindlessly straightened his waistcoat before he turned to look at her. "What do you mean, Claudia?" he asked evenly, despite the rage boiling in him just beneath the surface.

"You bitch," Stanwood breathed rabidly. "You came into *my* home and took *my wife* from me? That's a bloody crime, you stupid—"

Julian jerked around, pinning Stanwood to the wall with a murderous gaze as the footmen yanked him out of Julian's reach. "One more word, and I will kill you, so help me God!"

"Call me what you will, sir," Claudia said, her voice trembling. "But you won't lay a hand on her again!"

"Dear God! Where *is* she?" Eugenie cried hysterically. "What on earth have you done with her?"

Claudia looked wildly around her, her gaze skimming blindly across them all before settling on Stanwood again. "Sh-she is quite safe. But I won't tell you where, not until I am certain she is safe from him!" Her hands gripped her gown, balling the fabric.

Julian could sense the hysteria rising in her just as acutely as he felt the fury rising in himself. He could scarcely believe what he was hearing, unable to fathom how she might have done this, how she might have defied the law and him and stolen his sister. How she had neglected to tell him what she had done.

"You will pay for this, Lady Kettering! With your *life*, if I've anything to do with it!" Stanwood shouted.

"Take him!" Adrian roared. "Throw him out near the river. Shoot him if he causes a scene!"

"I'll go and make sure he doesn't," Arthur said, striding forward, and followed the servants out as they dragged Stanwood away.

"What of my wife!" he screamed as they forced him into the corridor. "I demand to know where she is!"

Julian jerked around to stare at *his* wife. Claudia gasped audibly for her breath; the expression on her face was one of terror. And he was struck with the notion that he had never felt more impotent than he did at this moment, incapable of controlling one goddam thing. Trying desperately to control his temper, he walked to her side. "We've got to get out of here."

"Julian, wait!" Ann cried. "We must know what she has done with Sophie!"

"I will speak with her, Ann!" he said gruffly, and glanced at Adrian, who seemed to sense how ridiculously sorry he was—he waved him on. Julian did not hesitate. Clamping an iron hold on Claudia, he pushed her into the corridor, propelling her forward when she stumbled on her hem. He said not a word other than to demand their coach, then stoically accepted their cloaks from a nervous footman, tossing Claudia's around her shoulders.

"Julian—" she started, but he was unable to speak, barely able to breathe, and stopped her from saying more by grabbing her arm and pushing her outside and into the coach as rage clawed at his throat.

Once inside, she tried again. "Julian, please, I—"

"No," he said simply, dangerously. She seemed to almost disappear into the squabs then, eyeing him warily as the coach pitched through the snow-covered streets of London.

The ride home was unbearable; silence stretched between them like an ocean. With each jolt the coach took over the icy roads, he despised her more. She had gelded him, publicly emasculated him. Jesus Christ, the whirlwind of emotion and confusion she had caused in him for two years now had exhausted him beyond reason or caring. There was simply nothing left in him, nothing else she could use up.

He wanted only to know where Sophie was.

When they reached Kettering House, Julian cut a scathing glance across her as he climbed out of the coach. When he extended his hand to help her down, Claudia grabbed his wrist and would not let go. His anger spiraled out of control; he jerked his arm up, yanking free of her and flinging her hand away from him. Ignoring the looks of astonishment on the faces of the driver and the two footmen, he stormed inside and up the grand staircase. The Demon's Spawn followed him.

Stalking into his rooms, he whirled around to face her, dragging ragged breaths of air as he clawed at his neckcloth and tossed it carelessly aside. "Where is she?" he managed to choke out.

"Please, listen to me—"

"Where is she?" he roared to the ceiling.

Claudia jumped several steps backward. "On my life, she is safe, Julian, I swear it—"

"How dare you swear *anything* to me! Do you even realize that you have committed a crime? *Where is she?*"

One arm curled protectively around her abdomen. "I—I won't tell you, not like this."

Rage blinded him; he pivoted sharply away from her, his hands on either side of his head, pressed against the ungodly throbbing in his temples. "Do not toy with me, Claudia!" he breathed. "What in God's name have you done with her?"

"He was *beating* her, Julian!" she cried. "I saw the bruises, and I . . . I feared for her life!"

All that was left of his composure shattered. The world stopped spinning; he had to fight the drag of inertia to turn and look at her. The color had bled from her face, the wetness in her eyes glistened in the candlelight. Bloody hell, it was true—his worst nightmare had become a reality. *"Bruises,"* he muttered hoarsely.

She nodded furiously, wiped her hands across her cheeks. "Lots of them. Up and down her body. She said . . . she said he hit her where it wouldn't show."

Why, God, did the earth not open and bury him now? Why must he endure this unspeakable anguish? "Why didn't you tell me?" he rasped, and when she did not answer immediately, his fury erupted anew. *"Why? Why didn't you tell me!"*

"B-because I was *afraid!*" she wailed. "I wanted to tell you, but I wasn't sure what you would do, and I could not bear it if you made her go back to him! And we had only a small window of opportunity—"

"How you must despise me, Claudia," he croaked. "You think me so heartless that I would leave my sister to a *monster?*"

"I only wanted to help Sophie—"

"You only wanted to geld me!" he spat. "If you'd had any sense at all you would have *told* me. I would have helped her! She is my *sister,* for God's sake! But no, you would prefer to announce to the world my impotence in this matter!"

Claudia gaped at him, dumbfounded. "Do I understand you correctly? You are angry because your male *pride* is injured?" she asked, incredulous.

"Thanks to you, madam, I have no pride. You have deprived me of even that. You win, Claudia. You have worn me down, physically and emotionally, and I scarcely know which end is up anymore."

"I have worn *you* down? Need I remind you, sir, that *you* seduced *me?* Your *lust* wore me down! It is the only reason we are standing here at all!"

"You seemed willing enough, lady," he retorted hotly, blatantly ignoring the truth of her statement.

She gasped with indignation. "Yes, *yes,* I was willing! I had drunk far too much champagne, and you—Oh, please *God,* don't remind me how poor my judgment has been all my life when it comes to *you!*"

His anger was now pounding like a drum in his chest and his throat and his temples, and Julian took a menacing step toward her. "Don't speak to me of poor judgment! I should have followed my instincts and left you to fend for your high and mighty self! I should *never* have allowed your father to talk me into protecting your honor! Had I known it would destroy my sister in the end, I would have let you *rot* in your scandal!"

"Had you at least *listened* to Sophie instead of thinking yourself so holy and infallible, this might never have happened!"

And now this was all *his* doing? "And had I listened to my head instead of my cock, this never would have happened, either, I assure you," he shot back.

That stung her. Claudia recoiled as if she had been slapped. "It's always the same with you, isn't it?" she muttered. "It's just lust—you don't really care where you relieve yourself of it, as long as it is warm and moving." A hysterical laugh bubbled up from her throat; her hand flew to her cheek. "Dear God, I *believed* you when you said you loved me! I truly believed you! But it was just another lie, wasn't it? Another lie to lure me to your bed! You *disgust* me!"

"It was a lie no worse than yours, Claudia. I wanted to believe you, too, but it seems we were ill-fated from the beginning. Well, you need not worry any longer—I would rather see myself strung up at Newgate before I have you in my bed again. The only thing I want from you is the whereabouts of my sister."

Her eyes narrowed dangerously. *"No."*

"Do you think this some sort of game?" he snapped irritably. "Another one of your little fantasies where women rule the world?"

"I told you, she is quite safe. But I won't tell you where, not until you have calmed yourself. You can't go after her, not like this."

He suddenly lunged at her, but Claudia quickly stepped beyond his reach. "There is nothing you can do to make me tell you!" she cried, and whirled, fleeing the rooms.

You can't make me stay in my rooms! The sudden

image of the defiant little girl shattered him; Julian fell to
one knee, covering his eyes with one hand as he tried to
steady himself with the other. The discomfort of his skin
was overpowering, tightening around his bones and his
skull. She had done it at last, destroyed him completely.
Funny, wasn't it, that all this time he'd been worried that
he would destroy *her.*

There was nothing left for them, except finding a way
to end this farce of a marriage once and for all.

Twenty-Four

Claudia was not invited to the family caucus that occurred the next afternoon, which was made exceedingly clear to her. Dejected, confused, and rather unsure of herself, she dismissed Brenda and spent the day in lonely solitude, moving woodenly to pack her things, knowing full well that it was over. The whole ugly mess was almost too complicated for her to fathom, and as hard as she tried, she could not put her finger on exactly what had ultimately destroyed his love for her.

There was so much distrust between them; doubts spanning years, too many untruths she could not seem to ferret her way through. Only one thing did she know with complete certainty.

She loved Julian.

Completely, with all her heart, as fiercely and futilely and fatally as she had when she was a young girl, if not more so. She loved him, but she loved Sophie, too, and she could not be entirely sorry for what she had done.

Nonetheless, Claudia intuitively understood that even if Sophie had never been, she would still be packing her things today. She and Julian were doomed from the moment they encountered one another in Dieppe, and if it hadn't been this, something else would eventually have caused her to stand on the outside looking in. She was too independent for this world, too involved in social causes, too irreverent of society's mores to have endured a marriage among the *ton*. Eventually, her school, or the town

house on Upper Moreland Street—*something*—would
have come between them.

Unfortunately, as much as she wanted to at this
moment, she could not change who she was.

It was late afternoon when someone finally rapped on
her door. Opening it, she found Tinley leaning against the
doorjamb. He motioned her aside and shuffled into her
room, easing himself down onto the couch at the hearth.
"Forgive me, milady, but I must catch my breath."

Claudia closed the door. "Tinley? Is something
wrong?"

Tinley stuck his bony hand into a breast pocket and
pulled out a piece of paper, extending it toward her with
his crooked arm. It was from Julian—he had taken to
writing things down rather than trust Tinley's memory.
Claudia did not want to read that note and watched it
taunt her from Tinley's wavering arm. "My *lady*," he
groaned when she made no move to take it.

She forced herself to take the note. Turning slightly so
that Tinley could not see her face, she opened it.

> *I will have your presence in the blue drawing*
> *room at precisely four o'clock. K.*

That was all—nothing more than a simple command.
Claudia glanced at the clock. A quarter of an hour. She
shifted her gaze to Tinley. "What does one usually wear to
a hanging, do you suppose?" she asked grimly.

"Black, I'd wager," Tinley responded affably.

At precisely four o'clock, Claudia was standing at the
door of the blue drawing room, drawing deep breaths into
her lungs in a futile attempt to calm her racing heart.
When that didn't work, she pressed her hands flat against
her abdomen, swallowing hard between breaths so that
her anxiety would not make her sick. She should knock,
go into that room and face the consequences of it all, but

apparently there was no force in the universe that could make her raise her arm.

No force was necessary; the door suddenly swung open and Julian glared down at her. "What are you waiting for?" he snapped as he stepped aside to give her entry.

Willing her legs to move, Claudia walked into the room. Julian shut the door with a resounding *thud,* clasped his hands behind his back, and began to pace in front of her. Back and forth he went, the hem of his coat flying out behind him with every violent turn. Too cowardly to speak or move, Claudia watched him, watched the muscles in his jaw bulge with the force of his bite, watched him glance at her, then to the floor again, as if her face burned him like the sun. It went on for what seemed like an eternity, but finally, he stopped and forced himself to look at her. "Where is she?"

Claudia released the breath she had been holding. "What will you do with her?"

His eyes roamed her face, searching, as if he had never really seen her before now. "I will protect her with my life, Claudia . . . how can you not *know* that?"

There was pain in his voice; she swallowed past a sudden lump of emotion, blinking rapidly against tears that all at once welled in her eyes. "I *do* know it," she admitted quietly. And she did—she knew it about him as well as she knew herself, and wondered madly why it had taken her so long to understand it. "I'll give you the directions."

Julian pivoted and strode quickly to a writing table, snatching paper and pencil, then strode back to her, thrusting them at her. "Write it down," he said anxiously, "the *exact* directions." He retrieved his spectacles and peered over her shoulder as she wrote the directions to 31 Upper Moreland Street, fairly snatching the paper from her hand when she had finished. He looked tired, she thought, much older than his thirty-three years. He frowned and glanced up at her. "I don't know the street."

"You wouldn't," she mumbled.

His frown deepened as he stuffed the paper into his

coat pocket, then walked swiftly to the door. "How far? I wonder if I might reach it before nightfall?" he muttered to himself, distracted. "I'll just send a note to Genie—"

"I intend to go to my father's house," Claudia said quietly.

With his back to her, Julian paused, his body visibly tensing. *Please say no. Say no, say no,* she silently begged him. "I won't stop you," he said without turning.

What was left of her heart crashed like a falling star to the earth. Tears slipped from her eyes and raced down her cheeks. "I was rather hoping you would," she said, and gulped back more tears.

Almost reluctantly, it seemed, he turned to look at her. His gaze faltered for a moment as he glanced at the paper in his hand, then at her again. "It's rather useless, don't you think?"

"Is it?" she whispered.

He nodded solemnly.

There it was—it was over, all hope gone, crushed— her husband plainly despised her. Claudia forced her gaze from his handsome face to the carpet at her feet—she never wanted to lay eyes on him again, not when he looked like this, so handsome, so virile . . . so distant and cold. "I've packed a few things. If you would be so kind as to send one of the footmen with it?"

"Of course."

She kept her gaze riveted to the floor, wishing he would just go now, leave her to her sorrow and misery.

"Claudia . . ."

He would not let her go, not like this! Her heart took wing, feebly attempting to resurrect itself.

"Is there anything I should know about this place? Will I encounter any obstacles if I want to see her?" he asked.

The wings on her heart broke and sent it plummeting to earth in a tailspin. "No, of course not," she managed. "She is quite safe. You need only knock on the door, and the rest is up to Sophie."

He nodded, turned away, and walked out of the room.

And Claudia collapsed onto a settee, doubled over in grief as the tears of her despair poured out of her heart.

Julian had but one thought upon seeing Upper Moreland Street: He was glad Claudia was gone, else he'd be tempted to have her head for subjecting Sophie to this place. Upper Moreland Street was clearly *far* beneath the standard of living Sophie was accustomed to, and Julian resented the hell out of it.

The coach pulled to a stop in front of Number 31; he alighted, closely watching the woman who appeared on the stoop. Small and thin, the gown she wore looked too big for her and had been patched in more than one place. Her graying brown hair was swept back and knotted tightly at her nape, making her look rather severe in countenance. She frowned as Julian walked toward her and folded her arms defensively beneath her bosom.

"Good evening," he called.

"Who are you?" she demanded.

"The Earl of Kettering," he informed her with an aristocratic air.

The woman, however, did not seem particularly impressed. "Ah," she remarked, as if they had met before. "So you're him, are you?"

Him? He let it go. "Might I inquire as to whom I have the pleasure of speaking?"

"Mrs. Conner."

"Mrs. Conner, I am given to understand that my sister, Lady Stanwood—"

"She's here all right. Come on, then," she said, and stepped into the little house.

Hesitating briefly, Julian walked up the steps of the little stoop, stepping into the tiny vestibule and passing through to the main corridor. Instantly, he encountered two young boys tumbling roughly in the narrow hallway as one of them rolled like a ball onto his foot. Julian cleared his throat, succeeded in gaining the lads' attention. Both turned startled expressions to him, tilting their heads as far back as they could to see him.

"Blimey," whispered one, his eyes as round as saucers.

"Blimey, indeed," Julian drawled, and carefully stepped over the two ruffians, snapping his greatcoat away from their grubby little hands. He had lost Mrs. Conner, of course, and paused as the two boys resumed their boisterous play, peering into one room on his left.

Two women were seated inside the small parlor, darning a mountain of stockings. One of them glanced at him and smiled broadly. "G'day, milord," she called out in a thick cockney accent.

Julian nodded curtly and quickly moved on. Rough lads and cockney women—what else had Sophie been subjected to? How had Claudia ever thought to bring her to such a place? Frustrated, he paused at the door to his right and looked inside. It was a dining area of some sort, except that bolts of cloth were strewn all over the place. Two young girls labored with a pair of shears over a bolt on the table, carefully cutting the cloth into large squares. The oldest girl paused in her work and peered curiously at him. "Are you the magistrate?" she asked.

"No," he responded instantly, shuddering to think why a girl of that age should have a need to know what a magistrate was, much less be expecting one. *Good God.* Where in the hell was Sophie? He headed for the stairs at the end of the corridor but noticed a door behind it. Leaning to one side to have a better look, he thought he ought to at least try the door before he went up and accidentally blundered into someone's bedchamber.

The door led to a narrow hall, which connected the front of the little house with another room in the back. As Julian squeezed into the narrow passageway, the scent of fresh-baked bread reached his nose. He had, apparently, stumbled onto the kitchens. He stuck his head in nonetheless to see three women baking, one up to her elbows in dough.

"Oh, my, look 'ere, Dorcus," one chirped cheerfully. " 'Av 'ye ever seen such a fine-lookin' bloke?"

The woman at a washtub quickly turned around. A gap-toothed grin spread her lips as she hastily wiped her hands on her apron. "Well then, come *in*, milord! We won't bite ye now, will we, Sandra?"

"I'm not making 'im any promises," Sandra replied coquettishly, and the three women howled their shared amusement.

"I beg your pardon—apparently I have the wrong room," Julian politely informed them, and received another round of cackling for it. He quickly backed out of the room, rolling his eyes at the laughter. What sort of strange place was this, filled with women and children? They were everywhere, in every room, engaged in every conceivable occupation. Julian mounted the stairs and paused to look in the first door he came to. Two more women, a stack of piecework between them, their needles flying over the cloth. He moved on before they could notice him, to a second door, where thankfully he found Mrs. Conner seated in a rocking chair, moving back and forth in time with her needle.

"Shall I pour a cup of tea for you?" she asked, never looking up from her piecework.

"Mrs. Conner," Julian said, feeling uneasier by the minute. "I have come to fetch my sister. If you would be so kind as to bring her to me, I'd be much obliged."

"She knows you're here, milord," Mrs. Conner casually informed him, still not looking up.

He seriously contemplated walking over and snatching the blasted sewing from her hand and demanding the attention that was his due. "Excuse me, Mrs. Conner, but I don't believe you understand. I am here to fetch my sister. *Now.*"

"Julian!"

Sophie's voice startled him; he whirled around, expecting to see . . . *anything but this*.

She was smiling, albeit rather thinly. The smile was marred by the black and purple bruise on her chin, its yellow edges spreading to the corner of her mouth. The sight of it sickened him; he silently vowed then and there that he would see Stanwood dead before he would ever see him near Sophie again.

"How did you find me?" she asked. "Claudia, I suppose. You see, Mrs. Conner? I knew she'd not keep it a secret for long."

"It's just as well," Mrs. Conner remarked casually.

"Are you all right?" he asked roughly. "Has he done more harm to you than . . ." He could not bring himself to say it, could only motion vaguely to her chin.

Sophie shook her head. "You mustn't worry about that, Julian. It's over now, and it shan't ever happen again. Really, I am fine."

She sounded so calm, so sincere, that he felt the painful prick of guilt run up his spine. *He* should be telling *her* not to worry, promising no one would ever harm her again! But when he opened his mouth to speak, no words came, and Sophie slipped her arm through his. "It's all right," she said softly. With a reassuring smile, she glanced over her shoulder at Mrs. Conner. "You wouldn't mind terribly if I showed him about, would you, Mrs. Conner?"

"Lord, no. It's high time he saw what she does for us," Mrs. Conner responded, and squinting, paused in her work to peer out the bowed window. "Time everyone knew what she does for us," she added quietly.

Julian had no idea who or what Mrs. Conner was talking about, nor did he particularly care to know—at the moment, he wanted only to take Sophie from this awful place, take her home where she belonged, where he could keep her safe. "There's no time now, darling," he said to her. "Where are your things?"

"There's all the time in the world," she gently contradicted him. "Another half-hour won't make a difference, Julian. Come. I want you to see it."

"I have seen—"

"No. No, you haven't. Not like you should," she said stubbornly, and with another, reassuring smile, she tugged on his arm, pulling him out of the small drawing room and into the little corridor. "Do you know what this place is?" she asked as she led him toward the end of the hall and another staircase leading upward.

"No," he grumbled irritably.

"I daresay there's not another place like it in all the world. It's a haven where women like me can come when they need shelter."

Julian huffed his opinion of that, and tossing a glance over his shoulder, he said tightly, "These women are not like you, Sophie—"

"Yes, they are," she said, cutting him off. "They are *just* like me. All of them have fallen on one sort of hardship or another, and all of them needed a place they could go, where they would be safe. They are just like me in that, Julian. Do you know how difficult it is, especially for *these* women?" she asked rhetorically as they reached the second floor.

Julian said nothing, but frowned at her back as she paused to open the door to a room where several small desks were crowded. He glanced around. "All right. It's a schoolroom," he said impatiently.

"It's the only education some of the children who come here shall ever receive," she said thoughtfully. Julian glanced again at the room and turned to leave— but something caught his eye. Reaching for his spectacles, he peered intently at a drawing tacked to the wall, and walked into the room.

He knew that drawing.

He had seen dozens just like it, in her sitting room at Kettering House. It was the drawing of a school that Claudia was constantly sketching. Here it was again, tacked to the wall, but this one had crude figures penciled in around the edges with names written in childish scrawl above each perfectly round head. Johnny, Sylvia, Carol, Belinda, Herman . . . "It's Claudia," he muttered.

"Why, of *course*, it's Claudia!" Sophie said, laughing.

Julian jerked his gaze to her. "What do you mean by that?"

Sophie's smile faded to confusion. "Surely you know!"

"Know what?" he demanded, feeling the disquiet come over him, the shift of his body inside his skin.

Sophie swept her arms wide. "*All* of this is Claudia! She is the one who made this place!"

Stunned, Julian stared at her. How could it be true? He'd never heard of this place, never so much as suspected its existence. Certainly he knew she donated to various causes, but he never in his wildest dreams—

"She started it more than a year ago. She pays for it with her allowance and Mrs. Conner keeps it for her. Mrs. Conner tells the most amazing story, really, of how Claudia rescued her from one of the textile factories. There's so much more to it, I think, but so many women have come through here. Janet said they all know about it now, you know—the women in the factories, that is. But they keep it a secret amongst themselves. If a woman should need sanctuary, regardless of the reason, they know there is a place they can go to be safe when they've got nowhere else to turn. Come," she said, and slipped her hand into his, pulling him along.

He followed, mute in his astonishment, trying to absorb the things Sophie proudly showed him. On the fourth floor, where the roof pitched sharply down, there were six beds along each wall in one long room. The children slept here, Sophie informed him. Sometimes the room was full, other times it was empty. All the beds were neatly made, and on the end of each of them were a woolen scarf and a pair of mittens. The women who stayed here were asked, in exchange for their keep, to contribute if they weren't too beaten down by life. Not money, she quickly informed him, never that, because Claudia believed they should keep every pence they earned. One woman had been so grateful for the shelter that, with the wool yarn Claudia supplied, she had knitted several pairs of mittens and scarves for the children who would come here.

Claudia apparently supplied everything, Julian quickly learned, with her own funds or by wrangling donations.

Sophie led him through the second floor, along a row

of small bedrooms each housing two beds all neatly made up, with cheerful pictures and little pots of violets gracing the dressers. In each room was a wardrobe with a handful of serviceable gowns for those women who arrived on the doorstep with nothing. The gowns, Sophie explained as she opened one wardrobe, came mostly from Mayfair, talked out of the wardrobes of Claudia's friends.

As they moved through the house, Sophie introduced him to several of the women in residence. Julian greeted them all with proper decorum. He couldn't help noticing little things about them, however, like how rough their hands were, or how one woman frequently caught her back, as if in pain. And there was Stella, Sophie's maid, happily tending two young girls. And Janet, Sophie's new friend, sporting a horrible black eye that sent a shudder of revulsion through him.

On the second floor was the main parlor where Mrs. Conner was still sitting, her needle flying in and out of her piecework. There was also a music room with a pianoforte and a harp donated by some Samaritan, and a library of sorts. As Julian wandered through the library full of novels and works of geography, astronomy, and etiquette, he spied a stack of basic children's primers. He picked up one child's book and thumbed through it.

"Many of the women who come here can't read a'tall," Sophie whispered. "Some can only read their letters. They like the children's books." Julian stared at the book he held, trying to imagine a grown woman struggling to read it. Such things he took for granted; he could not imagine how difficult or limited one's life would certainly be without the ability to read.

When they had completed the tour of the house, Sophie showed him the tiny little hothouse Claudia had talked a tradesman into erecting so that the women might have vegetables year round. As she wandered through a row of tomatoes, she said, "Mrs. Conner fears a long winter. Claudia's allowance isn't quite sufficient to keep them all clothed and fed, and unfortunately, the donations have dried up, what with the scandal."

The donations. He had thought they were all for her school project.

Julian was humbled into silence. He looked at Sophie as they stood in the little hothouse, a million thoughts, regrets, and sorrows rifling through him. "It's a remarkable place, I'll grant you that. But I'm sorry, nonetheless, Sophie. I'm so very sorry that you ever had to seek refuge here. I'm sorry that I didn't see—"

"No, Julian," she said with a firm shake of her head. "This is not your fault and I won't allow you to believe that it is. It was my decision to elope and there was nothing you could have said or done that would have changed my mind." She smiled tremulously and glanced away, her eyes focused on something very distant. After a long moment, she spoke again. "I am *very* glad I came here. I didn't want to at first, and I won't lie—I was frightened to death when Claudia left me alone here. But these women . . . oh God, I can't explain it. I just understand so much that I didn't know even two days ago, Julian. I never would have learned it had I not come here."

"Learned what?"

"That I am strong," she answered without hesitation. "I am strong, and I always have been. I just never realized that I could be me."

He really wasn't sure what she meant by that, but thought perhaps he understood it on some remote level. How strange it was, he thought, gazing at the youngest of his sisters, the last of his charges, that she seemed so . . . *grown-up* now, so very unlike the wailing, lovesick girl he had left at Kettering Park. Never had he seen Sophie so sure of herself. So *confident.*

Claudia had done that. Claudia had succeeded in doing what he had never been able to do. Not only had she given these women the means of finding their self-confidence, but she had given that precious gift to Sophie, too. That, and her life.

And all of it humbled him beyond comprehension, to the point that it was all he could do to keep from falling

to his knees in that tiny little hothouse and begging God
to let him take it all back, to start all over again.

Julian gave in to Sophie's pleas to allow her to remain at
Upper Moreland Street until it was time to sail to France.
Fortunately, she understood the family's decision to send
her there while he dealt with Stanwood and the Church
and various courts. The family, he explained, wanted to
help her seek a divorce if that was what she wanted.
Sophie remarked her great surprise that the family was
willing to face the scandal certain to befall them, and
Julian felt the pain of their upbringing pounding at his
temple—how deeply propriety had been drilled into them
all! But he assured her that what the family was willing
to endure was far less important than what *she* was willing to endure.

They would seek a parliamentary divorce, but it was
a long, highly public process, he informed her. If he could
not win it for her, the best the law afforded her was a separation. She would never be allowed to remarry, not as
long as Stanwood lived. Sophie nodded, gave his hand a
warm squeeze, and assured him that she was, indeed,
willing to risk everything to be free of Sir William
Stanwood.

What he did not tell her was that in France, Louis
would protect her should Stanwood think to exact his
revenge on her, or that he hoped the scandal would not
mark her so deeply there as it would in England. As far
as Eugenie was concerned, no one had to know that her
youngest sister had ever been married. Louis was less
confident that the scandal could be contained, but Julian
knew he would defend Sophie's reputation with all of his
considerable influence as if she were one of his own.

Sophie's decision was easily made; Julian kissed her
on the forehead, held her tightly to him for a long
moment, then bid her goodbye for a few more days.

Weary, his thoughts and emotions in complete disar-
ray, Julian dragged himself into Kettering House. As he

handed his hat to Tinley, the old man said, "He's come back," and brushed beads of water from Julian's hat with the sleeve of his coat.

"Who?" Julian asked.

"Can't recall the fellow's name. Lady Sophie's husband."

Good. He wanted this over with.

Stanwood was in the gold salon, sipping delicately from a glass of brandy. In addition to having helped himself to Julian's best liquor, he was wearing another new suit of clothes—yet another courtesy of the Kettering family fortune.

A sneer spread Stanwood's lips as Julian walked into the room. "Well, Kettering? Come to your senses yet?"

Lord God, he wanted to beat Stanwood within an inch of his sorry life. "Indeed I have," he drawled, strolled casually to where Stanwood stood, and removed the brandy from his hand, prompting a nasty chuckle from Stanwood.

"If I were you I wouldn't be so quick to insult me, my lord. I have the law on my side, as you well know."

"Do you?" Julian asked, tossing the brandy into the fire and watching it flare bright along with his temper.

"Naturally. The marriage is quite legal, whether you like it or not. She is mine, and there is not a damn thing you can do about it. Now, being the generous man that I am, I am willing to overlook your gross error in judgment for a small fee. I won't press my grievance in the courts and I'll even allow the wench to call on you occasionally."

Bloody bastard. Julian flexed his fist in a mighty struggle to maintain his composure. "I advise you to hold your tongue, Stanwood, lest I rip it out of your head. The fact of the matter is, on Sophie's behalf I intend to petition the Church for a divorce."

The scoundrel reacted with a sputtering laugh of disbelief. "You *what?* Oh, that's *marvelous!* On what grounds? You have no *grounds,* Kettering, and even if you did, you'd not stomach the scandal!"

"Just watch me," Julian said venomously.

Stanwood gaped at him as if he had just uttered a capital threat against the king. "But . . . but you have no *grounds*," he insisted wildly.

It was Julian's turn to smirk. "I will petition the Church for divorce *a mensa et a thoro*. Do you know what that is, Stanwood? The petition will cite grounds of extreme cruelty. And before you think to argue that, know that I have witnesses to the many bruises on her body."

Stanwood paled. "She fell!" he all but shouted, then looked frantically to the fire. "Nevertheless, what you threaten will gain you a legal separation, nothing more— it's not a divorce!"

"True," Julian said, nodding thoughtfully as he strolled nonchalantly to the middle of the room. "But then I shall bring suit in Parliament for dissolution of the marriage because of your adultery, as I am confident that you will find your way into a whore's bed before long . . ." —he paused to cast a scathing look of disgust across him—"if you haven't already." Stanwood blanched, revealing the truth in that statement, and Julian's smirk turned into a contemptuous scowl. "In the meantime, I will be watching you every minute of every day, Stanwood. My eyes will be everywhere, you may depend on it. When you breathe, I will know it. When you eat, I will know it. When you squat on a chamber pot, I will know it. And if you think for even a moment to defy me, I will bring the power of my name down on your head. No institution or man of standing will lend you money. No one will employ you. No one will house you or clothe you or feed you. There will be nowhere for you to turn, Stanwood. Do you quite understand me?"

The blackguard's chin began to tremble with his rage. "You can't do that!" he bellowed. "You don't have the power to do that!"

With a derisive chuckle, Julian folded his arms across his chest. "Try me," he drawled.

Stanwood's breathing was suddenly harsh and loud. "You can't do it," he repeated. "You and your sisters will not be able to abide the scandal I will cause! I will fight you—I can, you know—the law is on *my* side! Oh yes, I will fight you . . . if I want her, that is. Perhaps I don't want her any longer! Perhaps I am sick to death of the wench! What if I don't want her? What then?"

Julian shrugged indifferently, masking the cauldron of rage boiling in him. "I suppose, in that case, you may slink off and crawl back under the rock from which you came."

A curious shiver coursed Stanwood. "Don't *threaten* me, Kettering! You cannot win in this! The law gives her and all that is hers to me! She belongs to *me,* not you!" he blustered loudly, and stalked to the door.

Like hell he couldn't win in this. "Very well, then," he said casually. "Just remember—I'll be watching you. Mind that you do nothing to harm your cause," he said, and chuckled darkly. "There is, however, another way, should you choose to listen."

Stanwood faltered at the door, looking confused. "What way?"

"Fifty thousand pounds in exchange for dropping any claim to her annuity or disputing the accusation of adultery. Take it or leave it."

Stanwood bristled. "That's absurd! What of *me?*"

"It's your life, Stanwood. Fifty thousand pounds or a protracted fight in the courts. If you think your cause is sound, you can meet me on the floor of the House of Lords."

Stanwood turned red as he fidgeted with the watch fob at his waist. "What if I agreed? I don't say that I shall, but suppose I did—when exactly would I expect to receive this fifty thousand quid?"

Julian had won the first stage of the battle.

Twenty-Five

THE NEXT TWO days were a living hell for Julian in which old feelings of helplessness and grief were roused along with disturbing and emotional images of others lost to him. This was different, of course. Sophie was far from dead—she was merely going to France. Indefinitely. For the rest of her life, perhaps.

It felt like death, and Julian grieved for her loss of innocence, despairing of the road ahead for her. He moved through the long hours with a dozen distasteful tasks, from discussing Sophie's marriage in detail with his solicitors, to overseeing the packing of her things, to soothing his sisters' fears that the evolving scandal would potentially touch their own children.

He did not allow himself to think of anything but the task at hand, certainly not the many ways he might have spared Stanwood's fist on her, although that crept into his conscience more often than not.

And certainly not the extraordinary little house on Upper Moreland Street.

But he could not stop thoughts of Claudia invading him like an army, attacking every part of his mind and his heart. He forced those thoughts from his mind, smothered them under so much garbage in him, refused to acknowledge them or give them the light of the least bit of deliberation. How could he? He would crumble if he allowed himself to think, and he had to see to Sophie, to all of his sisters—everyone but himself.

On the morning Eugenie and Louis bundled their daughters in warm coats and waited patiently on St. Katherine's dock, Julian fetched Sophie from Upper Moreland Street. After a lengthy goodbye to all the women in residence there, including a teary farewell to Stella, who had opted to stay at the little town house, and Janet, who had no choice but to stay, Sophie stepped into the coach with a calmness that baffled Julian. Her new-found confidence had grown even more in the few days since he had last seen her, and as if to prove it, she assured him with a smile that she was quite all right and actually looking forward to her journey.

As the coach rolled away from Upper Moreland Street, Sophie asked, "Is Claudia with Eugenie? I want to thank her before I go."

Julian dragged his gaze away from the window. "Claudia has gone home to her father," he said simply.

The smile disappeared from Sophie's face; he could see the thoughts tumbling in her head. After a long moment she asked him why.

"Because, love, there was too much distrust between us."

"It's because of me, isn't it? Oh, Julian, don't be angry with her—she saved my life!"

As if he needed to be reminded of that.

"We *can't* lose Claudia! Whatever trouble there is between you, you can fix it, can't you?" she asked anxiously.

"I don't know," he answered honestly, and refrained from prolonging the conversation, unable to discuss what had happened—as if he really *knew* what had happened between them. It was struggle enough to keep his over-whelming dismay pushed down and buried in the darkest corner of his soul.

At the docks, his entire family was waiting. When he and Sophie walked down the boardwalk toward them, Ann and Eugenie broke away from the others, racing to their sister. The three of them held each other tightly with their arms around their shoulders, their faces pressed together as they whispered to one another. Watching them, Julian could remember how, as girls, they would hold one another just like that . . . except that there had been five of them then.

The rumbling disquiet in the pit of his belly almost doubled him over.

They milled around as they waited to board the ship that would take them to France, no one quite sure what to say, everyone stealing glimpses of Sophie, looking for more bruises, for some sign that she was broken. But her countenance was serene; she showed no signs of despair, nothing to suggest that the journey she was about to begin frightened her. When the ship's steward gave the signal to board, the girls hugged and kissed one another, promising to write often.

Julian exchanged a few final words with Louis before he lifted each niece to kiss their chubby cheeks. He held Eugenie in his arms and kissed the top of her head, extracting a promise that she would write at least weekly so he would know how Sophie fared. He then turned to Sophie, absolutely horrified that his eyes had started to water. She flung her arms around his neck, kissed his cheek. "I'll never forgive myself for all that I've put you through, Julian. I shall be quite all right, I swear it, and you must promise not to worry so."

He smiled into her hair. "I'll try, love, but I can't promise you that."

She pulled back, smiling up at him. "You will give my love to Claudia, won't you? You really must thank her for helping me. I am forever in her debt."

So were they all. With a nod, he kissed her forehead. And then Sophie was suddenly gone.

Julian was alone.

He did not return home immediately, but ordered the driver to take a turn around Hyde Park. And then another. He dreaded going back to that dark, empty house and its deathly quiet. There was no light or laughter there, no sound of children playing, or women gaily arguing, or target practice on the lawn.

Christ, he missed her.

Unthinking, he pressed his fists against his eyes. She was lost to him. In the end, he had lived up to his worst nightmare and failed her, too, just as badly as he had failed the others. The discomfort in him had grown to a raging fire since she had left, consuming his very spirit—at least he understood now from where the discomfort came.

It had taken Sophie's disaster to finally make him understand the ache that had plagued him since Valerie's death. It had dawned on him, crystal in its clarity, when he had returned from Upper Moreland Street to find Stanwood in his house. After the bastard had gone, Julian had sat with his head between his hands, aching until he thought he would go mad with it . . . because he *needed* her.

He had needed her then and there, to put her arms around him, to whisper something soothing in his ear. He needed to share his burden, to feel her comfort him. He needed her silly little violets on his desk, target practice on the lawn, teas with slightly deranged ladies. He needed her laughter, her dozen smiles, the warmth of her body at night. At last, a ray of light had finally shone on his battered heart, and he had understood the words of the vicar at Phillip's funeral, *"know ye in this death the light of our Lord, the quality of love . . ."*

He almost laughed aloud at his own stupidity as the coach creaked around a turn in the road. All this time he thought he knew the quality of love, that his was to lose those for whom he cared. Now he understood that the quality of love he yearned for, *ached* for, was with Claudia, a love without beginning or end, timeless, never ending, strong and pure in the face of the worst adversity. That was what he had so desperately wanted without even knowing it, perhaps since the time of his father's death. And it was a quality of love he had been unwilling to give himself, so foolishly convinced that he would harm her with it.

He had harmed her, all right—he had shut her out,

pushed her away when he needed her most. She could have turned her back on him, could have walked away from further scandal. But she hadn't—she had tried her best to hold on. And how goddamned ironic that was—when Phillip died, he had taken Julian to the edge of the abyss with him. He had clung to Claudia then, first the ideal, then the person. Whether she knew it or not, Claudia had pulled him back from the brink and kept him from falling.

He wanted nothing more than to bury the demons that plagued him and simply love her, believe in her, revel in her, help her. More than that, he desperately wanted her to love him. Yet that opportunity was perhaps lost to him forever.

Perhaps he would remain in that abyss after all.

The Danes were not the only family in Mayfair to have suffered the last few days. The Whitney household was in like turmoil over Sophie's tragedy, albeit from a very different perspective.

That perspective had to do with Earl Redbourne's steadfast belief that Claudia belonged to Kettering, and was, therefore, his problem. The moment the earl had given her to Kettering in marriage, her unorthodox behavior became his to discipline, her wild thinking his cross to bear, her extravagant allowance his expense. These opinions were rather loudly voiced to Claudia, along with a strongly worded admonishment that she could not simply walk out if the arrangements did not suit her. *Especially* not after another Dane woman had up and run from her lawful husband.

Claudia had argued fiercely with him, then cajoled him, then flatly begged him not to send her back. But the earl was insufferably determined in this—he would not allow her to leave her husband like some baseborn wench. However, if *Kettering* decided she was no longer wanted, then he would have no option but to send her to Redbourne Abbey until such time her husband could see his way clear to put her away at Kettering Hall. One way or another, he shouted, she would be dealt with. As if she was some distasteful object to be placed out of sight.

Claudia's degradation, then, was complete on the afternoon she was delivered to the Kettering House on St. James Square like a piece of old furniture that did not belong in her father's house. And while the earl thought it necessary to assure himself she actually boarded the coach as he had decreed, he did not think it necessary to actually deliver her to Kettering House, and therefore sent her on alone, in the company of a footman.

She arrived like a pauper, with nothing but the small bag she had left with. Much to her great relief, Tinley did not seem surprised to see her, and taking advantage of his faulty memory, she escaped to her rooms where she paced like a caged animal. Never in her life had she felt so insignificant, so contemptibly useless.

And never had she felt more alone.

Disheartened, Claudia was not as presumptuous as her father—she had no hope that Julian would allow her to stay. Even if he were feeling particularly generous, he would undoubtedly send her off somewhere so that he would not have to look at her. He would, at last, banish her from his sight.

Had he found Sophie? Where would he take her?

Her rooms were dark and cold, but Claudia made no move to call for a servant. She had no energy, no will. She collapsed into an overstuffed chair, tightened her cloak about her, and curled her feet under her gown for warmth. It occurred to her as she lay there in that enormous chair that she had lit a hearth fire only once in all her life. There had always been someone to do that for her, someone to tend to her every need. Someone to make her and keep her completely useless to the world. *She could not even light a fire.*

She dropped her forehead to her palm and closed her eyes, but there were no tears—the well was bone dry, used up. It didn't matter. She was far past tears—just . . . desolate. For the first time in her life, she had no idea which way to turn, no notion of how to cope, what to do. Helpless, vulnerable, and wretched, she had come to the realization that, in spite of all her efforts to improve her lot, it had all come down to the mercy of a man in the end, a man she loved with all her heart. A man who abhorred her.

The sound of someone entering the little vestibule of her suite filtered into her room and Claudia sighed wearily, trying to summon her strength for Brenda or Tinley—whoever had come to see after her. She listened to the muted footfall, felt it tread upon her heart. The bright flare of the match startled her, and she abruptly looked up, blinking.

"Claudia."

Oh, God. Julian.

Ashamed, she turned away and unsteadily brushed the back of her hand across her cheek, unable to look at him. "Tinley said you were here." He walked into the room, and Claudia glanced at him from the corner of her eye. His was an intimidating figure; he stared at her, his expression inscrutable. It was like a knife to her heart, shredding the last bit of her hope, and she was suddenly desperate to at least have her dignity.

"I'm sorry," she murmured, choking back dry tears. "Papa . . . he brought me back. H-he believes my place is here until you say otherwise. I'm really very sorry, Julian—I tried my best to dissuade him—"

"You must be freezing," he said softly.

Freezing. Not the response she had expected. She shook her head and slowly rose to her feet. "I'm not cold," she said dispassionately. "I can't really feel myself anymore."

"I am very sorry to hear that."

So was she. Looking at him now, at the sharp angles of his jaw, the thick hair that was still too long, black eyes boring into her, she was struck by just how sorry she was that she could not feel *him* any longer. There was a time she could feel his eyes on her from across a crowded room or his breath on the back of her neck when he wasn't even nearby. And now . . . now she couldn't feel a bloody thing. She was numb, deadened, her soul extinguished. *God, how she regretted it all!*

"Everything—this is all my fault, and I'm so very sorry," she suddenly blurted, and covered her face with her hands, mortified that he should see her like this, like a beggar. "I was so *stupid* about so many things! From the beginning, even, and you are quite right, you know, for I've known you near forever . . . but I . . . I just loved you so desperately that I wasn't thinking clearly all that time, and when the ladies would remark on your hands and your lips, and your beauty, I hated you for wanting them and not me—"

"Ah, Claudia," he murmured, and took a cautious step toward her.

She was aware that she was on the verge of blathering hysterically, but she couldn't stop herself, compelled by an unseen force to let the words tumble from her heart and into the open. She plunged on. "And then . . . then you were always with Phillip, always cavorting about, and it was no secret what the Rogues did, *especially* Phillip, and the night of Harrison Green's there was Lady Prather, you know. So when I came here, and you and Arthur went out, I assumed it was all the same again, and I should *never* have listened to Tinley, but women are supposed to accept it, and I wasn't supposed to mind terribly—but oh, God, I did!" she cried, covering her eyes with her hands again.

"Claudia—"

"I loved you so much that I couldn't *bear* for you to touch me, because when you touched me, I felt as if I was the only woman in the world to you, but I wasn't! There was always another whom you touched in the very same way—"

"I never touched another woman, Claudia—don't say more!" he begged her, taking another step toward her.

But she stumbled backward, out of his reach, unable to stop now until every last dark secret was out. "And I *lied* to you! Not just about Sophie, not only that, but about Phillip, too," she sobbed, lifting her head to look at him. "I lied to myself. I never loved Phillip, not like I have loved you, not like I love you now, and I am quite thankful I did not marry him, because I know what my life would have been, and it wouldn't have been *this*," she said, gesturing wildly about her. "It wouldn't have been you, and I would have been so sorry, so very sorry all my life! Yet I lied because I was hurt. I thought . . . I thought you didn't like me very much, that you thought something was infinitely wrong with me, and that you wished you had never known me, and perhaps you do, and I *surely* would understand if you were to go to my father right away and *demand* that he take me back—"

"I will never let you go again," he said hoarsely, moving forward until he was within arm's reach of her.

His nearness made her panic, as if she was standing too close to the edge—if he touched her, she would fall. She jerked her arm up, holding it straight in front of her. "This is . . . *so* humiliating," she muttered miserably. "To be sent back to someone who doesn't want you—"

"*I* want you—"

"Forced to grovel at your feet like some beggar—"

"It is I who am at your feet." He carefully reached for her, his fingers fluttering to her hand and closing around it.

With a violent shake of her head, Claudia said, "I can't bear this—I've ruined your life, I *know* it—"

"You have enriched it beyond measure—"

"I committed a crime when I took Sophie, with no thought to the consequence, and therefore, my crime is *your* crime—"

Julian suddenly jerked her toward him, grabbing her arms. "Claudia, *listen* to me," he said roughly, stooping down so that they were at eye level. "I love you! I have loved you hopelessly for far too long. There is not a single hour of the day that goes by that I do not think of you, not a moment I don't look for you or strain to hear your voice! All I want—" He stooped lower, forcing her to look at him. "All I want on this earth is for you to love me in return, if even just a little."

Her heart caught, suspended somewhere between heaven and earth. "Oh, *no,*" she moaned, and her legs buckled under the weight of those words. She went down on her knees, Julian with her, still holding her in a fierce grip. "I love you," he said again, his fingers curling deeper into her arms.

Inconceivable. After what she had done? "Don't say that," she begged him, squeezing her eyes shut against the poignant look in his eye. "Don't say it to me because I will fall to pieces—"

"No you won't," he said, shaking her once. "You *will* love me in return. You will love me as you tried to love me when I wouldn't let you. You will show me how to live, Claudia; you will show me how to give myself to everyone around me, never fearing the propriety or the consequences. You will show me how to care so deeply for others less fortunate than myself. You will show me how to love you, because God knows I haven't done it very well—"

"No!" she cried. "I'm afraid, Julian! You can't know how very much it hurts—"

"The hell I don't," he muttered angrily. "Don't give up on me, Claudia! It feels as if I have waited my whole *life* for you! I need you—can't you see just how desperately I do? I can't live without you. I can't *breathe* without you! I ache when you are away, I ache when you are near, I am consumed with longing for you! Lord God, I am sorry; from the depths of my pathetic soul, I am sorry that I didn't understand it all sooner. But I do now, and I swear to you, I swear I will do better, I will do whatever it takes . . . just *love* me."

The fragile shell of what was left of her heart shattered, and with a strangled cry, Claudia surged into his arms, groping for him, needing to anchor herself to him and the comforting warmth of his body.

With a moan, Julian pressed his mouth hard to hers, delving deeply, seeking refuge. With his hands, he cradled her jaw, holding her as if she was fragile . . . and God, she *was* fragile, on the verge of shattering with remorse, relief, and a euphoria that was sweeping her along on a tide, melding her against him.

He dragged his mouth across her cheek to her hair, his breath heavy in her ear as he pulled the pins from her hair. *"Love me, Claudia."*

The hint of desperation in his voice made her heart flail wildly. He didn't have to ask—she loved him, fiercely, deeply and still it was not enough. It could not be enough, she thought, and buried her face in his collar, breathing his scent, intoxicated by it as his hands pushed her cloak from her shoulders. She felt him shift, felt his arm behind her, and she instinctively threw her arms around his neck. He suddenly lifted her in his arms, carried her as he kissed her eyes, her forehead, her mouth, and laid her on the bed, coming over her, surrounding her in darkness and warmth. "Never leave me," he whispered, and descended hungrily to her mouth. Claudia eagerly sought the warmth of his body, clawing at the confining neckcloth, the waistcoat, and finally thrusting her hands deep inside his shirt to feel his hard chest and nipples.

Shuddering with her touch, his lips trailed down her neck to the top of her breasts, avidly tasting her until he could free her breast and bring it fully into his mouth. Instinctively, she arched into him, shamelessly indulging in the sweet sensation seeping through her skin to the fire burning in the pit of her stomach. With his mouth and hands he loved her, reverently caressed her and tasted her. Claudia returned his caress with one that grew more frantic, more insistent as a growing sense of elation and freedom overwhelmed her. With the one extraordinary exception of their wedding night, she had never allowed herself to *feel* him, to submerge herself entirely in the pleasure he gave her.

What had gone between them the last few weeks was seemingly forgotten, leaving nothing to inhibit their animal instincts. It was as if they were wild—her body felt feverish, the burning in the pit of her stomach now flaming, scorched every place he touched her, bewitched by unimaginable desire, obsessed with the need to feel *all* of him, to know love in its noblest and basest form.

Eagerly, anxiously, she pressed against him, her hands and mouth trailing across his hot flesh. With a guttural groan, Julian pressed his knee hard against the apex of her thighs. Claudia's hand drifted down his chest, along the wool of his trousers, stroking the hardness between his thighs.

When she cupped him, Julian tensed, arched his neck. "You will kill me yet," he rasped, and lowered his head, kissing her as she stroked him and felt him lengthen against her palm. Her fingers brushed against the buttons; she freed one, then another, and another, until his member sprang free, filling her hand with the heat of satin skin sliding over a marble core.

Suddenly, he jerked away from her, rearing back to discard his coat, and shirt. As he clawed at the pearl buttons on his shirt, he gazed down at her with dark intensity. "I can't wait. I have wanted you like this, just like *this* for so long that I can no longer remember a time I did not." Shoving out of his shirt, he caught her arm and yanked her up as one hand slipped behind her back, carelessly unfastening her gown so that he could pull it from her body.

When she wore nothing but a chemise and undergarments, Julian lowered her down, then lifted one ankle, flipping her shoe out into the dark room. His hand drifted up her calf, then to her ankle again, and slowly, carefully, he reached for the top of her stocking.

"If you had known how badly I wanted you like this," he murmured as he slowly rolled the stocking down, pausing to kiss the bare skin of her thigh, "you might very well have summoned the authorities." He tossed her stocking aside and kissed her toes, her ankle, her knee.

"If I had known you wanted me like this," she responded raggedly, "I would have summoned the authorities to bring you to me."

Julian chuckled against the soft inside of her knee, then bent her leg at the knee, pushing it aside so that he could skim his hand along her inner thigh and leave a path of white-hot sparks tingling in her skin. "From the moment I saw you in the Wilmington ballroom, I wanted to give you pleasure," he said, and leaned down, his breath brushing the springy curls between her legs.

The groan was hers, she realized. Julian smiled lazily, shifting downward so that he might kiss the level plane of her belly as he shoved her chemise aside. Claudia moaned; her body was a raging inferno, her mind numb to all but his hands, his lips, his voice. This was nothing like she had ever experienced; all her burdens, all the darkness that had surrounded her for the last few weeks was gone, vanquished by his kiss and his touch, his whisper of love. She caught his head in her hands as he dipped between her legs, his breath and tongue skirting over the inferno blazing within her, then probing the core of her heat.

"Julian!" she choked, but he seemed not to hear her, too intent on laving her with excruciating deliberateness. The inferno was suddenly blazing out of control, raging through her limbs and her mind. He was relentless, the silkiness of his touch a stark contrast to the intensity of it. Claudia pulled anxiously at his hair as her hips began to move against him, meeting each rush of his tongue until suddenly everything went white. She was flying and sinking all at once, a cry of pleasure on her lips.

Groaning, Julian lifted his head and positioned himself between her legs. He stared down at her, his black eyes almost indistinguishable from the dark of the room as he lightly pressed the tip of his manhood against her sheath, pulsing with need, sending dangerous shocks of pleasure through her. The muscles in his arms bulged with the exertion of holding himself just above her; his lips skimmed the tip of her nose, her mouth. "I love you," he whispered, and with the slightest move of his hips, slipped inside her.

"Desperately so," he added breathlessly as he slid

deeper. "And I always will." He paused, withdrew slowly, only to begin the maddening slide into her all over again. Lost in the pleasure he was giving her, Claudia moved beneath him, angling her hips so that he might reach the very center of her being. His hand covered hers, sprawled somewhere above her head, squeezing it tightly as his stroke began to lengthen and quicken. Deep into her he slid, drawn in like the tide, then ebbing out of her, only to swell and rush her again. The experience was staggering; Claudia could feel the roar inside her, as if the surf was actually pounding and pounding against her until she was suddenly plunging headlong into a pool of rapturous oblivion, bathing in wave after wave of pleasure all over again.

She rocked beneath him, flowing upward to meet his body's bearing into her. Her hands roamed his body, feeling the corded muscle of his neck, his back, and then the heavy sacs that swelled in her hand. Julian's breath came as a hiss between clenched teeth; his strokes were suddenly urgent, burrowing deeper into her until it seemed to her they were one body, one being, impossible to discern where one heart ended and the other began. Claudia could feel her body tighten around him as she experienced another shattering release into the dark, and as she lifted her hips to meet his powerful thrust, he tossed his head back and cried out, convulsing violently into her womb, giving over his life's blood.

With a final shudder, he lowered himself to his elbows, panting heavily, and touched his forehead to hers. Neither of them spoke. Claudia tenderly brushed damp hair from his temple, ran her fingers down the dewy skin covering the muscles of his arm, silently praying that this extraordinary moment would never end, that what had happened here would never ever leave her.

They remained that way, silently observing one another like two lovers, until the cold air began to chill them. Wordlessly, Julian left her to light a fire. He came back to the bed, pulled back the linens, and ordered her beneath them with a strong warning that she was to remain just there until he came back. Shoving into his trousers, he disappeared, returning a short time later in a long velvet dressing gown, carrying a tray of bread and cheese and wine. They feasted in her bed, whispering their love to one another, laughing softly about nothing and everything. And then Julian made love to her again, slowly and deliberately, prolonging the ecstasy until she thought she would go quite mad.

When he at last slept, he held her tightly in his arms as if he feared she would leave him while he slumbered. Burrowing into his side, Claudia closed her eyes, dreamily reliving each exceptional moment. Nothing had come between them tonight—it was as if they held the world at bay for a moment in time, and it had been the most wonderful moment of her life.

But as she drifted asleep, she felt the distant tug of reality on her conscience, the faint warning that it was an illusion, that it could never remain so sweet.

Twenty-Six

As HIS MIND slowly began to cast off the veil of sleep, Julian reached for her, but found the bed empty. Forcing his eyes open, he pushed himself up to his elbows with a groggy *harumph* and looked around. Claudia was crouched in front of the hearth wrapped in his dressing gown, her hair wild and flowing down her back, poking at the dying embers of the fire he had left flaming a few hours ago.

"Come back to bed, my love. I will warm you," he said, yawning.

She flashed a smile at him over her shoulder. "The sun is up," she informed him, and continued poking at the embers.

Damn.

Still smiling, she stood up and carefully wiped her hands on the outer folds of his dressing gown. Julian beckoned her to him. "Come here," he said gruffly. She obeyed him, moving gracefully across a floor strewn with clothing and wine bottles and a tray of stale bread and hard cheese to sit on the edge of the bed. Julian came up on his elbow to nuzzle her neck.

Claudia giggled, squirming away from him. "That tickles," she pleaded.

Reluctantly, Julian lay back against the pillows, letting his hand slip inside the voluminous sleeve of his dressing gown and drift up the inside of her arm over skin that felt like silk. She seemed awfully pensive, he thought, especially after the night of extraordinary love-making they had shared. He himself was feeling rather randy at the moment. "What is it, Claudia?"

"Nothing!" she declared, a little too adamantly. She blushed immediately and looked down at her lap. "All right," she said slowly. "I will not pretend. Last night was . . . it was the most beautiful, wonderful thing that has ever happened to me."

His groin responded to that with a faint reverberation. "That, my darling, is an understatement," he said, and absently fingered the end of a long strand of her hair.

"And nothing will ever take it from us—"

"Or those nights yet to come," he murmured, chuckling softly when she turned an appealing shade of pink.

"It was . . . wonderful," she said again, absently plucking at the piping of the dressing gown.

A warning flagged in Julian's brain—he suddenly sat up, put one arm around her and with the other forced her to look at him. "But?"

"But . . . but there is so much yet between us . . . and . . . and the world," she muttered miserably.

Panic. Small but certain, it was panic that made his stomach dip as if they had just encountered a rut in the road. "What do you mean?" he asked, trying hard to keep his voice even.

She dropped her gaze again, and he stared at the thick lashes fanning her cheeks. "Well . . . there is the matter of Sophie's running away, and . . . and the, ah, scandal. And my father's position with the king, which I must stress is paramount to all else in his mind," she said with a helpless glance to the ceiling.

"I don't care!" he said roughly. "I love you, Claudia. As long as I have you—as long as you love me, I don't give a damn what Redbourne or anyone else thinks."

She lifted her gaze to him, blue-gray eyes brimming with sorrow. "Oh, Julian," she whispered. "I *do* love you. More than my life, I swear it."

"All right, then!" he blustered, but the uneasiness in him was swelling. "What more is there to say? Come to bed now," he said, and wrapped her in his arms, pulling her head to his shoulder, unwilling to hear any more of her dangerous talk.

"But . . . but eventually we must rise, and when we do, there is scandal and disgrace to be borne. And for me, I . . ." Her voice trailed off; she pressed her face into his shoulder.

"What?"

"I've lost all credibility," she mumbled helplessly.

The image of the house on Upper Moreland Street suddenly invaded his mind's eye and he realized that in the last weeks, as he had suffered through some of the darkest moments of his life, he had never once thought how it all affected Claudia. As he stroked her hair, he recalled the sense of wonder he had felt as he had walked through that little house, the burgeoning sense of pride. He thought of the dozens of drawings of a schoolhouse that littered her sitting room, the many little speeches he had heard her give at more than one supper party on the subject of girls' education. He had agreed with her to gain her attention, never really giving any thought to the cause itself. But those things had meant something to her, and he knew she was right—between the humiliation of their forced marriage and Sophie's ruination, she had no credibility.

Hell, even her own father would not keep her.

She sighed into his shoulder, and Julian turned his face to her, kissing her temple as his hand floated to the slender column of her neck. "It will be all right," he whispered, but the words sounded empty. Brushing the curls from her face, he kissed her cheek . . . he would give anything to put this to rights for her, anything to make it all right.

"It won't be all right—"

"It will," he insisted, cupping her face and staring down at her.

Claudia smiled tremulously. "It's the way of things, Julian."

She said it so calmly and with such innocent belief that his heart wrenched. "I will find a way to make it all right." He kissed her quickly, before she could see by the look in his eye that he had no idea how he would fix this, no idea at all.

They made love again, reaching another pinnacle of bliss together. But when Julian heard a stirring in the corridor, he reluctantly rose, knowing that he could not put off the inevitable and that he would, eventually, be forced to face the reality of their life, just as she had said, and all that had gone on between them.

In the days that followed it seemed that there was no going back to the moment in her darkened bedroom when she had fallen into his arms, finally surrendering to him. Oh, they made love just as fiercely and quite often, as if there was an unspoken need between them to make up for lost time. Claudia blossomed in his arms, allowing herself to experience the magic of love, returning his desire with a fervent passion of her own that suddenly knew no bounds. She delighted in his body, torturing him with light caresses and the tantalizing trace of her lips on every conceivable part of him. The climaxes they shared were marked by a furious intensity that left him reeling.

But he could not, no matter how hard he tried, recreate the same freedom or unfettered feeling of euphoria that there had been that night. Not with everything that weighed down on them.

For Julian, of course, it was the abominable task of seeking Sophie's divorce, and in the course of it, he learned firsthand how very contemptuous the *ton* as a whole could be. Men who had known his father acted as if they had never met him. Mothers who had once offered money, lands, and anything else they thought might entice him, now made their daughters walk in the other direction when he approached.

Julian didn't give a damn for himself, but he did for Ann, who, had it not been for her confinement, might have suffered the worst of it. And he gave a damn for Sophie. It would be a long time before she could return to England, if at all.

But it was Claudia who was suffering their downright abandonment.

He realized just how frightfully true it was when he found her going over her ledgers. Frowning, she tapped the pen against the page, unaware that he had entered the room. The moment she realized it, however, she quickly shut the book and shoved it away. When he asked, Claudia had waved her hand dismissively, insisting she was merely passing the time. He had dropped it, but much later, after she had left to call on Ann, he withdrew the books and had a look.

With the exception of the four debts he had called in on behalf of her school project, there had not been a single donation made in two months, in spite of the fact that she had gone out almost every day to call on potential benefactors. She never spoke of it, and tried to seem unaffected by it, but Julian could sense her deep disappointment. Moreover, the drawings of the school disappeared—one morning, as he passed her sitting room, he felt as if something was different, as if a chair or table had been moved. Then he realized that the dozens of drawings were gone.

He wondered about the house on Upper Moreland Street, recalling that Sophie had said that contributions were dwindling. But when he tried to talk to Claudia about it, she wouldn't discuss it, insisting it was nothing and pretending that it was not an important part of her life—an important part of *her.*

What Claudia *did* want to discuss was Sophie, which was not a topic Julian was very keen to resurrect. He did not like being reminded of Claudia's role in Sophie's downfall, and worse, privately he wasn't completely certain he had forgiven her. He had forgotten it, certainly . . . but forgiven it? Yet she insisted, and one night, as they lay entwined in one another's arms, she forced the issue. Julian resisted as strongly as he could, but he was helpless against her soft voice and even softer lips. She pressed him until he was so very frustrated with her that he agreed *yes,* he was *still* angry and hurt by it.

Incredibly, Claudia had smiled. *"At last, then!"* she had exclaimed cheerfully, and in a sudden state of derangement, insisted that they speak of their respective feelings about what had happened, the reasons for their anger and distrust. He had done it for her, gritting his teeth and rolling his eyes quite frequently. But he had played along, listening to her ridiculous theory that he would have interceded and sent Sophie back to Stanwood, and the equally absurd notion that he was angry with her for doing what he had longed to do himself. Naturally, he argued with her, explaining to the little featherbrain the nonsense in her theories, and with a theatrical flare, even accepted her apology.

He would never admit, not to another living soul, that he had indeed felt quite relieved when it was all over.

Over the course of several nights, he was to learn much more, such as why Claudia thought him a rake. At the end of *that* discussion, he was rather convinced he *was* a rake. And much to his great surprise, he learned how the beastly little girl Claudia had been adored him. Amazingly, he had never even sensed it. *That,* Claudia huffed, was his greatest fault—he was obviously rather thickheaded when it came to a woman's affections. Later that evening, however, she begrudgingly admitted— while she lay naked in his arms—that he might have improved a tad bit on that front.

The most miraculous thing of all was that Phillip was finally beginning to fade away, and for that, Julian was eternally grateful. It did not happen easily—Julian had never been able to shake the sense that Phillip was watching him with Claudia. He must have said enough for her to gather what bothered him, because she had finally forced him to sit one night and listen to what had gone on with Phillip. Julian did *not* want to hear it ... but neither could he say no. He had listened with morbid fascination as she spoke of the increasing distance between her and Phillip, the drunkenness, the knowledge of his mistress. All of it surprised him—but she shocked him to his core when she told him of the last time she had ever seen Phillip, the assault on her person . . . and how that memory had overwhelmed her when she had seen Sophie's bruises, pushing her to act.

But Phillip's ghost did not truly begin to fade until she assured him with her words, and then with her body, that she never really loved him, not like this, and kissed away any lingering doubts.

Slowly but surely, Julian realized she was leading them through the maze of their past, putting events and perceptions in their proper place before locking them away forever, away from the living. With each passing day, they chiseled away a little more at the fear and doubts between them, growing more secure in one another. Julian reveled in it—for the first time in his life, he felt as if God was truly smiling on him, granting him the one thing that could make him ecstatically happy.

If only he could make her as happy.

For all her confessions to the contrary, Claudia did not sparkle as she once had. No matter how much she tried to convince him she was quite all right, there was something in her eyes that had been dulled, as if a light had gone out that could not be rekindled. No matter what he did, or how hard he loved her, he could not put the light back in her eyes.

He would die trying, he decided.

Having successfully petitioned the Doctor's Commons in Sophie's suit, the first step of an arduous journey to divorce, Julian returned home one afternoon in a state of elation—at last, he could see an end to this drama. No one blocked his petition—Stanwood had left London with his fifty thousand pounds, apparently convinced Julian could ruin him as he had threatened. Eugenie reported that Sophie grew stronger every day, that an inner peace had taken hold of her, and that she followed Claudia's example by spending her time in the villages, working with children and women less fortunate than she.

The sun was shining when Julian arrived home; anxious to write Eugenie with the latest news, he passed his butler asleep on a bench in the foyer, patting his shoulder as he walked briskly to his study. As he strode past the morning sunroom, he caught a glimpse of someone inside, and paused. Seated beside his wife on a settee was a woman Julian had never seen before. Claudia had her arm around her as the woman dabbed at her eyes with a kerchief. The woman wore a drab brown gown that had been patched along the hem. Her hands were rough and red; and although most of her hair was stuffed under a cap, limp gray strands of it fell around her ears. Claudia looked at her with great concern, seemingly oblivious to the difference in their rank, as if they were of equal class. As if they were sisters.

And in a rare moment of absolute brilliance, Julian instantly realized what he had to do and absently wondered why he had not thought of it before. With a faint smile, he continued his brisk walk to the study.

Claudia awakened Tinley sometime later, waiting patiently for him to rouse himself before she asked that a carriage be brought round. She returned to the little sitting room where Bernice Collier sat, her hands in a tight ball on her lap. The poor woman, who had the terrible misfortune of being penniless and with child, had rather miraculously found her way to St. James Square—the friend or sister of a servant somewhere, she had mumbled. It had taken her a quarter of an hour before she could swallow her shame and finally admit why she had come looking for Claudia. Having been abandoned by the child's father, she had no work, no funds, and no place to turn. Frightened to death by her predicament, she had sought Claudia in desperation, only to be turned away by Tinley and a footman. By chance, Claudia had seen her through the window, and had come out on the drive, beckoning her inside.

Now, she helped Miss Collier to her feet, put a comforting arm around her shoulders. "You will very much
like the house on Upper Moreland Street," she said as she
guided Miss Collier to the door of the sitting room. They
paused in the foyer and Claudia asked a footman to fetch
her blue cloak. When he returned, she wrapped the garment around Miss Collier's shoulders, smiling at the
woman's round-eyed look of surprise.

"Oh, no, I can't mu'um—"

"You must have a warm cloak, Miss Collier," Claudia
responded firmly. "I will not allow you to refuse it."

The woman's eyes brimmed with tears then. "It's true
what they say about you, milady. You are an angel."

Claudia laughed wholeheartedly. "I am hardly that,
you may trust me!" She pressed a small, folded piece of
paper in the woman's palm. "Give this to Mrs. Conner
when you arrive. You won't find a greater friend, I assure
you."

"The carriage, madam," a footman said from somewhere behind her, and Miss Collier very timidly went out
onto the drive, her mouth gaping open as she looked into
the interior of the plush carriage.

Claudia stood on the stoop and watched the carriage
pull out onto the Square, feeling an overwhelming sadness. She so longed to do more for women like Miss
Collier, but could scarcely manage to keep the little town
house on Upper Moreland Street afloat as it was—the
folly in her personal life had seen to that.

Damn it, but she could no longer garner enough in
donations to keep a pig afloat. What little had trickled in
had dragged to a complete halt two weeks ago when that
black-hearted Dillbey had written a letter to the editor of
the *Times* in response to a raging debate on women's suffrage. He argued that women who touted the same rights
as men meant no good by them.

" . . . Witness, then, our own Lord Redbourne's
daughter, Lady Kettering. If granted, her call for
the right to organize labor to protect women and

children in the factories would undoubtedly lead
to a call for more rights that, in Lady Kettering's
mind, perhaps, would include promiscuity in
hothouses and defying a husband's legal rule.
Gentlemen, we cannot allow feminine wailing
and gnashing of teeth to cloud our sound
reasoning. The platform is too radical . . ."

Since that article had appeared, even her most ardent
supporters had ceased their contributions. She could
hardly blame them; the threat of censure was quite real.
Unfortunately, the *ton* had a memory like an elephant.

When Miss Collier's conveyance disappeared from
sight, Claudia sighed wearily and retreated inside the
house in which she had lived like a virtual prisoner since
the news about Sophie had spread.

Her misery did not abate in the next few weeks.

Ann gave birth to a son just before the Christmas season, and Claudia had never seen Julian quite so jubilant.
He held the baby in one arm, beaming at him, reluctantly
giving him over to Victor when he asked, then shifting his
beaming smile to her. Claudia had inwardly cringed—the
whole cheery scene only made her sadder. Everything
seemed broken to her; she felt useless, as if she could not
do something even as simple as conceive.

For the first time in her life, she felt aimless, as if she
was drifting through every day with no particular destination. The only bright spot in her dreary world was, of
course, Julian. And as grateful as she was for that—she
thanked God for him every day—she had been so certain
his love would buoy her up in the worst of times. But
strangely, the more she felt his love, the more she felt her
own loss of purpose. She had nothing to offer him, could
only seem to cling to him like a child. She had lost her
bearings and she did not know how to get them back.
Every day, she sank a little farther into the black hole of
futility, struggling to find a lifeline.

The afternoon of Christmas Eve was dark; gray fog hovered just above the streets of London. Claudia stood at the long bank of windows in the gold salon, staring out into the Square. She had invited her father for supper but he had declined, said he was quite content to make a feast of it at his club. Ann and Victor, too, had declined, as Ann was understandably fearful of taking little Victor out into the cold. They would call in the morning after church services, thereby leaving Claudia and Julian alone on Christmas Eve. Completely alone, it seemed, as Julian had granted the servants at both Kettering House and Kettering Hall the evening free, as well as Christmas Day.

She glanced up at the leaden sky, then closed her eyes. *I will not allow melancholia to ruin this occasion for Julian.* At the very least, he deserved her spirit during the most festive of seasons. If she could only summon it! Julian had been very patient with her, accepting of her excuses lately for her lack of spirit. He deserved so much more than she was able to give him. Claudia glanced at the package resting on a small table next to his favorite chair. It was her Christmas gift for him, the one thing she had managed to do recently, and even that had required the help of her father.

"Ah, here you are." Julian's voice wrapped around her like a warm blanket, and Claudia smiled, turning to the door where he stood. Leaning against the frame, one leg crossed over the other, his arms folded across his chest. He was grinning; from across the room, she could see the glitter in his raven eyes. "Beautiful as always," he remarked.

Claudia glanced down at her gown of green and gold brocade.

"I am the most fortunate man on earth, I think," he said, shoving away from the door and strolling toward her. "My heart can scarcely bear it."

"You are a ruthless charmer, sir," she said, laughing softly as he slipped an arm around her waist. He smothered her laugh with a fierce kiss that left her feeling almost weightless, and when he at last lifted his head, he chuckled at her look of pure intoxication.

"I've a gift for you," she muttered dreamily.

"*You,* my darling, are the perfect Christmas gift."

Blushing, she pushed away from his embrace. "And you, my lord, are far too easy to please. Come." Taking him by the hand, Claudia led him to sit in the well-worn leather chair, then handed him the box wrapped in gold and silver ribbons. "Merry Christmas."

Grinning like a child, Julian eagerly accepted the box. "Shall I guess at it?" he asked, holding it up to shake it. "It's too heavy for a waistcoat, isn't it? Ah, I've got it. Cheroots rolled with American tobacco. I'm quite out, you know," he said, and lowered the box to his lap. "I've rather wondered if someone has been partaking of them when I'm not looking," he added with a playful frown.

"As a matter of fact, Tinley has taken quite a fancy to them."

Julian laughed as he untied the ribbon. "I swear it, the man will retire to his cottage this year if I have to carry him there myself," he said cheerfully, and lifted the lid to the box. He peered curiously at the contents, rooted around inside, and withdrew another, smaller box. "What have we here?" he muttered, and pulled off the lid. The smile faded from his face as he stared down at the ruby cuff links. The size of a farthing, they were cut to perfection and nestled in gold. "They are extraordinary," he mumbled, holding them up to the light.

"Do you like them?" Claudia asked anxiously.

His eyes flicked to her, then to the links, a smile creasing his face. "*Like* them? Darling, they are marvelous!"

A small surge of elation waved through her, and eagerly, she perched on the edge of the ottoman. "There is a shirt pin inside, too."

Julian rummaged through the box, extracting another, smaller box, and opened it. A shirt pin, topped with a ruby cut smaller but just as brilliantly as the links, winked back at him. "Oh, my," he said, clearly pleased. "Pin it on, will you?"

She affixed the pin very artfully in his black neckcloth as she had seen her father do, and Julian immediately stood, crossing to a small mirror near the sideboard to admire it. "Rather puts your father's to shame," he remarked with a chuckle. "Thank you, my love," he said, kissing the top of her head before resuming his seat. He turned his attention to one cuff and fastened the ruby link. When he started on the second cuff, he asked, "What would you like for Christmas, darling?"

You. Nothing more. Claudia shook her head. "I have everything I could want."

"Indeed? Everything? You are quite certain?"

Oh, she was certain. The greatest gift in her life was he—he was everything to her. "*Very* certain," she said, smiling.

"Come now. Surely there is *something* you would like to have." He fastened the second link and straightened his cuff, admiring the rubies at his wrist. "Something you have wanted and never received?"

No. She had more gowns than she could wear, more jewels, more shoes and hats and gloves and dressing gowns than a woman ought to have a right to own. If she wanted anything, it wouldn't come in a box, because it did not exist.

She wanted her life back.

She wanted to be Claudia Whitney again, capable of moving mountains for the less fortunate, able to extract pounds from families that were too wealthy by half and give to women and children who were in desperate need. She wanted to be the earl's favored daughter again, to have his respect and his support. Julian was her life, but she desperately wanted her own identity, too. "No," she repeated.

With a gentle chuck under her chin, Julian smiled. "Wait here, then, you silly girl."

He was gone in a flash and returned just as quickly, his hands behind his back. She supposed it was a piece of jewelry, something very expensive and exquisite, and she stood, smiling again.

"I see a dozen rainbows in that smile, do you know that?" he asked softly, and brought his hands around. "Here you are," he said, and moved to pin a little corsage of violets and white rosebuds on her breast.

Startled, Claudia stared at the little bundle of flowers, genuinely moved by the simplicity of it. "It's *beautiful.*" She truly meant it—it was the perfect gift for her, simple, pretty, unassuming. "The violets—"

"Are from the little pot at the edge of my desk." He flashed an irrepressible grin at her. "I vow to be as constant as that stubborn little plant," he informed her, and gathered her hands in his. "I will be forever at your side, supporting you in all that you do."

Claudia cocked her head to one side and looked at him suspiciously. "What exactly are you scheming, sir?"

That caused him to laugh, and he impulsively kissed her forehead. "I love you, Claudia. I will always be there with you, on that you may rely—but you must trust me."

The cheerful conversation had gone suddenly serious, and Claudia looked up at him, searched his eyes for an explanation.

"Do you trust me?"

"With my life," she solemnly responded.

Something sparked in his eyes; he kissed her hungrily, as if he had not seen her in days or weeks—then abruptly lifted his head. "Then come with me," he said, and grabbed her hand, pulling her toward the door.

He bustled her out into the foyer, fastened her cloak about her shoulders as she asked him where in God's name he intended to take her on Christmas Eve. "You shall see" was all he would say, ignoring her questions as he thrust his arms into his greatcoat and donned his hat and gloves.

"There is no place to go! Everyone is home with their families!"

Julian laughed as he dragged her outside, onto the stoop. A phaeton was at the ready in the drive; Julian waved to the groomsman who held the horse. "Thank you, Geoffrey. Merry Christmas to you and your family."

"Merry Christmas, my lord. Lady Kettering," he called back, and hopping down, jogged down the little path leading to the stables.

Julian looked at Claudia. "Well? What are you waiting for?"

"A bit of sense to strike you," she laughed, and allowed him to help her up.

As they drove through darkened streets, a thick woolen lap rug covering them, she rather enjoyed the game he had begun, and peppered him with questions he answered as evasively as he could. But when they crossed the river, she began to realize that her guess of a surprise visit to Ann and Victor's was wrong. Now she was wildly curious, and as they rolled to a stop in front of a crumbling brick building shoved in between two factories, she was absolutely perplexed.

"I think you've quite lost your mind," she remarked as he helped her down.

He smiled in the dark, kissed her temple. *"Trust me,"* he reminded her, and wrapping an arm around her, led her to the dark door.

She was certain the building would come tumbling down about them as he pushed the door open. It creaked loudly on rusty hinges and she was immediately assaulted by a damp mildew scent, as if the building hadn't been opened in years. It was pitch-black inside; she thought she heard the sound of rats scurrying across the floor, and unconsciously clutched Julian's arm. "Julian, what—"

"Merry Christmas!" The room suddenly erupted with the flare of a dozen or more candles and a host of voices. Claudia's great surprise was nearly fatal; with a shriek, she fell back against Julian, her heart pounding. More candles were lit as she held a hand over her pounding heart, gaping in astonishment at the crowded room.

It seemed almost everyone who mattered to her was in that room; Ann and Victor, Aunt Violet. Doreen— *Doreen?*—and several of the women and children from Upper Moreland Street, including Miss Collier. Her father, standing stiffly beside the Christian family; Mary Whitehurst and her husband, Adrian and Lilliana Spence and their baby daughter. Tinley, Brenda, and a handful of servants from Kettering House. As she looked around at their beaming faces, her gaze landed on a large, masonry sign that stood in the middle of the room.

THE WHITNEY-DANE SCHOOL FOR GIRLS

Suddenly, she understood. Her mind understood it but her heart could not absorb it. It was too much, too precious—speechless, she jerked her gaze to Julian.

He beamed at her, terribly pleased with himself. "I will admit, it needs an awful lot of work. But I rather thought it would give you something to do besides moping about, and as there is a seemingly endless supply of cheerful laborers at Upper Moreland Street, I supposed you would have enough help. I should warn you, however, that they have organized themselves into something of a labor union, and will not tolerate unsafe working conditions."

"You . . . you did this." It was not a question; it was a statement of wonder.

Julian laughed. "No darling, *you* did it, through your tireless and selfless work these last two years. I just helped it along a bit. Now listen to me—I can't be bothered with your new school," he said, reaching into his coat pocket. "I've far too many important things to tend to, such as card games and the annual races at Ascot. So I've deeded it over to you." He pressed a thick packet into her hand. "If you ask me kindly, I will help you, but I rather suspect you won't need me."

Claudia stared at the packet of paper he pressed into her hand. She could not begin to fathom how this man could have sensed what she needed when she herself could not put a word to it. But he had known it in that uncanny way he had of sensing all her needs before she did. More extraordinary than that, he had loved her enough, *believed* in her enough, to give her the single most glorious gift of her life. Claudia's vision suddenly blurred; a hot tear of joy slid down her cheek.

She lifted her gaze to her husband, saw the tears glimmering in his eyes, and smiled. "I could not possibly love you more than I do at this very moment," she choked, and threw her arms around his neck.

"Oh, God," he said, choking a bit, too, as his arms circled her waist. "I do hope you will remember that and tell me again when we are alone."

Her smile deepened, and she felt it in the very core of her soul. "Thank you for this gift—you cannot know what it means to me."

He slipped two fingers under her chin and tilted her head back. "I know. Trust me," he said, and kissed her, laughing into her mouth when their guests began to whistle, applauding and shouting for the guest of honor to cut their Christmas cake.

Twenty-Seven

Adrian and Arthur stood along one cold brick wall, each holding a glass of punch instead of the usual libations to which they were accustomed. They very stoically observed the festivities, which to Arthur seemed a bit out of control. Julian had brought Christmas gifts for all of the children—yet another sign that he had completely lost his mind—and they scampered in and around the legs of adults like little rats. One ruddy-cheeked little fellow lost control of his horse on wheels for the third time, and it came scudding across the stone floor, careening into Arthur's ankle. Very nonchalantly, he nudged the thing with his boot and sent it careening back to the little boy.

Across the room, Claudia, Lilliana, and a haggard-looking woman stood over the big masonry sign, talking with great animation, pointing to various places around the room as if they plotted a décor. The other women, whom Julian had brought up from some town house somewhere—Arthur was still a bit hazy on the exact details—were tending the gaggle of little monster children. In the midst of it all was Tinley, who had eaten two thick pieces of cake and then had promptly fallen asleep in his chair.

And Julian walked through the throng like a king, laughing with his servants, winking cheerfully at the women from the town house—all in all, strutting about like a peacock. Terribly pleased with himself, to be sure, he was apparently even more pleased with his wife, of whom he stole a glimpse every chance he got. It was obvious to everyone that Julian Dane was madly in love with the terror Claudia Whitney, which Arthur had, of course, predicted early on. He had just never guessed *how* madly in love—Julian Dane, the most unlikely man in all of England, was a lovesick, besotted fool.

"I rather suppose we can put to rest the notion that Julian might fall, wouldn't you say?" Adrian casually remarked, referring to their graveside vow to keep watch over one another.

With a nod as tepid as the punch, Arthur responded, "Unless we were to fret about him falling headlong into lovesickness from which he may never recover."

Adrian chuckled. "He's definitely gone round the bend."

"And toppled right off the cliff," Arthur added dryly.

"Which I suppose leaves us with you, Christian," Adrian remarked, casting a sidelong look at his friend. "Good God, what jolly fun this should be."

With a derisive chuckle, Arthur shook his head. "I am hardly of your ilk, Albright. I will not fall."

"I was referring to that 'headlong fall into lovesickness from which you may never recover.' Heart going pitter patter, that sort of thing."

The notion was so absurd that Arthur laughed roundly. "And Kettering calls me a sentimental fool!" he quipped, grinning. "Put your mind at ease, Albright. I am perfectly content with the way things are."

Adrian lifted a brow. "Oho! And I suppose you intend to remain a bachelor all your life? *That*, my friend, will never come to pass, mark my words!"

Arthur resisted the sudden urge to tug at his collar and shrugged indifferently. "What I shouldn't give for a bit of rum to put in this god-awful punch," he said, changing the subject and ignoring Adrian's wide, knowing grin. The subject, however, was hardly worthy of discussion—quite frankly, the thought of marrying one woman for all eternity was inconceivable to him. While he was perfectly reverent toward the fairer sex, he personally did not need them for anything more than to warm his bed. Which reminded him—the sooner he was gone from this cozy, touching little gathering, the better. Madame Farantino had promised a grand surprise for him.

About the Author

JULIA LONDON was raised on a ranch in West Texas, where she spent her formative years in the middle of vast wheat fields driving a tractor at the reckless speed of 5 mph. Scared to death she might actually have to plow for more than one summer, she studied hard and eventually got herself a real job. She now daydreams in Austin, Texas, where she lives with two enormous Labrador retrievers. You can write to Julia at P.O. Box 49315, Austin, Texas 78765, or visit her website at http://www.julialondon.com.